THE EMPEROR'S DICE

"But keep talking," said Ellery. "Just how was the murder concealed?"

"Simplest thing in the world. One of the sons was a medical doctor and the other was an undertaker. The son who was a doctor made out a false death certificate and the son who was an undertaker prepared the body for burial."

Mark Haggard laughed again. The lightning flashed, and for a photographic instant they saw his lumpish eyes, the blueness about the black stubble, the dance of his hands on the wheel.

Ellery heard Nikki's teeth. "M-Mister Haggard," she chattered, "what do you and your brother d-do for a living?"

"Tracy is a physician," Haggard cried, "and I'm an undertaker."

More Suspense from SIGNET

Calendar
of
Crime

ELLERY QUEEN

A SIGNET BOOK from
NEW AMERICAN LIBRARY
TIMES MIRROR

CONTENTS

The Adventure of the Inner Circle

IF YOU HOLD A degree from Eastern University and you have not been to New York since last year's All-University Dinner, you will be astounded to learn that the famous pickled-pine door directly opposite the elevators on the thirteenth floor of your Graduates' Club in Murray Hill is now inscribed: LINEN ROOM.

Visit The Graduates' Club on your next trip to New York and see for yourself. On the door now consigned to napery, in the area where the stainless steel medallion of Janus glistened for so long, you will detect a ghostly circumference some nine inches in diameter—all that is left of The Januarians. Your first thought will of course be that they have removed to more splendid quarters. Undeceive yourself. You may search from cellar to sun-deck and you will find no crumb's trace of either Janus or his disciples.

Hasten to the Club Steward for an explanation and he will give you one as plausible as it will be false.

And you will do no better elsewhere.

The fact is, only a very few share the secret of The Januarians' obliteration, and these have taken a vow of silence. And why? Because Eastern is a young—a very young—temple of learning; and there are calamities only age can weather. There is more to it than even that. The cataclysm of events struck at the handiwork of the architects themselves, that legendary band who built the tabernacle and created the holy canons. So Eastern's shame is kept steadfastly covered with silence, and if we uncover its bloody stones here, it is only because the very first word on the great seal of Eastern University is: *Veritas*.

To a Harvard man, "Harvard '13" means little more than "Harvard '06" of "Harvard '79," unless "Harvard

7

'13" happens to be his own graduating class. But to an Eastern man, of whatever vintage, "Eastern '13" is *sui generis*. Their names bite deep into the strong marble of The Graduate's Club lobby. A member of the Class is traditionally The Honourable Mr. Honorary President of The Eastern Graduates' Association. To the last man they carry gold, lifetime, non-cancellable passes to Eastern football games. At the All-University Dinner, Eastern '13 shares the Chancellor's parsley-decked table. The twined-elbow Rite of the Original Libation, drunk in foaming beer (the second most sacred canon), is dedicated to that Class and no other.

One may well ask why this exaltation of Eastern '13 as against, for example, Eastern '12, or Eastern '98? The answer is that there was no Eastern '12, and Eastern '98 never existed. For Eastern U. was not incorporated under the laws of the State of New York until A.D. 1909, from which it solemnly follows that Eastern '13 was the University's very first graduating class.

It was Charlie Mason who said they must be gods, and it was Charlie Mason who gave them Janus. Charlie was destined to forge a chain of one hundred and twenty-three movie houses which would bring Abbott and Costello to millions; but in those days Charlie was a lean weaver of dreams, the Class Poet, with a passion for classical allusion. Eastern '13 met on the eve of graduation in the Private Party Room of McElvy's Brauhaus in Riverdale, and the air was boiling with pipe smoke, malt fumes, and motions when Charlie rose to make his historic speech.

"Mr. Chairman," he said to Bill Updike, who was presiding in the Temporary Chair. "Fellows," he said to the nine others. And he paused.

Then he said: *"We are the First Graduates."*

He paused again.

"The eyes of the future are on us." (Stan Jones was taking notes, as Recording Secretary of the Evening, and we have Charlie's address verbatim. You have seen it in The Graduates' Club lobby, under glass. Brace yourself: It, too, has vanished.)

"What we do here to-night, therefore, will initiate a whole codex of Eastern tradition."

And now, the Record records, there was nothing to be heard in that smoky room but the whizz of the electric fan over the lithograph of Woodrow Wilson.

"I have no hesitation in saying—out loud!—that we men in this room, to-night . . . that we're . . . Significant.

8

Not as individuals! But as the Class of '13." And then Charlie drew himself up and said quietly: *"They will remember us and we must give them something to remember"* (the third sacred canon).

"Such as?" said Morry Green, who was to die in a French ditch five years later.

"A sign," said Charlie. "A symbol, Morry—a symbol of our Firstness."

Eddie Temple, who was graduating eleventh in the Class, exhibited his tongue and blew a coarse, fluttery blast.

"That may be the sign *you* want to be remembered by, Ed," began Charlie crossly . . .

"Shut up, Temple!" growled Vern Hamisher.

"Read that bird out of the party!" yelled Ziss Brown, who was suspected of holding radical views because his father had stumped for Teddy Roosevelt in '12.

"Sounds good," said Bill Updike, scowling. "Go on, Charlie."

"What sign?" demanded Rod Black.

"Anything specific in mind?" called Johnnie Cudwise.

Charlie said one word.

"Janus."

And he paused.

"Janus," they muttered, considering him.

"Yes, Janus," said Charlie. "The god of good beginnings——"

"Well, we're beginning," said Morry Green.

"Guaranteed to result in good endings——"

"It certainly applies," nodded Bill Updike.

"Yeah," said Bob Smith. "Eastern's sure on its way to big things."

"Janus of the two faces," cried Charlie Mason mystically. "I wish to point out that he looks in opposite directions!"

"Say, that's right——"

"The past and the future——"

"Smart stuff——"

"Go on, Charlie!"

"Janus," cried Charlie—"Janus, who was invoked by the Romans before any other god at the beginning of an important undertaking!"

"Wow!"

"This is certainly important!"

"The beginning of the day, month, and year were sacred to him! *Janus was the god of doorways!"*

9

"JANUS!" they shouted, leaping to their feet; and they raised their tankards and drank deep.

And so from that night forward the annual meeting of the Class of '13 was held on Janus's Day, the first day of January; and the Class of '13 adopted, by unanimous vote, the praenomen of The Januarians. Thus the double-visaged god became patron of Eastern's posterity, and that is why until recently Eastern official stationery was impressed with his two-bearded profiles. It is also why the phrase "to be two-faced," when uttered by Columbia or N.Y.U. men, usually means "to be a student at, or a graduate of, Eastern U."—a development unfortunately not contemplated by Charlie Mason on that historic eve; at least, not consciously.

But let us leave the profounder explorations to psychiatry. Here it is sufficient to record that something more than thirty years later the phrase suddenly took on a grim verisimilitude; and The Januarians thereupon laid it, so to speak, on the doorstep of one well acquainted with such changelings of chance.

For it was during Christmas week of last year that Bill Updike came—stealthily—to see Ellery. He did not come as young Billy who had presided at the beery board in the Private Party Room of McElvy's Brauhaus on that June night in 1913. He came, bald, portly, and opulently engraved upon a card: Mr. William Updike, President of The Brokers National Bank of New York, residence Dike Hollow, Scarsdale; and he looked exactly as worried as bankers are supposed to look and rarely do.

"Business, business," said Nikki Porter, shaking her Yuletide permanent. "It's Christmas week, Mr. Updike, I'm sure Mr. Queen wouldn't consider taking——"

But at that moment Mr. Queen emerged from his sanctum to give his secretary the lie.

"Nikki holds to the old-fashioned idea about holidays, Mr. Updike," said Ellery, shaking Bill's hand. "Ah, The Januarians. Isn't your annual meeting a few days from now—on New Year's Day?"

"How did you know——?" began the bank president.

"I could reply, in the manner of the Old Master," said Ellery with a chuckle, "that I've made an intensive study of lapel buttons, but truth compels me to admit that one of my best friends is Eastern '28 and he's described that little emblem on your coat so often I couldn't help but recognize it at once." The banker fingered the disk on his lapel nervously. It was of platinum, ringed with tiny garnets, and the gleaming circle enclosed the two faces of Janus. "What's the matter—is someone robbing your bank?"

"It's worse than that."

"Worse . . . ?"

"Murder."

Nikki glared at Mr. Updike. Any hope of keeping Ellery's nose off the grindstone until January second was now merely a memory. But out of duty she began: "Ellery . . ."

"At least," said Bill Updike tensely, "I *think* it's murder."

Nikki gave up. Ellery's nose was noticeably honed.

"Who . . .?"

"It's sort of complicated," muttered the banker, and he began to fidget before Ellery's fire. "I suppose you know, Queen, that The Januarians began with only eleven men."

Ellery nodded. "The total graduating class of Eastern '13."

"It seems silly now, with Eastern's classes of three and four thousand, but in those days we thought it was all pretty important——"

"Manifest destiny."

"We were young. Anyway, World War I came along and we lost two of our boys right away—Morry Green and Buster Selby. So at our New Year's Day meeting in 1920 we were only nine. Then in the market collapse of '29 Vern Hamisher blew the top of his head off, and in 1930 John Cudwise, who was serving his first term in Congress, was killed in a plane crash on his way to Washington—you probably remember. So we've been just seven for many years now."

"And awfully close friends you must be," said Nikki, curiosity conquering pique.

"Well . . ." began Updike, and he stopped, to begin over again. "For a long time now we've all thought it was sort of juvenile, but we've kept coming back to these damned New Year's Day meetings out of habit or—or something. No, that's not true. It isn't just habit. It's because . . . it's *expected* of us." He flushed. "I don't know—they've—well —deified us." He looked bellicose, and Nikki swallowed a giggle hastily. "It's got on our nerves. I mean—well, damn it all, we're not exactly the 'close' friends you'd think!" He stopped again, then resumed in a sort of desperation: "See here, Queen. I've got to confess something. There's been a clique of us within The Januarians for years. We've called ourselves . . . The Inner Circle."

"The what?" gasped Nikki.

The banker mopped his neck, avoiding their eyes. The Inner Circle, he explained, had begun with one of those dully devious phenomena of modern life known as a "business opportunity"—a business opportunity which Mr. Updike, a considerably younger Mr. Updike, had found himself unable to grasp for lack of some essential element, unnamed. Whatever it was that Mr. Updike had required, four other men could supply it; whereupon, in the flush of an earlier camaraderie, Updike had taken four of his six fellow-deities into his confidence, and the result of this was a partnership of five of the existing seven Januarians.

"There were certain business reasons why we didn't want our er . . . names associated with the ah . . . enterprise. So we organized a dummy corporation and agreed to keep our names out of it and the whole thing absolutely secret, even from our—from the remaining two Januarians. It's a secret from them to this day."

"Club within a club," said Nikki. "I think that's cute."

"All five of you in this—hrm!—Inner Circle," inquired Ellery politely, "are alive?"

"We were last New Year's Day. But since the last meeting of The Januarians . . ." the banker glanced at Ellery's harmless windows furtively, "three of us have died. *Three of the Inner Circle.*"

"And you suspect that they were murdered?"

"Yes. Yes, I do!"

"For what motive?"

The banker launched into a very involved and—to Nikki, who was thinking wistfully of New Year's Eve—tiresome explanation. It had something to do with some special fund or other, which seemed to have no connection with the commercial aspects of The Inner Circle's activities—a substantial fund by this time, since each year the five partners put a fixed percentage of their incomes from the dummy corporation into it. Nikki dreamed of balloons and noisemakers: "—now equals a reserve of around $200,000 worth of negotiable securities." Nikki stopped dreaming with a bump.

"What's the purpose of this fund, Mr. Updike?" Ellery was saying sharply. "What happens to it? When?"

"Well, er . . . that's just it, Queen," said the banker. "Oh, I know what you'll think . . ."

"Don't tell me," said Ellery in a terrible voice, "it's a

12

form of tontine insurance plan, Updike—*last survivor takes all?*"

"Yes," whispered William Updike, looking for a moment like Billy Updike.

"I knew it!" Ellery jumped out of his fireside chair. "Haven't I told you repeatedly, Nikki, there's no fool like a banker? The financial mentality rarely rises above the age of eight, when life's biggest thrill is to pay five pins for admission to a magic-lantern show in Stinky's cellar. This hard-eyed man of money, whose business it is to deal in safe investments, becomes party to a melodramatic scheme whereby the only way you can recoup your ante is to slit the throats of your four partners. Inner Circles! Januarians!" Ellery threw himself back on his chair. "Where's this silly invitation to murder cached, Updike?"

"In a safe-deposit box at The Brokers National," muttered the banker.

"Your own bank. Very cosy for *you*," said Ellery.

"No, no, Mr. Queen; all five of us have keys to the box——"

"What happened to the keys of the three Inner Circleites who died this year?"

"By agreement, dead members' keys are destroyed in the presence of the survivors——"

"Then there are only two keys to that safe-deposit box now in existence; yours and the key in the possession of the only other living Inner Circular?"

"Yes——"

"And you're afraid said sole-surviving associate murdered the deceased trio of your absurd quintet and has his beady eye on you, Updike?—so that as the last man alive of The Inner Circle he would fall heir to the entire $200,000 boodle?"

"What else can I think?" cried the banker.

"The obvious," retorted Ellery; "which is that your three pals travelled the natural route of all flesh. Is the $200,000 still in the box?"

"Yes. I looked just before coming here to-day."

"You want me to investigate."

"Yes, yes——"

"Very well. What's the name of this surviving fellow-conspirator of yours in The Inner Circle?"

"No," said Bill Updike.

"I beg pardon?"

"Suppose I'm wrong? If they *were* ordinary deaths, I'd have dragged someone I've known a hell of a long time into a mess. No, you investigate first, Mr. Queen. Find evidence of murder, and I'll go all the way."

"You won't tell me his name?"

"No."

The ghost of New Year's Eve stirred. But then Ellery grinned, and it settled back in the grave. Nikki sighed and reached for her notebook.

"All right, Mr. Updike. Who were the three Inner Circlovians who died this year?"

"Robert Carlton Smith, J. Stanford Jones, and Ziss Brown—Peter Zissing Brown."

"Their occupations?"

"Bob Smith was head of the Kradle Kap Baby Foods Korporation. Stan Jones was top man of Jones-Jones-Mallison-Jones, the ad. agency. Ziss Brown was retired."

"From what?"

Updike said stiffily: "Brassières."

"I suppose they do pall. Leave me the addresses of the executors, please, and any other data you think might be helpful."

When the banker had gone, Ellery reached for the telephone.

"Oh, dear," said Nikki. "You're not calling ... Club Bongo?"

"What?"

"You know? New Year's Eve?"

"Heavens, no. My pal Eastern '28, Cully? ... The same to you. Cully, who are the four Januarians? Nikki, take this down ... William Updike—yes? ... Charles Mason? Oh, yes, the god who fashioned Olympus ... Rodney Black, Junior—um-hm ... and Edward I. Temple? Thanks, Cully. And now forget I called." Ellery hung up. "Black, Mason, and Temple, Nikki. The only Januarians alive outside of Updike. Consequently one of those three is Updike's last associate in The Inner Circle."

"And the question is which one."

"Bright girl. But first let's dig into the deaths of Smith, Jones, and Brown. Who knows? Maybe Updike's got something."

It took exactly forty-eight hours to determine that Updike had nothing at all. The deaths of Januarians-Inner Circlers Smith, Jones and Brown were impeccable.

"Give it to him, Velie," said Inspector Queen at Headquarters the second morning after the banker's visit to the Queen apartment.

Sergeant Velie cleared his massive throat. "The Kradle Kap Baby Foods character——"

"Robert Carlton Smith."

"Rheumatic heart for years. Died in an oxygen tent after the third heart attack in eighteen hours, with three fancy medics in attendance and a secretary who was there to take down his last words."

"Which were probably 'Free Enterprise,'" said the Inspector.

"Go on, Sergeant!"

"J. Stanford Jones, the huckster. Gassed in World War I, in recent years developed T.B. And that's what he died of. Want the sanitarium affidavits, Maestro? I had photostats telephotoed from Arizona."

"Thorough little man, aren't you?" growled Ellery. "And Peter Zissing Brown, retired from brassières?"

"Kidneys and gall-bladder. Brown died on the operatin' table."

"Wait till you see what I'm wearing to-night," said Nikki. "Apricot taffeta——"

"Nikki, get Updike on the phone," said Ellery absently. "Brokers National."

"He's not there, Ellery," said Nikki, when she had put down the Inspector's phone. "Hasn't come into his bank this morning. It has the darlingest bouffant skirt——"

"Try his home."

"Dike Hollow, Scarsdale, wasn't it? With the new back, and a neckline that—— Hello?" And after a while the three men heard Nikki say in a strange voice: *"What?"* and then: "Oh," faintly. She thrust the phone at Ellery. "You'd better take it."

"What's the matter? Hello? Ellery Queen. Updike there?"

A bass voice said, "Well—no, Mr. Queen. He's been in an accident."

"Accident! Who's this speaking?"

"Captain Rosewater of the Highway Police. Mr. Updike ran his car into a ravine near his home here some time last night. We just found him."

"I hope he's all right!"

"He's dead."

"Four!" Ellery was mumbling as Sergeant Velie drove the Inspector's car up into Westchester. "Four in one year!"

"Coincidence," said Nikki desperately, thinking of the festivities on the agenda for that evening.

"All I know is that forty-eight hours after Updike asks me to find out if his three cronies of The Inner Circle who died this year hadn't been murdered, he himself is found lying in a gulley with four thousand pounds of used car on top of him."

"Accidents," began Sergeant Velie, "will hap——"

"I want to see that 'accident'!"

A state trooper flagged them on the Parkway near a cut-off and sent them down the side road. This road, it appeared, was a shortcut to Dike Hollow which Updike habitually used in driving home from the City; his house lay some two miles from the Parkway. They found the evidence of his last drive about midway. The narrow black-top road twisted sharply to the left at this point, but Bill Updike had failed to twist with it. He had driven straight ahead and through a matchstick guard-rail into the ravine. As it plunged over, the car had struck the bole of a big old oak. The shock catapulted the banker through his wind-shield and he had landed at the bottom of the ravine just before his vehicle.

"We're still trying to figure out a way of lifting that junk off him," said Captain Rosewater when they joined him forty feet below the road.

The ravine narrowed in a V here and the car lay in its crotch upside down. Men were swarming around it with crowbars, chains, and acetylene torches. "We're uncovered enough to show us he's mashed flat."

"His face, too, Captain?" asked Ellery suddenly.

"No, his face wasn't touched. We're trying to get the rest of him presentable enough so we can let his widow identify him." The trooper nodded toward a flat rock twenty yards down the ravine on which sat a small woman in a mink coat. She wore no hat and her smart grey hair was whipping in the Christmas wind. A woman in a cloth coat, wearing a nurse's cap, stood over her.

Ellery said, "Excuse me," and strode away. When Nikki caught up with him he was already talking to Mrs. Updike. She was drawn up on the rock like a caterpillar.

"He had a directors' meeting at the bank last night. I phoned one of his associates about 2 a.m. He said the meeting had broken up at eleven and Bill had left to drive home." Her glance strayed up the ravine. "At four-thirty this morning I phoned the police."

"Did you know your husband had come to see me, Mrs. Updike—two mornings ago?"

"Who are you?"

"Ellery Queen."

"No." She did not seem surprised, or frightened, or anything.

"Did you know Robert Carlton Smith, J. Stanford Jones, Peter Zissing Brown?"

"Bill's classmates? They passed away. This year," she added suddenly. "This year," she repeated. And then she laughed. "I thought the gods were immortal."

"Did you know that your husband, Smith, Jones, and Brown were an 'inner circle' in The Januarians?"

"Inner Circle." She frowned. "Oh, yes. Bill mentioned it occasionally. No, I didn't know they were in it."

Ellery leaned forward in the wind.

"Was Edward I. Temple in it, Mrs. Updike? Rodney Black, Junior? Charlie Mason?"

"I don't know. Why are you questioning me? Why——?" Her voice was rising now, and Ellery murmured something placative as Captain Rosewater hurried up and said: "Mrs. Updike. If you'd be good enough . . ."

She jumped off the rock. *"Now?"*

"Please."

The trooper captain took one arm, the nurse the other, and between them they half-carried William Updike's widow up the ravine toward the overturned car.

Nikki found it necessary to spend some moments with her handkerchief.

When she looked up, Ellery had disappeared.

She found him with his father and Sergeant Velie on the road above the ravine. They were standing before a large maple looking at a road-sign. Studded lettering on the yellow sign spelled out *Sharp Curve Ahead,* and there was an elbow-like illustration.

"No lights on this road," the Inspector was saying as Nikki hurried up, "so he must have had his brights on——"

"And they'd sure enough light up this reflector sign. I don't get it, Inspector," complained Sergeant Velie. "Unless his lights just weren't workin'."

"More likely fell asleep over the wheel, Velie."

"No," said Ellery.

"What, Ellery?"

"Updike's lights were all right, and he didn't doze off."

17

"I don't impress when I'm c-cold," Nikki said, shivering. "But just the same, how do you know, Ellery?"

Ellery pointed to two neat holes in the maple bark, very close to the edge of the sign.

"Woodpeckers?" said Nikki. But the air was grey and sharp as steel, and it was hard to forget Mrs. Updike's look.

"This bird, I'm afraid," drawled Ellery, "had no feathers. Velie, borrow something we can pry this sign off with."

When Velie returned with some tools, he was mopping his face. "She just identified him," he said. "Gettin' warmer, ain't it?"

"What d'ye expect to find, Ellery?" demanded the Inspector.

"Two full sets of rivet-holes."

Sergeant Velie said: "Bong," as the road-sign came away from the tree.

"I'll be damned," said Inspector Queen softly. "Somebody removed these rivets last night, and after Updike crashed into the ravine——"

"Riveted the warning sign back on," cried Nikki, "only he got careless and didn't use the same holes!"

"Murder," said Ellery. "Smith, Jones, and Brown died of natural causes. But three of the five co-owners of that fund dying in a single year——"

"Gave Number 5 an idea!"

"If Updike died, too, the $200,000 in securities would ... Ellery!" roared his father. "Where are you running to?"

"There's a poetic beauty about this case," Ellery was saying restlessly to Nikki as they waited in the underground vaults of The Brokers National Bank. "Janus was the god of entrances. Key were among his trappings of office. In fact, he was sometimes known as *Patulcius*— 'opener.' Opener! I knew at once we were too late."

"You knew, you knew," said Nikki peevishly. "And New Year's Eve only hours away! You can be wrong."

"Not this time. Why else was Updike murdered last night in such a way as to make it appear an accident? Our mysterious Januarian hotfooted it down here first thing this morning and cleaned out that safe-deposit box belonging to The Inner Circle. The securities are gone, Nikki."

Within an hour, Ellery's prophecy was historical fact.

The box was opened with Bill Updike's key. It was empty.

And of *Patulcius,* no trace. It quite upset the Inspector. For it appeared that The Inner Circle had contrived a remarkable arrangement for access to their safe-deposit box. It was gained, not by the customary signature on an admission slip, but through the presentation of a talisman. This talisman was quite unlike the lapel button of The Januarians. It was a golden key, and on the key was incised the two-faced god, with concentric circles. The outer circle was of Januarian garnets, the inner of diamonds. A control had been deposited in the files of the vault company. Anyone presenting a replica of it was to be admitted to The Inner Circle's repository by order of no less a personage, the vault manager informed them, than the late President Updike himself—who, Inspector Queen remarked with bitterness, had been more suited by temperament to preside over the Delancey Street Junior Spies.

"Anybody remember admitting a man this morning who flashed one of these doojiggers?"

An employee was found who duly remembered, but when he described the vault visitor as great-coated and muffled to the eyes, wearing dark glasses, walking with a great limp, and speaking in a laryngitical whisper, Ellery said wearily: "To-morrow's the annual meeting of The Januarians, Dad, and *Patulcius* won't dare not to show up. We'd better try to clean it up there."

These, then, were the curious events preceding the final meeting of The Januarians in the thirteenth-floor sanctuary of The Eastern Graduates' Club, beyond the door bearing the stainless steel medallion of the god Janus.

We have no apocryphal writings to reveal what self-adoring mysteries were performed in that room on other New Year's Days; but on January the first of this year, The Januarians held a most unorthodox service, in that two lay figures—the Queens, *pater et filius*—moved in and administered some rather heretical sacraments; so there is a full record of the last rites.

It began with Sergeant Velie knocking thrice upon the steel faces of Janus at five minutes past two o'clock on the afternoon of the first of January, and a thoroughly startled voice from within the holy of holies calling: "Who's there?" The Sergeant muttered an *Ave* and put his shoulder to the door. Three amazed, elderly male faces appeared. The heretics entered and the service began.

It is a temptation to describe in loving detail, for the satisfaction of the curious, the interior of the tabernacle—

its stern steel furniture seizing the New Year's Day sun and tossing it back in the form of imperious light, the four-legged altar, the sacred vessels in the shape of beakers, the esoteric brown waters, and so on—but there has been enough of profanation, and besides the service is more to our point.

It was chiefly catechistical, proceeding in this wise:

INSPECTOR: Gentlemen, my name is Inspector Queen, I'm from Police Headquarters, this is my son Ellery, and the big mugg on the door is Sergeant Velie of my staff.

BLACK: Police? Ed, do you know anything about——?

TEMPLE: Not me, Rodney. Maybe Charlie, ha-ha . . .?

MASON: What is it, Inspector? This is a private club-room——

INSPECTOR: Which one are *you*?

MASON: Charles Mason—Mason's Theatre Chain, Inc. But——

INSPECTOR: The long drink of water—what's *your* name?

TEMPLE: Me? Edward I. Temple. Attorney. What's the meaning——?

INSPECTOR: I guess, Tubby, that makes you Rodney Black, Junior, of Wall Street.

BLACK: Sir——!

ELLERY: Which one of you gentlemen belonged to The Inner Circle of The Januarians?

MASON: Inner what, what?

BLACK: Circle, I think he said, Charlie.

TEMPLE: Inner circle? What's that?

SERGEANT: One of 'em's a John Barrymore, Maestro.

BLACK: See here, we're three-fourths of what's left of the Class of Eastern '13 . . .

ELLERY: Ah, then you gentlemen don't know that Bill Updike is dead?

ALL: Dead! *Bill?*

INSPECTOR: Tell 'em the whole story, Ellery.

And so, patiently, Ellery recounted the story of The Inner Circle, William Updike's murder, and the vanished $200,000 in negotiable securities. And as he told this story, the old gentleman from Centre Street and his sergeant studied the three elderly faces; and the threatre magnate, the lawyer, and the broker gave stare for stare; and when Ellery had finished they turned to one another and gave stare for stare once more.

And finally Charlie Mason said: "My hands are clean, Ed. How about yours?"

20

"What do you take me for, Charlie?" said Temple in a flat and chilling voice. And they both looked at Black, who squeaked: "Don't try to make *me* out the one, you traitors!"

Whereupon, as if there were nothing more to be said, the three divinities turned and gazed bleakly upon the iconoclasts.

And the catechism resumed:

ELLERY: Mr. Temple, where were you night before last between 11 p.m. and midnight?

TEMPLE: Let me see. Night before last. . . . That was the night before New Year's Eve. I went to bed at ten o'clock.

ELLERY: You're a bachelor, I believe. Do you employ a domestic?

TEMPLE: My man.

ELLERY: Was he——?

TEMPLE: He sleeps out.

SERGEANT: No alibi!

INSPECTOR: How about you, Mr. Black?

BLACK: Well, the fact is . . . I'd gone to see a musical in town . . . between eleven and twelve I was driving home . . . to White Plains . . .

SERGEANT: Ha! White Plains!

ELLERY: Alone, Mr. Black?

BLACK: Well . . . yes. The family's all away over the holidays . . .

INSPECTOR: No alibi. Mr. Mason?

MASON: Go to hell. (*There is a knock on the door.*)

SERGEANT: Now who would that be?

TEMPLE: The ghost of Bill?

BLACK: You're not funny, Ed!

ELLERY: Come in. (*The door opens. Enter Nikki Porter.*)

NIKKI: I'm sorry to interrupt, but she came looking for you, Ellery. She was terribly insistent. Said she'd just recalled something about The Inner Circle, and——

ELLERY: She?

NIKKI: Come in, Mrs. Updike.

"They're here." said Mrs. Updike. "I'm glad. I wanted to look at their faces."

"I've told Mrs. Updike the whole thing," said Nikki defiantly.

And Inspector Queen said in a soft tone: "Velie, shut the door."

21

But this case was not to be solved by a guilty look. Black Mason, and Temple said quick ineffectual things, surrounding the widow and spending their nervousness in little gestures and rustlings until finally silence fell and she said helplessly, "Oh, I don't know, I don't know," and dropped into a chair to weep.

And Black stared out of the window, and Mason looked green, and Temple compressed his lips.

Then Ellery went to the widow and put his hand on her shoulder. "You recall something about The Inner Circle, Mrs. Updike?"

She stopped weeping and folded her hands, resting them in her lap and looking straight ahead.

"Was it the names of the five?"

"No. Bill never told me their names. But I remember Bill's saying to me once: 'Mary, I'll give you a hint.'"

"Hint?"

"Bill said that he once realized there was something funny about the names of the five men in The Inner Circle."

"Funny?" said Ellery sharply. "About their *names?*"

"He said by coincidence all five names had one thing in common."

"In common?"

"And he laughed." Mrs. Updike paused. "He laughed, and he said: 'That is, Mary, if you remember that I'm a married man.' I remember saying: 'Bill, stop talking in riddles. What do you mean?' And he laughed again and said: "Well, you see, Mary, *you're in it too.*'"

"You're in it, too," said Nikki blankly.

"I have no idea what he meant, but that's what Bill said, word for word." And now she looked up at Ellery and asked, with a sort of ferocious zest: "Does any of this help, Mr. Queen?"

"Oh, yes," said Ellery gently. "All of it, Mrs. Updike." And he turned to the three silent Januarians and said: "Would any of you gentlemen like to try your wits against this riddle?"

But the gentlemen remained silent.

"The reply appears to be no," Ellery said. "Very well; let's work it out *en masse*. Robert Carlton Smith, J. Stanford Jones, Peter Zissing Brown, William Updike. Those four names, according to Bill Updike, have one thing in common. What?"

"Smith," said the Inspector.

"Jones," said the Sergeant.

"Brown," said Nikki.

"Updike!" said the Inspector. "Boy, you've got me."

"Include me in, Maestro."

"Ellery, please!"

"Each of the four names," said Ellery, "has in it, somewhere, the name of a well-known college or university."

And there was another mute communion.

"Robert—Carlton—Smith," said the Inspector, doubtfully.

"Smith!" cried Nikki. "*Smith College,* in Massachusetts!"

The inspector looked startled. "J. Stanford Jones—That California university, *Stanford!*"

"Hey," said Sergeant Velie. "Brown, *Brown University,* in Rhode Island!"

"Updike," said Nikki, then she stopped. "Updike? There's no college called Updike, Ellery."

"William Updike was his full name, Nikki."

"You mean the 'William' part? There's a Williams, with an *s.* but no William."

"What did Updike tell Mrs. Updike? 'Mary, you're in it, too.' William Updike was in it, and Mary Updike was in it . . ."

"*William and Mary College!*" roared the Inspector.

"So the college denominator checks for all four of the known names. But since Updike told his wife the fifth name had the same thing in common, all we have to do now is test the names of these three gentlemen to see if one of them is the name of a college or university—and we'll have the scoundrel who murdered Bill Updike for the Inner Circle's fortune in securities."

"Black," babbled Rodney Black, Junior. "Rodney Black, Junior. Find me a college in that, sir!"

"Charles Mason," said Charles Mason unsteadily. "Charles? Mason? You see!"

"That," said Ellery, "sort of hangs it around your neck, Mr. Temple."

"Temple?"

"*Temple University* in Pennsylvania!"

Of course, it was all absurd. Grown men who played at godhead with emblems and talismans, like boys conspiring in a cave, and a murder case which was solved by a trick of nomenclature. Eastern University is too large for that sort of childishness. And it is old enough, we submit, to know the truth:

Item: Edward I. Temple, Class of Eastern '13, did not "fall" from the thirteenth floor of The Eastern Graduates' Club on New Year's Day this year. He jumped.

Item: The Patulcius Chair of Classics, founded this year, was not endowed by a wealthy Eastern man from Oil City who modestly chose anonymity. It came into existence through the contents of The Inner Circle's safe-deposit box, said contents having been recovered from another safe-deposit box rented by said Temple in another bank on the afternoon of December thirty-first under a false name.

Item: The Januarian room was not converted to the storage of linen because of the expanding housekeeping needs of The Eastern Graduates' Club. It was ordered so that the very name of the Society of the Two-faced God should be expunged from Eastern's halls; and as for the stainless steel medallion of Janus which had hung on the door, the Chancellor of Eastern University himself scaled it into the Hudson River from the George Washington Bridge, during a sleet storm, one hideous night this January.

The Adventure of
the President's Half Disme

THOSE FEW CURIOUS MEN who have chosen to turn off the
humdrum highway to hunt for their pleasure along the
back trails expect—indeed, they look confidently forward
to—many strange encounters; and it is the dull stalk
which does not turn up at least a hippogriff. But it remained for Ellery Queen to experience the ultimate excitement. On one of his prowls he collided with a President of the United States.

This would have been joy enough if it had occurred as
you might imagine: by chance, on a dark night, in some
back street of Washington, D.C., with Secret Service men
closing in on the delighted Mr. Queen to question his
motives by way of his pockets while a large black bullet-
proof limousine rushed up to spirit the President away.
But mere imagination fails in this instance. What is required is the power of fancy, for the truth is fantastic.
Ellery's encounter with the President of the United States
took place, not on a dark night, but in the unromantic
light of several days (although the night played its role,
too). Nor was it by chance: the meeting was arranged by
a farmer's daughter. And it was not in Washington, D.C.,
for this President presided over the affairs of the nation
from a different city altogether. Not that the meeting took
place in that city, either; it did not take place in a city at
all, but on a farm some miles south of Philadelphia.
Oddest of all, there was no limousine to spirit the Chief
Executive away, for while the President was a man of
great wealth, he was still too poor to possess an automo-
bile, and what is more, not all the resources of his Government—indeed, not all the riches of the world—could
have provided one for him.

There are even more curious facets to this jewel of
paradox. This was an encounter in the purest sense, and

25

yet, physically, it did not occur at all. The President in question was dead. And while there are those who would not blink at a rubbing of shoulders or a clasping of hands even though one of the parties was in his grave, and to such persons the thought might occur that the meeting took place on a psychic plane—alas, Ellery Queen is not of their company. He does not believe in ghosts, consequently he never encounters them. So he did not collide with the President's shade, either.

And yet their meeting was as palpable as, say, the meeting between two chess masters, one in London and the other in New York, who never leave their respective armchairs and still play a game to a decision. It is even more wonderful than that, for while the chess players merely annihilate space, Ellery and the father of his country annihilated time—a century and a half of it.

In fine, this is the story of how Ellery Queen matched wits with George Washington.

Those who are finicky about their fashions complain that the arms of coincidence are too long; but in this case the Designer might say that He cut to measure. Or, to put it another way, an event often brews its own mood. Whatever the cause, the fact is The Adventure of the President's Half Disme, which was to concern itself with the events surrounding President Washington's fifty-ninth birthday, actually first engrossed Ellery on February the nineteenth and culminated three days later.

Ellery was in his study that morning of the nineteenth of February, wrestling with several reluctant victims of violence, none of them quite flesh and blood, since his novel was still in the planning stage. So he was annoyed when Nikki came in with a card.

"James Ezekiel Patch," growled the great man; he was never in his best humour during the planning stage. "I don't know any James Ezekiel Patch, Nikki. Toss the fellow out and get back to transcribing those notes on Possible Motives——"

"Why Ellery," said Nikki. "This isn't like you at all."

"What isn't like me?"

"To renege on an appointment."

"Appointment? Does this Patch character claim——"

"He doesn't merely claim it. He proves it."

"Someone's balmy," snarled Mr. Queen; and he strode into the living room to contend with James Ezekiel Patch. This, he perceived as soon as James Ezekiel Patch rose

26

from the Queen fireside chair, was likely to be a heroic project. Mr. Patch, notwithstanding his mild, even studious eyes, seemed to rise indefinitely; he was a large, a very large, man.

"Now what's all this, what's all this?" demanded Ellery fiercely; for after all Nikki was there.

"That's what I'd like to know," said the large man amiably. "What did you want with me, Mr. Queen?"

"What did I want with you! What did you want with me?"

"I find this very strange, Mr. Queen."

"Now see here, Mr. Patch, I happen to be extremely busy this morning——"

"So am I." Mr. Patch's large thick neck was reddening and his tone was no longer amiable. Ellery took a cautious step backward as his visitor lumbered forward to thrust a slip of yellow paper under his nose. "Did you send me this wire, or didn't you?"

Ellery considered it tactically expedient to take the telegram, although for strategic reasons he did so with a bellicose scowl.

IMPERATIVE YOU CALL AT MY HOME TO-MORROW
FEBRUARY NINETEEN PROMPTLY TEN A.M. SIGNED
ELLERY QUEEN

"Well, sir?" thundered Mr. Patch. "Do you have something on Washington for me, or don't you?"

"Washington?" said Ellery absently, studying the telegram.

"*George* Washington, Mr. Queen! I'm Patch the antiquarian. I *collect* Washington. I'm an *authority* on Washington. I have a large fortune and I spend it all on Washington! I'd never have wasted my time this morning if your name hadn't been signed to this wire! This is my busiest week of the year. I have engagements to speak on Washington——"

"Desist, Mr. Patch," said Ellery. "This is either a practical joke, or——"

"The Baroness Tchek," announced Nikki clearly. "With another telegram." And then she added: "And Professor John Cecil Shaw, ditto."

The three telegrams were identical.

"Of course I didn't send them," said Ellery thoughtfully, regarding his three visitors. Baroness Tchek was a short, powerful woman, resembling a dumpling with grey hair; an angry dumpling. Professor Shaw was lank and long-jawed, wearing a sack suit which hung in some places and failed in its purpose by inches at the extremities. Along with Mr. Patch, they constituted as deliciously queer a trio as had ever congregated in the Queen apartment. Their host suddenly determined not to let go of them. "On the other hand someone obviously did, using my name . . ."

"Then there's nothing more to be said," snapped the Baroness, snapping her bag for emphasis.

"I should think there's a great deal more to be said," began Professor Shaw in a troubled way. "Wasting people's time this way——"

"It's not going to waste any more of *my* time," growled the large Mr. Patch. "Washington's Birthday only three days off——!"

"Exactly," smiled Ellery, "Won't you sit down? There's more in this than meets the eye . . . Baroness Tchek, if I'm not mistaken, you're the one who brought that fabulous collection of rare coins into the United States just before Hitler invaded Czechoslovakia? You're in the rare-coin business in New York now?"

"Unfortunately," said the Baroness coldly, "one must eat."

"And you, sir? I seem to know you."

"Rare books," said the Professor in the same troubled way.

"Of course. John Cecil Shaw, the rare-book collector. We've met at Mim's and other places. I abandon my first theory. There's a pattern here, distinctly unhumorous. An antiquarian, a coin-dealer, and a collector of rare books—Nikki? Whom have you out there this time?"

"If this one collects anything," muttered Nikki into her employer's ear, "I'll bet it has two legs and hair on its chest. A darned pretty girl——"

"Named Martha Clarke," said a cool voice; and Ellery turned to find himself regarding one of the most satisfying sights in the world.

"Ah, I take it, Miss Clarke, you also received one of these wires signed with my name?"

"Oh, no," said the pretty girl. "I'm the one who sent them."

There was something about the comely Miss Clarke which inspired, if not confidence, at least an openness of mind. Perhaps it was the self-possessed manner in which

28

she sat all of them, including Ellery, down in Ellery's living-room while she waited on the hearth-rug, like a conductor on the podium, for them to settle in their chairs. And it was the measure of Miss Clarke's assurance that none of them was indignant, only curious.

"I'll make it snappy," said Martha Clarke briskly. "I did what I did the way I did it because, first, I had to make sure I could see Mr. Patch, Baroness Tchek, and Professor Shaw to-day. Second, because I may need a detective before I'm through . . . Third," she added, almost absently, "because I'm pretty desperate.

"My name is Martha Clarke. My father Tobias is a farmer. Our farm lies just south of Philadelphia; it was built by a Clarke in 1761, and it's been in our family ever since. I won't go gooey on you. We're broke and there's a mortgage. Unless Papa and I can raise six thousand dollars in the next couple of weeks we lose the old homestead."

Professor Shaw looked vague. But the Baroness said: "Deplorable. Miss Clarke. Now if I'm to run my auction this afternoon——"

And James Ezekiel Patch grumbled: "If it's money you want, young woman——"

"Certainly it's money I want. But I have something to sell."

"Ah!" said the Baroness.

"Oh?" said the Professer.

"Hm," said the antiquarian.

Mr. Queen said nothing, and Miss Porter jealously chewed the end of her pencil.

"The other day while I was cleaning out the attic, I found an old book."

"Well, now," said Professor Shaw indulgently. "An old book, eh?"

"It's called *The Diary of Simeon Clarke*. Simone Clarke was Papa's great-great-great-something or other. His *Diary* was privately printed in 1792 in Philadelphia, Professor, by a second cousin of his, Jonathan, who was in the printing business there."

"Jonathan Clarke. *The Diary of Simeon Clarke*," mumbled the cadaverous book-collector. "I don't believe I know either, Miss Clarke. Have you . . . ?"

Martha Clake carefully unclasped a large Manila envelope and drew forth a single yellowed sheet of badly printed paper. "The title page was loose, so I brought it along."

Professor Shaw silently examined Miss Clarke's exhibit, and Ellery got up to squint at it. "Of course," said the Professor after a long scrutiny, in which he held the sheet up to the light, peered apparently at individual characters, and performed other mysterious rites, "mere age doesn't connote rarity, nor does rarity of itself constitute value. And while this page looks genuine for the purported period and is rare enough to be unknown to me, still . . ."

"Suppose I told you," said Miss Martha Clarke, "that the chief purpose of the *Diary*—which I have at home—is to tell the story of how George Washington visited Simeon Clarke's farm in the winter of 1791——"

"Clarke's farm? 1791?" exclaimed James Ezekiel Patch. "Preposterous. There's no record of——"

"And of what George Washington buried there," the farmer's daughter concluded.

By executive order, the Queen telephone was taken off its hook, the door was bolted, the shades were drawn, and the long interrogation began. By the middle of the afternoon, the unknown chapter in the life of the Father of His country was fairly sketched.

Early on an icy grey February morning in 1791, Farmer Clarke had looked up from the fence he was mending to observe a splendid cortège galloping down on him from the direction of the City of Philadelphia. Outriders thundered in the van, followed by a considerable company of gentlemen on horseback and several great coaches-and six driven by liveried Negroes. To Simeon Clarke's astonishment, the entire equipage stopped before his farmhouse. He began to run. He could hear the creak of springs and the snorting of sleek and sweating horses. Gentlemen and lackeys were leaping to the frozen ground and, by the time Simeon had reached the farmhouse, all were elbowing about the first coach, a magnificent affair bearing a coat of arms. Craning, the farmer saw within the coach a very large, great-nosed gentleman clad in a black velvet suit and a black cloak faced with gold; there was a cocked hat on his wigged head and a great sword in a white leather scabbard at his side. This personage was on one knee, leaning with an expression of considerable anxiety over a chubby lady of middle age, swathed in furs, who was half-sitting, half-lying on the upholstered seat, her eyes closed and her cheeks waxen under the rouge. Another gentleman, soberly attired, was stooping over the lady, his fingers on one pale wrist.

30

"I fear," he was saying with great gravity to the kneeling man, "that it would be imprudent to proceed another yard in this weather, Your Excellency. Lady Washington requires physicking and a warm bed immediately."

Lady Washington! Then the large, richly dressed gentleman was the President! Simeon Clarke pushed excitedly through the throng.

"Your Mightiness! Sir!" he cried. "I am Simeon Clarke. This is my farm. We have warm beds, Sarah and I!"

The President considered Simeon briefly. "I thank you, Farmer Clarke. No, no, Dr. Craik. I shall assist Lady Washington myself."

And George Washington carried Martha Washington into the little Pennsylvania farmhouse of Simeon and Sarah Clarke. An aide informed the Clarkes that President Washington had been on his way to Virginia to celebrate his fifty-ninth birthday in the privacy of Mount Vernon.

Instead, he passed his birthday on the Clarke farm, for the physician insisted that the President's lady could not be moved, even back to the nearby Capital, without risking complications. On His Excellency's order, the entire incident was kept secret. "It would give needless alarm to the people," he said. But he did not leave Martha's bedside for three days and three nights.

Presumably during those seventy-two hours, while his lady recovered from her indisposition, the President devoted some thought to his hosts, for on the fourth morning he sent black Christopher, his body-servant, to summon the Clarkes. They found George Washinton by the kitchen fire, shaven and powdered and in immaculate dress, his stern features composed.

"I am told, Farmer Clarke, that you and your good wife refuse reimbursement for the livestock you have slaughtered in the accommodation of our large company."

"You're my President, Sir," said Simeon. "I wouldn't take money."

"We—we wouldn't take money, Your Worship," stammered Sarah.

"Nevertheless, Lady Washington and I would acknowledge your hospitality in some kind. If you give me leave, I shall plant with my own hands a grove of oak saplings behind your house. And beneath one of the saplings I propose to bury two of my personal possessions." Washington's eyes twinkled ever so slightly. "It is my birthday— I feel a venturesome spirit. Come, Farmer Clarke and Mistress Clarke, would you like that?"

"What—what were they?" choked James Ezekiel Patch, the Washington collector. He was pale.

Martha Clarke replied: "The sword at Washington's side, in its white leather scabbard, and a silver coin the President carried in a secret pocket."

"Silver *coin?*" breathed Baroness Tchek, the rare-coin dealer. "What kind of coin, Miss Clarke?"

"The *Diary* calls it 'a half disme,' with an *s,*" replied Martha Clarke, frowning. "I guess that's the way they spelled dime in those days. The book's full of queer spellings."

"A United States of America half disme?" asked the Baroness in a very odd way.

"That's what it says, Baroness."

"And this was in 1791?"

"Yes."

The Baroness snorted, beginning to rise. "I thought your story was too impossibly romantic, young woman. The United States Mint didn't begin to strike off half dismes until 1792!"

"Half dismes or any other U.S. coinage, I believe," said Ellery. "How come, Miss Clarke?"

"It was an experimental coin," said Miss Clarke coolly. "The *Diary* isn't clear as to whether it was the Mint which struck it off, or some private agency—maybe Washington himself didn't tell Simeon—but the President did say to Simeon that the half disme in his pocket had been coined from silver he himself had furnished and had been presented to him as a keepsake."

"There's a half disme with a story like that behind it in the possession of The American Numismatic Society," muttered the Baroness, "but it's definitely called one of the earliest coins struck off by the Mint. It's possible, I suppose, that in 1791, the preceding year, some specimen coins may have been struck off——"

"Possible my foot," said Miss Clarke. "It's so. The *Diary* says so. I imagine President Washington was pretty interested in the coins to be issued by the new country he was head of."

"Miss Clarke, I—I want that half disme. I mean—I'd like to buy it from you," said the Baroness.

"And I," said Mr. Patch carefully, "would like to ah ... purchase Washington's sword."

"The *Diary,*" moaned Professor Shaw. "I'll buy *The Diary of Simeon Clarke* from you, Miss Clarke!"

"I'll be happy to sell it to you, Professor Shaw—as I

said, I found it in the attic, and I have it locked up in a highboy in the parlour at home. But as for the other two things . . ." Martha Clarke paused, and Ellery looked delighted. He thought he knew what was coming. "I'll sell you the sword, Mr. Patch, and you the half disme, Baroness Tchek, provided"—and now Miss Clarke turned her clear eyes on Ellery—"provided you, Mr. Queen, will be kind enough to find them."

And there was the farmhouse in the frosty Pennsylvania morning, set in the barren winter acres, and looking as bleak as only a little Revolutionary house with a mortgage on its head can look in the month of February.

"There's an apple orchard over there," said Nikki as they got out of Ellery's car. "But where's the grove of oaks? I don't see any!" And then she added sweetly: "Do you, Ellery?"

Ellery's lips tightened. They tightened further when his solo on the front-door knocker brought no response.

"Let's go around," he said briefly; and Nikki preceded him with cheerful step.

Behind the house there was a barn; and beyond the barn there was comfort, at least for Ellery. For beyond the barn there were twelve ugly holes in the earth, and beside each hole lay either a freshly felled oak tree and its stump, or an ancient stump by itself, freshly uprooted. On one of the stumps sat an old man in earth-stained blue jeans, smoking a corncob pugnaciously.

"Tobias Clarke?" asked Ellery.

"Yump."

"I'm Ellery Queen. This is Miss Porter. Your daughter visited me in New York yesterday——"

"Know all about it."

"May I ask where Martha is?"

"Station. Meetin' them there other folks." Tobias Clarke spat and looked away—at the holes. "Don't know what ye're all comin' down here for. Wasn't nothin' under them oaks. Dug 'em all up t'other day. Trees that were standin' and the stumps of the ones that'd fallen years back. Look at them holes. Hired hand and me dug down most to China. Washin'ton's Grove, always been called. Now look at it. Firewood—for someone else, I guess." There was iron bitterness in his tone. "We're losin' this farm, Mister, unless . . ." And Tobias Clarke stopped. "Well, maybe we won't," he said. "There's always that there book Martha found."

"Professor Shaw, the rare-book collector, offered your daughter two thousand dollars for it if he's satisfied with it, Mr. Clarke," said Nikki.

"So she told me last night when she got back from New York," said Tobias Clarke. "Two thousand—and we need six." He grinned, and he spat again.

"Well," said Nikki sadly to Ellery, "that's that." She hoped Ellery would immediately get into the car and drive back to New York—immediately.

But Ellery showed no disposition to be sensible. "Perhaps, Mr. Clarke, some trees died in the course of time and just disappeared, stumps, roots, and all. Martha"—Martha!—"said the *Diary* doesn't mention the exact number Washington planted here."

"Look at them holes. Twelve of 'em, ain't there? In a triangle. Man plants trees in a triangle, he plants trees in a triangle. Ye don't see no place between holes big enough for another tree, do ye? Anyways, there was the same distance between all the trees. No, sir, Mister, twelve was all there was ever; and I looked under all twelve."

"What's the extra tree doing in the centre of the triangle? You haven't uprooted that one, Mr. Clarke."

Tobias Clarke spat once more. "Don't know much about trees, do ye? That's a cherry saplin' I set in myself six years ago. Ain't got nothin' to do with George Washington."

Nikki tittered.

"If you'd sift the earth in those holes——"

"I sifted it. Look, Mister, either somebody dug that stuff up a hundred years ago or the whole yarn's a Saturday night whopper. Which it most likely is. There's Martha now with them other folks." And Tobias Clarke added, spitting for the fourth time: "Don't let me be keepin' ye."

"It reveals Washington rather er ... out of character," said James Ezekiel Patch that evening. They were sitting about the fire in the parlour, as heavy with gloom as with Miss Clarke's dinner; and that, at least in Miss Porter's view, was heavy indeed. Baroness Tchek wore the expression of one who is trapped in a cave; there was no further train until morning, and she had not yet resigned herself to a night in a farmhouse bed. The better part of the day had been spent poring over *The Diary of Simeon Clarke*, searching for a clue to the buried Washingtonia. But there was no clue; the pertinent passage referred merely to "a

34

Triangle of Oake Trees behinde the red Barn, which His Excellency the President did plant with his own Hands, as he had promis'd me, and then did bury his Sworde and the Half Disme for his Pleasure in a Case of copper beneathe one of the Oakes, the which, he said (the Case), had been fashion'd by Mr. Revere of Boston who is experimenting with this Mettle in his Furnasses."

"How out of character, Mr. Patch?" asked Ellery. He had been staring into the fire for a long time, scarcely listening.

"Washington wasn't given to romanticism," said the large man dryly. "No folderol about him. I don't know of anything in his life which prepares us for such a yarn as this. I'm beginning to think——"

"But Professor Shaw himself says the *Diary* is no forgery!" cried Martha Clarke.

"Oh, the book's authentic enough." Professor Shaw seemed unhappy. "But it may simply be a literary hoax, Miss Clarke. The woods are full of them. I'm afraid that unless the story is confirmed by the discovery of that copper case with its contents . . ."

"Oh, dear," said Nikki impulsively; and for a moment she was sorry for Martha Clarke, she really was.

But Ellery said: "I believe it. Pennsylvania farmers in 1791 weren't given to literary hoaxes, Professor Shaw. As for Washington, Mr. Patch—no man can be so rigidly consistent. And with his wife just recovering from an illness—on his own birthday . . ." And Ellery fell silent again.

Almost immediately he leaped from his chair. "Mr. Clarke!"

Tobias stirred from his dark corner. "What?"

"Did you ever hear your father, or grandfather— anyone in your family—talk of *another barn behind the house*?"

Martha stared at him. Then she cried: "Papa, that's it! It was a different barn, in a different place, and the original Washington's Grove was cut down, or died——"

"Nope," said Tobias Clarke. "Never was but this one barn. Still got some of its original timbers. Ye can see the date burned into the cross-tree—1761."

Nikki was up early. A steady *hack-hack-hack* borne on the frosty air woke her. She peered out of her back window, the coverlet up to her nose, to see Mr. Ellery

35

Queen against the dawn, like a pioneer, wielding an axe powerfully.

Nikki dressed quickly, shivering, flung her mink-dyed muskrat over her shoulders, and ran downstairs, out of the house, and around it past the barn.

"Ellery! What do you think you're doing? It's practically the middle of the night!"

"Chopping," said Ellery, chopping.

"There's *mountains* of firewood stacked against the barn," said Nikki. "Really, Ellery, I think this is carrying a flirtation too far." Ellery did not reply. "And, anyway, there's something—something gruesome and indecent about chopping up trees George Washington planted. It's vandalism."

"Just a thought," panted Ellery, pausing for a moment. "A hundred and fifty-odd years is a long time, Nikki. Lots of queer things could happen, even to a tree, in that time. For instance——"

"The copper case," breathed Nikki, visibly. "The roots grew *around* it. It's *in* one of these stumps!"

"Now you're functioning," said Ellery, and he raised the axe again.

He was still at it two hours later, when Martha Clarke announced breakfast.

At 11.30 a.m. Nikki returned from driving the Professor, the Baroness, and James Ezekiel Patch to the railroad station. She found Mr. Queen seated before the fire in the kitchen in his undershirt, while Martha Clarke caressed his naked right arm.

"Oh!" said Nikki faintly. "I *beg* your pardon."

"Where are you going, Nikki?" said Ellery irritably. "Come in. Martha's rubbing liniment into my biceps."

"He's not very accustomed to chopping wood, is he?" asked Martha Clarke in a cheerful voice.

"Reduced those foul 'oakes' to splinters," groaned Ellery. "Martha, ouch!"

"I should think you'd be satisfied *now*," said Nikki coldly. "I suggest we imitate Patch, Shaw, and the Baroness, Ellery—there's a 3.05. We can't impose on Miss Clarke's hospitality forever."

To Nikki's horror, Martha Clarke chose this moment to burst into tears.

"Martha!"

Nikki felt like leaping upon her and shaking the cool look back into her perfidious eyes.

36

"Here—here, now, Martha." That's right, thought Nikki contemptuously. Embrace her in front of me! "It's those three rats. Running out that way! Don't worry—I'll find that sword and half disme for you yet."

"You'll never find them," sobbed Martha, wetting Ellery's undershirt. "Because they're not here. They *never* were here. When you s-stop to think of it ... *burying* that coin, his sword ... if the story were true, he'd have given them to Simeon and Sarah ..."

"Not necessarily, not necessarily," said Ellery with a hateful haste. "The old boy had a sense of history, Martha. They all did in those days. They knew they were men of destiny and that the eyes of posterity were upon them. Burying 'em is *just* what Washington would have done!"

"Do you really th-think so?"

Oh ... *pfui*.

"But even if he did bury them," Martha sniffled, "it doesn't stand to reason Simeon and Sarah would have let them *stay* buried. They'd have dug that copper box up like rabbits the minute G-George turned his back."

"Two simple countryfolk?" cried Ellery. "Salt of the earth? The new American earth? Disregard the wishes of His Mightiness, George Washington, First President of the United States? Are you out of your mind? And anyway, what would Simeon do with a dress-sword?"

Beat it into a ploughshare, thought Nikki spitefully—*that's* what he'd do.

"And that half disme. How much could it have been worth in 1791? Martha, they're here under your farm somewhere. You wait and see——"

"I wish I could b-believe it ... Ellery."

"Shucks, child. Now stop crying——"

From the door Miss Porter said stiffly: "You might put your shirt back on, Superman, before you catch pneumonia."

Mr. Queen prowled about the Clarke acres for the remainder of that day, his nose at a low altitude. He spent some time in the barn. He devoted at least twenty minutes to each of the twelve holes in the earth. He reinspected the oaken wreckage of his axework like a palaeontologist examining an ancient petrifaction for the impression of a dinosaur foot. He measured off the distance between the holes; and, for a moment, a faint tremor of emotion shook him. George Washington had been a surveyor in his youth; here was evidence that his passion for exactitude

had not wearied with the years. As far as Ellery could
make out, the twelve oaks had been set into the earth at
exactly equal distances, in an equilateral triangle.

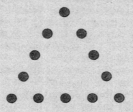

It was at this point that Ellery had seated himself upon
the seat of a cultivator behind the barn, wondering at his
suddenly accelerated circulation. Little memories were
knocking at the door. And as he opened to admit them, it
was as if he were admitting a personality. It was, of
course, at this time that the sense of personal conflict first
obtruded. He had merely to shut his eyes in order to
materialize a tall, large-featured man carefully pacing off
the distances between twelve points—pacing them off in a
sort of objective challenge to the unborn future. George
Washington . . .

The man Washington had from the beginning possessed
an affinity for numbers. It had remained with him all his
life. To count things, not so much for the sake of the
things, perhaps, as for the counting, had been of the
utmost importance to him. As a boy in Mr. William's
school in Westmorland, he excelled in arithmetic, long
division, subtraction, weights and measures—to calculate
cords of wood and pecks of peas, pints and gallons and
avoirdupois—young George delighted in these as other
boys delighted in horseplay. As a man, he merely directed
his passion into the channel of his possessions. Through his
possessions he apparently satisfied his curious need for
enumeration. He was not content simply to keep accounts
of the acreage he owned, its yield, his slaves, his pounds
and pence. Ellery recalled the extraordinary case of Washington and the seed. He once calculated the number of
seeds in a pound troy weight of red clover. Not appeased
by the statistics on red clover, Washington then went to
work on a pound of timothy seed. His conclusions were:
71,000 and 298,000. His appetite unsatisfied, he thereupon
fell upon the problem of New River grass. Here he

tackled a calculation worthy of his prowess: his mathematical labours produced the great, pacifying figure of 844,800.

This man was so obsessed with numbers, Ellery thought, staring at the ruins of Washington's Grove, that he counted the windows in each house of his Mount Vernon estate and the number of "Paynes" in each window of each house, and then triumphantly recorded the exact number of each in his own handwriting.

It was like a hunger, requiring periodic appeasement. In 1747, as a boy of fifteen, George Washington drew "A Plan of Major Law: Washington's Turnip Field as Survey'd by me," In 1786, at the age of fifty-four, General Washington, the most famous man in the world, occupied himself with determining the exact elevation of his piazza above the Potomac's high-water mark. No doubt he experienced a warmer satisfaction thereafter for knowing that when he sat upon his piazza looking down upon the river he was sitting exactly 124 feet 10½ inches above it.

And in 1791, as President of the United States, Ellery mused, he was striding about right here, setting saplings into the ground, twelve of them in an equilateral triangle, and beneath one of them he buried a copper case containing his sword and the half disme coined from his own silver. Beneath one of them . . . But it was not beneath one of them. Or had it been? And had long ago been dug up by a Clarke? But the story had apparently died with Simeon and Sarah. On the other hand . . .

Ellery found himself irrationally reluctant to conclude the obvious. George Washington's lifelong absorption with figures kept intruding. Twelve trees, equidistant, in an equilateral triangle.

"What is it?" he kept asking himself, almost angrily. "Why isn't it satisfying me?"

And then, in the gathering dusk, a very odd explanation insinuated itself. *Because it wouldn't have satisfied him!*

That's silly, Ellery said to himself abruptly. It has all the earmarks of a satisfying experience. There is no more satisfying figure in all geometry than an equilateral triangle. It is closed, symmetrical, definite, a whole and balanced and finished thing.

But it wouldn't have satisfied George Washington . . . for all its symmetry and perfection.

Then perhaps there is a symmetry and perfection beyond the cold beauty of figures?

39

At this point, Ellery began to question his own postulates . . . lost in the dark and to his time . . .

They found him at ten-thirty, crouched on the cultivator seat, numb and staring.

He permitted himself to be led into the house, he suffered Nikki to subject him to the indignity of having his shoes and socks stripped off and his frozen feet rubbed to life, he ate Martha Clarke's dinner—all with a detachment and indifference which alarmed the girls and even made old Tobias look uneasy.

"If it's going to have this effect on him," began Martha, and then she said: "Ellery, give it up. Forget it." But she had to shake him before he heard her.

He shook his head. "They're there."

"Where?" cried the girls simultaneously.

"In Washington's Grove."

"Ye found 'em?" croaked Tobias Clarke, half-rising.

"No."

The Clarkes and Nikki exchanged glances.

"Then how can you be so certain they're buried there, Ellery?" asked Nikki gently.

Ellery looked bewildered. "Darned if I know *how* I know," he said, and he even laughed a little. "Maybe George Washington told me." Then he stopped laughing and went into the firelit parlour and—pointedly—slid the doors shut.

At ten minutes past midnight Martha Clarke gave up the contest.

"Isn't he ever going to come out of there?" she said, yawning.

"You never can tell what Ellery will do," replied Nikki.

"Well, I can't keep my eyes open another minute."

"Funny," said Nikki. "I'm not in the least bit sleepy."

"You city girls."

"You country girls."

They laughed. Then they stopped laughing, and for a moment there was no sound in the kitchen but the patient sentry-walk of the grandfather clock and the snores of Tobias assaulting the ceiling from above.

"Well," said Martha. Then she said: "I just *can't*. Are you staying up, Nikki?"

"For a little while. You go to bed, Martha."

"Yes. Well. Good night."

"Good night, Martha."

40

At the door Martha turned suddenly: "Did he say *George Washington told him?*"

"Yes."

Martha went rather quickly up the stairs.

Nikki waited fifteen minutes. Then she tiptoed to the foot of the stairs and listened. She heard Tobias snuffling and snorting as he turned over in his bed, and an uneasy moan from the direction of Martha's bedroom, as if she were dreaming an unwholesome dream. Nikki set her jaw grimly and went to the parlour doors and slid them open.

Ellery was on his knees before the fire. His elbows were resting on the floor. His face was propped in his hands. In this attitude his posterior was considerably higher than his head.

"Ellery!"

"Huh?"

"Ellery, what on earth——?"

"Nikki. I thought you'd gone to bed long ago." In the firelight his face was haggard.

"But what have you been *doing*? You looked exhausted?"

"I am. I've been wrestling with a man who could bend a horseshoe with his naked hands. A very strong man. In more ways than one."

"What are you talking about? Who?"

"George Washington. Go to bed, Nikki."

"George . . . Washington?"

"Go to bed."

". . . *Wrestling* with him?"

"Trying to break through his defenses. Get into his mind. It's not an easy mind to get into. He's been dead such a long time—that makes the difference. The dead are stubborn, Nikki. Aren't you going to bed?"

Nikki backed out shivering.

The house *was* icy.

It was even icier when an inhuman bellow accompanied by a thunder that shook the Revolutionary walls of her bedroom brought Nikki out of bed with a yelping leap.

But it was only Ellery.

He was somewhere up the hall, in the first glacial light of dawn, hammering on Martha Clarke's door.

"Martha. *Martha!* Wake up, damn you, and tell me where I can find a book in this damned house! A biography of Washington—a history of the United States—an almanac . . . *anything!*"

The parlour fire had long since given up the ghost. Nikki and Martha in wrappers, and Tobias Clarke in an ancient bathrobe over his marbled long underwear, stood around shivering and bewildered as a dishevelled, daemonic Ellery leafed eagerly through a 1921 edition of *The Farmer's Fact Book and Complete Compendium.*

"Here it is!" The words shot out of his mouth like bullets, leaving puffs of smoke.

"What is it, Ellery?"

"What on earth are you looking for?"

"He's loony, I tell ye!"

Ellery turned with a look of ineffable peace, closing the book.

"That's it," he said. "That's it."

"What's it?"

"Vermont. The State of Vermont."

"Vermont . . . ?"

"Ver*mont*?"

"Vermont. What in the crawlin' creepers's Vermont got to do with———"

"Vermont," said Ellery with a tired smile, "did not enter the Union until March fourth, 1791. So that proves it, don't you see?"

"Proves *what*?" shrieked Nikki.

"Where George Washington buried his sword and half disme."

"Because," said Ellery in the rapidly lightening dawn behind the barn, "Vermont was the fourteenth State to do so. The *fourteenth*. Tobias, would you get me an axe, please?"

"An axe," mumbled Tobias. He shuffled away, shaking his head.

"Come on, Ellery, I'm d-dying of c-cold!" chattered Nikki, dancing up and down before the cultivator.

"Ellery," said Martha Clarke piteously, "I don't understand *any* of this."

"It's very simple, Martha—oh, thank you, Tobias—as simple," said Ellery, "as simple arithmetic. Numbers, my dears—numbers tell this remarable story. Numbers and their influence on our first President who was, above all things, a number-man. That was my key. I merely had to discover the lock to fit it into. Vermont was the lock. And the door's open."

Nikki seated herself on the cultivator. You had to give

42

Ellery his head in a situation like this; you couldn't drive him for beans. Well, she thought grudgingly, seeing how pale and how tired-looking he was after a night's wrestling with George Washington, he's earned it.

"The number was wrong," said Ellery solemnly, leaning on Tobias's axe. "Twelve trees. Washington apparently planted twelve trees—Simeon Clarke's *Diary* never did mention the number twelve, but the evidence seemed unquestionable—there were twelve oaks in an equilateral triangle, each one an equal distance from its neighbour.

"And yet . . . I felt that *twelve* oaks couldn't be, perfect as the triangle was. Not if they were planted by George Washington. Not on February the twenty-second, New Style, in the year of our Lord 1791.

"Because on February the twenty-second, 1791—in fact, until March the fourth, when Vermont entered the Union to swell its original number by one—there was *another* number in the United States so important, so revered, so much a part of the common speech and the common living—and dying—that it was more than a number; it was a solemn and sacred thing; almost not a number at all. It overshadowed other numbers like the still-unborn Paul Bunyan. It was memorialized on the New American flag in the number of its stars and the number of its stripes. It was a number of which George Washington was the standard-bearer!—the head and only recently the strong right arm of the new Republic which had been born out of the blood and muscle of its integers. It was a number which was in the hearts and minds and mouths of all Americans.

"No. If George Washington, who was not merely the living symbol of all this but carried with him that extraordinary compulsion toward numbers which characterized his whole temperament besides, had wished to plant a number of oak trees to commemorate a birthday visit in the year 1791 . . . he would have, he could have, selected only one number out of all the mathematical trillions at his command—*the number thirteen.*"

The sun was looking over the edge of Pennsylvania at Washington's Grove.

"George Washington planted thirteen trees here that day, and under one of them he buried Paul Revere's copper case. Twelve of the trees he arranged in an equilateral triangle, and we know that the historic treasure was not under any of the twelve. Therefore he must have buried the case under the thirteenth—a thirteenth oak

43

sapling which grew to oakhood and, some time during the past century and a half, withered and died and vanished, vanished so utterly that it left no trace, not even its roots.

"Where would Washington have planted that thirteenth oak? Because beneath the spot where it once stood—there lies the copper case containing his sword and the first coin to be struck off in the new United States."

And Ellery glanced tenderly at the cherry sapling which Tobias Clarke had set into the earth in the middle of Washington's Grove six years before.

"Washington the surveyor, the geometer, the man whose mind cried out for integral symmetries? Obviously, in only one place: *In the centre of the triangle*. Any other place would be unthinkable."

And Ellery hefted Tobias's axe and strode toward the six-year-old tree. He raised the axe.

But suddenly he lowered it, and turned, and said in a rather startled way: "See here! Isn't to-day . . . ?"

"Washington's Birthday," said Nikki.

Ellery grinned and began to chop down the cherry tree.

The Adventure of
the Ides of Michael Magoon

IT WAS PASSSED in the third session of the 65th Congress and approved as of 6.55 p.m. on the twenty-fourth of February, 1919, and its title is Public—No. 254 [H.R. 12863].

Nor is there anything alarming in its subtitle, which happens to be *An Act To provide revenue, and for other purposes.* The fifth word may raise a few scattered goose pimples, but hardly more.

It is necessary to read on.

Nothing will be clear until you come upon the phrase, "on or before the fifteenth day of March."

Then everything will be clear, clear as the clap of the tocsin. There is only one calamity which befalls America, *urbs et suburbs,* on or before the fifteenth day of March, and that is the income tax.

Before going on to Michael Magoon and his unusual tax problem, it is tempting to take a short detour into the statutes, which concern not Mike alone but very nearly all of us. There was income-tax legislation before the Revenue Act of 1918, and there has been income-tax legislation since, but Public—No. 254 [H.R. 12863] bears a curious distinction. It was the first income-tax law which pronounced the annual Judgment Day to be March the fifteenth. Its predecessors designated March the first.

Why the change in dates?

There is a reason, of course, and it is not the reason your tax expert, for all his awful knowledge, can give you.

Someone—perhaps it was Mr. Secretary of the Treasury, or a Gentleman from Indiana or Ohio, or even some lowlier lackey of the Peopl with a finger in the legislative pie—someone with a frightening lack of humour remembered great Ceasar and the bloody daggers. Someone remembered the signs and the portents and the gathering crimson thunderheads over the full Capitoline moon. He may even have recalled that *postridie idus.*, the day following the Ides, was held by the ancient Romans to be unlucky.

And who among us, after rendering unto Caesar, will deny on any given March the sixteenth that the Romans were right?

The whole thing was certainly unlucky for Magoon.

Mike was what the fancy boys like to call a private "op," or "eye." These fascinating terms inevitably materialise a slim-hipped, narrow-eyed, cigarette-dragging character in a Finchley custom-drape, a Sulka tie and a $35 Dobbs, who is greased death on the draw, kills five thugs and one master mind on every case, is as irresistible with dames as a fox in a hen-coop, carries a self-refillable flask of Scottish dew on the other hip, and speaks, when he speaks at all, in insolent monosyllables—something out of Chandler by Bogart.

Alas. Mike Magoon was a sagging 63 with a 48 waist, very large flat feet, and blinky brown eyes covered by tortoiseshell glasses, which gave him an air of groping astonishment. He wore Adam hats, suits from Barney's and shoes by W. L. Douglas. And he neither smoked nor drank—asthma barred the one and, as for the other, his good wife had the nasal infallibility of a beagle. He had never manhandled a lady client in his life; not that he lacked a libido, but he cherished his license more. And in the sudden-death department, he had discharged his Police Positive exactly twice since resigning from the Force four years before, and one of those times he was cleaning his pistol in the fire escape when a neighbour's pride and joy whanged his shooting hand with a well-directed B.B. shot.

No cases came Mike's way involving mysterious fat men with inscrutable eyes, or Maltese falcons, or gangster chieftains in luxurious penthouses. For the most part he spent his time trailing thirtyish ladies for suspicious husbands or putting the grab on shop clerks allergic to the boss's till. On those Saturday nights when he was not working, he took his wife to the movies. On Sundays, after church, there was always The Little Ukraine on Fordham Road—Mike was mad about *shashlik* and *borscht* with sour cream. And on Wednesday nights, bingo.

The first three years Mike was a private eye he operated out of his three-room Bronx flat to cut the overhead, picking up what cases he could through tips from old friends in brass buttons. Then he and Mrs. Magoon decided that a front and a midtown telephone number might pay for more bingo games, so Mike sublet one room of a four-office suite in a 42nd Street office building, sharing the premises with a public stenographer, a commercial artist and a little bald man with a gold tooth who had four phones which were always ringing. A week after *Michael Magoon, Confidential Investigations,* had sprouted in gilt on his pebbled-glass door, Mike opened it to admit Mrs. Clementa Van Dome, the kind of client the Magoons of this world lie awake nights praying for: the client who pays an annual retainer for continuous services rendered. It was a klep case in which—but more of Mrs. Van Dome anon.

Three times since that gold letter day the Ides of Martius came and went, and Casesar was satisfied. And then came the fourth time.

The fourth time it was Mike who went, hurrying as fast as his asthma and flat feet would permit, to the Queen apartment.

A detective consulting a detective struck Nikki's funny-bone. And poor Mike's manner as he looked around at the Queen walls somehow made it even funnier.

But the best was still to come.

"Ellery," said Mike, blushing. "I have been robbed."

"Robbed." said Ellery with a straight face. "Robbed of what, Mike?"

"My income tax return."

Nikki excused herself heroically. When she came back, Ellery was putting his handkerchief away.

"Forgive me, Mike," he was saying. "My old pleurisy. Did you say your tax return has been stolen?"

"That's what I said, and you're healthy as a horse," said Mike Magoon doggedly. "Oh, I don't blame you for goin' into hysterics. But it ain't funny, McGee. To-day's the fourteenth of March. How am I gonna make the March fifteenth deadline?"

"Well, your—hrm!—return can't be terribly complicated, Michael," said Ellery gravely. "Get another blank and fill it in, and so on."

"With what, I ask you!"

"With what?"

"You gotta have data!"

"Well, certainly. Don't you have data?"

"No!"

47

"But——"

"Listen, Ellery. All my papers and records—everything I was usin' to make out my return—it's all been swiped!"

"Oh."

"It was in this brief-case, the whole business. It'd take me weeks to round up duplicates of my records! Meanwhile, what do I say to the Collector of Internal Revenue?" And Mike, because he was an old stable-mate of Inspector Queen's and had known Ellery when he was a cigar in the Inspector's pocket, added: "Wise guy?"

"Ellery, that is a nuisance." said Nikki, glancing over at the table to make sure that her own records and return were still there.

"Records and all . . . Where were the contents of your brief-case stolen from. Mike?"

"My office. You been up there, Ellery—you know there's three other tenants——"

"And you all use a common reception-room," Ellery nodded. "Were you in your office at the time, Mike?"

"Yes. Well, no—not exactly. Look. I better tell you the whole thing, just the way it happened. It's got me loopin'."

It had happened around 6 p.m. the previous day. Mike had been working on his tax return. Just before six he had decided to give up the struggle for the day. He had collected his cancelled checks, memoranda, receipted bills and so on and had put them, together with his return. into his brief-case.

"I'd just put on my overcoat," said Mike, "when Mrs. Carson—she's the public steno who leases the suite and rents out the offices—Mrs. Carson comes runnin' into my office yellin' there's a fire in the reception-room. So I run out there and, sure enough, the settee's on fire. Somebody'd dropped a match into a waste-paper basket right next to it, and it blazed up and the settee caught fire. Well, it wasn't much—I put it out in five minutes—then I go back to my office, pick up my hat and brief-case, and amble on home."

"And of course," sighed Ellery, "when you got home you opened your brief-case and your return and records were gone."

"With the wind," said Michael Magoon bitterly. "Cleaned out and a newspaper stuffed inside instead."

"Could the transfer have been made, Mike, en route from your office to your home?"

"Impossible. I walked over from the office to the garage where I park my car with the brief-case under my arm. Then I drove home, the case next to me on the car seat."

"You're sure this is the same brief-case?"

"Oh, sure. It's an old one. It's my case, all right."

"Then it wasn't a wholesale substitution," said Ellery thoughtfully. "Someone opened your case on your office desk, removed its contents, substituted a newspaper, and closed the case again, all while you were putting out the fire in the reception-room."

"It must have been that Mrs. Carson," said Nikki, wondering how the obvious could have escaped even such a pedestrian sleuth as Mike Magoon.

"How about it, Mike?" asked Ellery.

"Not a chance. She ran out in front of me and stayed with me in the reception-room, runnin' back and forth from the watercooler to the settee with a vase she keeps on her desk. Didn't leave my sight for a second."

"Who else was in the suite, Mike?"

"The two other tenants. One of 'em's a commercial artist named Vince, Leonardo Vince, a screwball if I ever saw one. The other's a little crumb calls himself Ziggy, Jack Ziggy. He thinks I don't know it, but he's a bookie."

"Didn't Vince and Ziggy run out of their offices when you and Mrs. Carson tackled the fire?"

"Sure. But they didn't help put it out—just stood around givin' advice. I didn't pay any attention to either of 'em."

"Then it's possible one of *them*——?"

"It's possible. But I can't be sure. Anyway, I drove right back down to the office again last night, thinkin' maybe I'd left my tax stuff on my desk or somethin'——"

"But of course it wasn't there."

"I didn't sleep last night," said Mike miserably, "and if I could have slept, the old lady's jawin' would have kept me awake."

"Have you been to the office this morning, Mike?"

"No. I came right down here, Ellery."

"Well," Ellery rose and began to fill his pipe. "A very unusual problem, Mike."

"Huh?"

"Unusual!" said Nikki. "All right, Mr. Queen, I'll bite. What's unusual about it?"

"Why should someone steal a man's income-tax return—the return of a man like Mike? To find out what Mike's

49

income was last year? With all respect to your industry, Michael, that could hardly interest anyone; and more to the point, if that was what the thief was after, he wouldn't have to *steal* the return—a quick look would tell him what he wanted to know."

"Then why," asked Nikki, "did he steal it?"

"That," replied Ellery, "is what makes the problem interesting. Mike." He eyed Mike sternly. "Have you been up to anything illegal?"

"Illegal!"

Ellery chuckled. "Routine question, Michael. Of course, if you were finagling, you'd hardly report it to Uncle Sam. No." Ellery puffed on his pipe. "The only thing that makes sense is the source of your income."

"I don't get it," complained the eye.

"Now, now. After all, Mike, you're a private dick. Your own shingle advertises the confidential nature of your work. Tell me: Which paper or papers in your brief-case referred to a client or case in which *secrecy* is of the essence?"

Mike looked doubtful. "Well, all my cases are what you might call confidential——"

"Mike, I'm willing to bet your tax against mine that you have at least one client who's extremely wealthy, who came to you under a pledge of absolute secrecy . . . and whose records, or a record of whose case, were in your brief-case yesterday."

"Mrs. Van Dome," said Magoon, gaping.

"Mrs. Van Dome," said Ellery briskly. "Sounds as if I've hit the jack-pot, Mike. Nikki—notes!"

And Michael Magoon told the story of his very best client, Mrs. Clementa Van Swicken Van Dome.

Mrs. Clementa Van Swicken Van Dome, had she been either a Van Swicken or a Van Dome, would have occupied a position of high altitude on the social pyramid. Being both a Van Swicken and a Van Dome, she reigned alone at the very apex, surrounded by the stratosphere and God. She was so far out of sight of mere earthlings that Nikki, who was Ellery's Almanach de Gotha, had never heard of her, whereas Ellery had. She considered Park Avenue gauche, and the D.A.R. upstarts. A Van Swicken had helped build Fort Amsterdam in ye Manhatas, and a Van Dome had led the trek to Gowanus Bay nine years before he became restless and moved on to establish a settlement which was named Breuckelen. The measure of Mrs. Clementa Van Swicken Van Dome's social standing was that she was invited to all the most exclusive functions in New York and never went to any. She herself gave one party each year; her guest-list was more carefully scrutinized than the personnel at Oak Ridge, Tennessee, and only those were invited whose forefathers had settled in the New World before 1651 and whose fortunes had not been tainted by trade for at least six generations.

Mrs. Van Dome was a widow, and she had one child, a daughter.

"You ought to see this Margreta," said Mike Magoon. "Skinny as a pretzel-stick, pimples all over her map, forty-five if she's a day, and she's a poetess."

"A what?" said Nikki.

"She writes poetry," said Mike firmly.

"Under the name of Hollandia," nodded Ellery. "Brutal stuff. I take it, Mike, mama consulted you about Margreta?"

"That's it."

"Just because she writes bad poetry?" said Nikki.

"Because she's a klep, Miss Porter."

Nikki looked excited, "What's that? It sounds——"

"Relax, Nikki," said Ellery. "Mike means a kleptomaniac. It all begins to be too, too, clear, Michael. Stop me if I'm wrong. If there's one thing Mrs. Van Dome fears, it's scandal. The unlovely Margreta does not merely commit the crime of writing bad poetry, she also develops a yearning to take things belonging to other people. There have been polite complaints, perhaps, discreetly made to mama. Mama pays, but begins to worry. Margreta shows no signs of reform. The habit grows. It will soon be in the papers. Mama comes to a relatively unknown private detective—no doubt after checking your personal reputation, Mike, with your old pals at Headquarters—and puts Margreta into your hands on a one-hundred-per-cent. hush-hush basis."

"That's it, that's it," said Mike. "My job is to protect Margreta from arrest and publicity. I trail her whenever she hits the street. When I see her take somethin', I quietly pay for it after she drifts on. Mrs. Van Dome gives me an expense account—which, believe me, she looks over with an eagle eye! I get an annual retainer—not a heck of a lot, but it's good steady dough."

"And among your income tax records," nodded Ellery,

"were the various accounts, receipted bills, *et cetera,* pertaining to the misadventures of Margreta."

"Somebody," cried Nikki, "trailed Mr. Magoon or something, saw what was going on, then stole his income tax records to . . ." Nikki stopped. "To what?"

"To make use of them," said Ellery dryly, "obviously."

"Blackmail!" roared Mike, jumping up as if he had just been given the hot-foot. "By cripes, Ellery, with those receipted bills, and correspondence and stuff—whoever it was could blackmail old lady Van Dome till she was . . . black in the face! She'd pay anything to keep that yarn from gettin' out! That's it!"

"Somebody," said Nikki. "Who's somebody?"

Mike sat down.

But Ellery, knocking his pipe out on the fire screen, said: "Mrs. Carson."

"But Ellery, Mr. Magoon says she couldn't possibly——"

"Nikki. A fire starts in a waste-basket which ignites an office settee which sends Mrs. Carson running into Mike's office yelling for him to . . . what? Run out—with her. Mike does so. And Mrs. Carson sticks with him." Ellery shrugged. "By the same token, Mike sticks with Mrs. Carson . . . while Mrs. Carson's accomplice slips into Mike's office and, having no time to winnow the Van Dome papers from the rest, lifts the entire contents of Mike's brief-case, puts a newspaper stuffing in their place, and slips out. Mike," said Ellery, setting his pipe into the mantelpiece rack, "let's go down to your office and give that public stenographer a little dictation."

So Collector of Internal Revenue *v.* Magoon was a simple business after all.

Only, it wasn't.

When they opened Mrs. Carson's door they found Mrs. Carson taking dictation from a higher Authority.

"Feeling better now?" asked Ellery, drinking the rest of the bourbon in the paper cup.

"Oh Ellery," moaned Nikki. "That dead woman."

"Is a dead woman."

"But a dead woman without a face!"

"I should think you'd be used to that sort of thing by now, Nikki."

"I suppose that's why you finished my drink."

"I was thirsty," said Ellery with dignity; and he strolled through Mrs. Carson's doorway waging a heroic battle with his stomach.

They were standing around the typewriter desk staring down at Mrs. Carson's ruins. Nobody was saying anything.

"Oh, Ellery."

"Dad."

"Six inches," said Inspector Queen in a wondering voice. "The rod was fired not more than six inches from her pan."

"There's no question but that it's Mrs. Carson?"

"It's her all right." Mike was slugging it out too.

"Mrs.," said Ellery, looking at her left hand. "Where's Mr.?"

"In Montefiore Cemetery," said Mike, still swallowing powerfully. "He kicked off six years ago, she told me."

"How old was she, Mike?" Funny how hard it was to tell a woman's age when her face was not there for reference.

"I'd have said round thirty-six, thirty-eight."

"Ever mention a boy friend?" asked the Inspector.

"Nope. And she never seemed to have a date, Inspector. Always workin' in here late."

"Michael, Michael," said Inspector Queen. "That's *why* she worked in here late. Only she wasn't working. Not at a typewriter, anyway."

Through the greenish overcast. Mike looked puzzled.

The old gentleman said impatiently: "We know she decoyed you with that fire she set herself; we know somebody lifted the Van Dome stuff from your brief-case during the fire. And who was here at the time? The other two tenants. So one of *them* was the Carson woman's accomplice. Does it fit? Sure, Mike. When she was 'working late,' she was playing hoopla with either Leonardo Vince or Jack Ziggy right here in the office."

"But then," muttered Mike Magoon, "who plugged her last night? You mean Vince, or Ziggy . . .?"

The Inspector nodded.

"But why, Inspector!"

"Michael, Michael."

"The double-cross, Dad?" asked Ellery, not sceptically— just asking.

"What else? She helps him swipe the documents he can blackmail Mrs. Van Dome with, so then he rubs the girl friend out. He's got it all to himself and no blabbermouth to worry about besides. Ellery, why are you looking as if you smell something."

"He must be very stupid," said Ellery.

"Sure," said his father cheerfully. "They're only smart in the fairy tales you write. Now if this were one of your mystery plots, Ellery, you know who'd be the criminal?"

"Mike," said Ellery.

"*Me!*" Mike immediately looked guilty.

"Sure, Mike," chuckled the Inspector. "By the way, what time was it when you got back here last night? Your return trip, Mike—when you came back to see if you'd left your papers behind?"

"So that's it," growled Mike. "Listen here, Inspector . . .!"

"Oh, don't be an ass, Mike," said Ellery irritably. "What time was it? Was she alive? Was her light on? What?"

"Oh. Yeah, sure. Must have been a quarter of eight or so. She was workin' in her office here. I says Mrs. Carson did you find any papers of mine around from my briefcase and she says no Mr. Magoon I didn't. I says where's Ziggy and that nut artist and she says oh they went home long ago. So I says good night and goes back home myself."

"How did she seem to you at the time, Mike?"

"Okay."

"Not nervous?"

"Hell, I don't know. She was always nervous."

"Well." The Inspector scratched his head. "The best Doc Prouty can give us is that she was killed between seven and nine last night. The cleaning woman's no help— she was through giving the offices a lick and a promise by seven o'clock, she says, and she says Mrs. Carson was here alone. So, Mike if you left her alive near eight, then she was bopped between eight and nine."

"By one of these two characters," said Sergeant Velie from the doorway.

The first man was a tall, frayed, decayed-looking fellow with prehensile dirty fingers and half-slices of lemon under his eyes. The second was a little bald-headed man with a very gold tooth. Their eyes bugged at the thing lolling on the typewriter and they both back-pedalled fast. But Sergeant Velie was leaning in the doorway, licking a cigar.

The tall man went over to the window and opened it and stuck his face out into the cold March airstream. The small man went over to Mrs. Carson's waste-basket and bent over, almost embracing it.

"How can you stand it? How can you stand it?" the tall man kept saying.

"Arrrgh," said the little man.

54

"That's Vince the artist," said Mike. "That's Jack Ziggy the bookie," said Mike.

"I didn't kill her," said the tall man. "I'm an artist. I'm interested in life. I couldn't kill a spider crawling up my leg. Ask anybody. Don't think you'll make me say I did it. Cut pieces out of me——" Leonardo Vince was getting worked up, blood in his musty face again.

"You've made your point, Vince," said the Inspector mildly. "I suppose, Ziggy, you didn't kill her either."

The little bald man raised his head to reply, but then he stooped quickly again and repeated "Arrrgh!"

Sergeant Velie drawled: "Inspector."

"Huh?" The old gentleman did not glance at him.

"The night man here says Vince and Ziggy both came back to the buildin' last night. He can't remember the exact time, but he says they came separate, and they came between eight and nine."

Mrs. Carson was a pall, definitely. Even Sergeant Velie sucked on his cigar with more enjoyment when she floated out of the office between two Welfare men.

Leonardo Vince shut the window, shivering, and the little bookmaker straightened up with the waste-basket, glancing around apologetically. The Inspector nodded to a detective and Jack Ziggy went out holding the basket high and wide.

"Cobalt blue," said the Inspector to the artist. "You were saying . . . ?"

"You can't make it out red or ochre or any damned thing but what I say it was," said Vince wearily. "It was cobalt blue. Go into my office and see if you can find the tube. You can't. It's not there. I took it home last night. That's why I came back. I may serve commerce during the day, and damn the shrivelled souls of all agency men!—but my nights are dedicated to Art, gentlemen, with a capital and profitless A. I got home, had a bite, went to my easel, and found I had no cobalt blue which I happened to need for a purpose which would be far above your vulgar understanding. The supply stores were closed. I returned to the office here for a tube of——"

"Cobalt blue," said the Inspector, nodding. He stared at Vince hard. Vince stared back, with hate. "And Mrs. Carson was——?"

"Am I supposed to contradict myself?" asked the artist bitterly. "But how could I? A child could repeat this story *ad infinitum.* I didn't even see Mrs. Carson. There was a light on in her office, but the door was shut. Don't bother to ask the next question. It was about eight-fifteen. No, the homunculus wasn't here—I refer to the creature who calls himself Zigggy—at least, I didn't see him. And I have no idea if the woman was alive or dead; I heard not a whisper from her office. And lastly, I am a woman-hater. Now what do I do—say it all over again?"

On the heels of this remarkable soliloquy came the homunculus, with the detective but without the wastebasket.

"And me," whined Ziggy, "me, I don't know——"

"Nuttin."

"—nuttin. But from nuttin."

"You had a couple of parties to ring up," prompted Inspector Queen politely, "and——?"

"Yeah. Private calls, see? Confidentially, some of my clients owe me some back dough and they been tryin' to sucker me, so I come back at eight-thirty to use my own phone, see? More private, like. And I don't remember a thing, not a thing. No light, no Mrs. Carson, no nuttin. I don't remember nuttin. I don't see nobody, I don't hear nobody——"

"Oh, hell," said the Inspector. "Ellery, have you got anything?"

"I see no reason," said Ellery absently, "to hold these two men any longer."

His father frowned.

"You've established no connection between these fellows and Mrs. Carson, beyond a common tenancy. The woman was obviously killed by someone else. Get them out of here, Dad—I'm sicker of them than you are."

When Leonardo Vince and Jack Ziggy were gone, the old gentleman said: "All right, Master Mind. What's the great big plot?"

"And why'd you warn us not to say anything about Mike's income tax stuff on Mrs. Van Dome bein' swiped?" demanded Sergeant Velie.

"Suppose," said Ellery, "suppose thief-killer-potential-blackmailer is in desperate need of ready cash." He looked at them.

"He wouldn't dare," breathed his father. "Not *now*."

"Maestro, he's hot!"

"He doesn't know we've made the least connection between the theft of Mike's records and the murder of Mrs. Carson."

Inspector Queen trotted around the office, pulling at his moustache.

Then he stopped and said: "Mike, phone that Mrs. Van Dome. I want to talk to her."

The next morning, when Ellery hung up, he said to his audience: "It's a curious experience, speaking to Mrs. Van Dome. Didn't you find it so yesterday, Dad?"

"Never mind how I found that snooty, upstaging, cop-hating old battle-axe," grunted the Inspector. "What did she just say, Ellery?"

"Like a dream-trip through outer space. It leaves you with an exhilarating memory of indescribable grandeurs and only the vaguest sense of reality. Mike, does she really exist?"

"Never mind the fancy stuff," growled Magoon. "What did she *say*?"

"She received the note in the first mail this morning."

"Really, Ellery," said Nikki, "your omniscience is disgusting."

"I better ankle over there," said Sergeant Velie, "see her Nibs, get the note, and arrange for——"

"You will not be received," said Ellery dreamily. "Mrs. Clementa Van Swicken Van Dome has just passed a Law. It is to the effect that if she wants to pay blackmail, she'll pay blackmail, and if the City of New York sends so much as one policeman or detective to the rendezvous, she'll sue said City for a large number of millions."

"You mean——" cried the Inspector.

"She's afraid that you'd scare off the blackmailer, Dad. Then he'd give the full and documented story of Margreta's little vice to the newspapers. To prevent that, she's ready to pay ten thousand dollars, and so on. She was quite nasty about it in an imperial sort of way."

"So our hands are tied," groaned the Inspector. "If only we knew what was in that note."

"Oh, that. I have it here on my pad, word for word."

"She *read* it to you?"

"It seems that I," said Ellery, "am a gentleman—of a lower order, to be sure—but still ... Oh, you heard my line. Here's the note: 'Mrs. Van Dome. I have the proof your daughter is a crook. Be in the south Waiting Room at Penn Station at eight p.m. tonight. Bring ten thousand dollars in nothing bigger than twenties. Wear a black hat with a purple nose-veil. Wrap the dough in red paper, hold it under your left arm. Don't tell police. If there's any sign of gumshoes or cops to-night I'll see to it every paper in town gets the lowdown—with photostats—on how your

57

daughter's been lifting stuff from New York department stores for years. Be smart. Play ball. I mean business.' No signature."

"It sounds like that gold-tooth man," said Nikki, but doubtfully.

"I think it's Vince," said Mike excitedly.

"Might be either," grunted the Inspector. "Ziggy being extra-careful about his English, or Vince being purposely sloppy. Good work, son. We'll be there and——"

"Oh, no, you won't."

"You think I won't?"

"City. Suit."

His father ground the inspectorial jaws.

"Besides," said Ellery, "I gave Mrs. Van D. my word as a gentleman that no policeman or city detective would be at the rendezvous tonight."

"Ellery," groaned his father.

"On the other hand, I'm not a policeman or city detective, am I? Nor is Mike. And certainly Nikki isn't."

"Ellery!"

"Mike, you don't look pleased."

"Pleased! To-day is March the fifteenth," said Mike through his teeth, "the rat won't show till eight p.m.—the deadline for income-tax returns is midnight—and he says I don't look pleased."

"Why, Michael," said Ellery soothingly. "That gives us all of four hours."

"To collar this skunk, find out where he's hid my tax stuff, get 'em, finish workin' out my return, and have it in the mail—all between eight and twelve!"

"Cinch," said Ellery. "Michael, my boy, it's as good as in the bag—the mail bag—right now."

Prophecy is a perilous art.

At twelve minutes of eight o'clock on the evening of March fifteenth a large stout woman wearing a black hat and a purple nose-veil, carrying a fat parcel wrapped in red paper under her left arm, appeared suddenly in the entrance to the south Waiting Room at Pennsylvania Station.

Mrs. Clementa Van Swicken Van Dome surveyed her fellow-Americans. There was an expression of excitement on those remote features. So these were the People, it said. One gathered that this was at least as great an adventure.

The People stared back, rather uneasily. The steamfitter

58

jaw bunched, and Mrs. Van Dome swept regally to the nearest bench. A Negro soldier moved over to make room for her. On the other side a young mother was struggling to diaper a kicking, screaming infant. Mrs. Van Dome was seen to take a long, deep breath. Then she sat down, and she sat rigidly. She grew red in the face.

She was trying not to breathe.

At twelve minutes of ten she was still seated there. By now her neighbours were an old man without a tie who was carrying a paper bag, and a girl in a mink coat and no hat who was smoking a cigarette.

The three watchers crossed glances over their newspapers.

"All this excitement," muttered Nikki, "is killing me"—she stirred tenderly—"and you know where."

"He couldn't have spotted us," mumbled Mike. "Ellery, he couldn't have."

"It's unlikely," said Ellery. "Unless he was here at six o'clock and saw us enter the station. If he wasn't, it's even unlikelier because, from where we're sitting, we're invisible unless you come *into* the Waiting Room, or at least stand in the entrance. That's why I picked this spot."

"But then we'd have seen *him,*" winced Nikki.

"Exactly." Ellery rose. "We've either been gulled, or he got cold feet at the last moment."

"But what about Mrs. Van Dome?" asked Nikki.

"Let her stay here inhaling the odours of America," said Ellery. "Do her good. Come on."

"My income tax," groaned Mike Magoon.

And the first people they saw when they entered Inspector Queen's ante-room at Police Headquarters were Leonardo Vince and Jack Ziggy.

"Ellery——" cried Nikki; but then she saw the Inspector's face, and she stopped.

"Ah, here's a man who'll be interested in your yarn, Mr. Vince," said the Inspector genially. "Ellery, guess what. Oh, by the way, son. Did you have a good *dinner?*"

"Disappointing."

"You can't always tell from those fancy menus, can you? As I was saying. At seven-thirty this evening, Mr. Vince marches into Headquarters here. Mr. Vince, tell my son what you told me."

"I was home painting," said Leonardo Vince wearily. "About a quarter of seven my phone rang. It was Western Union. They read me a telegram. It said: 'Want to

59

commission daughter's portrait. Am leaving town to-night but will have few minutes discuss it with you before train time. Meet me eight to-night south Waiting Room Penn Station. Will be wearing black hat and purple nose-veil and carrying red parcel.' "

"Signed," said Inspector Queen, " 'Clementa Van Swicken Van Dome.' "

"Have you——" began Ellery.

"Sure, Maestro," said Sergeant Velie. "That's the copy I myself got from the telegraph office this evenin' when I checked. The message was phoned in to a mid-town station in the middle of the afternoon. They can't tell us who phoned it in. They had instructions to deliver the wire to the addressee at a quarter of seven tonight."

Then Ellery turned to the artist and asked pleasantly: "Well, why didn't you keep the appointment, Mr. Vince."

The artist bared his woody-looking teeth. "Oh, no," he grinned. "Not little Leonardo. You develop an animal instinct for danger when you've been hunted in this world as long as I have. Riches descend on me the very same day I become a suspect in a murder case? Ha, ha! I came straight to Inspector Queen."

"And he's been here," said Inspector Queen dryly, "ever since."

"Can't get him out of the office," complained the Sergeant.

"It's such a nice, safe office," said Leonardo Vince.

"And Mr. Jack Ziggy?" asked Ellery suddenly.

The little bookmaker started. Then he said: "It's a frame. I don't know——"

"Nuttin," said the Inspector. "Mr. Jack Ziggy, Ellery, was picked up at seven-thirty this evening in a routine raid on a big bookie joint on 34th Street and Eighth Avenue."

"When the boys found out who they had," said Velie, "they brought him right here." He looked baleful.

"Where he's been keeping Mr. Vince company. Velie, stay here and entertain these gentlemen. We're going into my office."

"My income tax," muttered Mike Magoon.

"The way I see it," said the Inspector comfortably, putting his feet up on his desk, "is that this is pretty smart stuff. Vince is our baby. He's a cutie. He knows we've connected the theft and the murder. Or he suspects we have, maybe because we haven't handled Mike as a suspect, too. He decides to play it safe."

60

"Sends that letter to Mrs. Van Dome," said Nikki, "making the appointment at Penn Station—then to-day he wires *himself* to keep it!"

"And of course, promptly comes hot-footing it down to me with it instead," nodded the Inspector. "Effect? He's an innocent man being framed for theft, intended extortion, murder—the book."

"But then," protested Mike, "how's he ever figure to blackmail Mrs. Van Dome? I thought that was the whole idea!"

"I think he's a cutie, Mike," replied the Inspector. "He weighs relative values. Decides his original hunch was a bad mistake and this is his way of covering up while he backs out. How does it sound to you, Ellery?"

"Admissible, but rather on the involved side, don't you think?" Ellery scowled. "There's an alternate theory which is much simpler. Mr. Jack Ziggy. Mr. Ziggy, too, develops chilled feet. Mr. Ziggy therefore decides to give us a fall guy. Writes the note to Mrs. Van Dome, sends the wire to Leonardo Vince."

"Maybe he even heard a rumour about that raid," cried Nikki, "and purposely went to that bookie place to be picked up before the eight o'clock meeting to-night at Penn Station! With Vince meeting Mrs. Van Dome, and himself arrested on a minor charge——"

"What's wrong with that, Dad?"

"Not a thing," snarled his father. "*Two* theories. Why couldn't there be just one?"

"My income tax," moaned Mike. "Ain't anybody interested in my income tax? Look at the time!"

"Oh, there are more than two theories, Dad," said Ellery absently.

"I can think of at least two others—either of which would satisfy my plot appetite considerably more. The trouble is——" But then Ellery stopped. He was starting at his father's feet.

"What's the matter?" said the Inspector, sighting along his legs. "Hole in my shoe?"

"That brief-case you've got your feet on," said Ellery.

"What?"

"That's mine," said Mike. "You remember, Ellery, the one I brought when I came to you."

"We took it from Mike after we got down to the offices," said the Inspector. "Here, Mike, we're through with it."

"Wait a minute, Mike," said Ellery. "You know, come

to think of it, I never did examine this brief-case while you were at the apartment, and finding Mrs. Carson dead at the office as soon as we got there ... Dad, may I have that?"

"Sure. But it won't tell you anything."

"Is this the newspaper that the thief stuffed into it?" asked Ellery, drawing out a rather crumpled copy of the *New York Times*.

"Lemme see," said Mike. "Yeah. I remember that tear just over the *T*."

"You're sure, Mike."

"Sure I'm sure!"

"What are you looking so eagled-eyed about?" sniffed Nikki, peering over Ellery's shoulder. "It's just a copy of yesterday's *New York Times*."

"And there isn't an identifiable fingerprint on it," said the Inspector.

"So now tell us you've made a great big blinding deduction."

Ellery opened his mouth, but something else opened simultaneously—the door to Inspector Queen's anteroom. Sergeant Velie stood there.

"Her Highness," said the Sergeant, "is back from the front—madder'n hell."

"Ah, Mrs. Van Dome!" said Ellery, jumping to his feet. "Come in, come in—you're just in time."

"I imagine, Mike," said Ellery, "that your original plan didn't include the concept of an accomplice at all."

"What's that?" said Mike. "What did you say, Ellery?"

"When you set fire to the reception-room settee, it was in a less involved plot. You would smell smoke, you would come running out of your office raising an outcry, Ziggy and Vince and—yes—Mrs. Carson would dash out of *their* offices to see what was the matter, you would put the fire out yourself, and meanwhile any of the three— yes, including Mrs. Carson—might have been the 'thief' who slipped into your office and stole the Van Dome kleptomania-case records. You would have given us three red herrings instead of two—a more nourishing diet."

"What are you talkin' about, Ellery?"

"But something went wrong. In fact, Mike, the most interesting part of your plot to extort money from Mrs. Van Dome is that it never really got started. Something went wrong at the outset. Since Mrs. Carson is the one you murdered, it takes no great intellect to infer that it was Mrs. Carson who threw the monkey-wrench. What was it, Mike? *Did Mrs. Carson accidentally see you set the fire with your own hands?*"

Mike sat very straight in the honoured chair beside the Inspector's desk. But then, all at once, he sagged.

"Yes. She saw you do it, Mike. But you didn't know that till you came back to the office that evening ostensibly to 'see' if you hadn't left your tax records there by mistake. You found Mrs. Carson there alone, you asked her about the tax records . . . and she told you she had seen you set the fire. Did she also perceive dimly that you had taken your own property? I think so, Mike. I think Mrs. Carson accused you of skullduggery, and I think it was then and there that you gave up all thoughts of bleeding Mrs. Van Dome of considerably more than she was paying you to protect her daughter's name. You took your gun and shot Mrs. Carson to death. Very stupid, Mike. Lost your head. But that's the way it is with honest men who go wrong. You'd have been better off to let Mrs. Carson talk. The worst that would have happened is that you might lose your licence—you had still not committed any crime! And even if you had already tried to extort, would Mrs. Van Dome have prosecuted? No, indeed. Your very plot in its origin—setting up a straw man who 'stole' your tax records and so got into the position of being able to blackmail Mrs. Van Dome—was predicated on Mrs. Van Dome's willingness to do anything rather than let the story of her daughter's kleptomania come out.

"All this must have been obvious to you—and still you shot Mrs. Carson. Mike, Mike."

The Inspector was sitting there with his mouth open.

"The rest," said Ellery, scowling, "followed logically. Having killed, you then had to direct attention away from yourself. You'd already made a beginning with the fire. The killing made it look as if Mrs. Carson had been murdered by an 'accomplice.' The 'accomplice' was what you had to work with. And you worked it to death, winding up with a frame of Leonardo Vince—who was supposed to take the rap for you, but—so unpredictable are plots, Mike—who refused to fall into the trap. That was another bad mistake, Mike—picking Mr. Vince. But you made a mistake that was even worse."

The Inspector tried twice to speak, nothing coming out but a bray and a croak. The third time he made it. "But Ellery, this is all speculation! You haven't *deduced* anything. It's guesswork!"

63

This was the most repulsive word in the Queen lexicon.

"Wrong, Dad. There's a clue which, taken at the source, leads on to the logical conclusion. This newspaper." Ellery waved the *New York Times* from Mike's brief-case.

Even Mike looked curious at that. Out of the stupor into which he had fallen he roused himself to blink and lick his lips and glance uneasily at the paper.

"Nikki," said Ellery, "what day is to-day?"

Nikki jumped. "Day? Why, March fifteenth."

"And what is the date on this newspaper?"

"Why, you saw it yourself. And I remarked on it. Yesterday's paper, I said."

"Yesterday's. Then it's the *New York Times* of *March fourteenth*. When did Mike come to consult me?"

"Yesterday morning."

"The morning of March *fourteenth*. When, according to Mike's story, had the theft of his income-tax taken place—the fire, the theft, the substitution of a newspaper for the records in his brief-case?"

"Why the evening before that."

"March *thirteenth*. And what did Mike say?" cried Ellery. "That the fire and substitution of newspaper for records had taken place around six p.m.—six p.m. on March thirteenth! How could a *New York Times* dated March *fourteenth* have been put into Mike Magoon's brief-case at six p.m. on March *thirteenth*? It couldn't have been. Not possibly. No *New York Times* comes out that early the previous day! Mike Magoon lied. The substitution hadn't been made the previous day at all—it had been made on the morning of the fourteenth—just before Mike came to see me . . . obviously by Mike himself. Then Mike's whole story collapses, and all I had to do was re-examine the known facts in the light of Mike's duplicity." Ellery glanced at the clock. "There's still time to send your tax return to Uncle Sam, Mike," he said, "although I'm afraid you'll have to change your address."

The Adventure of
the Emperor's Dice

WHEN CALIGULA BECAME emperor of the world he nominated Incitatus his consul, Incitatus being his horse. On evidence such as this, the grandson of Tiberius is considered by historians to have been crazy. The conclusion is questionable. Consuls in Caligula's day exercised high criminal jurisdiction; obviously, a man could turn his back on his horse. There have been appointments, and not only in Roman history, far less astute.

We are told, too, that Caligula nad his adopted son, Lucius, murdered; that he commanded citizens who displeased him to enter the arena; that at the imperial gaming tables this legate of Tiberius's mighty treasury played with crooked dice; and so on. That these are the historical facts seems indubitable, but do the facts warrant the historians' conclusions? We have already disposed of the episode of the praetorian horse. As for Lucius, by Tiberius's will he was Caligula's co-heir; and an emperor who murders his co-heir before his co-heir can murder him may be considered of nervous temperament, or overcautious, but he is certainly not irrational. Turning one's enemies into gladiators combines private interest with the public pleasure and is the sign of a political, not a psychotic, mind. And while loading one's dice is indefensible on moral grounds, there is no denying the fact that the practice reduces the odds against the dicer.

In short, far from being a lunatic, Caligula was a man of uncommon sense; demonstrating what was to be proved —namely, *Caveat lector*.

We now leap nineteen centuries.

It was the time of the vernal equinox, or thereabout; in fine, the last day of the third month of the Queenian calendar, and a night of portents it was, speaking in wind, thunder, and rain. Even so, Mark Haggard's voice could be heard above the uproar. Haggard was driving a leaky station-wagon along the Connecticut road with the hands of a charioteer, sawing away at the wheel and roaring oaths against the turbulent heavens as if he were Martius himself. The Queens and Nikki Porter could only embrace one another damply and pray for midnight and the rise of a saner moon.

Ellery did not pine for Connecticut weekends at unmapped homes occupied by unexplored persons. He had too cartographic a memory of hosts floating about in seas of alcohol or, as happened with equal frequency, forty-eight becalmed hours of Canasta. But the Inspector appeared sentimental about this one.

"Haven't seen Mark, Tracy, or Malvina Haggard since their dad kicked off ten years ago," the Inspector had said, "and I hadn't much contact with Jim's children before that except when they were little. But if they've turned out anything like Jim or Cora . . ."

"They rarely do," Ellery had said nastily. "Anyway, did Mark Haggard have to include me in?"

"Jim and I went through the police academy together, son. I was Jim Haggard's best man when he married Cora Maloney in—yep, 1911, just forty years ago. I can see the big lug now," said the Inspector mistily, "standing in front of the preacher in his monkey suit. . . . Cora buried Jim in that suit, Ellery."

"Hadn't he gained any weight? But I still don't see why——"

"Ellery's too lofty to mix with ordinary folks, Inspector," Nikki had put in gently. "Too much of a brain, you know. It gets *so* bored. Besides, he knows I can't go unless he does——"

"All right!" howled Ellery; and so here they were, and he hoped they were both thoroughly satisfied.

It had begun with a train that was late, a whistle-stop station that was wrong, no taxi service, and an hour's wait in splashy darkness. Then their host found them, and even the Inspector began to look as if he regretted the whole thing. Haggard was a staring man with a week's black stubble, given to sudden convulsions of laughter, and he drove like a madman.

"Can't tell you how happy I was to hear from you, Mark," said the old gentleman, bouncing and hanging on to his denture. "I feel like a heel having neglected your mother so long. It'll be good seeing Cora again."

66

"In hell," screamed Mark Haggard, rocketing over a patch of ice left over from the last snowfall.

"What did you say, Mark?"

"Ma's in hell!"

"Oh, I'm sorry to hear it," the Inspector said confusedly. "I mean, when did she——?"

"Two years ago."

"But not in the hot place," muttered the Inspector. "Not Cora."

Mark Haggard laughed. "You didn't know her. You don't know any of us."

"Yes, people change," sighed the Inspector. Then he tried to sound chatty again. "I remember when your father resigned from the Force, Mark. Your mother was against it. But he'd inherited all that money, and I guess it went to his head."

"What makes you think his head was any different before, Inspector? He was crazy. We're all crazy!"

Ellery thought that was an extremely bright remark.

"Is it much further, Mark?" asked the old gentleman desperately.

"Yes, I'm so very wet," said Nikki in a gay voice.

"Threw money around like a maniac," said Mark Haggard angrily. "The great collector! Who did he think he was—Rosenbach?"

"Books?" asked Ellery, rousing himself.

"My father? He could hardly read. Gambling collection! Crummy old roulette wheels, medieval playing cards, ancient dice—junk filled the whole Gun Room. Get over on your side of the road, you—— ——!"

"Sounds like a—harmless enough—hobby," said Nikki jouncily. The other car was lost in the weeping night. Lightning showed them Haggard's face. Nikki closed her eyes.

"Harmless?" chortled their host. "Nothing about our family is harmless. Including the ancestral dump that Pop inherited from Uncle Jonas."

"I suppose," said Nikki, keeping her eyes shut, "you live in a haunted house, Mr. Haggard?"

"Yes!" said Mark Haggard gleefully.

Nikki screeched. But it was only another icy drop pelting the side of her neck.

"Any ghost I know?" asked the Inspector wittily.

"It's the ghost of an unsolved murder mystery."

"Murder mystery!"

"Unsolved?" said Ellery.

"The house was then occupied by a family of five," chuckled their chauffeur, "a father, a mother, and three grown children. The two sons were bugs on hunting and they had a regular arsenal. One night the father's body was found in the gun-room. He'd been shot to death. It couldn't have been suicide, the servants were away, and from the physical evidence an outside murderer was out of the question. It had to be someone in the house that night, and the only ones in the house that night were the mother and the three grown children. Revolting, hey?"

Ellery stirred.

"Humour him!" whispered Nikki.

"Mark's just making this up," said Inspector Queen heartily." Mark, I'm soaked to the hide. Have you lost your way?"

Haggard laughed again. But then he hurled the station-wagon around another car, cursing, and Ellery shuddered. "And the best part of it was that nobody ever suspected the father'd been murdered. Not even the police."

"You see?" said the Inspector in a beamy voice. "Fairy tales, Mark, get there!"

"But keep talking," said Ellery. "Just how was the murder concealed?"

"Simplest thing in the world. One of the sons was a medical doctor and the other was an undertaker. The son who was a doctor made out a false death certificate and the son who was an undertaker prepared the body for burial." Haggard's laugh mingled with the rain and the thunder. "So murder didn't out after all. And it won't unless somebody can read those three clues."

"Oh, there were clues," said Ellery.

"This has gone far enough," said the Inspector sharply. "Are you sure, Mark, you're not driving around in circles?" He peered through a window, but they might have been crossing the Styx.

"What were they, Mark?"

"Ellery," moaned Nikki.

"The bullet which killed the father came from a .38 revolver. There were two .38 revolvers in the Gun Room. So the two .38s were clues——"

"Ballistics check-up," mumbled the Inspector.

"Oh, no," chuckled Mark Haggard. "The bullet passed right through the body and smashed against the bricks of the fireplace. And both guns had been cleaned after the murder."

"And the third clue?"

"You'll love it, Ellery. It was found by the sons in their father's hand."

"Oh? What was it?"

"A pair of dice. Very famous bones they are, too, bloody as hell." And Haggard laughed and laughed.

After a moment Ellery said, "All this happened . . . when did you say, Mark?"

"I didn't. Ten years ago."

"Ten——!" The Inspector checked himself.

"Would you care to see the two revolvers and the dice?"

"Do you have them?"

"Oh, yes," said Mark. "In a wooden box at home."

"Now that's going too far!" exploded the Inspector. "Mark, either stop this foolishness or turn around and drive us back to the railroad station!"

Mark Haggard laughed again. The lightning flashed, and for a photographic instant they saw his lumpish eyes, the blueness about the black stubble, the dance of his hands on the wheel.

Ellery heard Nikki's teeth. "M-Mister Haggard," she chattered, "what do you and your brother d-do for a living?"

"Tracy is a physician," Haggard cried, "and I'm an undertaker." The station-wagon slid to a cascading stop, throwing them violently forward. Mark Haggard sprang into the darkness, and from the darkness they heard him shout, "Get out, get out. We're here!" like some demon commanding them to his pleasure.

This was the beginning of an historic night . . . darkest history. They could make out nothing of the house, but a porch creaked underfoot and things banged somewhere gleefully. Ellery could feel the revolt in Nikki as she held on to him. Mark Haggard's right fist crashed repeatedly against an invisible door.

"Damn you, Malvina, open the door! Why'd you lock it?"

A creature in a white negligee of the flowing drapery variety stood there, holding aloft in her left hand—Nikki giggled something about a left-handed Statue of Liberty— a candle in a black candlestick. The face behind the candle was blanker than her robe. Only the eyes had life, a peering kind of life.

"I'm glad you've come back, Mark," she said in a perfectly lifeless voice. "The lights went out and then a hot flash followed me all over the house. Wherever I went, it was hot, and it burned, Mark, it burned me. Why did the lights go out?"

"Hot *what*?" muttered the Inspector.

Haggard tried a wall switch. "Power failure——!"

"It burns, Mark," his sister intoned.

"Malvina, these are some people visiting us. Give me that candle! I'll get a couple of flashlights." Mark Haggard's right hand seized the candlestick and the flame darted off, leaving them in darkness, with the white-robed woman.

"Malvina, you remember me, don't you?" The Inspector might have been wheedling a child. "Your father's friend? Richard Queen?"

"No." That was all she said, in the toneless tones; after that inhuman sound, no one said anything. They shivered in the dark among their weekend bags, waiting dully for Mark Haggard's return. The house was deathly cold, with a dampness that attacked like acid.

Mark returned in another rage. "No lights, no heat, no dinner prepared, Tracy gone out on a sick call, servants off somewhere—Malvina! Where the devil are Bessie and Connors?"

"They left. They were going to kill me. I chased them with a kitchen knife and they ran away. And Tracy went away, too. My own brother a doctor, and he doesn't care that the hot flashes burn me ..." They heard a horrible snuffling and they realized the creature was crying.

Mark thrust a flashlight into Ellery's hand, wielding his own in crazy swoops that touched bare floors, shrouded furniture, his weeping sister. "Stop it or you'll have another fit——" She had it, on the floor, writhing like a crying soul, and screaming, screaming. "——! If Tracy hadn't——*No!* I'll handle 'er alone. Go to your rooms—head of the stairs. You'll find some bread and a can of sardines in the kitchen——"

"Couldn't eat a thing," mumbled Inspector Queen. "Wet clothes ... go to bed ..."

But Haggard was gone, running with his sister in his arms, her draperies trailing, the beam of light painting wild parabolas on the darkness. The Inspector said simply, "We'd better get dry, rest awhile, and then clear out."

"How about now?" said Nikki. "I sometimes enjoy being wet, and I'm not in the least bit tired. I'm sure we could call a cab——"

"While a ten-year-old unsolved murder drifts around

the premises crying for its mate?" Ellery glanced up into the black hole of the staircase, his jaw out. "I'm sticking the week-end."

Inspector Queen was stretched on one of the icy twin beds, and Nikki whimpered in the bedroom beyond—she had promised hysterics at the suggestion that in the interests of propriety the communicating door be shut—when the men's door burst open and light invaded the room. From the other room Nikki squealed, and the Inspector heaved twelve inches toward the ceiling. Ellery dropped a shoe, definitely.

But it was only Mark Haggard, grinning. He was carrying an electric lantern in one hand and a battered old wooden box the size of a cigar humidor in the other. "The clues to the murder," he chuckled. "Old Mark Elephant!" He slammed the box down on the highboy nearest the door.

Haggard kept looking at Ellery, teeth glittering from the underbrush of stubble. The Inspector scrambled out of bed in his nightshirt as Ellery slowly opened the box.

Two rusty revolvers, Colt .38s, nested in the box. On them lay a small squarish case that looked like gold.

"The dice," said Mark Haggard, smiling. "Open it."

"Hold the light higher," Ellery said. His father craned over his shoulder.

Two crystalline red dice incised in gold sparkled up at them from a bed of purple velvet.

"They look like jewels," exclaimed the Inspector.

"That's what they are," said Mark. "Square-cut rubies with pure gold dots inset. These dice are almost as old as the Christian era. Supposed to have been the personal property of the Roman Emperor Caligula. We gave them to Pop for his gambling collection."

"This inscription in the case?" Ellery squinted. "Hold the lantern up a bit, Mark . . . *To Dad, from Mark, Malvina, and Tracy, on his Ruby Wedding Anniversary.* In what way, Mark, were these dice a clue to——?"

But Haggard was gone in the arctic night of the hall.

The Inspector heard the sounds first. He reached across the abyss between their beds and touched Ellery on the shoulder. It was a little past three. Ellery awoke instantly.

"Ellery. Listen."

It was still raining, jungle music by a thousand drums. The wind slammed a shutter somewhere. In the next room

71

Nikki's bed springs complained as she turned desperately over.

Then Ellery heard a floorboard give way and in the same moment ghastly lightning made the bedroom spring alive. A man was standing at the highboy, his right hand reaching for the box Mark Haggard had brought to the room a few hours before. With the first crack of thunder Ellery jumped out of bed and hurled himself across the room. His shoulder hit the intruder below the knees and the man toppled with a cry, striking his head against the highboy.

Ellery sat on him.

"Tracy Haggard!" Inspector Queen leaned over them, trying to hold the beam of his flash steady. From the other room Nikki was wailing. "What was that? What happened?" Dr. Haggard was a small, neat, greying man with a clever face; when his eyes opened they were pale and rather glassy. "This is a fine way to meet again after all these years, Tracy," growled the Inspector. "What's the idea of playing sneak thief in your own house?"

"Mark's box of clues, Dad," murmured Ellery. "Apparently when Tracy Haggard got home, he learned that his brother had blabbed to us about the ten-year-old murder and left the clues in here. He's tried to get them back and dispose of them before we can dig too deeply into the crime."

"I don't know why I didn't destroy those guns and dice years ago," said Dr. Tracy Haggard, calmly enough. "Ellery—you are Ellery, aren't you?—would you mind removeing the *derrière* from my alimentary canal? You're not exactly a featherweight."

"Then it's true." Ellery did not stir.

"And I attended Jim's funeral and never suspected," said Inspector Queen bitterly. "Tracy, which one of you shot your father? And for God's sake, why?"

"I don't know the answer to either question, Inspector. It's been unholy hell . . . the four of us living together all these years, knowing one of us did it . . . It sent Mother to her grave." Tracy Haggard tried to rise, failed, and hardened his stomach muscles. "I'm glad she's dead and out of it. And I suppose you saw what it's done to Malvina and Mark. Mark was always a little batty, but Malvina had a promising career in the theatre when this happened, and she cracked."

"What's going *on* in there?" shrieked Nikki.

"Dr. Haggard, your brother made no bones about the

72

murder of your father," said Ellery. "Does Mark want the truth to come out?"

"When Mother died," said Tracy Haggard coolly, "the three of us split the income of a very large trust fund. By will, if there were only two of us, the income would be that much greater per individual. Mark is always broke—gambling mostly. Does that answer your question?"

"Won't anybody talk?" howled Nikki. "I *can't* come in there!"

"That's why he asked us up here, is it?" snarled the Inspector. "To pin Jim's death on you or Malvina. Mark must feel pretty safe. . . ."

"We're going to try to oblige your brother, Doctor." Ellery got off his host and reached for the box of clues.

Dr. Haggard rose, tight-lipped. "In the middle of the night?"

"Dad, get a robe on and throw me mine . . . Why, yes, Doctor. Would you take us to the room where your father was shot to death?"

They trooped downstairs to the nervous accompaniment of the electric lantern, Ellery hugging the box, Nikki in a woolly robe and scuffs insisting that death would be instantaneous if she were to stay upstairs alone. Toward the rear of the main hall Tracy Haggard paused before a heavy door.

"Understandably, none of us ever goes in here. Nothing's been touched since the night of the crime." Dr. Haggard unlocked the door, threw it open, and stepped aside. "I might add," he said dryly, "that neither Mark nor I has done any hunting since . . . at least with any of these weapons."

The walls of the gun-room flanking the one door were hung with racks of shotguns, rifles, and small arms. On the other walls were cases containing James Haggard's gambling collection, and a great many larger gambling objects were grouped about the room. A thick coat of dust covered everything.

"Just where was your father's body found?" Ellery murmured.

"Seated behind that desk."

The desk was an elaborate production of inlaid woods, with gunstock-shaped legs and a sheathing of hammered gunmetal. A matching chair with a braided leather seat stood behind it.

"Was he facing this door, Dr. Haggard?"

"Squarely."

73

"The only door, notice," snapped Inspector Queen, "so the odds are the killer stood in the doorway when he fired the shot. Just one shot, Tracy?"

"Just one shot."

Ellery opened Mark's box and removed the two rusty revolvers. "I see the gunracks are numbered. In which rack, Doctor, were these .38s normally kept?"

"This one came from the rack immediately to the right of the door."

"To the right of the door, Doctor? You're positive?"

"Yes, this rack is numbered 1. The other .38 was kept in the rack immediately to the left of the door. This one here, the rack numbered 6."

"Gun Exhibit A, right of door, rack number 1. Gun Exhibit B, left of door, rack number 6." Ellery frowned. "And it must have been done by one of those two guns, Mark said ... These ruby dice, Doctor—what did they have to do with the murder?"

"Caligula's dice? We found them in Dad's hand."

"In his *hand?*" exclaimed Nikki. "I didn't really believe your brother when he said that——"

"My examination of his body indicated that he lingered a few minutes before dying. You'll notice that one of the wall cases behind the chair is open and empty. That's where the Emperor's Dice, as Dad used to call them, were displayed. When the shooter left, Dad must have managed to reach up, open the case, and take out the ruby dice. Then he died."

"But why would he do a thing like that?" asked Nikki.

"Dad had police training. He was leaving a clue to his killer's identity. But we never could figure out whom the dice indicated. They'd been a gift from all three of us."

"Seems like an awfully peculiar anniversary gift to one's parents," Nikki said coldly.

"The dice were for Dad. We gave Mother a ruby pendant."

"Well, I don't get it," the Inspector said irritably. "Clues, ruby dice, emperors! Ellery, can you make anything out of this hash?"

"Let's hope he won't," said Dr. Haggard. "I could kill Mark for this stunt . . ."

"The way you killed your father, Dr. Haggard?" asked Nikki.

Tracy Haggard smiled. "Shows how insidious Mark's little propaganda scheme is." He shrugged and disappeared in the black hall.

The Inspector and Nikki were staring into the darkness when Ellery said abruptly. "You and Nikki go to bed."

"What are you going to do?" asked his father.

"Stay down here," said Ellery, rolling the historic dice between his palms, "until I throw a natural."

Malvina Haggard screamed on and off for the remainder of the night, and the angry voices of the brothers raised in bitter argument penetrated to the gun-room, but from that room there was no sound but the sound of rattling bones, as if the bimillennial ghost of the gambling Emperor himself and returned to dice with Ellery. And finally, at the first smudge of the cold and streaming dawn, the sound stopped, and Ellery came upstairs and methodically roused the household, inviting them all—even the demented woman—to join him on the scene of the old crime. Something in his manner quieted Malvina, and she drifted downstairs with the others docilely.

They took places about the desk in the dusty gun-room, Mark viciously alive, Malvina somnolent, the doctor suspended watchfully, and Nikki and Inspector Queen trying to contain their excitement.

"The case," announced Ellery, "is solved."

Mark laughed.

"Damn you, Mark!" That was his brother.

Malvina began to croon a wailing tune, smiling.

"I've been throwing these ruby dice for hours," continued Ellery, "with the most surprising result." He shook the dice briskly in his cupped right hand and rolled them out on the desk.

"Nine," said Tracy Haggard. "What's surprising about that?"

"Not merely nine, Dr. Haggard. A 3 and a 6."

"Well that's nine!"

"Temper, Tracy," laughed Mark. Ellery rolled again.

"Eleven. Remarkable!"

"Not merely eleven, Dr. Haggard—a 5 and a 6." And Ellery rolled a third time. "And there's seven—a 1 and a 6. Never fails."

"What never fails?" asked Nikki.

"The 6, my pet. I've made several hundred rolls while you were tossing around upstairs, and while one of these dice behaves with self-respecting variability, the other comes up 6 every time."

"Crooked! Loaded!" said Inspector Queen. "Who'd you say these dice used to belong to?"

"According to Mark, to Gaius Cæsar, better known as Caligula, Emperor of Rome from A.D. 37 to 41. And it may well be true, because Caligula was one of history's most distinguished dicing cheats."

"And what does all this mean to you, Ellery?" asked Mark Haggard softly.

"Your father left these dice as a clue to the one of you who shot him. There are two dice, there were two .38 revolvers. Theory: The dice were meant by your father to refer to those two revolvers. But we now find that one of these dice is 'loaded'—your word, Dad—while the other is not. Conclusion: Jim Haggard meant to convey the message that *the murderer loaded one of these revolvers.*"

"Wonderful," said Mark Haggard.

"Ridiculous," said Tracy Haggard. "Of course he loaded one of them! But which one?"

Malvina Haggard kept smiling and crooning her little tune, keeeping time with her sharp white fingers.

"The loaded dice," explained Ellery, "always turns up at the number 6, and one of the revolvers comes from a gunrack numbered 6. It seems obvious that the revolver associated with the number 6 was the one the murderer 'loaded' . . . in other words, the one he chose to fire the fatal bullet into Jim Haggard."

"And a fat lot of good that does you," sneered Tracy Haggard. "How can knowing which of the two .38s killed Dad possibly tell you which one of us murdered him?"

"In which direction in relation to the door," inquired Ellery, "is rack number 6 located?"

"The rack to the left of the doorway," the Inspector said slowly. "To the *left* . . ."

"Killer opens door, to his right is a rack with a .38, to his left a rack with a .38. We now know he chose the .38 from the left-hand rack. What kind of person, when he has a choice of either side, automatically chooses an object to his left side? Why, a left-handed person, of course. And that pins the murder on . . ." Ellery stopped.

"Just marvellous," gloated the Inspector. "How this boy of mine comes through! Eh, Nikki?"

"Every time!" said Nikki worshipfully.

"And that pins the job on which one, son?" The old gentleman rubbed his palms together.

"It was *supposed* to pin the crime on Malvina," said Ellery, "who held the candle prominently aloft in her left hand when she greeted us—as commented upon by Miss Nikki Porter, aloud—whereas the brothers conscientiously demonstrated by various actions during the night that they're both right-handed. Unfortunately, gentlemen and ladies, I'm going to prove a disappointment to you. Aside from a number of tremendous, not to say laughable, improbabilities in the plot, there was one enormous flaw."

"Plot? Flaw?" spluttered Inspector Queen.

The brothers glared. Even Malvina's clouded intelligence seemed shocked to clarity by Ellery's tone.

"I was told," murmured Ellery, "that the ruby dice were a gift to Jim Haggard on the occasion of Mr. and Mrs. Haggard's ruby wedding anniversary——"

"Sure they were, Ellery," said the Inspector. "You saw the inscription in the case yourself!"

"And you told me, Dad, that you'd been the best man at your old friend Jim Haggard's wedding forty years ago. You even mentioned the date—1911."

"Yes, but I don't see," began his father doubtfully.

"You don't? How long ago was Jim Haggard murdered?"

"Ten years ago, Ellery," said Nikki. "That's what they said."

"Married forty years ago, died ten years ago—so Jim Haggard could have been married no longer than thirty years at the time of his death. But ruby weddings commemorate which anniversary? Don't strain yourselves—ruby wedding is the *fortieth*. I must therefore inquire," said Ellery politely, "how Mr. and Mrs. Hggard could have been presented with gifts commemorating forty years of marriage if when Mr. Haggard died he'd only been married thirty years. No answer being forthcoming, I must conclude the error in mathematics lies in the figures surrounding Mr. Haggard's 'death'; and this is confirmed by the dice, which these two innocent eyes saw in their gold case, dear children, proving that your parents celebrated an anniversary this year. So I'm delighted to announce—as if you didn't know it—that your parents are very much alive, my friends, and that the whole thing has been a hoax! You lied, Mark. You lied, Tracy. And Malvina, your performance as Ophelia completely vindicates Mark's judgement that you had a promising career on the stage.

"And *you*, my worthy father." Inspector Queen started. "You ought to apply for an Equity card yourself! Didn't you tell me emotionally that you attended Jim Haggard's funeral ten years ago? So you're one of this gang, too . . . and so are you, Nikki, with your screams and your squeals and the dramatic way in which you pointed out for my benefit the crucial fact that Malvina is left-handed."

There was a vast silence in Jim Haggard's gun-room.

"All cooked up," said Ellery cheerfully. "The wild night ride, the prevailing lunacy, the lights that atmospherically failed, the carefully desposited dust in the gun-room, and all the rest of it—cooked up by my own father, in collusion with his precious pals, the Haggard family! Object: Apparently to lead me to deduce from the herrings strewn across the trail, that Malvina killed her father. Then Jim Haggard could pop out of whatever closet he's skulking in with dear Cora and show me up for the gullible fathead I presumably am. My own father! Not to mention my faithful amanuensis. Reason totters and whimpers: Why? I restored her to her throne when I remembered the date."

Ellery grinned. "Yesterday was the last day of March. Which makes to-day," and Ellery applied his outspread hand to the end of his nose and, using his thumb as a pivot, gently waved his celebrated fingers in their petrified direction, *"April Fool!"*

The Adventure of
the Gettysburg Bugle

THIS IS A VERY old story as Queen stories go. It happened in Ellery's salad days, when he was tossing his talents about like a Sunday chef and a red-headed girl named Nikki Porter had just attached herself to his typewriter. But it has not staled, this story; it has an unwithering flavour which those who partook of it relish to this day.

There are gourmets in America whose taste buds leap at any concoction dated 1861–1865. To such, the mere recitation of ingredients like Bloody Angle, Minié balls, Little Mac, "Tenting To-night," the brand of Ulysses Grant's whisky, not to mention Father Abraham, is sufficient to start the passionate flow of juices. These are the misty-hearted to whom the Civil War is "the War" and the blue-grey armies rather more than men. Romantics, if you will; garnishers of history. But it is they who pace the lonely sentry-post by the night Potomac, they who hear the creaking of the ammunition wagons, the snap of camp-fires, the scream of the thin grey line and the long groan of the battlefield. They personally flee the burning hell of the Wilderness as the dead rise and twist in the flames; under lanterns, in the flickering mud, they stoop compassionately with the surgeons over quivering heaps. It is they who keep the little flags flying and the ivy ever green on the graves of the old men.

Ellery is of this company, and that is why he regards the case of the old men of Jacksburg, Pennsylvania, with particular affection.

Ellery and Nikki came upon the village of Jacksburg as people often come upon the best things, unpropitiously. They had been driving back to New York from Washington, where Ellery had had some sleuthing to do among the stacks of the Library of Congress. Perhaps the Potomac, Arlington's eternal geometry, giant Lincoln frozen in sadness brought their weight to bear upon Ellery's decision to veer towards Gettysburg, where murder had been national. And Nikki had never been there, and May was coming to its end. There was a climate of sentiment.

They crossed the Maryland-Pennsylvania line and spent timeless hours wandering over Culp's Hill and Seminary Ridge and Little Round Top and Spangler's Spring among the watchful monuments. It is a place of everlasting life, where Pickett and Jeb Stuart keep charging to the sight of those with eyes to see, where the blood spills fresh if colourlessly, and the high-pitched tones of a tall and ugly man still ring out over the graves. When they left, Ellery and Nikki were in a mood of wonder, unconscious of time or place, oblivious to the darkening sky and the direction in which the nose of the Duesenberg pointed. So in time they were disagreeably awakened by the alarm clock of nature. The sky had opened on their heads, drenching them to the skin instantly. From the horizon behind them Gettysburg was a battlefield again, sending great flashes of fire through the darkness to the din of celestial cannon. Elery stopped the car and put the top up, but the mood was drowned when he discovered that something ultimate had happened to the ignition system. They were marooned in a faraway land, Nikki moaned; making Ellery angry, for it was true.

"We can't go on in these wet clothes, Ellery!"

"Do you suggest that we stay here in them? I'll get this crackerbox started if . . ." But at that moment the watery lights of a house wavered on somewhere ahead, and Ellery became cheerful again.

"At least we'll find out where we are and how far it is to where we ought to be. Who knows? There may even be a garage."

It was a little white house on a little swampy road marked off by a little stone fence covered with rambler rose vines, and the man who opened the door to the dripping wayfarers was little, too, little and weather-skinned and gallused, with eyes that seemed to have roots in the stones and springs of the Pennsylvania countryside. He smiled hospitably, but the smile became concern when he saw how wet they were.

"Won't take no for an answer," he said in a remarkably deep voice, and he chuckled. "That's the doctor's orders, though I expect you didn't see my shingle—mostly overgrown with ivy. Got a change of clothing in your car?"

"Oh yes!" said Nikki abjectly.

Ellery, being a man, hesitated. The house looked neat and clean, there was an enticing fire, and the rain at their backs was coming down with a roar. "Well, thank you ... but if I might use your phone to call a garage——"

"You just give me the keys to your car trunk."

"But we can't turn your home into a tourist house——"

"It's that, too, when the good Lord sends a wanderer my way. Now see here, this storm's going to keep up most of the night and the roads hereabout get mighty soupy." The little man was bustling into waterproof and overshoes. "I'll get Lew Bagley over at the garage to pick up your car, but for now let's have those keys."

So an hour later, while the elements warred outside, they were toasting safely in a pleasant little parlour, full of Dr. Martin Strong's home-made poppy-seed twists, scrapple, and coffee. The doctor, who lived alone, was his own cook. He was also, he said with a chuckle, mayor of the village of Jacksburg and its chief of police.

"Lots of us in the village run double harness. Bill Yoder of the hardware store's our undertaker. Lew Bagley's also the fire chief. Ed MacShane——"

"Jacksburger-of-all-trades you may be, Dr. Strong," said Ellery, "but to me you'll always be primarily the Good Samaritan."

"Hallelujah," said Nikki, piously wiggling her toes.

"And make it Doc," said their host. "Why, it's just selfishness on my part, Mr. Queen. We're off the beaten track here, and you do get a hankering for a new face. I guess I know every dimple and wen on the five hundred and thirty-four in Jacksburg."

"I don't suppose your police chiefship keeps you very busy?"

Doc Strong laughed. "Not any. Though last year——" His eyes puckered and he got up to poke the fire. "Did you say, Miss Porter, that Mr. Queen is sort of a detective?"

"Sort of a!" began Nikki. "Why, Dr. Strong, he's solved some simply unbeliev——"

"My father is an inspector in the New York police department," interrupted Ellery, curbing his new secretary's enthusiasm with a glance. "I stick my nose into a case once in a while. What about last year, Doc?"

"What put me in mind of it," said Jacksburg's mayor thoughtfully, "was your saying you'd been to Gettysburg to-day. And also you being interested in crimes. . . ." Dr. Strong said abruptly, "I'm a fool, but I'm worried."

"Worried about what?"

"Well . . . Memorial Day's to-morrow, and for the first time in my life I'm not looking forward to it. Jacksburg makes quite a fuss about Memorial Day. It's not every village can brag about three living veterans of the Civil War."

"Three?" exclaimed Nikki. "How thrilling."

"Gives you an idea what the Jacksburg doctoring business is like," grinned Doc Strong. "We run to pioneer-type women and longevity. . . . I ought to have said we *had* three Civil War veterans—Caleb Atwell, ninety-seven, of the Atwell family, there are dozens of 'em in the county; Zach Bigelow, ninety-five, who lives with his grandson Andy and Andy's wife and seven kids; and Abner Chase, ninety-four, Cissy Chase's great-grandpa. This year we're down to two. Caleb Atwell died last Memorial Day."

"A, B, C," murmured Ellery.

"What's that?"

"I have a bookkeeper's mind, Doc. Atwell, Bigelow, and Chase. Call it a spur-of-the-moment mnemonic system. A died last Memorial Day. Is that why you're not looking forward to this one? B following A sort of thing?"

"Didn't it always?" said Doc Strong with defiance. "Though I'm afraid it ain't—isn't as simple as all that. Maybe I better tell you how Caleb Atwell died.

"Every year Caleb, Zach and Abner have been the star performers of our Memorial Day exercises, which are held at the old burying ground on the Hookerstown road. The oldest of the three——"

"That would be A. Caleb Atwell."

"That's right. As the oldest, Caleb always blew taps on a cracked old bugle that's 'most as old as he was. Caleb, Zach, and Abner were in the Pennsylvania Seventy-second of Hancock's Second Corps, Brigadier General Alexander S. Webb commanding. They covered themselves with immortal glory—the Seventy-second, I mean—at Gettysburg when they fought back Pickett's charge, and that bugle played a big part in their fighting. Ever since it's been known as the Gettysburg bugle—in Jacksburg, anyway."

The little mayor of Jacksburg looked softly down the years. "It's been a tradition, the oldest living vet tootling that bugle, far back as I remember. I recollect as a boy standing around with my mouth open watching the G.A.R.s—there were lots more then—take turns in front of Maroney Offcut's general store . . . been dead thirty-eight years, old Offcut . . . practising on the bugle, so any one of 'em would be ready when his turn came." Doc

Strong sighed. "And Zach Bigelow, as the next oldest to Caleb Atwell, he'd be the standard-bearer, and Ab Chase, as the next-next oldest, he'd lay the wreath on the memorial monument in the burying ground.

"Well, last Memorial Day, while Zach was holding the regimental colours and Ab the wreath, Caleb blew taps the way he'd done nigh on to twenty times before. All of a sudden, in the middle of a high note, Caleb keeled over. Dropped in his tracks deader than church on Monday."

"Strained himself," said Nikki sympathetically. "But what a poetic way for a Civil War veteran to die."

Doc Strong regarded her oddly. "Maybe," he said. "If you like that kind of poetry." He kicked a log, sending sparks flying up his chimney.

"But surely, Doc," said Ellery with a smile, for he was young in those days, "surely you can't have been suspicious about the death of a man of ninety-seven?"

"Maybe I was," muttered their host. "Maybe I was because it so happened I'd given old Caleb a thorough physical check-up only the day before he died. I'd have staked my medical license he'd live to break a hundred and then some. Healthiest old copperhead I ever knew. Copperhead! I'm blaspheming the dead. Caleb lost an eye on Cemetery Ridge. . . . I know—I'm senile. That's what I've been telling myself for the past year."

"Just what was it you suspected, Doc?" Ellery forbore to smile now, but only because of Dr. Strong's evident distress.

"Didn't know what to suspect," said the country doctor shortly.

"Fooled around with the notion of an autopsy, but the Atwells wouldn't hear of it. Said I was a blame jackass to think a man of ninety-seven would die of anything but old age. I found myself agreeing with 'em. The upshot was we buried Caleb whole."

"But, Doc, at that age the human economy can go to pieces without warning like the one-hoss shay. You must have had another reason for uneasiness. A motive you knew about?"

"Well . . . maybe."

"He was a rich man," said Nikki sagely.

"He didn't have a pot he could call his own," said Doc Strong. "But somebody stood to gain by his death just the same. That is, if the old yarn's true.

"You see, there's been kind of a legend in Jacksburg about those three old fellows, Mr. Queen. I first heard it when I was running around barefoot with my tail hanging out. Folks said then, and they're still saying it, that back in '65 Caleb and Zach and Ab, who were in the same company, found some sort of treasure."

"Treasure . . ." Nikki began to cough.

"Treasure," repeated Doc Strong doggedly. "Fetched it home to Jacksburg with them, the story goes, hid it, and swore they'd never tell a living soul where it was buried. Now there's lots of tales like that came out of the War"— he fixed Nikki with a stern and glittering eye—"and most folks either cough or go into hysterics, but there's something about this one I've always half-believed. So I'm senile on two counts. Just the same, I'll breathe a lot easier when to-morrow's ceremonies are over and Zach Bigelow lays Caleb Atwell's bugle away till next year. As the oldest survivor Zach does the tootling to-morrow."

"They hid the treasure and kept it hidden for considerably over half a century?" Ellery was smiling again. "Doesn't strike me as a very sensible thing to do with a treasure, Doc. It's only sensible if the treasure is imaginary. Then you don't have to produce it."

"The story goes," mumbled Jacksburg's mayor, "that they'd sworn an oath——"

"Not to touch any of it until they all died but one," said Ellery, laughing outright now. "Last-survivor-takes-all department. Doc, that's the way most of these fairy tales go." Ellery rose, yawning.

"I think I hear the feather-bed in that outer guest-room calling. Nikki, your eyeballs are hanging out. Take my advice, Doc, and follow suit. You haven't a thing to worry about but keeping the kids quiet to-morrow while you read the Gettysburg Address!"

As it turned out, the night shared prominently in Doc Martin Strong's Memorial Day responsibilities. Ellery and Nikki awakened to a splendid world, risen from its night's ablutions with a shining eye and a scrubbed look; and they went downstairs within seconds of each other to find the mayor of Jacksburg, galluses dangling on his pants bottom, pottering about the kitchen.

"Morning, morning," said Doc Strong, welcoming but abstracted. "Just fixing things for your breakfast before catching an hour's nap."

"You lamb," said Nikki. "But what a shame, Doctor. Didn't you sleep well last night?"

"Didn't sleep at all. Tossed around a bit and just as I

was dropping off my phone rings and it's Cissy Chase. Emergency sick call. Hope it didn't disturb you."

"Cissy Chase." Ellery looked at their host. "Wasn't that the name you mentioned last night of——?"

"Of old Abner Chase's great-granddaughter. That's right, Mr. Queen. Cissy's an orphan and Ab's only kin. She's kept house for the old fellow and taken care of him since she was ten." Doc Strong's shoulders sloped.

Ellery said peculiarly: "It was old Abner . . . ?"

"I was up with Ab all night. This morning, at six-thirty, he passed away."

"On Memorial Day!" Nikki sounded like a little girl in her first experience with a fact of life.

There was a silence, fretted by the sizzling of Doc Strong's bacon.

Ellery said at last, "What did Abner Chase die of?"

Doc Strong looked at him. He seemed angry. But then he shook his head. "I'm no Mayo brother, Mr. Queen, and I suppose there's a lot about the practice of medicine I'll never get to learn, but I do know a cerebral hæmorrhage when I see one, and that's what Ab Chase died of. In a man of ninety-four, that's as close to natural death as you can come. . . . No, there wasn't any funny business in this one."

"Except," mumbled Ellery, "that—again—it happened on Memorial Day."

"Man's a contrary animal. Tell him lies and he swallows 'em whole. Give him the truth and he gags on it. Maybe the Almighty gets tired of His thankless job every once in an æon and cuts loose with a little joke." But Doc Strong said it as if he were addressing, not them, but himself. "Any special way you like your eggs?"

"Leave the eggs to me, Doctor," Nikki said firmly. "You go on up those stairs and get some sleep."

"Reckon I better if I'm to do my usual dignified job to-day," said the mayor of Jacksburg with a sigh. "Though Abner Chase's death is going to make the proceedings solemner than ordinary. Bill Yoder says he's not going to be false to an ancient and honourable profession by doing a hurry-up job undertaking Ab, and maybe that's just as well. If we added the Chase funeral to to-day's pro-gramme, even old Abe's immortal words would find it hard to compete! By the way, Mr. Queen, I talked to Lew Bagley this morning and he'll have your car ready in an hour. Special service, seeing you're guests of the mayor." Doc Strong chuckled. "When you planning to leave?"

"I *was* intending . . ." Ellery stopped with a frown. Nikki regarded him with a sniffy look. She had already learned to detect the significance of certain signs peculiar to the Queen physiognomy. "I wonder," murmured Ellery, "how Zach Bigelow's going to take the news."

"He's already taken it, Mr. Queen. Stopped in at Andy Bigelow's place on my way home. Kind of a detour, but I figured I'd better break the news to Zach early as possible."

"Poor thing," said Nikki. "I wonder how it feels to learn you're the only one left." She broke an egg viciously.

"Can't say Zach carried on about it," said Doc Strong dryly. "About all he said, as I recall, was: 'Doggone it, now who's goin' to lay the wreath after I toot the Gettysburg bugle!' I guess when you reach the age of ninety-five, death don't mean what it does to young squirts of sixty-three like me. What time'd you say you were leaving, Mr. Queen?"

"Nikki," muttered Ellery, "are we in any particular hurry?"

"I don't know. Are we?"

"Besides, it wouldn't be patriotic. Doc, do you suppose Jacksburg would mind if a couple of New York Yanks invited themselves to your Memorial Day exercises?"

The business district of Jacksburg consisted of a single paved street bounded at one end by the sightless eye of a broken traffic signal and at the other by the twin gas pumps before Lew Bagley's garage. In between, some stores in need of paint sunned themselves, enjoying the holiday. Red, white, and blue streamers crisscrossed the thoroughfare overhead. A few seedy frame houses, each decorated with an American flag, flanked the main street at both ends.

Ellery and Nikki found the Chase house exactly where Doc Strong had said it would be—just around the corner from Bagley's garage, between the ivy-hidden church and the firehouse of the Jacksburg Volunteer Pump and Hose Company No. 1. But the mayor's directions were a superfluity; it was the only house with a crowded porch.

A heavy-shouldered young girl in a black Sunday dress sat in a rocker, the centre of the crowd. Her nose was as red as her big hands, but she was trying to smile at the cheerful words of sympathy winged at her from all sides.

"Thanks, Mis' Plum ... That's right, Mr. Schmidt, I

know ... But he was such a spry old soul, Emerson, I can't believe ..."

"Miss Cissy Chase?"

Had the voice been that of a Confederate spy, a deeper silence could not have drowned the noise. Jacksburg eyes examined Ellery and Nikki with cold curiosity, and feet shuffled.

"My name is Queen and this is Miss Porter. We're attending the Jacksburg Memorial Day exercises as guests of Mayor Strong"—a warming murmur, like a zephyr, passed over the porch—"and he asked us to wait here for him. I'm sorry about your great-grandfather, Miss Chase."

"You must have been very proud of him," said Nikki.

"Thank you, I was. It was so sudden—— Won't you set? I mean—— Do come into the house. Great-grandpa's not here ... he's over to Bill Yoder's, on some ice ..."

The girl was flustered and began to cry, and Nikki took her arm and led her into the house. Ellery lingered a moment to exchange appropriate remarks with the neighbours, who, while no longer cold, were still curious; and then he followed. It was a dreary little house, with a dark and damp parlour.

"Now, now, this is no time for fussing—may I call you Cissy?" Nikki was saying soothingly. "Besides you're better off away from all those folks. Why, Ellery, she's only a child!"

And a very plain child, Ellery thought, with a pinched face and empty eyes; and he almost wished he had gone on past the broken traffic light and turned north.

"I understand the parade to the burying ground is going to form outside your house, Cissy," he said. "By the way, have Andrew Bigelow and his grandfather Zach arrived yet?"

"Oh, I don't know," said Cissy Chase dully, "it's all such a dream, seems like."

"Of course. And you're left alone. Haven't you any family at all, Cissy?"

"No."

"Isn't there some young man——?"

Cissy shook her head bitterly. "Who'd marry me? This is the only decent dress I got and it's four years old. We lived on Great-grandpa's pension and what I could earn hiring out by the day. Which ain't much, nor often. Now ..."

"I'm sure you'll find something to do," said Nikki, very heartily.

"In Jacksburg?"

Nikki was silent.

"Cissy." Ellery spoke casually, and she did not even look up. "Doc Strong mentioned something about a treasure. Do you know anything about it?"

"Oh, that." Cissy shrugged. "Just what Great-grandpa told me, and he hardly ever told the same story twice. But near as I was ever able to make out, one time during the War him and Caleb Atwell and Zach Bigelow got separated from the Army—scouting, or foraging, or something. It was down South somewhere, and they spent the night in an old empty mansion that was half-burned down. Next morning they went through the ruins to see what they could pick up, and buried in the cellar they found the treasure. A big fortune in money, Great-grandpa said. They were afraid to take it with them, so they buried it in the same place in the cellar and made a map of the location and after the War they went back, the three of 'em, and dug it up again. Then they made the pact."

"Oh, yes," said Ellery. "The pact."

"Swore they'd hold on to the treasure till only one of them remained alive, I don't know why, then the last one was to get it all. Leastways, that's how Great-grandpa told it. That part he always told the same."

"Did he ever say how much of a fortune it was?"

Cissy laughed. "Couple of hundred thousand dollars. I ain't saying Great-grandpa was cracked, but you know how an old man gets."

"Did he ever give you a hint as to where he and Caleb and Zach hid the money after they got it back North?"

"No, he'd just slap his knee and wink at me."

"Maybe," said Ellery suddenly, "maybe there's something to that yarn after all."

Nikki stared. "But Ellery, you said——! Cissy, did you hear that?"

But Cissy only drooped. "If there is, it's all Zach Bigelow's now."

Then Doc Strong came in, fresh as a daisy in a pressed blue suit and a stiff collar and a bow tie, and a great many other people came in, too. Ellery and Nikki surrendered Cissy Chase to Jacksburg.

"If there's anything to the story," Nikki whispered to Ellery, "and if Mayor Strong is right, then that old scoundrel Bigelow's been murdering his friends to get the money!"

"After all these years, Nikki? At the age of ninety-five?" Ellery shook his head.

"But then what——?"

"I don't know." But when the little mayor happened to look their way, Ellery caught his eye and took him aside and whispered in his ear.

The procession—near every car in Jacksburg, Doc Strong announced proudly, over a hundred of them—got under way at exactly two o'clock.

Nikki had been embarrassed but not surprised to find herself being handed into the leading car, an old but brightly polished touring job contributed for the occasion by Lew Bagley; for the moment Nikki spied the ancient, doddering head under the Union Army hat in the front seat she detected the fine Italian whisper of her employer. Zach Bigelow held his papery frame fiercely if shakily erect between the driver and a powerful red-necked man with a brutal face who, Nikki surmised, was the old man's grandson, Andy Bigelow. Nikki looked back, peering around the flapping folds of the flag stuck in the corner of the car. Cissy Chase was in the second car in a black veil, weeping on a stout woman's shoulder. So the female Yankee from New York sat back between Ellery and Mayor Strong, against the bank of flowers in which the flag was set, and glared at the necks of the two Bigelows, having long since taken sides in this matter. And when Doc Strong made the introductions, Nikki barely nodded to Jacksburg's sole survivor of the Grand Army of the Republic, and then only in acknowledgment of his historic importance.

Ellery, however, was all deference and cordiality, even to the brute grandson. He leaned forward, talking into the hairy ear.

"How do I address your grandfather, Mr. Bigelow? I don't want to make a mistake about his rank."

"Gramp's a general," said Andy Bigelow loudly. "Ain't you, Gramp?" He beamed at the ancient, but Zach Bigelow was staring proudly ahead, holding fast to something in a rotted musette bag on his lap. "Went through the War a private," the grandson confided, "but he don't like to talk about that."

"General Bigelow——" began Ellery.

"That's his deef ear," said the grandson. "Try the other one."

"General Bigelow!"

89

"Hey?" The old man turned his trembling head, glaring. "Speak up, bub. Ye're mumblin'."

"General Bigelow," shouted Ellery, "now that all the money is yours, what are you going to do with it?"

"Hey? Money?"

"The treasure, Gramp," roared Andy Bigelow. "They've even heard about it in New York. What are you goin' to do with it, he wants to know?"

"Does, does he?" Old Zach sounded grimly amused. "Can't talk, Andy. Hurts m'neck."

"How much does it amount to, General?" cried Ellery.

Old Zach eyed him. "Mighty nosy, ain't ye?" Then he cackled. "Last time we counted it—Caleb, Ab, and me—came to nigh on a million dollars. Yes, sir, one million dollars." The old man's left eye, startlingly, drooped. "Goin' to be a big surprise to the smart-alecks and the doubtin' Thomases. You wait an' see."

Andy Bigelow grinned, and Nikki could have strangled him.

"According to Cissy," Nikki murmured to Doc Strong, "Abner Chase said it was only two hundred thousand."

"Zach makes it more every time he talks about it," said the mayor unhappily.

"I heard ye, Martin Strong!" yelled Zach Bigelow, swivelling his twig of a neck so suddenly that Nikki winced, expecting it to snap. "You wait! I'll show ye, ye durn whippersnapper, who's a lot o' wind!"

"Now, Zach," said Doc Strong pacifyingly. "Save your wind for that bugle."

Zach Bigelow cackled and clutched the musette bag in his lap, glaring ahead in triumph, as if he had scored a great victory.

Ellery said no more. Oddly, he kept staring not at old Zach but at Andy Bigelow, who sat beside his grandfather grinning at invisible audiences along the empty countryside as if he, too, had won—or was on his way to winning—a triumph.

The sun was hot. Men shuckled their coats and women fanned themselves with handkerchiefs and handbags.

It is for us the living, rather, to be dedicated . . .

Children dodged among the graves, pursued by shushing mothers. On most of the graves there were fresh flowers.

"—that from these honoured dead . . ."

Little American flags protruded from the graves, too.

". . . gave the last full measure of devotion . . ."

Doc Martin Strong's voice was deep and sure, not at all like the voice of that tall, ugly man who had spoken the same words apologetically.

"*. . . that these dead shall not have died in vain . . .*"

Doc was standing on the pedestal of the Civil War Monument, which was decorated with flags and bunting and faced the weathered stone ranks like a commander in full-dress uniform.

"*—that this nation, under God . . .*"

A colour guard of the American Legion, Jacksburg Post, stood at attention between the mayor and the people. A file of Legionnaires carrying old Sharps rifles faced the graves.

"*—and that government of the people . . .*"

Beside the mayor, disdaining the simian shoulder of his grandson, stood General Zach Bigelow. Straight as the barrel of a Sharps, musette bag held tightly to his blue tunic.

"*. . . shall not perish from the earth.*"

The old man nodded impatiently. He began to fumble with the bag.

"*Comp'ny! Present—arms!*"

"Go ahead, Gramp!" Andy Bigelow bellowed.

The old man muttered. He was having difficulty extricating the bugle from the bag.

"Here, lemme give ye a hand."

"Let the old man alone, Andy," said the mayor of Jacksburg quietly. "We're in no hurry."

Finally the bugle was free. It was an old Army bugle, as old as Zach Bigelow, dented and scarred in a hundred places.

The old man raised it to his earth-coloured lips.

Now his hands were not shaking.

Now even the children were quiet.

Now the Legionnaires stood more rigidly.

And the old man began to play taps.

It could hardly have been called playing. He blew, and out of the bugle's bell came cracked sounds. And sometimes he blew and no sounds came out at all. Then the veins of his neck swelled and his face turned to burning bark. Or he sucked at the mouthpiece, in and out, to clear it of his spittle. But still he blew, and the trees in the burying ground nodded in the warm breeze, and the people stood at attention listening as if the butchery of sound were sweet music.

And then, suddenly, the butchery faltered. Old Zach

91

Bigelow stood with bulging eyes. The Gettysburg bugle fell to the pedestal with a tinny clatter.

For an instant everything seemed to stop—the slight movements of the children, the breathing of the people, even the rustling of the leaves.

Then into the vacuum rushed a murmur of horror, and Nikki unbelievingly opened the eyes which she had shut to glimpse the last of Jacksburg's G.A.R. veterans crumpling to the feet of Doc Strong and Andy Bigelow.

"You were right first time, Doc." Ellery said.

They were in Andy Bigelow's house, where old Zach's body had been taken from the cemetery. The house was full of chittering women and scampering children, but in this room there were only a few, and they talked in low tones. The old man was laid out on a settee with a patchwork quilt over him. Doc Strong sat in a rocker beside the body, looking very old.

"It's my fault," he mumbled. "I didn't examine Caleb's mouth last year. I didn't examine the mouthpiece of that bugle. It's my fault, Mr. Queen."

Ellery soothed him. "It's not an easy poison to spot, Doc, as you know. And after all, the whole thing was so ludicrous. You'd have caught it in autopsy, but the Atwells laughed you out of it."

"They're all gone. All three." Doc Strong looked up fiercely. "Who poisoned their bugle?"

"God almighty, don't look at me," said Andy Bigelow. "Anybody could of, Doc."

"Anybody, Andy?" the mayor cried. "When Caleb Atwell died, Zach took the bugle and it's been in this house for a year!"

"Anybody could of," said Bigelow stubbornly. "The bugle was hangin' over the fireplace and anybody could of snuck in durin' the night ... Anyway, it wasn't here before old Caleb died; *he* had it up to last Memorial Day. Who poisoned it in *his* house?"

"We won't get anywhere on this tack, Doc," Ellery murmured.

"Bigelow. Did your grandfather ever let on where that Civil War treasure is hidden?"

"Suppose he did." The man licked his lips, blinking, as if he had been surprised into the half-admission. "What's it to you?"

"That money is behind the murders, Bigelow."

"Don't know nothin' about that. Anyway, nobody's got

92

no right to that money but me." Andy Bigelow spread his thick chest. "When Ab Chase died, Gramp was the last survivor. That money was Zach Bigelow's. I'm his next o' kin, so now it's mine!"

"You know where it's hid, Andy." Doc was on his feet, eyes glittering. "Where?"

"I ain't talkin'. Git outen my house!"

"I'm the law in Jacksburg, too, Andy," Doc said softly. "This is a murder case. Where's that money?"

Bigelow laughed.

"You didn't know, Bigelow, did you?" said Ellery.

"Course not." He laughed again. "See, Doc? He's on your side and he says I don't know, too."

"That is," said Ellery, "until a few minutes ago."

Bigelow's grin faded. "What are ye talkin' about?"

"Zach Bigelow wrote a message this morning, immediately after Doc Strong told him about Abner Chase's death."

Bigelow's face went ashen.

"And your grandfather sealed the message in an envelope——"

"Who told ye that?" yelled Bigelow.

"One of your children. And the first thing you did when we got home from the burying ground with your grandfather's corpse was to sneak up to the old man's bedroom. Hand it over."

Bigelow made two fists. Then he laughed again. "All right, I'll let ye see it. Hell, I'll let ye dig the money up for me! Why not? It's mine by law. Here, read it. See? He wrote my name on the envelope!"

And so he had. And the message in the envelope was also written in ink, in the same wavering hand:

Dear Andy now that Ab Chase is ded to—if sumthin happins to me you will find the money we been keepin all these long yeres in a iron box in the coffin *wich we beried Caleb Atwell in.* I leave it all to you my beluved grandson cuz you been sech a good grandson to me. Yours truly Zach Bigelow.

"In Caleb's coffin," choked Doc Strong.

Ellery's face was impassive. "How soon can you get an exhumation order, Doc?"

"Right now," exclaimed Doc. "I'm also deputy coroner of this district!"

And they took some men and they went back to the old

93

burying ground, and in the darkening day they dug up the remains of Caleb Atwell and they opened the casket and found, on the corpse's knees, a flattish box of iron with a hasp but no lock. And, while two strong men held Andy Bigelow to keep him from hurling himself at the crumbling coffin, Doctor-Mayor-chief of Police-Deputy Coroner Martin Strong held his breath and raised the lid of the iron box.

And it was crammed to the brim with mouldy bills of large denominations.

In Confederate money.

No one said anything for some time, not even Andy Bigelow.

Then Ellery said, "It stood to reason. They found it buried in the cellar of an old Southern mansion—would it be Northern greenbacks? When they dug it up again after the War and brought it up to Jacksburg they probably had some faint hope that it might have some value. When they realized it was worthless, they decided to have some fun with it. This has been a private joke of those three old rascals since, roughly, 1865. When Caleb died last Memorial Day, Abner and Zach probably decided that, as the first of the trio to go, Caleb ought to have the honour of being custodian of their Confederate treasure in perpetuity. So one of them managed to slip the iron box into the coffin before the lid was screwed on. Zach's note bequeathing his 'fortune' to his 'beloved grandson'—in view of what I've seen of his beloved grandson to-day—was the old fellow's final joke."

Everyone chuckled; but the corpse stared mirthlessly and the silence fell again, to be broken by a weak curse from Andy Bigelow and Doc Strong's puzzled: "But Mr. Queen, that doesn't explain the murders."

"Well, now, Doc, it does," said Ellery; and then he said in a very different tone: "Suppose we put old Caleb back the way we found him, for your re-exhumation later for autopsy, Doc—and then we'll close the book on your Memorial Day murders."

Ellery closed the book in town, in the dusk, on the porch of Cissy Chase's house, which was central and convenient for everybody. Ellery and Nikki and Doc Strong and Cissy and Andy Bigelow—still clutching the iron box dazedly—were on the porch, and Lew Bagley and Bill Yoder and everyone else in Jacksburg, it seemed, stood about on the lawn and sidewalk, listening. And there

94

was a touch of sadness to the soft twilight air, for something vital and exciting in the life of the village had come to an end.

"There's no trick to this," began Ellery, "and no joke, either, even though the men who were murdered were so old that death had grown tired waiting for them. The answer is as simple as the initials of their last names. Who knew that the supposed fortune was in Confederate money and therefore worthless? Only the three old men. One or another of the three would hardly have planned the deaths of the other two for possession of some scraps of valueless paper. So the murderer has to be someone who believed the fortune was legitimate and who—since until to-day there was no clue to the money's hiding place—knew he could claim it legally.

"Now of course that last-survivor-take-all business was pure moonshine, invented by Caleb, Zach, and Abner for their own amusement and the mystification of the community. But the would-be murderer didn't know that. The would-be murderer went on the assumption that the *whole* story was true, or he wouldn't have planned murder in the first place.

"Who would be able to claim the fortune legally if the last of the three old men—the survivor who presumably came into possession of the fortune on the deaths of the other two—died in his turn?"

"Last survivor's heir," said Doc Strong, and he rose.

"And who is the last survivor's heir?"

"Zach Bigelow's grandson, Andy." And the little mayor of Jacksburg stared hard at Bigelow, and a grumbling sound came from the people below, and Bigelow shrank against the wall behind Cissy, as if to seek her protection. But Cissy only looked at him and moved away.

"You thought the fortune was real," Cissy said scornfully, "so you killed Caleb Atwell and my great-grandpa so your grandfather'd be the last survivor so you could kill him the way you did to-day and get the fortune."

"That's it, Ellery," cried Nikki.

"Unfortunately, Nikki, that's not it at all. You all refer to Zach Bigelow as the last survivor——"

"Well, he was," said Nikki in amazement.

"How could he not be?" said Doc Strong. "Caleb and Abner died first——"

"Literally, that's true," said Ellery, "but what you've all forgotten is that Zach Bigelow was the last survivor *only by accident*. When Abner Chase died early this morning,

95

was it through poisoning or some other violent means? No, Doc, you were absolutely positive he'd died of simple cerebral hæmorrhage—not by violence, but a natural death. Don't you see that if Abner Chase hadn't died a natural death early this monring, *he'd still be alive this evening?* Zach Bigelow would have put the bugle to his lips this afternoon, just as he did, just as Caleb Atwell did a year ago ... *and at this moment Abner Chase would have been the last survivor.*

"And who was Abner Chase's only living heir, the girl who would have fallen heir to Abner's 'fortune' when, in time, or through her assistance, he joined his cronies in the great bivouac on the other side?"

"You lied to me, Cissy," said Ellery to the shrinking girl in his grip, as a horror very like the horror of the burying ground in the afternoon came over the crowd of mesmerized Jacksburgers. "You pretended you didn't believe the story of the fortune. But that was only after your great-grandfather had inconsiderately died of a stroke just a few hours before old Zach would have died of poisoning, and you couldn't inherit that great, great fortune, anyway!"

Nikki did not speak until they were twenty-five miles from Jacksburg. Then all she said was, "And now there's nobody left to blow the Gettysburg bugle," and she continued to stare into the darkness toward the south.

The Adventure of
the Medical Finger

IN WATCHING OVER THE special interests of women since
early Roman times, the queen of heaven has had more
names, shapes, and identies than the notorious Sophie
Lang. As Caprotina, Juno was worshipped by female
slaves. As Sospita, the saviour, she was invoked by women
in their perils. Under titles like Cinxia, Unxia, and Pronu-
ba she played the leading role in the ritual of marriage; as
Iuno Lucina, her protection was implored by occupants of
the labour stools; and on the Matronalia the married
ladies with their maiden daughters met at her temple in a
grove on the Esquiline and made offerings. Also, not to be
sentimental about it, Juno is found represented as a war
goddess—a fine recognition by the ancients that, where
the fairer sex is concerned, all is not moonlight and roses.
The animals sacred to her were the goose, which is silly;
the peacock, which is beautiful; the cuckoo, which has a
monotonous voice and lays its eggs in other bird's nests;
and the serpent, whose nature is too well-known for in-
dictment. She is the goddess of advice and of money—of
all things peculiarly interesting to women; and of course,
ever since the hapless judgment of Paris, when—as Hera—
Juno was outbribed by Aphrodite, she has been the most
jealous and unforgiving of the deities.

In short, Juno is all things to all women, and that is
why the poet Ovid has Juno say that the month of June
was named in her honour—June being the season of the
year most favourable to marriages. "Prosperity to the man
and happiness to the maid when married in June," was a
proverb in ancient Rome. Multi-millions of the sisterhood
have put their maiden faith in it ever since, and the elder
daughter of Richard K. Troy of Sutton Place and Palm
Beach was no exception. She had always wanted a June
wedding, and she got one—not quite, perhaps, as she had

dreamed. But the calendar was right, she was dressed as a bride, and there was a ring; so the old saying came true, if only for a very short time.

Her father had named her Helen, for Richard K. Troy was that most dangerous of people, a practising sentimentalist. To Mr. Troy, in the beginning was the word; and since he had an easy vocabulary and a cliché for everything, he had made his fortune in the greeting card business. His first child's name was a sentimental inspiration of his youth, and when Helen Troy grew to be a marvellously beautiful young woman, her father was not surprised; it was simply another proof, in the whole argument of his life, of the word made flesh.

He always regretted that he had not had the foresight to perform a similar service for his younger daughter Effie, the selection of whose name he had imprudently left to his wife. Mrs. Troy had leaned heavily toward propriety; and Euphemia, the dictionary told her, signified "of good report." Effie indeed grew up to be well spoken of, but the trouble was she entered conversations very seldom, being plain and always looking as if she were about to get down on all fours. Effie was Mr. Troy's cross.

But Helen was the apple of his eye—"the golden apple," he liked to say whimsically. "You'll remember that was the real reason the Trojan War was fought, ha-ha!" Peaceable as he was, Mr. Troy said it not without a glow; an army of young men had fought over Helen from the time she was beginning to bud above the waist, and she arrived at Junoesque maturity by stepping lightly over a battlefield littered with bloodied noses and broken hearts. Mr. Troy had a moment of uneasiness after Mrs. Troy died when Helen, the vigilant mother-eye finally lidded over, promptly trifled with the wrong kind of man. But Helen laughed and assured her father that she could handle the fellow, and Mr. Troy was fatuous enough to let the moment pass.

That was a mistake.

Victor Luz was a chunky young European with sprouting black eyebrows and really formidable hands. They were the hands of a peasant and he was ashamed of them, because his father—who was attached to one of the United Nations delegations—came from a Louvre of aristocrats and had long, slim, golden fingers like women's cigarette-holders. Victor had come to the United States as a college student. At Princeton he had been persuaded to put his hands to use, and as he was agile and athletic, with a naturally lethal left hook, he had no difficulty making the boxing team. But intercollegiate competition brought out the depressing fact that when he was hurt, Luz forgot the rules and became a killing animal, gouging and punching wildly low and all but using his powerful teeth. In one bout he rolled to the mat with his opponent, a bewildered junior from Rutgers, and he was disqualified and dropped from the team. But he was charming and handsome, with Continental manners and a great deal of money, and he was a social success from the moment he sublet a bachelor apartment on Park Avenue after his graduation. He made rare appearances at Lake Success, where he was known vaguely to have some connection with his country's delegation. But he was seen regularly at horse shows and hunt clubs and he was a favourite of café society—even being interviewed under his full name, which included a titular prefix, on the Stork Club television programme by Sherman Billingsley himself.

Luz was introduced to the Troys by Henry Middleton Yates, who had known him at Princeton and now sold bonds for a Wall Street house. Yates had been in love with Helen Troy since his first crew-cut. He was one of the warriors whose nose had been bloodied, but his heart remained intact; being a born bond salesman, Henry was undiscourageable. Long after most of his rivals had consoled themselves with lesser prizes, he was still in dogged pursuit of the Troy beauty. Helen was fond of him; he was good-natured, good-looking, comfortably manageable, and he had just the right promise of static electricity; she might in fact have married him long before if the battle had still not warmed her blood a little and . . . of course . . . her mother had approved, which she had not. Henry was aware of the two impediments to his happiness, but he was patient; he knew time would remove both of them. When Mrs. Troy died, Henry was ready. He threw Victor Luz at Helen.

Henry was a planner, and his plan depended on his knowledge of Helen and his shrewd appraisal of her state of mind. Adoration at arm's length would not satisfy her forever, and there were signs that the Trojan wars were palling. What she needed, he reasoned, was a final passage of arms, in which her appetite for conquest would be glutted. Victor Luz, thought Henry, was just the man for the job. Luz could hardly fail to be smitten, and Helen would lead him on automatically. There was no danger that she would fall in love with him or that his name would tempt her to do something silly; Luz was too foreign for Helen's emotional tastes and she was too sensible to sell her freedom for a title. He would amuse her for a while; then she would drop him, expecting him to accept his dismissal, as the others had done, with a broken heart and a sporting smile. What she would not know until it was too late was that Luz, when baulked, forgot the rules. So he would be a bad loser, and the whole episode would end disagreeably. Henry was sure such an experience at this period in Helen's life would drop her, finally and gratefully, into his lap.

And that was a mistake also, even though it all came to pass exactly as Henry hoped.

He brought Victor Luz to the Troy house, Luz was enchanted, Helen was interested, they began to see a great deal of each other, Luz pressed an ardent courtship. Helen played with him until her interest dribbled away, she broke it off—and Luz hung on. Helen looked at him then really for the first time. There was something alarming in the quality of his persistence, the quivering intensity of a sealed tank building up a pressure. He did not hang on like a gentleman, unobtrusively. He took to following her, threatening her escorts with violence, sending her wild notes, hounding her on the telephone, proposing suicide pacts, weeping on the garden wall outside her bedroom window, jumping out at her from doorways in broad daylight and falling at her feet. The climax came one night at El Morocco, when Luz made a scene so outrageous and humiliating that Helen fled in tears—into Henry Middleton Yates's arms.

As far as Henry Middleton Yates was concerned, that was the end of the day. Unfortunately, Victor Luz was following a script of his own.

The morning after the scandalous scene in the night club, Richard K. Troy was peacefully finishing his decaffeinized coffee when his younger daughter, Euphemia, came in and said with unfamiliar vivacity, "Victor Luz is in the library asking for you."

"That fellow?" said Mr. Troy, frowning. "What's he want?"

"I don't know, Father," said Effie. "But he looks awfully stiff and correct. Maybe he wants to apologize for last night."

100

"I suppose I ought to punch him in the nose," said her father helplessly. "Where's Helen?"

"She won't see him. Anyway, she's in the garden with Henry Yates. I'll bet Henry would punch him in the nose?"

"I'm entirely capable of handling my children's affairs," said Mr. Troy, sounding the reverse; and he went to the library unhappily.

Victor Luz was seated on the edge of a chair, knees spread slightly, big hands grasping suède gloves and a Homburg over the head of a furled umbrella. His dark skin was quite yellow. He rose immediately.

"See here, Luz——" began Mr. Troy with a scowl.

"Excuse me, Mr. Troy," said Luz, "but I call this morning for two purposes. I wish to abase myself before your daughter for having been so gauche as to make a public scene last night. But she will not see me. Therefore, sir, I address my apologies to you."

"Well, ah, yes. Yes, I see," said Mr. Troy.

"The second purpose of my visit is to seek your permission to ask your daughter's hand in marriage," said Victor Luz. "I am madly in love with Helen, Mr. Troy. I cannot——"

"——live without her. Yes, yes," sighed Mr. Troy. "It's surprising, though, how many of you fellows manage to survive. Mr. Luz, my only mission in life is to see my daughters happy. If Helen thinks you'd do it, it doesn't matter what I think. Go ahead and ask her."

"Ah, you are a great man!" cried Luz joyfully.

"Not at all," said Mr. Troy with a grin. "I'm just passing the buck to more capable hands."

But Luz was raptly soliloquizing, "I have spoken to her of my love, of her beauty, and so on, but the word 'marriage' . . . How could she have failed to misunderstand? I'll ask her now!"

At this moment the library door opened and the fair Helen appeared, followed by Henry Middleton Yates. Behind Henry hovered Effie, trembling.

Luz blinked as if at an unbearable radiance. He went to her swiftly, engulfing her hand. "Helen. I must speak to you!"

Helen laughed, withdrawing her hand and wiping it carefully with her handkerchief. Then she went up to her father and she said, "Dad, Henry has something to say to you."

"Henry," said Mr. Troy. "Oh! Oh, yes, yes."

"I've asked Helen to marry me, Mr. Troy," said Henry Middleton Yates, "and she's said yes. Is it kappazootic with you?"

Mr. Troy looked bewildered. For a cry came from an unexpected quarter, the throat of his daugher Effie. After that single noise, Effie became silent and mousier than ever; then she scurried down the hall as if cats were after her. Helen looked thoughtful and Henry Yates blank.

It was all too much for Mr. Troy, especially since in the very next instant Henry Yates was on his back on the library floor, giving an incredible imitation of a man fighting for his life. He had been bowled over by the ninepin head of Victor Luz, and Luz now had his great hands about Henry's throat and was banging Henry's head against the floor. Mr. Troy was conscious of his daughter Helen making some unpleasantly shrill sounds.

"Descendant of bloody lice!" shouted Luz, his dark skin now magenta. "You will never have her! I will kill her first!"

Henry gurgled something indignant, and Helen whacked Luz's head with the handle of his umbrella. Mr. Troy found himself growing strong with anger. He had always believed in the brotherhood of man, and he had supported the United Nations wholeheartedly, but this episode . . .

Mr. Troy throttled Victor Luz so vigorously that, between the grip on his throat and the blows on his head, Luz released his hold on poor Henry Yates and fell back blanched and impotent.

Helen was on her knees beside her gasping cavalier, crooning solace. Luz got to his feet, fumbling for his umbrella. He did not look at either of them.

"I said I would kill her," he said in a bubbly voice to no one in particular, "and if she marries Yates I will."

"But that isn't all of it, Mr. Queen," Mr. Troy said a month later. "When my prospective son-in-law got to his feet, he knocked the fellow kicking, and you'd have thought that would be the end of it. But it was only the beginning."

"More threats?" said Ellery. "Or actual attempts on your daughter's life?"

"No, no, it was the beginning of an entirely new relationship. I don't pretend to understand young people nowadays," said Mr. Troy, using his handkerchief. "In my day he'd have been horsewhipped or put in jail, and no amount of crawling on his—I beg your pardon, Miss Porter, is it?—but this has really got me down."

"I don't think we follow, Mr. Troy," said Nikki corporately.

"Why, he no sooner recovered from Henry's knockout than Luz was a changed man. Butter wouldn't melt in his mouth. Sucking dove—ate humble pie as if he enjoyed it. Apologized practically on his knees. Positively embarrassed me. The next day he sent Helen a bushel of orchids with the inscription, *With Best Wishes for the Coming Event, Your Friend, Victor Luz*—he wouldn't go very far in the greeting card business, I'm afraid, ha-ha!—and he sent Henry Yates a case of sixty-five-year-old cognac, and the result of all this was that within a week Helen had forgiven him and Henry was saying he wasn't such a bad scout after all."

"And within two weeks?" asked Ellery. "Because it's evident it didn't stop there."

"You're darned right it didn't," said Mr. Troy indignantly. "Within two weeks Helen had invited him to the wedding, because Luz threw a big party at the Versailles at which Helen and Henry were guests of honour and, as I understand it, the fellow spent most of the evening proposing champagne toasts to their happiness."

"How very sweet," said Nikki.

"Mr. Troy, I think, Nikki," said Ellery, "detects a dry bouquet."

"Mr. Queen, I yield to no man in loving-kindness," said Mr. Troy earnestly, "and I'm not saying this because the fellow comes from Europe—some of my best friends are Europeans—but I tell you this particular individual isn't to be trusted. He'd be dangerous if he were a one hundred per cent American. I consider myself a judge of character, and I saw his face when he heard that Helen was going to marry Henry Yates. There was murder there!"

"Clarence Darrow once remarked that he'd never killed anyone, but he frequently got satisfaction reading the obituary notices," murmured Ellery. "However. You distrust this man——"

"I know his kind!"

"——and he's to be at your daughter's wedding——"

"He's not only going to be at it," howled Mr. Troy, "he's going to be the best man!"

There was a silence.

"Oh, dear," said Nikki. "How did he get to be that?"

"He's stuck close to Henry ever since the fight in my

library," said Mr. Troy wildly, "and apparently he's made Henry feel that the only way Henry can show there are no hard feelings is to let him be best man at the wedding. I've appealed to Helen, but she's walking on clouds these days and she thinks it's simply too romantic! I tell you, it's enough to——"

"When and where is the wedding, Mr. Troy?" asked Ellery thoughtfully. "And what kind of wedding will it be?"

"Quiet, Mr. Queen, very quiet. My wife died recently, and of course a big church wedding is out of the question. I wanted Helen to wait a few months, but June starts on Friday, and she insists on a June wedding—June weddings *are* lucky, of course—and she won't wait another year till next June. So it's to be at home, with a small, select guest list—immediate family and a few friends—this coming Saturday. . . . I'd have gone to the police, Mr. Queen," said Mr. Troy glumly, "except that . . . Would you consider coming to the wedding to sort of keep an eye on things?"

"I really don't think you have much to worry about, Mr. Troy," said Ellery with a smile, "but if it will ease your mind——"

"Thank you!"

"But wouldn't this man Luz," asked Nikki, "be suspicious of the presence of a complete stranger?"

"Let him!" said Mr. Troy violently.

"Mr. Troy's right, Nikki. If Luz knows he's being watched, he's much less likely to try anything. If, of course," added Ellery indulgently, "he has any such intention."

Indulgent or not, Ellery did not wait for Saturday to make the acquaintance of Victor Luz. He set about getting to know him immediately, by remote control. In addition, Ellery confided in Inspector Queen, and the Inspector assigned Sergeant Thomas Velie of his staff to special duty, which consisted in following Mr. Luz conspicuously wherever he went. The Sergeant executed his assignment as ordered, grumbling at the affront to his professional pride. As a result, by the day of the Troy-Yates nuptials, Ellery had an approximate knowledge of Mr. Luz's life and habits, and Mr. Luz had the certain knowledge that he was being shadowed. As for the dossier on Luz, Ellery found nothing in it of interest beyond repeated evidence that Luz had a beastly temper and went berserk occasionally, and that he came from a long line of European noblemen with a history of elegant sadism and, in the older days, refined savagery toward peasants, *pour le sport*. For the rest, Luz lived well and honourably on his father's money, and his personal life was neither more nor less questionable than that of any other young Park Avenue bachelor.

Nevertheless, because he was thorough, Ellery arranged with Richard K. Troy for Sergeant Velie to attend the wedding too.

"Acting the part of a detective," Ellery explained.

"What d'ye mean, acting?" growled the Sergeant.

"Private detective, Sergeant, ostensibly watching the wedding presents."

"Oh," said Sergeant Velie; but he went to the wedding unmollified.

The June day was as rare as any bride could have yearned for. It was a garden wedding, with the high Troy walls invisible under thousands of roses and the river invisible beyond the walls. The bride's gown was by Mainbocher, the floral decorations and bouquets were by Max Schling, the catering was by the Ritz, the presiding clergyman was a bishop, and there were no more than five dozen wedding guests. And Juno Regina smiled down from the battlements of heaven.

As far as Ellery could see, he was merely wasting an afternoon healthily. He and Velie, in striped trousers, had arrived early and they had elaborately searched the house and grounds, making sure that Mr. Luz saw them at their labours. Mr. Luz had paled slightly on seeing the heroic figure of Sergeant Velie, and he had made some remark to the bride's father.

"Oh, detectives," growled Mr. Troy, trying to sound careless.

Luz had bitten his lip and then, impeccable in his cutaway, he had gone upstairs to the rooms set aside for the groom. When he found Ellery at his heels, he ground his teeth. Ellery waited patiently outside the door. When Luz, after a long time, emerged with Henry Yates, Ellery followed them downstairs.

"Who the devil is that?" he heard Yates ask Luz.

"A detective, Mr. Troy said."

"What on earth for?"

In the crowded room downstairs Ellery nodded to Sergeant Velie, and Sergeant Velie collided with Luz.

"Here, fellow! What are you doing?" cried Luz angrily.

"Pardon," said the Sergeant; and he reported to Ellery that their man was not heeled.

Neither man took his eyes off Luz for an instant.

When the ceremony began, Ellery was in the front row of chairs, directly behind Luz. Sergeant Velie was in the doorway of the reception-room off the terrace, one hand tucked under his coat in Napoleon's classic pose.

Ellery concentrated on the best man, letting the bishop's murmur trickle over him. It had all long since begun to seem unreal and silly. Luz stood a little behind and to the side of the groom looking properly solemn, and quite conscious of the watchful stranger behind him. Yates's big body was between him and Helen Troy; he could not possibly have reached her without interception. And the bride was too beautiful in her wedding gown to give credence to thoughts of death—far more beautiful than any woman there, in particular her maid of honour, who was her sister Euphemia and seemed precariously on the verge of tears. And Mr. Troy, to the side of the bride, kept his beetled glance directly on the best man, as if challenging him to violate the loveliness of the moment by so much as a thought.

Too silly for words . . .

"And now the ring, if you please," the bishop was saying.

The groom turned to the best man, and the best man's fingers automatically went to the left-hand lower pocket of his vest. They probed. They probed deeper. They stopped probing, paralysed. A horrified titter ran through the garden. Victor Luz began to search frantically through all his pockets. The bishop glanced heavenward.

"For—for God's sake, Victor," whispered Henry Yates. "This is no time to gag!"

"Gag!" choked Luz. "I assure you . . . I could have sworn . . ."

"Maybe you left it in your topcoat!"

"Yes. Yes! But where . . . ?"

Effie Troy stretched her skinny neck their way and hissed, "Your topcoat's in the clothes closet in the upstairs hall, Victor. I put it there myself when you got here."

"Hurry up," groaned the groom. "Of all the idiot . . . Darling, I'm so sorry . . . Bishop please forgive . . ."

"It's quite all right, young man," sighed the bishop.

"Won't be a minute," stammered Luz. "So terribly sorry . . ."

106

Ellery pinched his nose, so when Victor Luz disappeared in the reception-room Sergeant Velie clumped after him.

When Luz emerged from the house Ellery quietly rose and made his way to the terrace, where the Sergeant stood waiting. Luz was advancing across the lawn holding a ring aloft shamefacedly, and everyone was smiling. He handed it to Henry Yates with careful ceremony, looking relieved. The bishop, looking martyred, resumed.

"Now if you will repeat after me . . ."

"What did Luz do, Sergeant?" whispered Ellery.

"Went upstairs to a hall closet, fished around in a man's topcoat, came up with the ring——"

"That's all he did?"

"That's all. Just beat it back downstairs with it."

They watched.

"It's all over!"

"And I had to miss my Turkish bath for this." Sergeant Velie sounded disgusted.

Ellery hurried out on to the lawn. The bride and groom were surrounded by laughing people, kissing and being kissed, shaking hands, everyone talking at once. The newly minted Mrs. Henry Middleton Yates had never looked more mythically happy, her sister Effie more realistically plain, the groom more dazedly successful, the bride's father more puzzled and relieved. As for Luz, he had quietly congratulated the bride and groom and he was now on the edge of the crowd, smiling and saying something to the white-cheeked Effie, whose eyes were tragically on her sister's husband. Mr. Troy was conversing animatedly with the bishop. Waiters were beginning to wheel out veritable floats of tables, others were beginning to circulate with portable bars. Two photographers were busy setting up. The sun was mild, the roses sugared the air, and a barge beyond the river wall hooted its good wishes.

Ellery shrugged. Now that Helen Troy was safely Mrs. Yates, the gyrations of the past two hours seemed infantile. He would have to see Mr. Troy . . .

"Darling! What's the matter?"

The voice was the groom's. Ellery craned. The mob around the couple had stopped milling with a curious suddenness. Mr. Troy and the bishop had turned inquiringly.

With violence, Ellery shoved through the crowd.

"Henry . . ." The bride was leaning against her husband. Her cheeks were chalky under the make-up. She had a hand to her eyes, as if shading them from an intolerable sun.

"What is it dearest? . . . *Helen!*"

"Catch her!" Ellery shouted.

But the bride was already on the grass in a broken white pile, staring into the sun.

Inspector Queen was definitely a menace that day. He had an unusually bitter altercation with Dr. Prouty of the medical examiner's office, a few searing words for the bewildered Sergeant Velie, and deathly sub-temperatures for his son. Having already been exposed to absolute zero in the person of Richard K. Troy before the poor man was put to bed by his physician, Ellery was thoroughly refrigerated. He hung about the proceedings like a fugitive drip of stalactite. Effie Troy was in her room in hysterics, in care of a nurse; Henry Yates sat on a chair in the reception room vacantly, drinking brandy by the water glass and not even looking up when addressed; Victor Luz was in Troy's library chain-smoking under the murderous eye of Sergeant Velie; there was no one to talk to, no one at all. Ellery wandered miserably about, yearning for Nikki Porter.

About the only thing everyone agreed on without argument that abrasive afternoon was that it had been the quickest June marriage in society history.

Finally, after a century, the Inspector beckoned.

"Yes, Dad!" Ellery was at his father's side like an arrow. "Why the freeze-out?"

Inspector Queen looked positively hostile.

"I still don't know how it happened." Ellery sounded as if he were about to cry. "She just dropped, Dad. She was dead in a few minutes."

"Seven minutes from the time the poison was administered," the Inspector said frigidly.

"How? She hadn't had time to eat or drink anything!"

"Directly into the bloodstream. With this." And the Inspector opened his fist. "And you let him!"

Her wedding ring?

The ring gleamed on his father's palm. It was a plain, very broad and massive gold band.

"You can handle it. The sting's removed."

Ellery shook his head, then he seized the ring and scrutinized it fiercely. He looked up, incredulous.

"That's right," nodded the Inspector. "A poison ring. Hidden automatic spring on the inner surface of the band

108

that ejects a hollow needle point under pressure. Like the fang of a snake. And this was loaded, brother. Right after the ceremony everybody was congratulating her, kissing her, shaking her hand ... Quite a gimmick. The hand-shaker exerts just the right amount of pressure on the hand wearing the ring, and wham—a dead bride in seven minutes. If she felt the sting, she was too excited to call attention to it. I've heard of the kiss of death, but the hand-shake of death—that's a new one!"

"Not so new," muttered Ellery. "Poison rings go back at least to the time of Demosthenes. And Hannibal, who killed himself with one. But those weren't like this. This is the *anello della morte* with reverse Venetian. In the medieval model the hollow point was in the bezel and scratched the person with whom the wearer of the ring was shaking hands. This one pricks the wearer."

"Medieval Europe." The Inspector sounded very grim; he was an incurable softie, and the sight of the beautiful young corpse in her wedding gown under the June sun had infuriated him. "It's an antique; I've had it expertized. This is the kind of cute gadget an Old World blueblood like Luz might have had in his family locker for centuries."

"It's also the kind of thing you might pick up in a New World Third Avenue pawnshop," said Ellery. "Is it an exact duplicate—except for the mechanism—of the ring Yates had bought?"

"I haven't been able to get much out of Yates, but I gather it's not quite the same. It wouldn't be. Yates's ring, of course, is gone. The killer counted on the excitement and tension of the ceremony preventing Yates from notic-ing that the poison ring was a bit different when Luz handed it to him. Yates bought his ring two weeks ago and showed it to all of them except Helen, so the killer had plenty of time to dig up a poison ring resembling it ... if he didn't have one handy all the time."

"When did Yates turn the regular ring over to Luz?"

"Last night. Luz claims, of course, that he knows nothing about this poison ring. He says—he *says*—when he went upstairs to the hall closet during the ceremony and fished around in his topcoat and felt the ring, he just took it out and hurried downstairs with it without taking a good look at it, and Velie confirms that."

"And then he handed it to Yates, who may have palmed it," said Ellery.

"Yates? The *groom*? Palmed it? I don't——"

"Suppose Henry Yates had the poison ring concealed in

109

his hand. Luz hands him the innocent ring. Yates palms it and puts the poison ring on Helen's finger."

The Inspector seemed to pop from all directions. "Are you out of your mind? That boy want to kill the girl he was marrying? And what a girl. And in such a way!"

"I don't say he did, but you'll find," said Ellery, "that Helen Troy came into a wad of money the instant she got married. By the will of her mother, who had an independent fortune. And Henry Yates is, after all, merely a bond salesman—a very smart bond salesman, incidentally, or he'd never have snagged the Troy girl. And you can't ignore the corollary fact that such a time and method of murdering his bride would give Yates the perfect fall guy ... the man who handed him the ring, the man who had been rejected by the bride, the man who had actually threatened to kill her if she married Yates. Not to mention the psychological advantages to Yates in picking such a time for his crime——"

Inspector Queen said through his dentures: "You know what your trouble is, son? A degenerate imagination."

"It's not imagination at all. It's logic."

"Its—it's corruption!"

"And then there's Effie Troy," Ellery continued surgically. "Effie is hopelessly in love with Yates—a strabismic jackass could see that. And it was Effie, by her own admission, who hung Luz's topcoat in the upper hall closet. Velie says none of the wedding guests or hired help had access to that closet, Dad. He had the staircase in view the whole time and he says only Luz and the immediate family used those stairs from the time Luz arrived at the house."

The Inspector fixed his son with a skewering eye. "Then you don't believe Luz did this?"

"I don't see anything that pins it on him. There are at least two other possible theories, either of which makes more sense."

"To you on cloud eighty-eight," rasped his father. "To my simple brain it's simple. Luz threatened to kill Helen Troy if she married Yates. That's motive——"

"One motive," said Ellery patiently.

"As best man Luz had charge of the wedding ring and had the best chance to substitute the poison ring for the real one. That's opportunity."

"One opportunity, and only equally as good as Effie Troy's and Henry Yates's," mumbled Ellery. "Not best at all."

"Luz shook hands with the bride right after the ceremony——"

"So did dozens of other people."

The Inspector glared, turning an eggplant colour. "If no evidence to the contrary turns up in the next twenty-four hours," he snarled, "father of a genius or no father of a genius, I'm arresting Luz for the murder of that girl!"

It must be faced: Ellery did not shine in the Troy-Yates-Luz case. In a lesser way, that June wedding was as unlucky for him as for the bride. Not only had he failed to prevent the tragedy he had been commissioned to prevent, not only was he an honourless prophet in his own house, but he found that he had suddenly lost caste in the eyes of his secretary. Nikki was Juno's messenger to her mortal sex; licit love and blessed betrothal had no more fanatical advocate on earth. The murder of a beautiful bride on her wedding day—more, with the first holy kiss of her husband still warm on her lips—struck Miss Porter as a more inhuman crime than the drawing and quartering of newborn babes. She was all for applying vigilante law to the monster Luz—she was positive he was a monster— and after reading the details in the Sunday paper she came to the Queen apartment, notwithstanding it was her day off, expressly to whip Mr. Queen into the proper bloodthirsty frame of mind ... after telling him, of course, what she thought of his bungling.

"How could you have let it happen, Ellery?" cried Miss Porter scathingly. "Under your high-priced nose! When you were supposed to be *watching!*"

"Surely," said Mr. Queen wearily, "I can be forgiven for not anticipating that somebody was going to bump her off with a wedding ring? Even geniuses—to quote a certain relative of mine—can't be expected to think of wedding rings as dangerous weapons. We're not living in the days of the Borgias, Nikki." Ellery jumped up and began to walk about his cell violently. "It was diabolical. The whole body of myth and folk belief that surrounds the institution of marriage got in the way. Did you ever hear of the medical finger?"

"What an odd way to change the subject," said Miss Porter coldly, and colouring slightly.

"It is the subject. The medical finger was what the English centuries ago called the third finger—not counting the thumb. Their leeches used that finger in stirring drugs and potions——"

111

"Educational," began Nikki.

"—and it was believed that that finger was connected with the heart directly by a special nerve and that no poisonous substance could come in contact with it without giving a warning. And that's the finger, Nikki, wedding rings are worn on."

"And poetic," finished Nikki, "but considering what happened, a lot of horse malarkey, don't you agree? And it hardly puts Victor Luz where he belongs, does it? Why isn't he in the clink? Why did the Inspector grill poor Effie Troy and that poor, poor Henry Yates last night till all hours? What is everybody waiting for? What's the matter?"

For Ellery had stopped in the middle of the room, stealthy-still and starting as if he were peering into the fourth dimension and being revolted by what he saw there.

"Ellery, what's wrong?"

Ellery came back to the solar system with an unmistakable shudder. "Wrong?" he said feebly. "Did I say anything is wrong?"

"No, but you looked——"

"Electrified, Nikki. I'm always electrified by my own stupidity. Get Dad on the phone," he muttered. "Try headquarters. I've got to talk to him . . . God help me."

"He's tied up," Nikki said when she had put the phone down. "He'll call you back. You're acting awfully strange, Ellery."

Ellery backed into a chair and fumbled unseeingly for his cigarettes. "Nikki, a premise of this case has been that the pressure of a hand-shake, exerted a certain way, was required to release the spring in the poison ring. When you shake hands with somebody, which hand do you offer?"

"Which hand do I offer?" said Nikki. "My right, of course."

"And which hand does the other person offer?"

"His right. He has to."

"But on which hand does a woman wear her wedding ring?"

"Her . . . left."

"Merest detail, you see. Trivial. The only thing is, it solves the case and, of course, I forgot it until just now." From his tone, Nikki expected him to produce scorpions and iron-tipped whips. "How could a normal right-handed

112

hand-shake have released that poisoned needle when the ring was on Helen's left hand?"

"Impossible," said Nikki excitedly. "So it wasn't done by a handshake at all!"

"That's not the alternative, Nikki—it had to be done by a handshake. The alternative is that, since the poisoned ring was on Helen's left hand, *it was her left hand which was shaken.*"

Nikki looked blank.

"Don't you see? In the press of people around her just after the ceremony, the murderer came up and extended his left hand, forcing Helen to extend hers."

"So what?"

"So the murderer was left-handed."

Miss Porter considered this. "Come, come," she said at last, with no respect at all. "Being a wedding ring, it *had* to be on her left hand, therefore the killer *had* to give her a left-handed handshake, therefore he isn't necssarily left-handed at all."

The master, sorely tried as he was, managed a smile. "His crime, Nikki, necessitated a left-handed hand-shake. The brain is modified and restrained by the nature of the machine it runs. If a right-handed man were planning a crime that depended on the use of a hand, he'd instinctively plan a crime that depended on the use of his right hand. The very conception of a left-handed crime indicates a left-handed criminal." Ellery shrugged. "When the bishop asked for the ring during the ceremony and the groom turned to his best man, *his best man's hand automatically went to the lower* left-hand *pocket of his vest.* Had he been right-handed, he would have searched, or pretended to search, his right-hand pocket, because a right-handed man—when he has a free choice of sides and there are no conditioning factors present—will automatically reach for a right-side pocket. Victor Luz automatically reached for a left-hand side pocket, so he's left-handed."

"So for once," Ellery sighed, "logic comes to the support of a circumstantial case. Luz meant his threat, and left the ring in his top-coat deliberately to make it look later as if anyone could have switched rings, not merely himself. Dad was ri——"

The telephone rang.

"Ellery?" It was Inspector Queen's sharp voice.

"Dad——" began Ellery, inhaling manfully.

But the Inspector said, "I told you Luz was our man. Dumb as hell, besides. We traced that poison ring to an

113

antique shop on Madison Avenue, and when Luz was faced with the evidence he broke. I've just got through blotting the ink on his signed confession. All that fancy big-brain stuff about Henry Yates and Effie Troy! What did you want, Ellery?" Ellery swallowed. Then he said, "Nothing, Dad," humbly, and hung up.

The Adventure of
the Fallen Angel

THAT EVERLASTING CICERONE of the world forum, Marcus Tullius, somewhere tells us amicably that Fire and Water are "proverbial"; which is to say, these ancient elements of life are truly elementary. If it is further presumed that where life burns, death with his sprinkler cannot be far behind, the case of Miles Senter *et al.* may be considered classic. In that case there was Fire to the point of pyrotechnics, for though the New York summer was officially a mere ten days old, the sun was already baking the Senter garden to the charred crispness of an overlooked piecrust and barbecuing the stones of the garden walls in a temperature more commonly associated with the Underworld. As for Water, below the east wall flowed a whole stream of it, for the Senter house was one of those marginal Manhattan affairs clinging splendidly to the island's shore and staring with hauteur at the untidy commercial profile of the Borough of Queens across the commonplace swells of the East River.

Nor was antique harmony restricted to geography and the season. Mythology shared in the Senter case, and art. The house had been designed in the highfalutin era, when architecture was cathedral and structural decoration full of monsters. The Senter pharmaceutical fortune had been baptized in the font of a purgative whose pink-on-black prose still illuminated the barns and jakes of rural America; and in building his mansion the progenitor of the Senter wealth—possibly in extenuation of its ephemeral source— had turned his eyes heavenward and builded for eternity. Or at least for greater permanence than was promised by cathartic pills. He had had his architect go for inspiration to the Cathedral of Notre Dame in Paris. Unfortunately, for all the laxative riches at his command, the architect had neither an *Ile de la Cité* on which to build nor the papal

115

resources of the twelfth century; consequently the astonished neighbours found themselves rubbing walls with a sort of gigantic architectural dwarf, an ecclesiastical Quasimodo of a building, vulgar, ugly, and unbelievably uncomfortable. Miles Senter, who had been born in it, once spent an uneasy six months on his analyst's couch recollecting the horrid Gothic dreams which it had visited on his childhood.

The most frightening of these concerned the grotesque stone carvings which stuck out from the tower roofs like abnormal growths. These were the Senter architect's versions of the *chimères* of Notre Dame Cathedral. And the Chimaera, if you remember your Bullfinch and Bellerophon, breathed a particularly effective kind of fire. Thus Fire again. As for Water, unhappily the architect had confused chimaeras with gargoyles, and the monsters he had had hewn and installed on the cornices of the Senter towers, while they had the lion's head, goat's body, and dragon's behind of the true Chimaera, served the traditional gargoyle purpose of providing outlets for the rain which collected on the roof. In a word, they were waterspouts. To complete the chaos, the founding Senter to his dying day persisted in calling them "angels," and his grandson Miles, as he settled substantially into the Founder's shoes, canonized the heresy. Not so Miles's younger brother, David, who broke images as easily as he made them. David was a painter, with a studio on the roof of what—to his brother's vague annoyance—he would call "the Cathedral." David unfailingly remarked before guests, when Miles referred to the waterspout monsters as angels, that it gave an educational insight into their grandfather's view of heaven . . . if not Miles's.

But these are trifling, if pleasant, divagations. We were at a more serious business in the Senter garden on a recent broiling summer evening, with the East River lapping thirstily at the wall.

Two young ladies were perspiring under the sun-lamp moon. One was Miles's wife, the reigning Mrs. Senter; the other was Nikki Porter, who had exercised the private secretarial right of deserting her employer in his evening of direst need—it had something silly to do with a book publisher, and a deadline. But Nikki had run into Dorothy the day before, after a separation of years, and could auld acquaintance be forgot? Thus desertion, and the garden by the river. The reunion was scented for Nikki with the aromatic news that Dorothy was now Mrs. Miles Senter, which she had certainly not been when Nikki had known her last, and with a something else that defied analysis and so challenged it. There were moribund shadows under otherwise lively eyes and a kind of "To the barricades!" gaiety which had struck Nikki as out of tune with recent wedding harmonies. Indeed, dinner had had a faintly royal *émigré* flavour—a taste of *noblesse oblige* and tumbrils at the door. Even Miles Senter's confidential secretary, a Mr. Hart, a Princeton-type man with a crew-cut and the well-greased manners of an advertising agency junior executive, took the first opportunity to make a discreet—and relieved—retreat to his room. And thereafter the young matron, with a female smile, had sent her husband packing and steered Nikki into the dark garden and immediately burst into tears.

Nikki let Dorothy cry, wondering if it might not be the house. The house was frightful—musty and catlike, with great clanging rooms, bedrooms uniformly exposed to the noise and damp of the river, and a colossal dinginess; it had not seen decorators for a generation. It was evident that Miles Senter, though kindly and agreeable, was a man of uncompromising conservatism and no imagination. In fact, Nikki had been rather shocked by him. He claimed forty-five, looked sixty, and was probably in mid-fifties. And Dorothy was twenty-six years old. Of course it could be that, although Dorothy had always been a practical girl with no nonsense about her and a wonderful respect for accomplishment; it was quite like her to fall in love with a rich man twice her age. Or was it David? Nikki had heard a great deal about David Senter at dinner, although the artist had not joined them—"Has a watercolour on his mind," Miles Senter had said. "David's always up to something in his studio." Nikki had gathered that David was a lovable scamp with all the absurd ideas of extreme youth— "the Greenwich Village type," his brother had said fondly. "Practically a Red." So she was surprised to learn—from Dorothy—that David was thirty-five years old. To Miles, he would evidently always be a teenager, to be indulged or spanked by the hand that held the purse-strings. There was a self-portrait of David in oils in the living-room—"the Nave, David calls it," Dorothy had laughed as Miles frowned—and he certainly looked Byronic enough to explain Dorothy's tears in the garden. He was a dark, handsome fellow with the devil in his eye, or at least he had painted the devil there. Yes, it might well be David.

And apparently it was. For when Dorothy began to

explain her tears, the first thing she did was to praise her husband. Miles was the finest, tenderest, most considerate, most generous husband in the world. And she, Dorothy, was the most ungrateful, confused, irresponsible little bitch who had ever lured a good man into marriage. Oh, she'd thought she was in love with him, and Miles had been so . . . *solid*. And persistent, of course . . . She hadn't really lured him, he'd sort of lured himself; but then it was equally true that she hadn't been trueblue honest with herself, she'd only thought she was being . . . "Oh, Nikki, don't think horrible things of me. I've fallen in love with Somebody Else."

So there it was.

Nikki sipped her Bombay Cooler, which she had had the providence to take into the garden with her. "Well, suppose you have," she said, as brightly and illusively as the long reflections on the river. "Those things happen, Dorothy."

"But Nikki, what shall I do? I don't want to hurt Miles. He's a little limited, of course, but salt of the earth, really a darling, and I'm afraid if I ran out on him now . . . so soon . . . I mean, I'm afraid——"

"You're afraid what?"

Dorothy began to cry again.

"See here, Dotty," said Nikki. "You've eaten your cake and now you want it back. That's bound to be messy."

"What a horrid way to put it," said Dorothy, wiping her eyes a little peevishly.

"It's the man I work for," said Nikki, taking another sip. "Spells out every spade, and it's catching. Dotty dear, we're a couple of the girls, and no men around. How much do you want this character, S.E.?"

"S.E.?"

"Somebody Else."

"Nikki, I love him! I do!"

"And what is Somebody Else's view of the siuation?"

"He says——"

"Wait." Nikki put her hand on her friend's bare arm. She said suddenly, "Smile, Dotty. Someone's coming."

Miles Senter's broad figure appeared from around the northeast corner of the house. The lights from the front of the building silhouetted him as he paused in the path, dabbing his half-bald head with a handkerchief, peering into the gloom of the garden.

"Dorothy?" he called uncertainly. "You out there with Miss Porter?"

"Yes, Miles!" said Dorothy.

"Oh," said her husband, and he was silent. Then he cleared his throat. "So stifling indoors ... radio says there's no relief in sight. ... I thought maybe you and Miss Porter might like to play some Canasta ..." Senter took a slight step toward them, handkerchief in hand.

Nikki found herself thinking aqueously that the poor fish was out of his natural element, and it occurred to her that Miles Senter might not be entirely insensitive after all. And because she felt sorry for him, Nikki looked away as he stepped forward, and that was how she happened to glimpse the descent of the angel—one of the gargoyle-throated chimaeras which had thrust its unlovely form from the tower roof over the garden for three-quarters of a century. The glimmering mass was falling straight for where Miles Senter's head would be in another step. And Nikki cried out, and the mass fell, and Senter fell, and Dorothy began to shriek with an automatic vitality as if she were possessed. The burden of her dark litany was death and disenchantment, and the response from the Senter physician, old Dr. Grand, who lived next door and had been dozing in his garden, was more in the nature of a retort. Devil or angel, Dr. Grand remarked as he stooped over the fallen man, it had missed its mark; and he instructed Miles Senter to get off his backside and on to his knees, in a more fitting attitude to thank his Maker.

At this Dorothy's husband scrambled to his feet, paler than the stone monster in the path, and turned his eyes to the heavens. But it was not out of gratitude for his deliverance. A black head projected from the roof, another gargoyle against the moon, and its owner was demanding in a curious voice what the devil all the noise was about. When neither Miles nor his wife replied, Dr. Grand explained in his crickety way, and there was a silence from the roof, and then David Senter's dark head vanished. To Nikki the air seemed suddenly chill, and she took no pleasure in it. And when David bounded around the corner to help his brother into the house, Nikki found him even more Byronic-looking than his portrait. And this gave her no pleasure, either.

The next day Ellery patiently pointed out that he made his livelihood inventing far cleverer crimes than Nikki was ever likely to encounter among her acquaintances, and would she please stick to his typing, for her social life was interfering with his contractual obligations—not to mention his publisher's advance, which was not payable until delivery of the finished manuscript.

"But Ellery, it wasn't an accident," said Nikki, using the typewriter as an elbow-rest.

"It wasn't? I suppose," said Ellery, falling back helplessly on irony, "that's a demonstrable conclusion, like most of your conclusions?"

"I've been trying to tell you. I examined that tower roof last night, where the thing fell from——"

"With Lens and Calipers Among the Lotus-Eaters. And you found?"

"I told you. Weren't you listening?"

"You found that the cement holding the doodad to the whatsis was worn as friable as Roquefort. Astounding! And the waterspout weighed—how much, did you say?"

"About a hundred pounds, Mr. Senter said."

"I refer you to Sir Isaac and the law of gravity. Shall we get back to mere fiction?"

"Be logical, but I still say it was no accident," declared Miss Porter, unmoved. "And that's why I suggested to Miles Senter last night——"

The doorbell trilled, and Nikki stopped.

A terrible suspicion darkened her employer's countenance. "Nikki," he said in a Basil Rathbone voice, "you suggested *what* to Miles Senter last night?"

Nikki glanced mutely toward the foyer, which was in full cry.

Ellery groaned.

"You angel, I knew you wouldn't mind!" and Nikki flew. A moment later Ellery heard her assuring someone that Mr. Queen could hardly wait.

To his astonishment, Ellery found himself immediately feeling sorry for the fellow. The president of Senter Pharmaceuticals all but crawled into view. It was a sort of nervous slither, and it went perfectly with his windy eyes and greying stubble; in fact, Miles Senter gave a creditable impersonation of a dope-pedlar about to consummate a sale. He offered a trembling hand, refused a drink—"on principle, Mr. Queen"—accepted a cigarette, failed to puff on it, and through it all he was grateful, abjectly grateful that Mr. Queen was bothering to see him at all. The fact was ... it was damned awkward ... Miss Porter's being Dorothy's friend and so on ... if Nikki hadn't saved his life the night before ...

"Mr. Senter," said Ellery, "what are you trying to say?"

Senter studied the dead cigarette in his hand; then he

120

8 mg. "tar," 0.7 mg. nicotine
av. per cigarette by FTC Method.
© Lorillard 1976
NEW
Low Tar & Nicotine Famous Micronite Filter
KENT
Golden
Lights
8 Mgs. Tar. 0.7 Mgs. Nicotine
KENT GOLDEN LIGHTS
ONLY 8 MG TAR.
YET TASTES SO GOOD,
YOU WON'T BELIEVE THE NUMBERS.
Warning: The Surgeon General Has Determined
That Cigarette Smoking Is Dangerous to Your Health.

Newport

Alive with pleasure!

Newport
20 CLASS A CIGARETTES

Newport

MENTHOL KINGS

17 mg. "tar," 1.2 mg. nicotine av. per cigarette, FTC Report April 1976.

crumpled and crushed it between his fingers. "Queen, I think my wife and my brother are in love with each other." There was an ashtray at his elbow, but rather remarkably he placed the remains in his pocket. "In love with each other," he repeated, and he stopped as if he expected Ellery to say something devastating.

But Ellery said nothing at all. And Nikki was finding one of her fingernails interesting.

"Nothing I've been able really to get hold of," Senter mumbled on. "It's just that Dorothy's been acting ... well, I can't quite name it, but something's come between us lately. She's too darned polite to me!" he blurted. "And David's a handsome young artist and a devil with the women. Suppose I oughtn't to have expected much else— what do they say about old fools?—but why didn't they come to me? Instead of ... Well, Mr. Queen," cried Miles Senter, "what would *you* think?"

"Using your major premise? Let's see. Your brother and your wife are in love, and last night a heavy waterspout parted from the roof where your brother has his studio and missed braining you by a hair. It would seem, Mr. Senter, that your brother tried to murder you."

"Then you agree with me." He sagged against the chair.

"Oh, no," said Ellery, smiling. "I've drawn a possible conclusion from a pair of facts, one of which is not a fact, but an opinion."

"Well, there's a third fact I failed to mention," said Senter, and now his voice was hard, "and this one would satisfy a bank examiner. My father left the Senter enterprises to me during my lifetime. But when I die, David gets them."

Ellery sighed. "People will do odd things, won't they?" He rose. "While I can't share your certainty, Mr. Senter, I certainly appreciate your fears. How and when can I examine the roof without your brother David's knowledge? The sooner, I should say, the better."

Miles Senter promised to notify Ellery when the condition could be met, and later that day he telephoned naming that very night for the investigation. "I'll have my secretary meet you at the side gate at midnight," he said, and he hung up before Ellery could raise his brows.

Ellery left his car on First Avenue and he and Nikki walked toward the river, slowly, for they were a few minutes early and the night steamed. There was a simmering lambency over the world that made straight lines fluid,

121

so that when they came to the Senter house the whole incredible mass seemed in motion, as if it were about to change into something else. Ellery felt his arm clutched and he murmured something about heat waves and optical illusions, but Nikki's hold did not relax until a man stepped from the wrought-iron gateway and she recognized Miles Senter's secretary.

"I'm certainly glad it's you, Mr. Hart, and not some priest of the Black Mass!"

Mr. Hart looked baffled. But then he shook hands footballishly with Ellery, made a hearty remark about the heat, and ushered them across the front lawn. Ellery walked rubber-necking. But at the skyline the mansion was still doing tricks.

Nikki clung.

"I take it you know why I'm here to-night, Mr. Hart?"

"Mr. Senter's just told me." The secretary sounded secretarial.

"What's your opinion?"

"Fellow in my spot has no opinions. Right, Miss Porter? ... David? Oh, David has a shack in Westport where he gets away from it all when we poor goofs bore him or he wants to paint Connecticut barns. He was to leave to-night for over the holiday, but Mr. Senter didn't know what train he was making, so he set midnight as ... I'm sure he must have. I haven't seen him—just got in from a party—but it's so late. ... This way, please. Mr. Senter's waiting upstairs for you. His own rooms. He's given the servants the night off, so you'll have a clear field. Mrs. Senter? I really couldn't say. I'd assume Mr. Senter's seen to—er—that arrangement personally." Mr. Hart, it appeared, was urbanely determined to be the most confidential—and uninvolved—of secretaries.

There were three doors, as in Paris. Little early Gothic imitations surmounted by twenty-eight reduced kings of Israel and Judah, a skimpy rose window, and other shrunken wonders. Having passed through the central door, they entered a sort of medieval never-never land which was mercifully in darkness, or at least in that curious negation of light passing for illumination by which material objects are guessed at rather than seen. No one was about, and the great hall was as deeply hushed as a Hollywood sound-stage; in fact, Ellery would not have been surprised had someone suddenly appeared in puttees and in a loud voice ordered the set to be struck. For all its age, blackened oak, and inky iron, it looked as insubstantial as a backdrop.

They were halfway up the grand staircase and Ellery was just remarking respectfully, "Is that a *bona-fide* suit of Norman armour, Mr. Hart, or are we in the Metropolitan Museum?" when from somewhere above, slightly damped, came a short explosive *kwap*! like a little clap of thunder.

It brought them to a military halt, and for a moment they listened. But the angry sound was not repeated, and they looked at one another.

"What," asked Nikki in the strangest voice, "was *that*?"

"It couldn't be," said Miles Senter's secretary, with an uneasy laugh, "what it sounded like."

"Why not?" snapped Ellery; and he was away.

They found him a moment later in a sitting-room upstairs, kneeling beside an outstretched man who seemed to have run head on into a copious quantity of tomato purée.

"Oh, no," said Hart idiotically.

"Oh, yes," said Nikki. "I was right. He was right. Murdered."

"Not quite." Ellery glanced quickly about. "Head wounds are often a bloody mess. No sign of the gun . . . I don't think it's fatal. Nikki, poke your head out the window and yell."

"Yell?"

"For that doctor! Next door, didn't you say? Hart, you come with me." Ellery was already in the hall.

"But Mr. Senter," began the secretary.

"Don't touch him!" Hart blundered into the hall. "Whoever shot Senter can't have got far. Hart, where's the other way down?"

"Other way down?"

"Damn it, Hart! We came up the front stairs and didn't see anyone, so Senter's assailant must have escaped another way! Isn't there a second stairway?"

"Oh! Yes, Mr. Queen. Backstairs. Up the hall there——"

Ellery ran, and Hart trotted dismally after. Behind them Nikki's demoniac voice shrieked for Dr. Grand.

The backstairs went gloomily down to an iron-clasped oak door which opened on the rear of the great hall.

"Hart, you search the front—lawn, shrubbery, street. I'll take the rear." He gave the man a shove.

The kitchens were dark. Ellery blundered through several coppery caverns, bumping into things and cursing.

Finally he sighted a star, set a straight course, and in a moment was plunging through a doorway. He found himself in a stingy strip of back garden, and the first thing he spied was a spidery figure not ten feet away, clinging to the top of the wall separating the Senter property from its neighbour.

Ellery jumped, clutching. His hands closed triumphantly about a bony ankle.

"Oh, thank you," said a testy voice. "I'm not as spry getting over this wall as I used to be when Elmo Senter imagined himself dying, which was regularly once a week. Catch me, please," and Ellery received in his arms first a medical bag and then a panting old gentleman who was chiefly bones. "Well, well? What's happened now? Speak up, man! That woman yelled bloody murder. And who, by the way, are you?"

"Miles Senter first, Doctor—his upstairs sitting-room. Gunshot scalp wound. You'd better hurry."

Dr. Grand looked incredulous. Snatching his bag, he scurried into the house.

Ellery followed the Senter-Grand wall toward the river. When he met the river wall he turned north and toed his way among the Senter flowerbeds. Two upper windows glared out of the dark mass on the other side of the garden; Ellery saw Nikki swoop across one of them like an agitated fly. Then his hand encountered the splintery side of a wooden structure, which interrupted the river wall apparently for some distance. Exploring it cautiously, he discovered that it was a long low shed, with its back to the garden and a flight of wooden steps along its north side that went down to the river. A boathouse . . . It struck him that a guilty man might find it irresistible.

Taking a grip on his slippery flashlight, and wishing wistfully that he were Dan'l Boone, Ellery began to edge down the steps. But the steps squeaked and groaned abominably, as he had known they would, so he jumped the rest of the way, scrambled around the corner of the boathouse, found a doorway, and went in sidewise to sweep the interior with his light and catch in its beam the frightened face of a young woman. There was no one else in the building, and it was stifling, so Ellery sat down on a coil of nylon rope and he asked, "Has anyone come this way in the last few minutes? Besides yourself, I mean?"

"Why do you ask?"

"Because I take it you're Mrs. Miles Senter and, if you are," said Ellery regretfully, "it's my melancholy job to inform you that your husband has just stopped a bullet upstairs. And now would you mind answering my question, Mrs. Senter?"

"No one."

"You don't seem surprised."

"Is Miles dead?"

"I couldn't wait for the returns. So you've seen no one, Mrs. Senter. In that case, may I ask——"

"You needn't," said Dorothy Senter. "I shot him."

When Inspector Queen arrived, there was blood in his sleepy eyes. "You can take this homicidal high life," he snorted to his son, "but I'm old enough to be your father. Couldn't you have let the local men handle this?"

Ellery said thoughtfully, "I thought it was a case that called for more elevated skull-work," and the Inspector immediately looked wakeful. Ellery followed him about, remaining thoughtful.

In proper course Dorothy Senter and Nikki Porter had hysterics and got over them, Inspector Queen had settled what facts there were to his peculiar satisfaction, men came and went, telephones rang and were silent, and at last they waited upon the pleasure of old Dr. Grand. At a few minutes before 2 a.m. Dr. Grand opened the door of Miles Senter's bedroom, drying his hands on a monogrammed towel. "Nothing to it," he chirruped. "It's going to give him an interesting part in what hair he's got left, and that's about all, gentlemen. Wonderful constitutions, these Senters. Takes a lot to kill 'em." Then he saw Dorothy Senter's face, and his own changed. "Short as you can make it, Inspector Queen." He stepped aside.

There was an odd illusion of headlessness in the man who lay on the great testered bed, but when they came near they saw that it was only the effect of bandages against the pillows and a face from which all colour had been washed.

Miles Senter looked at his wife with a sort of feeble eagerness, but after a moment the eagerness died and he shut his eyes.

"Mr. Senter," said Inspector Queen, "can you tell us what happened?"

"I don't know. I had been talking to my secretary, Mr. Hart, and I sent him downstairs to wait for Mr. Queen. I was alone. The door opened. I was about to turn around when something exploded and everything went black."

"Then you didn't see who fired at you?"

125

"No." The man on the bed sounded remote.

"Well, then, Mrs. Senter," said the Inspector, "suppose you tell your husband what you told me."

Miles Senter opened his eyes quickly.

Dorothy Senter said in a high singsong, "I left the house after dinner saying I was going to visit some friends. I walked over to Central Park and sat down on a bench. After a while I got up and walked some more. Then I walked back to the house. It was almost midnight. I went up to my room, passing Miles's sitting-room. He was in there talking to Harry Hart; they didn't hear me. I waited till Harry went downstairs. Then I got a gun from my room that I have had for a long time and I went to Miles's room and I shot him." The man on the bed made a slight movement, then he was still again. "I ran down the backstairs to the garden. I saw the boathouse. I threw the gun as far as I could out into the water and I ran to the boathouse and stayed in there. I don't know why."

Miles Senter was squinting, as if the light hurt him.

"And now about the gun, Mrs. Senter," said the Inspector, swabbing his face. "A .22 revolver, didn't you tell me?"

"Yes."

"The kind that has a cylinder that turns—that holds the bullets? That's the kind it was, Mrs. Senter?"

"Yes. But I threw it into the river."

"And a .22, you said," said the Inspector, reaming his collar.

"That's really interesting, Mrs. Senter. Because when my son found your husband on the floor, he also found the shell of the cartridge. Mrs. Senter, revolvers don't eject shells on being fired; the shell stays in the chamber. It's automatics that eject shells, Mrs. Senter. And another interesting thing . . . this shell didn't come from a .22, it came from a .38. So I regret to say you've been lying your head off, Mrs. Senter, and now what I would like to know is: Whom are you covering up?"

Dorothy gripped the footrail of her husband's bed.

"I'll tell you whom she's covering up," said her husband, staring at the canopy of his tester. "She's covering up my brother David. Instead of going to Westport, David hid somewhere and then shot me. And Dorothy saw him do it. And because she's crazy in love with him——"

"Harry, no!" screamed Dorothy.

But Miles Senter's secretary was shaking his head. "It's

no use, Dotty. I can't let this go on. Senter, David isn't the man. I am."

Miles Senter involuntarily raised himself. He stared at Harry Hart as if for the first time he was aware of more than a suit of clothes. In that stare he seemed to see everything at once, like a camera. When the wounded man sank back he turned his face away.

Hart was pale to the roots of his crew-cut. "We tried our best to avoid it. But how can you stop a thing like that? It happened, and there it was. I wanted to tell you——"

"But there was always the salary," said the man on the bed. "Eh, Harry?"

Hart went on with an effort. "Dorothy thinks I tried to kill you to-night because of it. That's why she said she did it herself."

"Noble."

The other man was silent.

"So this has all been for love, Harry?"

"All for love," said Hart steadily.

"Touching. But I'm a business man, Harry. I have the commercial mind. The way I see it, you knew I'd willed my estate to Dorothy. Life, liberty, and the pursuit of idle luxury—that's what I think you were after, Harry, and all that stood in the way was a simple-minded husband who's losing his hair. One shot, and the problem was solved——"

"If it only were," said a voice; and, startled, they looked around, even Senter. But it was Ellery, looking thoughtful still. "Harry Hart is unquestionably a talented fellow, Mr. Senter, but to have shot you to-night he'd have to have been a wizard. Hart was coming up the stairs down there between Nikki Porter and me when we heard the report of the gun over our heads. So maybe it's true love, after all. . . . Human interest in quantity, Dad, but homicidally a famine. Could we have been right in the first place?"

"Looks like it," said Inspector Queen grouchily. "Well, Mr. Senter, I think you've had enough of us for one night, and Dr. Grand's looking fidgety. We shan't disturb you again unless we get a line on your brother."

"My brother?" repeated Miles Senter painfully.

"On your death, I understand, Senter Pharmaceuticals goes to David Senter by the will of your father. And from what I've heard of Senter Pharmaceuticals, that's a goal worth shooting for . . . so to speak. I'm afraid, Mr. Senter, we're going to have to start looking for your brother."

127

That was an unmarked night, and when Nikki drifted into the garden she had no idea how much time had passed, if time had passed at all, except that the darkness was greyer, a boiling greyness that reduced everything to a glutinous mass, tasteless and unrecognizable. She groped for one of the bamboo chairs and a human hand clamped on her wrist.

Nikki squealed.

"It's only me," said a voice; and after a moment Nikki made out the long lines of Ellery, lying on the bamboo chaise on one elbow. "Nikki——"

"You fool," said Nikki angrily. "Does failure bring out the card in you?"

"I wanted action," said Ellery. "Nikki, look at those stars. . . ."

"I've had all the action I want for one night," said Nikki, dropping into the bamboo chair. "Yes, and romance, too. I finally got Dorothy to sleep with a pill Dr. Grand gave me, and I didn't neglect to tell Mr. Hart a thing or two, either. I know *his* type. Plays golf like a professional—and women—and the stock market like a yokel. Do you suppose New York will ever stop cooking?"

"It looks," said Ellery intently, "as if it's only just begun." He pointed. "The stars, Nikki, the stars."

"*What* stars?" Nikki sighted along his ghostly arm. "Oh, I'm in no condition for games!"

"Nor I." Ellery was still squinting obliquely skyward. "But this game has its points. I was lying here simmering away, waiting for you and wondering how a man who was merely going to Westport could disappear as thoroughly as David Senter seems to have done, when I began to realize there was something new under the moon. Nikki, look at the roof . . . Over there. Above the . . . the apse, I suppose you'd call it. That penthouse thing."

"That's David Senter's studio," said Nikki. "What's come over you?"

"See his chimney?"

"Of course I see his chimney."

"What's hovering over it?"

"A . . . sort of haze, it looks like."

"It's smoke."

"Well, of all things," sniffed Nikki. "What should come out of a chimney?"

"Not smoke, Nikki. Definitely not smoke, when we're a week and a half into what can be described with perfect decorum as a hell of a summer, the hour is almost 3 a.m.

and the thermometer sticks at ninety-one. Or are you sitting there gasping like a television wrestler because you find my proximity overpowering?" Ellery rose from the bamboo chaise, still craning. "Nikki, someone's been playing with fire up there and I'm feeling just deep-fried enough to want to know why. Coming along?"

"Yes," said Nikki. "Maybe it's cooler on the roof."

A few minutes later Ellery was on his hands and knees on David Senter's hearth, inspecting the smouldering remains of a fireplace fire with the jerky fixity of an aroused hound. The studio, which was in Byronic disorder, was otherwise dedicated to thermal science and Gabriel Fahrenheit; but Ellery's perspiration hissed on to the grate unnoticed in the profounder concerns absorbing him. Nikki, hung up in the doorway, thought she could see him dwindling by the inch. The roof was not cooler, Nikki had learned; it was merely less infernal than the studio, whose door and windows they had found shut.

"Who the devil would start a fire in this heat?" moaned Nikki. "Or rather, who but the devil?"

"Exactly," said Ellery, turning his nose this way and that. "Therefore heat wasn't the desideratum. Leaving combustion. Leaving ashes. And the ashes tell me this curious conflagration," said Ellery, "was set in motion around three hours ago. It was green wood and slow-burning. Also, the damper is partially closed——"

"What," said Nikki wearily, "no Trichinopoly cigars?"

"No," said Ellery, his tone glinting like his skin, "but there's this," and he held up what Nikki thought for a horrified instant was a severed, charred human hand. But it was only a thick white cotton glove, one of those sexless mitts which are purchasable at the gardening counter of any emporium. It was singed, soot-streaked, and spattered with mysterious-looking black specks, and immediately upon relieving Nikki it depressed her. For it sustained the crime story of the long night and made the unspeakable fire not merely devilish but, what was possibly worse, irrelevant. And when Ellery tasted several of the black specks, savoured them like a gourmet, and pronounced them grains of gunpowder, Nikki nodded gloomily.

"Then that's the glove he wore when he shot his brother. Had a fire laid, ran up here, tossed the glove on it, and a match, and got away while we were finding Miles. Trust an artist to be inefficient. The least he could have done was make sure it burned up."

"He was in a hurry." Ellery replaced the burned glove meticulously. "He was also unlucky. Look here, Nikki."

Nikki looked. But all she could see were some tiny red scraps of paper or cardboard, clinging like confetti to one of the side walls of the fireplace.

"What are they?"

"Unholy relics, Nikki. A rather perverted miracle. Stay here a minute, will you? I'll send Dad up. Some fur's going to fly around here. The roof's supposed to have been searched."

"Where are you going?"

"I'll be in the garden," said Ellery, and he went out so quickly Nikki had no time to assure him that she wasn't going to stay upon the roof alone and he could put *that* in David Senter's fireplace and smoke it. As it was, she had to stay until the Inspector appeared, roaring, and then she left quickly, too, with her hands over her ears.

She found Ellery at the north-east corner of the mansion, prodding the path and nearby shrubbery with the beam of his flashlight, like a man who has lost something.

"Where is it, Nikki?" Ellery demanded without looking around.

"Where is what?"

"The waterspout. That gargoyle that almost conked Miles Senter."

"Well, for heaven's sake," said Nikki crossly. "How should I know?"

"Wasn't it here that it fell?"

Nikki recognized a certain urgency in the casual Queen manner. It certainly wasn't there. "It was right here on the path last time I saw it. Night before last. See? Where the flags are chipped?"

"I see where the flags are chipped," said Ellery, suddenly austere, and he went back into the house.

The next hour bubbled. Ellery went about demanding the waterspout, waking people up, whipping them to feats of memory and muscle, and generally making himself unpopular. Why he was so bent on locating an object which, after all, had failed to be lethal he chose not to explain, and the victims of his inquisition went about muttering while they searched. Harry Hart was roused, Dorothy Senter was slapped awake, Dr. Grand was routed from his aged bed next door; not even Miles Senter was spared, although his questioning was executed with tactful dispatch. In the end, the waterspout was not found, although the house was gone over from cellar to roof and the grounds inch by inch. Nor could anyone remember having seen it since late afternoon of the day before, when the butler had stumbled over it on the spot in the path where it had crashed the night previous and, being the butler and not the gardener, had merely cursed and gone about his business. The gardener, a hickory-necked Irishman with the succinct philosophy of his profession, merely said, "Nobody told me to take the dom thing away," and went back to bed.

So there it was, or rather wasn't, as Inspector Queen said, and what difference its presence or absence made——

"Except that it's absent," and Ellery absently.

"All *right*, Ellery. So whoever tried to knock Senter's brains out took the dom—the damn thing away because somehow it left a clue to his identity——"

"His fingerprints," said Nikki with a flicker of life.

"On stone, Nikki? And anyway, if that was it, why didn't he just wipe it off? And, anyway, if he used a glove once he'd use it twice, and that reminds me of something a lot more import nt than missing angels, which is missing brothers who try to burn up evidence in fireplaces. Velie!" shouted the Inspector.

Sergeant Velie came wearily, drying his vast face with a crib-sized handkerchief.

"What did you find out?"

"From the Westport police nothin' except a couple of new cuss words. They swear there's no evidence he's been to his shack, in a month. Anyway, he ain't in Westport. The N.Y.N.H. and H. trains stopping at Westport that left New York beginning last night can't remember anyone of his description. The New Haven ticket sellers at Grand Central can't remember ditto. Our taxi investigation——"

"You satisfied now?" demanded Inspector Queen, turning around. "Now where the devil did he go?"

"Miles Senter's study," said Nikki.

At this moment the study door opened and Ellery appeared.

"Senter's definitely missing. You satisfied now?"

"That he's definitely missing? Definitely."

"Velie, general alarm for David Senter. Put it through and then let's all go home and take a shower. I'm not coming back till he's found, and that's that."

"Make it . . ." Ellery glanced at his wrist-watch. "Make it seven or eight hours, Dad. Take some time at this hour to get the equipment here that I phoned for in your name . . . oh, say, noon."

"Equipment? Noon?"

"You want David Senter, don't you?"

"Certainly I want David Senter!"

"Noon."

"Here?"

Ellery sat down on a settee, his knees apart and his palms supporting him, like an old lady who had been climbing stairs. "It's the old arithmetic," he said. "Two and two, no trick to it . . . A solid stone object weighing one hundred pounds is missing. A man is missing. And beside the house runs a river. Missing man, missing weight, deep water. David Senter was murdered and his body sunk in the East River, and as soon as the harbour police can get their diver and dragging apparatus here . . . Does anyone mind if I catch my forty?"

They fished David Senter out with twenty-five minutes to spare; and Inspector Queen, who had not gone home after all, stamped in to announce with bleary wrath that Miles Senter's artist-brother had an artistic bullet-hole through his head and had had same, from all the superficial signs, for at least twelve hours.

"They're still looking for the gun," said the Inspector, glaring about Miles Senter's bedroom, where everyone was congregated. "But we'll get it, we'll get it, and when we do——"

"I don't think," said Ellery, "we'll have to wait that long. Mrs. Senter, wouldn't you prefer a chair? The evidence of who murdered David and almost murdered you, Mr. Senter—the logical evidence—is all in; we merely have to assemble it. And by the way, Mr. Senter, are you sure you're feeling well enough to go through this? It consists of four elements: the grains of gunpowder peppering the cotton glove which failed to be consumed in David's fireplace; the little scraps of red cardboard clinging to the fireplace wall; the shot that was fired in the upper part of the house while we were coming up the stairs, and, of course, the date."

"The date," said Inspector Queen.

"The date?" said Nikki.

"That's very nearly the best part of it," Ellery said enthusiastically. "Summer became official as usual on June twenty-first, a week and a half ago, so the holiday David Senter meant to spend reproducing a Westport barn was obviously the Fourth of July, as it's hardly necessary to point out. And putting an incipient Fourth of July holiday

132

together with gunpowder grains, pieces of red cardboard, and a loud noise, you can scarcely avoid getting ... a firecracker.

"Now it was midnight when we got here, Nikki," said Ellery, "and I told you at 3 a.m. that the fire in the roof studio was about three hours old. So that noise we heard coming up the stairs on our arrival, Nikki, which we took to be a revolver shot, must have been a firecracker exploding in David Senter's studio fireplace. And since there was only one explosion that we heard, you couldn't have been shot at that time, Mr. Senter. You must have been shot a few minutes earlier."

"Then why didn't we hear the real shot?" Nikki demanded. She knew she looked like the wrath, her clothes felt leprous, and her friend Dorothy insisted on reminding her of something repulsive at Madame Tussaud's. So there was a snap in her voice. "Everything was so quiet we'd certainly have heard it, even from the street."

"The answer to that, I think," said Inspector Queen grimly, "is coming this way right now. The gun, Velie? Wrapped up in a pillow." And now he said, an amiable old gentleman; "*All* right, Sergeant. Wrap it up, and shut the door behind you."

And there was nothing to be heard in that room but Sergeant Velie's weighty tread and the life-cutting switch of the closing door. And the Inspector patted himself under the left arm, looking around.

"An explosion that was planned to be heard," said Ellery pleasantly, "and a prior explosion that was planned not to be heard. What was achieved? A miracle. The firecracker going off was taken to be the revolver shot. A simple illusion designed to make us think you were being shot while we were coming up the stairs, Mr. Senter, when actually you'd been shot a few minutes before. A falsification of time of the shooting which could have had only one purpose: to seem to give the shooter an alibi, an alibi for the false time, when the firecracker went off.

"And who had an alibi when the firecracker went off?" Ellery went on, smiling. "You, Dorothy Senter? No, you were alone in the boathouse. You, Mr. Senter—to be absurd? No, you were alone in your sitting-room with a well-creased scalp. You, Dr. Grand—to be fantastic? No, even you were alone, dozing in your garden. And David Senter was also alone—alone at the bottom of the East River.

"So I'm afraid," said Ellery, and now he was not

smiling, "I'm afraid that leaves you, Hart, and by a curious coincidence you did have an alibi for the time when the firecracker went off. A very strong alibi, Hart, in fact, the strongest possible. You were walking up the stairs between Nikki Porter and me. An excellently planned bit of stagecraft.

"But as a technician I find you wanting. You had two tries at Miles Senter and you flubbed both. First you loosened the gargoyle waterspout and pushed it off the roof while Miles Senter was passing along the path below. You chose that method because his brother David's studio was on the roof, and David, with his money motive, would be the natural suspect. When that didn't work you rather extended yourself. Yesterday you hid the waterspout and last night you shot David to death, weighted his body with the waterspout, and sank it in the river, thinking he would make the perfect scapegoat, since he would presumably never be found. Then you went to Miles Senter's sitting-room, had your chat, walked out, and immediately walked back in and shot him in the head through a muffling pillow—and did you witness that, Mrs. Senter? I think you did—and you left your heroine's husband for dead, Hart, which was criminally careless of you. The rest was timing. You hurled the gun into the river from one of the windows, dashed up to the studio where you had a firecracker ready on a fuse, dropped the glove with which you'd handled everything into the fireplace, tossed a match on the prearranged fire which was to destroy all the evidence—and didn't—and you hurried downstairs to meet me and Nikki at the gate and copper-rivet your alibi when the firecracker went off. Clever, Harry, clever; but a little on the intricate side, don't you agree . . . *post mortem*? The hard ones are the simple ones."

Thus Fire, and Water, in a case which *aficionados* say will become proverbial. Should time bear them out Ellery will be pleased, for he has always considered Marcus Tullius Cicero one of the soundest old ear-benders in the business.

The Adventure of
the Needle's Eye

THIS BEING A TALE of pirates and stolen treasure, it is a gratification to record that it all happened in that season of the year to which the moonstone and the poppy are traditionally dedicated. For the moonstone is a surprisingly moral object. To its lawful owner it brings nothing but good. Held in the mouth at the full of the moon, it reveals the future; it heats the lover and it cools the heated; it cures epilepsy; it fructifies trees; and so on. But rue and blight upon him who lays thievish hands on it, for then it invokes the black side of its nature and brings down upon the thief nothing but evil. Such exact justice is unarguably desirable in a story of piracy which, while boasting no moonstones—although there were buckets of other gems— did reach its apogee in Augustus Caesar's month, which is the moonstone's month. And the poppy springs from the blood of the slain, its scarlet blooms growing thickest on battlefields and in places of carnage. So it is a poetic duty to report that there is murder in this August tale, too.

The sea-robber involved was master of the galley *Adventure,* a Scotsman who was thoroughly hanged in London's execution Dock two centuries and a half ago—alas, on a day in May—and whose name ever since has stood for piracy in general. Ellery had tangled with historical characters before, but never with one so exciting as this; and it must be confessed that he embarked on the case of Captain Kidd's treasure with a relish more suitable to a small boy in his first hot pursuit of Mr. Legrand's golden *scarabæus* than to a weary workman in words and the case-hardened son of a modern New York policeman.

And then there was Eric Ericsson.

Ericsson was the most tragic of men, an explorer in an age when nothing of original note remained on earth to be explored. He had had to content himself with being, not

135

the first in anything, but the farthest, or the highest, or the deepest. Where five channels in the North-West Passage were known, Ericsson opened a sixth. He found a peak in Sikang Province of western China, in the Amne Machin Range, which was almost a thousand feet higher than Everest, but he lost his instruments and his companions and Mount Everest remained on the books the highest mountain on the planet. Ericsson went farther and wider in the great Juf depression of the Sahara than the Citroën expedition, but this did not salve the nettling fact that other men had blazed the trail. And so it had gone all his life. Now in middle age, broken in health, Ericsson rested on his bitter fame—honorary fellowships and medals from all the proper learned societies, membership and officership in clubs like the Explorers', Cosmos, Athenaeum—and brooded over his memories in his New York apartment or, occasionally, at the fireside of the old stone house on the island he owned off Montauk Point, Long Island.

Ellery had heard the story of William Kidd and Ericsson's Island as a result of his first meeting with Ericsson at the Explorers' Club. Not from Ericsson—their introduction had been by the way and their conversation brief; if any discoveries had been made it was by Ericsson, who explored Ellery with far swifter economy than that explorer in other spheres would have believed possible of anyone but himself. Then the large, burned, bowed man had shuffled off, leaving Ellery to quiz his host of the evening, a cartographer of eminence. When this amiable personage mentioned Ericsson's Island and the buccaneer of the *Adventure* in adjoining breaths, Ellery's bow plunged into the wind.

"You mean you've never heard that yarn?" asked the cartographer with the incredulity of the knowledgeable man. "I thought everyone had!" And he gripped his glass and set sail.

An Ericsson had taken possession of the little island in the fourth quarter of the seventeenth century, and he had managed to hold on to it through all the proprietary conflicts of that brawling era. Along the way the Northman acquired a royal patent which somehow weathered the long voyage of colonial and American history.

"Now did Kidd know Ericsson's Island?" asked the cartographer, settling himself as if for argument. "The circumstantial evidence is good. We know that in 1691, for instance, he was awarded £150 by the council of New

York for his services during the disturbances of the colony 'after the rebellion of 1688.' And then, of course, there was the treasure found on Gardiner's Island off the tip of Long Island after Kidd's arrest in 1699 on a charge of murder and piracy. On a clear day you can see Ericsson's Island from Gardiner's Island with a glass. How could he have missed it?"

"It's your story," said Ellery judicially. "Go on."

William Kidd served respectably against the French in the West Indies, the cartographer continued, and in 1695 he was in London. Recommended as fit to command a vessel for the king, Captain Kidd received the royal commission to arrest all freebooters and *boucaniers,* and he sailed the galley *Adventure* from Plymouth in 1696 into a life, not of arresting pirates, but of outpirating them.

"The rest is history," said the cartographer, "although some of it is dubious history. We do know that in 1698 or thereabout he was in these parts in a small sloop. Well, the story has persisted for two hundred and fifty years that during this period—when Kidd deserted the *Adventure* in Madagascar and took to the sloop, eventually working his way to these waters—he paid a visit to Ericsson's Island."

"To Gardiner's Island," corrected Ellery.

"And Ericsson's," said his host stubbornly. "Why not? About £14,000 was recovered from Kidd's vessel and from Gardiner's Island afterward; there must have been a great deal more than that. Why, John Avery—'Long Ben' —once grabbed off 100,000 pieces of eight in a single haul, and a Mogul's daughter to boot!

"What happened to the rest of Kidd's booty? Is it likely he'd have cached it all in one place? He knew he was in for serious trouble—he tried to bribe Governor Bellomont, you'll recall. And with Ericcson's Island so handy ..."

"What's the story?" murmured Ellery.

"Oh, that he put into the cove there with a small boat one night, by a ruse got into the Ericsson house—the original's still standing, by the way, beautifully preserved— gave Ericsson and his family fifteen minutes to get off the island and used the place as his headquarters for a few days. When Kidd cleared out, to be seized and shipped to England shortly after, the Ericssons went back to their island——"

"And perforated it fore and aft and amidships for the

treasure Kidd presumably buried there," said Ellery, trying to sound amused.

"Well, certainly," said the cartographer peevishly. "Wouldn't you have?"

"But they never found it."

"Neither they nor their heirs or assigns. But that doesn't mean it isn't there, Queen."

"Doesn't mean it is, either."

Nevertheless, Ellery went home that night feeling as if he had spent the evening in a hurricane off the Spanish Main, clinging to the wild rigging.

It was not quite two weeks later, in a mid-August spell of Dry Tortugan weather, that Eric Ericsson telephoned. The explorer sounded remote, as if deep—at least six fathoms deep—affairs were on his mind.

"Could you see me confidentially, Mr. Queen? I know you're a busy man, but if it's possible——"

"Are you calling from town, Mr. Ericsson?"

"Yes."

"You come right on over!"

Nikki could not understand Ellery's excitement. "Buried treasure," she sniffed. "A grown man."

"Women," pontificated Mr. Queen, "have no imagination."

"I suppose that's true," said his secretary coolly, "if you mean the kind that heats up at a bucket of nasty gore and a couple of rum-soaked yo-ho-hos. Who ever heard of a lady pirate?"

"Two of the bloodiest pirates in the business were Anne Bonny and Mary Read."

"Then they were no ladies!"

Twenty minutes later the doorbell rang and Nikki, still sniffishly, admitted the owner of the island whose clam-shells had once been crunched by the tread of Captain Kidd and his cutthroat crew.

"Glad you didn't waste any time getting here, Mr. Ericsson," said Ellery enthusiastically. "The sooner we get going on it——"

"You know why I'm here?" The explorer frowned.

"It doesn't take a math. shark to put a couple of twos together."

"What on earth are you talking about."

"Oh, come, Mr. Ericsson," chortled Ellery. "If it's Nikki you're worried about, I assure you that not only is she the custodian of all my secrets, she also has no interest whatsoever in buried treasure."

"Buried treasure?" Ericsson waved a charred hand impatiently. "That's not what I wanted to see you about."

"It's . . . not?"

"I've never put any stock in that yarn, Mr. Queen. In fact, the whole picture of Kidd as a pirate, in my opinion, is a myth and a historical libel. Kidd was the goat of a political intrigue, I'm convinced, not a pirate at all. Dalton's book presented some pretty conclusive evidence. If it's real pirates you're after, look up Bartholomew Roberts. Roberts took over four hundred ships during his career."

"Then the story of Kidds' seizure of Ericsson's Island ——?"

"He may have visited the island around 1698, but if it was to bury anything I've never seen the slightest evidence of it. Mr. Queen, I'd like to tell you why I came."

"Yes," sighed Ellery, and Nikki felt almost sorry for him.

Ericsson's problem involved romance, it appeared, but not the kind that glittered under pirate moons. His only sister, a widow, had died shortly after Ericsson's retirement, leaving a daughter. The explorer's relationship with his sister had been distant, and he had last seen her child, Inga, as a leggy creature of twelve with a purple pimple on her nose. But at the sister's funeral he found himself embraced as "Uncle Eric" by a golden Norse goddess of nineteen. His niece was alone in the world and she had clung to him. Ericsson, a bachelor, found the girl filling a need he had never dreamed existed. Inga left college and came to live with him as his ward, the consolation of his empty retirement, and the sole heir of his modest fortune.

At first they were inseparable—in Ericsson's New York household, at the stone house on the island during long week-ends. But Inga began to glow, and the moths came. They were young moths and they rather interfered. So Ericsson—selfishly he admitted—had his yacht refurbished and sailed Inga away on a cruise of the Caribbean.

"Biggest mistake of my life," the explorer shrugged. "We stopped over in the Bahamas, and there Inga met a young Britisher, Anthony Hobbes-Watkins, who was living a gentlemanly beachcomber sort of existence out on Lyford Cay, at the other end of New Providence Island. It was Inga's first serious love affair. I should have taken her away immediately. When I woke up, it was too late."

"Elopement?" asked Nikki hopefully.

"No, no, Miss Porter; it was a cathedral wedding. I

couldn't stand in Inga's way. And I really had nothing definite to go on."

Ellery said: "There's something fishy about Hobbes-Watkins?"

"I don't know, Mr. Queen." Ericsson's heavy, burned-out face remained expressionless, but not his eyes. "That's what I want you to find out."

"What do you know about him?"

"Only what he's told me and a few things I've picked up. Captaincy in the R.A.F. during the war, and not much of anything since—I don't hold that against him, it's a rocky world. All the British upper-class attainments—shoots well, plays an earnest game of polo, grouses about the fading star of empire; that sort of thing. Knew all the right people in Nassau; but he hadn't been there long.

"His father, a Colonel Hobbes-Watkins, came on from somewhere—England, he said—for the wedding," continued the explorer, and he shrugged again. "A stout, red, loud, horsy specimen, nearly a caricature of his type. They seem to have plenty of money so it can't be that. But there *is* . . . something, a mystery, a vagueness about them that keeps disturbing me. They're like figures on a movie screen—you see them move, you hear them talk, but they never seem flesh and blood. Two-dimensional . . . I'm not saying this well," said Ericsson, flushing. "When a man's tramped mountains and deserts and jungles all his life, as I have, he develops an extra sense." He looked up. "I don't trust them."

"I suppose," said Nikki, "your niece does."

"Well, Inga's young and unsophisticated, and she's very much in love. That's what makes it so awkward. But she's become important to me, and for her sake I can't let this go on unless I'm satisfied she hasn't made some awful mistake."

"Have you noticed anything different since the wedding, Mr. Ericsson?" asked Ellery. "A change in their attitude?"

The explorer scraped the back of his neck with a limp handkerchief. But he said defiantly, "They whisper together."

Ellery raised his brows.

But Ericsson went on doggedly. "Right after the wedding Colonel Hobbes-Watkins left for the States. On business, he said. I gave the yacht to Inga and Tony for a three-week honeymoon. On their way back they picked me up in Nassau and we sailed up to New York, meeting Tony's father here . . . On three different occasions I've come on the Hobbes-Watkinses having whispered conversations which break off like a shot. I don't like it, Mr. Queen. I don't like it to such an extent," said Ericsson quietly, "that I've deliberately kept us all in the city instead of doing the sensible thing in this heat and living down at the island. My island is pretty isolated, and it would make the ideal setting for a . . . Instead of which, Tony and Inga have my apartment, I'm stopping at one of my clubs, and the Colonel is sweating it out politely in a midtown hotel—business, unspecified, still keeping him in the States. But I can't stall any longer. Inga's been after me now for weeks to shove off for the Point, and she's beginning to look at me queerly. I've had to promise we'd all go down this week-end for the rest of the summer."

"It would make the ideal setting," said Ellery, "for a what?"

"You'll think I'm cracked."

"For a what, Mr. Ericsson?"

"All right!" The explorer gripped the arms of his chair. "For a murder," he muttered.

Nikki stared. "Oh, I'm sure——" she began.

But Ellery's foot shifted and somehow crushed Nikki's little toe. "Murder of whom, Mr. Ericsson?"

"Inga! Me! Both of us—I don't know!" He controlled himself with an effort. "Maybe I'm hallucinated. But I tell you those two are scoundrels and my island would be a perfect place for whatever they're up to. What I'd like you to do, Mr. Queen, is come down this week-end for an indefinite stay. Will you?"

Ellery glanced at his secretary; Nikki was often his umpire when he was playing the game of working. But she was regarding him with the grim smile of a spectator.

"Come down, too, Miss Porter," said the explorer, misinterpreting the glance. "Inga will love having you. Besides, your coming will make it appear purely social. I don't want Inga having the least suspicion that . . . Don't bother about a wardrobe; we lead the most primitive life on the island. And there's plenty of room; the house has tripled its original size. About the fee, Mr. Queen——"

"We'll discuss fees," murmured Ellery, "when there's something to charge a fee for. We'll be there, Mr. Ericsson. I can't leave, however, before Saturday morning. When are you planning to go down?"

"Friday." The explorer looked worried.

"I don't imagine they'd try anything the very first

141

night," said Ellery soothingly. "And you're not exactly a helpless old gaffer."

"Good lord! You don't think it's myself I'm concerned about! It's Inga ... married and ..." Ericsson stopped abruptly. Then he smiled and rose. "Of course you're right. I'll have the launch waiting for you at Montauk Point. You don't know how this relieves me."

"But won't your niece suspect something by the mere fact of Ellery's being invited down?" asked Nikki. "Unless, Ellery, you cook up one of your stories."

"How's this?" beamed Ellery. "I met Mr. Ericsson at the Explorers' Club recently, heard the family tale about Captain Kidd's treasure. I couldn't resist it, and I'm coming down to try to solve a two-hundred-and-fifty-year-old-mystery. Simple?"

"Simply perfect," exclaimed Ericsson. "Inga's had them half believing this yarn ever since the Bahamas, and if I talk it up for the rest of the week you'll have them under your feet—they'll follow you around like tourists. See you both Saturday."

"It's simple, all right," said Nikki, when the explorer had gone. "The simple truth! Shall I pack your extra cutlass, my bucko—and a couple of all-day suckers!"

Eric Ericsson and his niece met them at Montauk Point Saturday morning and hurtled them over blue water in a noisy launch. It was hard to think of wickedness. Inga was a big, solid blonde girl with the uncomplicated loveliness of the North, friendly and charming and—Nikki thought—happy as a newlywed could be. The day was stainless, the sun brilliant, the horizon picketed with racing sails; a salt breeze blew the girls' hair about, and the world looked a jolly place. Even Ericsson was composed, as if he had slept unexpectedly well or the presence of serene, golden-legged Inga gave him the strength to dissemble his fears.

"I think it's so thrilling," Inga cried over the roar of the launch. "And Tony and the Colonel have talked of nothing else since Uncle Eric told us why you were coming down, Mr. Queen. Do you really feel there's hope?"

"I'll try to," Ellery shouted. "By the way, I'm disappointed. I thought your husband and father-in-law might be with you in the launch."

"Oh, that's Uncle Eric's fault," the girl said, and the explorer smiled. "He kidnapped me before I could scream for help."

"Guilty." Ericsson's grip on the wheel gave the lie to his

142

smile. "I don't see much of you now that you're Mrs. Hobbes-Watkins."

"Darling, I'm glad you kidnapped me. I really am."

"Even though Mr. Hobbes-Watkins is probably fit to be tied?"

Inga looked happy.

But Nikki, the sun notwithstanding, felt a chill. Ericsson had been afraid to leave Inga alone on the island with her husband and father-in-law.

Ellery kept chattering to Inga about the paragon she had married, while Ericsson stood quietly over the wheel. Nikki could have told the great man that he was wasting his celebrated breath: the girl was in the first heaven of wedded bliss, where the beloved hangs in space clothed in perfect light and there is no past.

From the horizon rose a seaweed-hung otter with a fish in its mouth, which changed rapidly into a long low-lying island thinly wooded and running down to a white beach and a pretty cove. As the launch drew near, they made out a shed, a boathouse, and a jetty. A lank, disjointed something stuck up from the jetty like a piece of drift-wood. It turned surprisingly into a one-legged old man. His left leg was gone at the knee; the trouser of his bleached fishy jeans was pinned back over the stump; and to the stump there was strapped a crude, massive pegleg. With a skin resembling the shed's corrugated roof, a nose that was a twist of bone, crafty and secretive eyes, and a greasy bandana tied behind his ears against the sun, the peglegged old man looked remarkably like a pirate; and Nikki said so.

"That's why we call him Long John," Inga said as her uncle manœuvred the launch toward the jetty. "At least Tony and I do. Uncle Eric calls him Fleugelheimer, or something as ridiculous, though I suppose it's his name. He's not very bright, and he has no manners at all. Hi, Long John!" she called. "Catch the line."

The old man hopped sidewise with great agility and caught the line, poorly tossed, in his powerful right hand. Immediately he wheeled on Ericsson, his bony jaws grinding.

"Bloodsucker!" he yelled.

"Now, John," said the explorer with a sigh.

"When ye givin' me more money?"

"John, we have guests . . ."

"Or d'ye want me to quit? Ye want me to quit!"

"Make the line fast," said Ericsson with a faint smile.

"I'm a poor man," whined the old pirate, obeying. Suddenly he squinted sidewise at Ellery. "This the great detective?"

"Yes, John."

"Henh!" said Long John, and he spat into the water, grinning evilly. He seemed to have forgotten all about his grievance.

"He's been on the island for years," Ericsson explained as they went up a rough path in the woods. "My caretaker. Surly old devil—not all there. He's a miser—hoards every penny I give him, and keeps dunning me for more with the regularity of a parrot. I ignore him and we get along fine."

And there was the stone house at the hump of the island's back. Clean wings stretched from a central building whose stones were grimy with weathered age. The old part of the house rose in a clapboard tower. The tower was square, with several small windows from which, Ellery thought, the whole island and a great spread of the sea must be visible. Undoubtedly the lookout tower of the orginal structure.

To one side of the house someone—Ericsson, or one of his more recent forebears—had built a rough but comfortable terrace. It was paved with oyster shells and there was a huge barbecue pit.

Two men—one portly and middle-aged, the other slim and young—rose from deck-chairs, waving frosty glasses.

And the instant Ellery laid eyes on the Hobbes-Watkinses he knew Eric Ericsson had been right.

It was hard to say why. They were almost professionally British, especially Colonel Hobbes-Watkins, but that did not account for it and for the rest of the day Ellery devoted himself to this riddle. He did not solve it.

On the surface the men were plausible. Inga's husband was handsome in a thin, underdone way; he slouched and lolled as if he were hopelessly tired; speech seemed forced out of him and he drank a good deal. This was the very picture of the younger postwar European, spoiled, sick, and disenchanted. Still . . . The elder Hobbes-Watkins was Colonel Blimp to the life, fussing and blustery and full of old-fashioned prejudices. A warmed-over mutton roast, as Nikki promptly dubbed him in a mumble. But there was something in the Colonel's bloated eye and occasionally in his blasting tone that had a lean and cynical energy in it, not at all in character.

During the afternoon Ellery, playing his role of historical detective, set off on a survey of the island. Inga, Tony, and the Colonel insisted on accompanying him.

Long John was fishing from a dory off the cove. When he spied them, he deliberately turned his back.

Ellery began to saunter along the beach, the others trotting eagerly behind.

"Needn't be bashful," he called, mindful of Inga between the two ogres at his back. "I'm merely casing the joint. Come up here, Inga."

"Casing the joint," wheezed Colonel Hobbes-Watkins. "Very good, ha-ha! But I say, won't we trample the clues?"

"Not much danger of that, Colonel," said Ellery cheerfully, "after two and a half centuries. Inga, do join me."

"Glad I ambled along," said Tony Hobbes-Watkins in a languid voice. It sounded queerly dutiful for a groom. Ellery was conscious of the man's eyes; they kept a staring watch.

They went around the island in an hour. It was long and narrow and swelled to a ridge in the middle. The vegetation was scrubby and poor. There was no close anchorage except off the cove. None of the trees, which might have been landmarks, looked old; the island was exposed to the sea, and centuries of winter gales had kept it pruned.

"I don't suppose," Ellery asked Inga as they climbed the path back to the house in the dusk, "the story has ever had any documentation? Chart, map—anything like that?"

"Nothing that still exists. But it's said that there was once a letter or diary page or something left by the 1698 Ericsson—it's been lost, if it ever existed at all—telling about the clue in Captain Kidd's room, and of course that's been the big mystery ever since."

"Clue? Kidd's room?" exclaimed Ellery. "No one's mentioned that!"

"Didn't Eric tell you?" murmured the younger Englishman. "Fantastic fellow, Eric. No imagination."

"I wondered why you hadn't steamed up there immediately," panted the Colonel. "Fancy your uncle's not telling Mr. Queen the most exciting part of it, Inga! It's the chamber the pirate watched the sea from when he took the island over—didn't you say, my dear?"

"The tower room," said Inga, pointing through the dusk. "*That* was in the lost letter, and the reference to the clue Kidd left there."

"Clue left in the tower room?" Ellery squinted through the twilight hungrily. "And that's the original room up there, Inga?"

"Yes."

"What was the clue?"

But the terrace and Long John at the barbecue pit intervened; and since the one-legged caretaker was brandishing a veritable trident as he glowered at the latecomers, Ellery was not answered.

They had dinner. A great moon rose, and the air turned chilly. Ellery wandered to the edge of the terrace with his plate, and a moment later Eric Ericsson joined him.

"Well?" the explorer asked.

"Nothing tangible, Mr. Ericsson. But I agree—there's something in the wind."

"What about to-night? I've put you next to the Colonel's room, and I have an automatic, but Inga ... alone with ..."

"I've already fixed that. By a happy coincidence Nikki is going to be so nervous to-night in this primeval setting that she'll just have to sleep with somebody. Since she's had a strict upbringing, that means with Inga, the only other female here. A dirty trick to play on a new husband," said Ellery dryly, "but Tony can console himself with the prospect of a good night's sleep in the room next to mine." Ericsson pressed Ellery's arm rather pathetically. "For the rest of the evening, Mr. Ericsson," murmured Ellery, "please follow my lead. I'm going to be treasure-hunting like mad."

"Ha. Caught you whispering," said a voice at Ellery's elbow; it was young Hobbes-Watkins with a glass in his hand. "Pumping Eric about that clue, eh, Queen?"

"We were just getting round to it," said Ellery. "Girls couldn't take it, I see." Inga and Nikki were gone.

"Driven to cover by the mosquitoes and gnats," boomed the Colonel, slapping himself. "Lovely children, but females, what? Ah, there, you dog, don't shake your head at your old bachelor father! The moon's bloody, and it's the hour for high adventure, didn't some chap say? About that clue Mr. Queen ..."

"Yes, you never said a word to me about Captain Kidd's room, Mr. Ericsson," said Ellery reproachfully. "What's all this about a clue he's supposed to have left up there?"

"It's characteristically cryptic," said the explorer, pouring coffee. "The legend says that just before Kidd was to be hanged in London he sent a letter to my ancestor admitting that he'd buried a treasure on Ericsson's Island in '98, and saying that 'to find it you must look through the eye of the needle."

"Eye of the needle," said Ellery. "Eye of which needle?"

"Ah!" said Colonel Hobbes-Watkins ominously. "There's the rub, as the Bard says. No one knows—eh, Ericsson?"

"I'm afraid not, Colonel, and no one ever will, because it's all moonshine."

"Don't see why you say that, Eric, at all," said Tony, almost energetically. "Could have been a needle!"

"Even if there had been," Ericsson smiled in his moonshine, "two hundred and fifty years make a large haystack."

"One moment!" said Ellery. "Look through the eye of the needle *in the tower room,* Mr. Ericsson?"

"That's how it goes."

"What's in that room?"

"Nothing at all. Just four walls, a floor, and a ceiling. I assure you, Mr. Queen, everything's been tried—unsuccessfully—from hunting for a peculiar rock formation to conjuring up a tree fork viewed from a certain angle from the windows."

Ellery stared up at the tower. Suddenly he sprang to his feet. "How do I get up there?"

"There's the sleuth for you!" cried Colonel Hobbes-Watkins, hurling himself from his chair. "Been itching to have a go at that ruddy room myself!"

"But Eric's been so discouraging," murmured his son.

Nikki and Inga had their heads together before the fireplace, where Long John was laying a fire. Inga fell behind to say something to her young husband, who glanced quickly at Nikki and then shrugged.

The explorer led the way up a tiny narrow coiling staircase, holding a kerosene lamp high. "The tower's never been electrified," he called down, his deep voice reverberating. "Better use those flashlights or you'll break your necks on these stairs."

"Eeee," said Nikki convincingly; but it was only a dried-up wasps' nest. The stairs sagged perilously at every step.

The climb ended in a little landing and a heavy door of blackened oak and hand-forged iron. Ericsson set his big shoulder to the door. It gave angrily. The lamp bobbed off.

147

"A couple of you had better stay on the landing. This floor may not hold up under so much weight. Come in, Mr. Queen."

It was scarcely more than a large closet with miniature square windows. A floor of dirt-glazed random boards, undulant like the sea; a raftered ceiling only a few inches above the men's heads; and four papered walls. And that was all, except for dust and cobwebs. The windows, of imperfectly blown glass, were closed.

"Open them, Ellery," choked Nikki from the doorway. "You can't breathe up here."

"You can't open them," said Inga. "They've been stuck fast for six generations."

Ellery stood in the middle of the room looking about.

"Aren't you going to get down on all fours, Mr. Queen?" bellowed the Colonel from the landing. "Like the fellow from Baker Street?"

"I find these walls much more interesting."

But the only thing Nikki could see on the walls was the wallpaper. The paper showed an imitation coloured marble design on a grainy background—ugly as sin, Nikki thought, and even uglier for being faded and mildewed in great patches.

Ellery was at one of the walls now, actually caressing it, holding the lamp close to the marbled paper. Finally he began at a corner and went over the paper inch by inch, from ceiling to floor. At one point he examined something for a long time. Then he resumed his deliberate inspection, and he neither spoke nor looked around until he had completed his tour of the room.

"This wallpaper," he said. "Do you know, Mr Ericsson, what you have here?"

"Dash it all, sir," interrupted the Colonel explosively, "are you treasure-hunting, or what?"

"The wallpaper?" Ericsson frowned. "All I know about it is that it's very old."

"To be exact, late seventeenth century," said Ellery. "This is genuine flock paper, made by the famous Dunbar of Aldermanbury. It's probably quite valuable."

"There's a treasure for you," wailed Inga.

"If so," shrugged her uncle, "it's the first I've run across on the island."

"There may be a second," said Ellery. "If we look through the eye of the needle."

"Don't tell me, Queen," said Inga's husband with what might have been animation, "you've spotted something."

148

"Yes."

The Hobbes-Watkinses made admiring sounds and Inga embraced her spouse. The explorer seemed stunned.

"Do you mean to say," demanded Nikki in a loud voice, "that you walk into a strange room and in ten minutes solve a mystery that's baffled everybody for two hundred and fifty years? Come, come, Mr. Q!"

"It's still only theory," said Ellery apologetically. "Inga, may I borrow a broom?"

"A broom!"

Inga, Tony, and the Colonel shouted chaotically down the tower stairs for Long John to fetch the best broom on the premises. Then they ran into the little room and danced around Ellery, reckless of the aged floor.

"If the yarn is true at all," Ellery said, "Kidd couldn't have meant it literally when he instructed your ancestor, Mr. Ericsson, to 'look through the eye of the needle.' The early treasure-hunters saw that at once, or they wouldn't have looked for peculiar rock and tree formations. They just didn't look close enough to home. It was under their noses all the time."

"*What* was under their noses all the time?" asked Nikki.

"The marble design on this wallpaper. Marble's unique characteristic is its veining. Look at these veins in the pattern. Some are long and thin, tapering to a point——"

"*Like needles,*" said the explorer slowly.

Everyone began scuttling along a wall.

"But where's one with an opening?" shrieked Inga. "Oh, I can't find a—a bloody eye!"

"An eye, an eye," mumbled the Colonel feverishly. "There must be one with an eye!"

"There is," said Ellery. "Just one, and here it is near this window."

And while they stared in awe at the place on the wall beyond the tip of Ellery's forefinger, Long John's boot and pegleg stumped into the tower room.

"Broom." He flung it.

Ellery seized it, placed the end of the broom handle on the open space in the needle-shaped vein, said with piety, "Let us pray," and pushed.

There was a ripping sound and the broomhandle burst through the wallpaper and sank into the wall. Ellery kept pushing gently. The handle slid out of sight up to the sweep.

Ellery withdrew the broom and stepped back.

149

"Mr. Ericsson." he said, not without emotion, "the honour of the first look is yours."

"Well, don't just crouch there, Uncle Eric!" moaned Inga. "What do you see?"

"Can you see *anything*?"

"But he must—there's a bright moon!"

"Now, my dears, give the old chap a chance——"

"I see," said Eric Ericsson slowly, "a bit of the north-east shoreline. You know the place, Inga. It's that postage stamp patch of beach with the slight overhang of flat rock. Where you've sunbathed."

"Let me see!"

"Let me!"

"It is!"

"It can be. By George, not really——"

"What luck!"

There was a great deal of confusion.

Ellery said rapidly, "Mr. Ericsson, since you know just where the place is, take a hurricane lamp and a stake and get down there. We'll keep watch through the peephole. When we've got your lamp in the centre of our sight, we'll signal with a flashlight three times from this window. Drive your stake into the sand at that point, and we'll join you there with shovels."

"I'll get 'em!" shrieked a voice; and they turned to see Long John's peg vanishing. Fifteen minutes later, with Inga sprinting ahead, they thrashed through the scrub toward the explorer's light.

They found Ericsson standing on an outcrop of silvery rock, smiling. "No hurry," he said. "And no treasure—not till low tide to-morrow morning, anyway."

Ericsson's stake was protruding from four and a half feet of ocean.

Nikki found herself able to play the part of a nervous city female with no difficulty at all. How could Inga *sleep*? she thought as she thrashed about in the twin bed. When in a few hours she was going to be the heiress of a pirate's treasure? ... The ... *piracy* of that pirate ... to bury it so that for half the elapsed time the Atlantic rolled over it ... He ought to be hanged. ...

Then Nikki remembered that he *had* been hanged; and that was her last thought until a hand clamped over her mouth and a light flashed briefly into her eyes and Ellery's voice said affectionately in her ear, "You certainly sleep soundly. Get into some clothes and join me outside. And don't wake anyone or I'll give you a taste of the cat."

Nikki slipped out of the house into a dead and lightless world. She could not even make out the terrace. But Ellery rose out of the void and led her down the path and into the woods, his grip forbidding noise. Not until they had gone several hundred yards did he turn on his flashlight, and even then he cupped its beam.

"Is it all right to talk now?" Nikki asked coldly. "What time is it? Where are we going? And why are you practically naked? And do you think this is cricket? After all, Ellery, it's not your treasure."

"It's not quite four, we're getting the jump on our friends, I expect it will be wet and mucky work, and pirate loot calls for pirate methods. Would you rather go back to your hot little bed?"

"No," said Nikki. "Though it all sounds pretty juvenile to me. How can you dig through sea water?"

"Low tide at 4.29 a.m.—I checked with the tide table at the house."

Nikki began to feel excited all over again.

And she almost burst into a yo-ho-ho when they came out on the flat rock and saw Ericsson's stake below them lapped by a mere inch or two of water.

The sun made its appearance with felicity. The first sliver of fried-egg radiance slipped over the edge of the sea's blue plate just as Ellery's spade rang a short of breakfast bell. Nikki, who was flat on the wet sand with her head in the hole, and Ellery, whose salted hair bobbed a foot below Nikki's chin, responded to the sound with hungry cries.

"It's a metal box, Nikki!"

"Whee!"

"*Don't* come down here! Get that windlass ready."

"Where? What? What's a windlass?"

"That drum up there for hoisting!" Before turning in the previous night the men had lugged all the portable paraphernalia they could find in the shed down to the site of the treasure. "And unwind the line and pay it down to me——"

"Yaaaaa-hoo!" Nikki ran around in her little bare feet madly.

Twenty minutes later they knelt panting on the sand at the edge of the hole, staring at a brassbound iron chest with a fat convex lid. It was a black and green mass of

151

corruption. Shreds of crumbled stuff told where leather had once been strapped. And the chest was heavy——"

"Can you open it?" whispered Nikki.

Ellery set the heels of his hands on the edge of the lid and got his shoulders ready. The lid cracked off like a rotten nutshell.

Nikki gulped. The celestial egg was sunnyside up now, and beneath it a million little frying lights danced.

The chest was heaped with jewels.

"Diamonds." said Nikki dreamily. "Rubies. Emeralds. Pearls. Sapphires. So pretty. Look, Ellery. The booty of a real pirate. Wrenched from the throats and arms of dead Spanish women——"

"And the jewels in turn wrenched from their settings," muttered Ellery, "most of which were probably melted down. But here are some they overlooked. An empty gold setting. A silver one——"

"Here are more silver ones, Ellery . . ."

"Those aren't silver." Ellery picked up one. "This is platinum, Nikki . . ."

"And look at those old coins! What's this one?"

"What?"

"This coin!"

"Oh? *El peso duro*. A piece of eight."

"Gosh . . ." Nikki suddenly thrust both hands into the chest.

And at this precise moment, through the young air of the island's morning, there came a dull crack, like the faraway slam of a door, and quickly after—so quickly it sounded like an echo of the first—another.

Ellery vaulted across the hole and leaped onto the flat rock. "Nikki, those were gunshots——"

"Huh?" Nikki was still on the quarterdeck with her jewels. "But Ellery—the treasure! You can't leave——" But Ellery was gone.

They found Eric Ericsson in a robe and slippers lying in the doorway of Captain Kidd's roost, across the sill. He had tumbled head first into the empty room. In his right hand there was a .38 automatic pistol.

When they turned him over they saw a red hole in his forehead and red thickening fluid on the floor where the forehead had rested.

His body was still warm.

Ellery got up, and he said to the Hobbes-Watkinses and the marble-faced girl and the one-legged caretaker and

Nikki, "We will go downstairs now we will bar the tower door." So they went downstairs quietly, and Ellery excused himself for a moment and disappeared in his room, and when he appeared again he had a police revolver in his hand. "Nikki, you and Inga will take the launch and go over to the mainland and notify the Coast Guard and the Suffolk County police; there's no phone here. You won't come back until someone in authority can come with you. You gentlemen will wait here with me—with me, that is, and my shooting iron."

Late that day Ellery came downstairs from the tower room and conferred with the Coast Guard officer and the police captain from the mainland. Finally he said, "I appreciate that. It's something I owe poor Ericsson," and he waited until the people were brought in and seated before him.

The hearty bloat had gone out of Colonel Hobbes-Watkins; it was supplanted wholly by the muscular alertness Ellery had glimpsed the day before. Tony Hobbes-Watkins was very still, but he was no longer remotely languid. Inga was the palest projection of herself. Even Long John jiggled his peg nervously.

"Fifteen minutes or so after sunrise this morning," Ellery began, "just about the time I was down at the beach opening the treasure chest, Eric Ericsson was climbing the stairs in this house to the tower room. He was in his robe and slippers, and he carried his .38 automatic, with a full clip. His bedroom is below the tower shaft, which acts as an amplifier; evidently he was awakened by some noise from the tower room and decided to investigate. He took a gun with him because, even in his own house, he was afraid to be without it."

"I say——" began the Colonel furiously; but he did not say after all; he wiped the rolls on his neck.

"Someone was in the tower room. What was this person doing there—at dawn, in an empty room? There is only one thing of utility in that room—the peephole I punctured through the wall last night. The person Ericsson heard was watching me through the peephole. Watching me dig up the treasure."

They stared at him.

"Ericsson came to the landing and flung open the door. The man at the peephole whirled. Maybe they talked for a little while; maybe Ericsson was put off his guard. His gun came down and the man across the room whipped out a

153

revolver and fired a .22 calibre bullet into Ericsson's head, killing him instantly. But Ericsson's automatic had come up again instinctively as his murderer drew, and it went off, too—a split second after the murderer's! We know two shots were fired almost simultaneously because Miss Porter and I heard them, and because we found a .22 calibre bullet in Ericsson's head and a .38 shell on the floor near Ericsson's .38 automatic."

And Ellery said clearly, "The murderer ran down the tower stairs after the shots, heard the others coming— you'd all been awakened by the shots and dashed out of your rooms at once, you've said—realized he was trapped, and thereupon did the only thing he could: he pretended that he, too, had been awakened by the shots and he ran *back* up the stairs with the rest of you. The gun he managed to dispose of before I got back to the house from the beach.

"One of you," said Ellery, "was that murderer.

"Which one was it?"

There was no sound in the room at all.

"We found the empty shell of Ericsson's discharged cartridge, as I say, near his body. He had fired once at his murderer, his automatic had ejected the shell, and the bullet had sped on its way.

"But here is the interesting fact: *We haven't found Ericsson's bullet.*"

Ellery leaned their way. "The tower room has been gone over all day by these officers and me. The bullet isn't there. There is no sign of it or its passage anywhere in the room—floor, walls, ceiling. The windows remain intact. They weren't open at the time of Ericsson's shot; as you remarked yesterday, Inga, they've been stuck fast for generations; and when we tried to open them today without breaking something, we failed.

"Nor did Ericsson's shot go wild. He was killed instantly, falling into the room head first; this means that when he fired, he was facing into the room. But just to be thorough, we went over the landing and the tower shaft, too. No bullet, no bullet mark, and no slightest opening through which the bullet might have passed."

"The peephole!" Nikki said involuntarily.

"No. There is considerable thickness to the walls. Ericsson in the doorway was at an extremely acute angle to the peephole. So while the bullet conceivably might have passed through the opening of the hole inside the tower room, it would have to have lodged inside the wall, or at least left some sign of its passage if it went clear through. We've torn down part of the wall to get a look inside. There is no bullet and no mark of a bullet.

"So the extraordinary fact is that while Ericsson's bullet must have struck something in that room, there is no sign of its having done so.

"Impossible? No.

"There is one logical explanation."

And Ellery said, "The bullet must have struck the only thing in that room which left it—the murderer. *One of you is concealing a bullet wound.*"

Ellery turned to the silent officers. "Let's have these three men stripped to the skin. And Nikki," he added, "go you somewhere with Inga—yes, I said Inga!—and do likewise."

And when the Colonel, raging, had been reduced to his fundamental pinkness, and his intent son stood similarly unclothed, and when what there was of Long John was grimly revealed also—and no wound was found on any of them, not so much as a scratch—Ellery merely blinked and faced the door through which Nikki had taken the murdered man's niece, the heir to his fortune and the treasure.

And the men redressed quickly, as if time were at their heels.

And when Nikki came back with Inga the police captain asked, "Where is Mrs. Hobbes-Watkins's wound, Miss Porter?"

"Mrs. Hobbes-Watkins," replied Nikki, "has no wound."

"No . . .?"

"Maybe," said the Coast Guard officer awkwardly, "maybe you didn't look—uh——"

"And maybe I did," said Nikki with a sweet smile. "I work for the great Ellery Queen . . . you know?"

So now the two officers turned to look at the great Ellery Queen, but with no appreciation of his greatness at all.

And the Coast Guard officer said, "Well," and the police captain from the mainland did not say even that but turned on his heel.

He turned immediately back. For Ellery was growling, "If that's the case, it's obvious who killed Ericsson."

And Ellery produced a cigarette and a lighter and went to work on them, and then he said, "It all goes back to

155

what I dug up this morning. And what did I dig up? An old chest, some old coins, a great number of unmounted gems, and some empty gem settings. Nikki, you saw the empty settings. Of which materials were they made?"

"Gold, silver, platinum——"

"Platinum," said Ellery, and he waved his cigarette gently. "The metal platinum wasn't introduced into Europe until about 1750—*over fifty years after Kidd supposedly buried the chestful of jewels on this island*. It's even worse than that: *Platinum wasn't used for jewel settings until the year 1900*, at which time Kidd had been dead a hundred and ninety-nine years.

"A phony, gentlemen. A plant. The whole thing.

"The 'treasure' I unearthed this morning was buried in that sand very recently, I'm afraid. It has no more connection with William Kidd or any other seventeenth-century pirate than the loose change in my pocket. Oh, it was meant to be taken for a treasure Kidd buried—the chest is authentically old, and some old coins were strewn among the jewels. But the jewels, as proved by those platinum settings, are modern.

"Why should modern jewels be buried on an island in the guise of old pirate treasure? Well, suppose they were stolen property. As stolen property, they'd have to be disposed of through fences for a small portion of their value. But as buried treasure they could be disposed of openly at market prices. Very clever.

"Eric Ericsson, gentlemen, suspected that Anthony Hobbes-Watkins and his 'father,' Colonel Hobbes-Watkins —who's probably not his father at all—were not what they seemed. He was tragically right—they're a pair of European jewel thieves and, from the size of their accumulations, they must hold some sort of record for prowess in their exacting profession.

"They were cooling off in the Bahamas, wondering how best to turn their loot into cash, when Eric Ericsson and his niece stopped over at New Providence Island for a visit. Hearing the purely mythical yarn about how Kidd had buried treasure on Ericsson's Island two hundred and fifty years ago—treasure that had never been found— these worthies got a remarkably ingenious idea. They would plant the jewels in a real old chest—the Bahamas were the headquarters of the buccaneers and are full of pirate relics; they would salt the stolen jewels with a few authentic old coins; and they would bury the chest on Ericsson's Island, to be 'discovered' by them at a later date. The plan revolved about Inga's infatuation for this fellow here; he pretended to reciprocate her love and he married her. As Ericsson's sole heir, Inga would inherit his entire estate, which included this island, when Ericsson died. And as Inga's husband, Tony Hobbes-Watkins would control it all, and when Inga died—an early and untimely death, eh, gentlemen?—our friends would be in the rosy clear . . . I'm sorry, Inga, but it seems to be a day for crushing blows."

Inga sat pallid and blank, her hand clutching Nikki's.

"If you're trying to pin Ericsson's murder on me——" began the younger man in a swift and nasal voice.

But the Colonel said harshly, "Be quiet."

"Oh, that?" said Ellery. "Let's see. We know that Ericsson's bullet struck his murderer. Yet none of his four possible murderers exhibits a wound. Obviously, the bullet buried itself in a part of the murderer which couldn't be wounded"—Ellery smiled—*"which couldn't be wounded because it's not flesh and blood.* Only one of you four fits that curious specification. The one who uses a wooden leg to compensate for his—— *Stop him!"*

And when they had subdued the struggling caretaker and dug Eric Ericsson's bullet out of the pegleg, the police captain—who was glassy-eyed—said, "Then these two men here, Mr. Queen . . . they weren't in on Ericsson's murder . . .?"

"The whole plot, Captain, was geared to Ericsson's murder," said Ellery with a shrug, "though I'm afraid Long John rather jumped the gun.

"Don't you see that they were all in the plot together? How could our friend the Colonel, when he left the Bahamas after the wedding to smuggle the jewels into the States and get them to Ericsson's Island before the others sailed up to join him—how, I say, could the Colonel have planted the chest on the island unless the caretaker was taken into the gang? Also, the stage had to be set for the 'discovery' of the treasure: a hole bored through the tower room wall to sight on the chosen spot, the wallpaper doctored to implement the mythical clue of 'the needle's eye,' and so on—none of it possible unless Long John were declared in. He was, I suppose, to be paid off when Ericsson was disposed of and they got control, through Inga, of the estate and the island.

"What these gentry didn't figure on was the stupidity and avarice of Long John. They're far too clever operators to have planned to kill Ericsson the very night the

157

treasure was located. Even if that had been their plan, they'd hardly have devised such a crude and obvious murder—especially with a trained investigator on the island. An 'accident' would have been more their style. At their leisure, under selected conditions . . . like a storm, say, and an overturned boat . . . perhaps even with Inga a victim of the same accident, in that way gaining their objective in one stroke and with no danger to themselves.

"But Long John is simple-minded and, as Ericsson told me, a miser. He just couldn't wait. He heard me leave in the dark, realized my purpose, saw the dawn coming up, and hurried to the tower room to spy on me. He watched me dig the jewels up, probably saw them sparkling in the sun. When Ericsson surprised him in the tower at that very moment, all he could see were those jewels and his share of them when Ericsson should be killed. So Long John killed him—then and there. Speeding up the great day. . . .

"Haste makes waste, eh, Colonel? And Tony, I regret to inform you that I'm going to take your wife to the best lawyer in New York and see what can be done about an immediate annulment.

"And now, gentlemen, if you'll remove these pirates," said Ellery to the officers, but looking soberly at Inga, "Nikki and I have some holes to refill."

The Adventure of
the Three R's

HAIL MISSOURI! WHICH IS North and also South, upland
and river-bottom, mountain, plain, factory, and farm. Hail
Missouri! for MacArthur's corncob and Pershing's noble
mule. Hail! for Hannibal and Mark Twain, for Excelsior
Springs and Jesse James, for Barlowe and ... Barlowe?
Barlowe is the site of Barlowe College.

Barlowe College is the last place in Missouri you would
go to (Missouri, which yields to no State in the historic
redness of its soil) if you yearned for a lesson in the fine
art of murder. In fact, the subject being introduced, it is
the rare Show Me Stater who will not say, with an
informative wink, that Barlowe is the last place in Missouri, and leave all the rest unsaid. But this is a smoke-room
witticism, whose origin is as murky as the waters of the
Big Muddy. It may well first have been uttered by an old
grad. of some Missouri university whose attitude toward
learning is steeped in the traditional embalming fluid—
whereas, at little Barlowe, learning leaps: Jove and jive
thunder in duet, profound sociological lessons are drawn
from "Li'l Abner" and "Terry and the Pirates," and in the
seminars of the Philosophy Department you are almost
certain to find faith, as a matter of pedagogic policy, paired
with Hope.

Scratch a great work and find a great workman.

Dr. Isaiah St. Joseph A. Barlowe, pressed for vital
statistics, once remarked that while he was old enough to
have been a Founder, still he was not so old as to have
calcified over a mound of English ivy. But the good man
jested; he is as perennial as a sundial. "Even a cynic," Dr.
Barlowe has said, "likes his grain of salt." And the truth
is, in the garden where he labours, there is no death and a
great deal of healthy laughter.

One might string his academic honours after him, like

dutiful beads; one might recount the extraordinary tale of how, in the manner of Uther Pendragon, Dr. Barlowe bewitched some dumbfounded Missourians and took a whole series of substantial buildings out of their pockets; one might produce a volume on the subject of his acolytes alone, who have sped his humanistic gospel into the far corners of the land. Alas, this far more rewarding reportage must await the service of one who has, at the very least, a thousand pages at his disposal. Here there is space merely to record that the liveliness of Barlowe's alarming approach to scholarship is totally the inspiration of Dr. Isaiah St. Joseph A. Barlowe.

Those who would instruct at Barlowe must pass a rather unusual entrance examination. The examination is conducted *in camera,* and its nature is sacredly undisclosable as the Thirty-Third Rite; nevertheless, leaks have occurred, and it may be significant that in its course Dr. Barlowe employs a 16-millimetre motion-picture projector, a radio, a portable phonograph, one copy each of The Bible, *The Farmer's Almanac,* and *The Complete Sherlock Holmes;* and the latest issue of *The Congressional Record*—among others. During examinations the voices of Donald Duck and Young Widder Brown have been reported; and so on. It is all very puzzling, but perhaps not unconnected with the fact that visitors often cannot distinguish who are Barlowe students and who are Barlowe professors. Certainly a beard at Barlowe is no index of dignity; even the elderly among the faculty extrude a zest more commonly associated with the fuzzy-chinned undergraduate.

So laughter and not harumphery is rampant upon the Gold and the Puce; and, if corpses dance macabre, it is only upon the dissection tables of Bio III, where the attitude toward extinction is roguishly empirical.

Then imagine—if you can—the impact upon Barlowe, not of epic murder as sung by the master troubadours of Classics I; not of romantic murder (Abbott, Anthony, to Zangwill, Israel) beckoning from the rental shelves of The Campus Book Shop; but of murder loud and harsh.

Murder, as young Professor Bacon of the Biochemistry Department might say, with a stink.

The letter from Dr. Barlowe struck Ellery as remarkably woeful.

"One of my faculty has disappeared," wrote the president of Barlowe College, "and I cannot express to you,

Mr. Queen, the extent of my apprehension. In short, I fear the worst.

"I am aware of your busy itinerary, but if you are at all informed regarding the institution to which I have devoted my life, you will grasp the full horror of our dilemma. We feel we have erected something here too precious to be befouled by the nastiness of the age; on the other hand, there are humane—not to mention legal—considerations. If, as I suspect, Professor Chipp has met with foul play, it occurred to me that we might investigate *sub rosa* and at least present the not altogether friendly world with *un mystère accompli*. In this way, much anguish may be spared us all.

"Can I prevail upon you to come to Barlowe quietly, and at once? I feel confident I speak for our Trustees when I say we shall have no difficulty about the coarser aspects of the association."

The letter was handwritten, in a hasty and nervous script which seemed to suggest guilty glances over the presidential shoulder.

It was all so at variance with what Ellery had heard about Dr. Isaiah St. Joseph A. Barlowe and his learned vaudeville show that he scribbled a note to Inspector Queen and ran. Nikki, clutching her invaluable notebook, ran with him.

Barlowe, Missouri, lay torpid in the warm September sunshine. And the distant Ozarks seemed to be peering at Barlowe inquisitively.

"Do you suppose it's got out, Ellery?" asked Nikki *sotto voce* as a sluggish hack trundled them through the slumbering town. "It's all so still. Not like a college town at all."

"Barlowe is still in its etesian phase," replied Ellery pedantically. "The fall term doesn't begin for another ten days."

"You always make things so darned uninteresting!"

They were whisked into Dr. Barlowe's sanctum.

"You'll forgive my not meeting you at the station," muttered the educator as he quickly shut the door. He was a lean, grey-thatched man with an Italianate face and lively black eyes whose present preoccupation did not altogether extinguish the lurking twinkle. Missouri's Petrarch, thought Ellery with a chuckle. As for Nikki, it was love at first sight. "Softly, softly—that must be our watchword."

161

"Just who is Professor Chipp, Dr. Barlowe?"

"American Lit. You haven't heard of Chipp's seminar on Poe? He's an authority—it's one of our more popular items."

"Poe," exclaimed Nikki. "Ellery, that should give you a personal interest in the case."

"Leverett Chisholm Chipp," nodded Ellery, remembering. "Monographs in *The Review* on the Poe prose. Enthusiasm and scholarship. That Chipp . . ."

"He's been a Barlowe fixture for thirty years," said the doctor unhappily. "We really couldn't go on without him."

"When was Professor Chipp last seen?"

Dr. Barlowe snatched his telephone. "Millie, send Ma Blinker in now. . . . Ma runs the boarding-house on the campus where old Chipp's had rooms ever since he came to Barlowe to teach, Mr. Queen. Ah! Ma! Come in. And shut the door!"

Ma Blinker was a brawny old Missourian who looked as if she had been summoned to the council chamber from her Friday's batch of apple pies. But it was a landlady's eye she turned on the visitors from New York—an eye which did not surrender until Dr. Barlow uttered a cryptic reassurance, whereupon it softened and became moist.

"He's an old love, the Professor is," she said brokenly. "Regular? Ye could set your watch by that man."

"I take it," murmured Ellery, "Chipp's regularity is germane?"

Dr. Barlowe nodded. "Now Ma, you're carrying on. And you with the blood of pioneers! Tell Mr. Queen all about it."

"The Professor," gulped Ma Blinker, "he owns a log cabin up in the Ozarks, 'cross the Arkansas line. Every year he leaves Barlowe first of July to spend his summer vacation in the cabin. First of July, like clockwork."

"Alone, Mrs. Blinker?"

"Yes, sir. Does all his writin' up there, he does."

"Literary textbooks," explained Barlowe. "Although summer before last, to my astonishment, Chipp informed me he was beginning a novel."

"First of July he leaves for the cabin, and one day after Labour Day he's back in Barlowe gettin' ready for the fall term."

"One day after Labour Day, Mr. Queen. Year in, year out. Unfailingly."

"And here 'tis the thirteenth of September and he ain't showed up in town!"

162

"Day after Labour Day. . . . Ten days overdue."

"All this fuss," asked Nikki, "over a measly ten days?"

"Miss Porter, Chipp's being ten days late is as unlikely as—as my being Mrs. Hudson in disguise! Unlikelier. I was so concerned, Mr. Queen, I telephoned the Slater, Arkansas, authorities to send someone up to Chipp's cabin."

"Then he didn't simply linger there past his usual date?"

"I can't impress upon you too strongly the inflexibility of Chipp's habit-pattern. He did not. The Slater man found no sign of Chipp but his trunk."

"But I gathered from your letter, Doctor, that you had a more specific reason for suspecting——"

"And don't we!" Ma Blinker broke out frankly now in bosomy sobs. "I'd never have gone into the Professor's rooms—it was another of his rules—but Dr. Barlowe said I ought to when the Professor didn't show up, so I did, and—and——"

"Yes, Mrs. Blinker?"

"There on the rug, in front of his fireplace," whispered the landlady, "was a great . . . big . . . stain."

"A stain!" gasped Nikki. "A *stain*?"

"A bloodstain."

Ellery raised his brows.

"I examined it myself, Mr. Queen," said Dr. Barlowe nervously. "It's—it's blood, I feel certain. And it's been on the rug for some time. . . . We locked Chipp's rooms up again, and I wrote to you."

And although the September sun filled each cranny of the president's office, it was a cold sun suddenly.

"Have you heard from Professor Chipp at all since July the first, Doctor?" asked Ellery with a frown.

Dr. Barlowe looked startled. "It's been his habit to send a few of us cards at least once during the summer recess . . ." He began to rummage excitedly through a pile of mail on his desk. "I've been away since early June myself. This has so upset me, I . . . Why didn't I think of that? Ah, the trained mind . . . Mr. Queen, here it is!"

It was a picture postcard illustrating a mountain cascade of improbable blue surrounded by verdure of impossible green. The message and address were in a cramped and spidery script.

July 31.

Am rewriting my novel. It will be a huge surprise to you all. Regards—

CHIPP.

163

"His 'novel' again," muttered Ellery. "Bears the post-mark Slater, Arkansas, July thirty-first of this year. Dr. Barlowe, was this card written by Professor Chipp?"

"Unmistakably."

"Doesn't the writing seem awfully awkward to you, Ellery?" asked Nikki, in the tradition of the detectival secretary.

"Yes. As if something were wrong with his hand."

"There is," sniffled Ma Blinker. "Middle and forefinger missin' to the second joint—poor, poor old man!"

"Some accident in his youth, I believe."

Ellery rose. "May I see that stain on Chipp's rug, please?"

A man may leave more than his blood on his hearth, he may leave his soul. The blood was there, faded brown and hard, but so was Professor Chipp, though *in absentia*.

The two small rooms overlooking the campus were as tidy as a barrack. Chairs were rigidly placed. The bed was a sculpture. The mantelpiece was a shop-window display: each pipe in the rack had been reamed and polished and laid away with a mathematical hand. The papers in the pigeonholes of the old pine desk were ranged according to size. Even the missing professor's books were disciplined: no volume on these shelves leaned carelessly, or lolled dreaming on its back! They stood in battalions, company after company, at attention. And they were ranked by author, in alphabetical order.

"Terrifying," Ellery said; and he turned to examine a small ledger-like volume lying in the exact centre of the desk's dropleaf.

"I suppose this invasion is unavoidable," muttered Barlowe, "but I must say I feel as if I were the tailor of Coventry! What's in that ledger, Mr. Queen?"

"Chipp's personal accounts. His daily outlays of cash ... Ah. This year's entries stop at the thirtieth day of June."

"The day before he left for his cabin!"

"He's even noted down what one postage stamp cost him ..."

"That's the old Professor," sobbed Ma Blinker. Then she raised her fat arms and shrieked: "Heavens to Bessie, Dr. Barlowe! It's Professor Bacon back!"

"Hi, Ma!"

Professor Bacon's return was in the manner of a charge from third base. Having pumped the presidential hand

164

violently, the young man immediately cried: "Just got back to the shop and found your note, Doctor. What's this nonsense about old Chipp's not showing up for the fall brawl?"

"Its only too true, Bacon," said Dr. Barlowe sadly, and he introduced the young man as a full professor of chemistry and biology, another of Ma Blinker's boarders, and Chipp's closest faculty friend.

"You agree with Dr. Barlowe as to the gravity of the situation?" Ellery asked him.

"Mr. Queen, if the old idiot's not back, something's happened to him." And for a precarious moment Professor Bacon fought tears. "If I'd only known," he mumbled. "But I've been away since the middle of June—biochemical research at Johns Hopkins. Damn it!" he roared. "This is more staggering than nuclear fission!"

"Have you heard from Chipp this summer, Professor?"

"His usual postcard. I may still have it on me . . . Yes!"

"Just a greeting," said Ellery, examining it. "Dated July thirty-first and postmarked Slater, Arkansas—exactly like the card he sent Dr. Barlowe. May I keep this, Bacon?"

"By all means. Chipp not back . . ." And then the young man spied the brown crust on the hearthrug. He collapsed on the missing man's bed, gaping at it.

"Ellery!"

Nikki was standing on tiptoe before Chipp's bookshelves. Under Q stood a familiar phalanx.

"A complete set of *your* books!"

"Really?" But Ellery did not seem as pleased as an author making such a flattering discovery should. Rather, he eyed one of the volumes as if it were a traitor. And indeed there was a sinister air about it, for it was the only book on all the shelves—he now noted for the first time—which did not exercise the general discipline. It stood on the shelf upside down.

"Queer . . ." He took it down and righted it. In doing so, he opened the back cover; and his lips tightened.

"Oh, yes," said Barlowe gloomily. "Old Chipp's quite unreasonable about your books, Mr. Queen."

"Only detective stories he'd buy," muttered Professor Bacon.

"Rented the others."

"A mystery bug, eh?" murmured Ellery. "Well, here's one Queen title he didn't buy." He tapped the book in his hand.

"The Origin of Evil," read Nikki, cranning. "Rental library!"

"The Campus Book Shop. And it gives us our first confirmation of that bloodstain."

"What do you mean?" asked Bacon quickly, jumping off the bed.

"The last library stamp indicates that Professor Chipp rented this book from The Campus Book Shop on June twenty-eight. A man as orderly as these rooms indicate, who moreover scrupulously records his purchase of a postage stamp, would scarcely trot off on a summer vacation and leave a book behind to accumulate eleven weeks' rental-library charges."

"Chipp? Impossible!"

"Contrary to his whole character."

"Since the last entry in that ledger bears the date June thirtieth, and since the bloodstain is on this hearthrug," said Ellery gravely, "I'm afraid, gentlemen, that your colleague was murdered in this room on the eve of his scheduled departure for the Ozarks. He never left this room alive."

No one said anything for a long time.

But finally Ellery patted Ma Blinker's frozen shoulder and said: "You didn't actually see Professor Chipp leave your boarding house on July first, Mrs. Blinker, did you?"

"No, sir," said the landlady stiffly. "The expressman came for his trunk that mornin', but the Professor wasn't here. I . . . thought he'd already left."

"Tell me this, Mrs. Blinker: did Chipp have a visitor on the preceding night—the night of June thirtieth?"

A slow change came over the woman's blotchy features.

"He surely did," she said. "He surely did. That Weems."

"Weems?" Dr. Barlowe said quickly. "Oh, no! I mean . . ."

"Weems," said Nikki. "Ellery, didn't you notice that name on The Campus Book Shop as we drove by?"

Ellery said nothing.

Young Bacon muttered: "Revolting idea. But then . . . Weems and old Chipp were always at each other's throats."

"Weems is the only other one I've discussed Chipp's nonappearance with," said the college president wildly. "He seemed so concerned!"

"A common interest in Poe," said Professor Bacon fiercely.

"Indeed," smiled Ellery. "We begin to discern a certain unity of plot elements, don't we? If you'll excuse us for a little while, gentlemen, Miss Porter and I will have a chat with Mr. Weems."

But Mr. Weems turned out to be a bustly, bald little Missouri countryman, with shrewdly-humoured eyes and the prevailing jocular manner, the most unmurderous-looking character imaginable. And he presided over a shop so satisfyingly full of books, so aromatic with the odours of printery and bindery, and he did so with such a naked bibliophilic tenderness, that Nikki—for one—instantly dismissed him as a suspect.

Yep, Mr. Queen'd been given to understand correctly that he, Claude Weems, had visited old Chipp's rooms at Ma Blinker's on the night of June thirty last; and, yep, he'd left the old chuckle-head in the best of health; and, no, he hadn't laid eyes on him since that evenin'. He'd shut up shop for the summer and left Barlowe on July fifteenth for his annual walking tour cross-country; didn't get back till a couple of days ago to open up for fall.

"Doc Barlowe's fussin' too much about old Chipp's not turnin' up," said little Mr. Weems, beaming. "Now, I grant you he's never done it before, and all that, but he's gettin' old, Chipp is. Never can tell what a man'll do when he passes a certain age."

Nikki looked relieved, but Ellery did not.

"May I ask what you dropped in to see Chipp about on the evening of June thirtieth, Mr. Weems?"

"To say goodbye. And then I'd heard tell the old varmint'd just made a great book find——"

"Book find! Chipp had 'found' a book?"

Mr. Weems looked around and lowered his voice. "I heard he'd picked up a first edition of Poe's *Tamerlane* for a few dollars from some fool who didn't know its worth. You a collector, Mr. Queen?"

"A *Tamerlane* first!" exclaimed Ellery.

"Is that good, Ellery?" asked Nikki with the candour of ignorance.

"Good! A *Tamerlane* first, Nikki, is worth at least $25,000!"

Weems chuckled. "Know the market, I see. Yes, sir, bein' the biggest booster old Edgar Allan ever had west of the Mississip', I wanted to see that copy bad, awful bad. Chipp showed it to me, crowin' like a cock in a roostful.

Lucky dog," he said without audible rancour. " 'Twas the real article all right."

Nikki could see Ellery tucking this fact into one of the innumerable cubbyholes of his mind—the one marked *For Future Consideration*. So she was not surprised when he changed the subject abruptly.

"Did Professor Chipp ever mention to you, Weems, that he was engaged in writing a novel?"

"Sure did. I told ye he was gettin' old."

"I suppose he also told you the *kind* of novel it was?"

"Dunno as he did." Mr. Weems looked about as if for some goal for his spittle, but then, with his indignation, he swallowed it.

"Seems likely, seems likely," mumbled Ellery, staring at the rental-library section where murder frolicked.

"What seems likely, Ellery?" demanded Nikki.

"Considering that Chipp was a mystery fan, and the fact that he wrote Dr. Barlowe his novel would be a 'huge surprise,' it's my conclusion, Nikki, the old fellow was writing a whodunit."

"No! A Professor of Literature?"

"Say," exclaimed Mr. Weems. "I think you're right."

"Oh?"

"Prof Chipp asked me—in April, it was—to find out if a certain title's ever been used on a detective story!"

"Ah. And what was the title he mentioned, Weems?"

"The Mystery of the Three R's."

"Three R's ... Three R's?" cried Ellery. "But that's incredible! Nikki—back to the Administration Building!"

"Suppose he was," said Professor Bacon violently. "Readin'! 'Ritin'! 'Rithmetic! Abracadabra and Rubadub-dub. What of it?"

"Perhaps nothing, Bacon," scowled Ellery, hugging his pipe.

"And yet ... see here. We found a clue pointing to the strong probability that Chipp never left his rooms at Ma Blinker's alive last June thirtieth. What was that clue? The fact that Chipp failed to return his rented copy of my novel to Weems's lending library. Novel ... book ... *reading*, gentlemen! The first of the traditional Three R's."

"Rot!" bellowed the professor, and he began to bite his fingernails.

"I don't blame you," shrugged Ellery. "But has it occurred to you that there is also *a writing clue*?"

At this Nikki went over to the enemy.

168

"Ellery, are you sure the sun . . .?"

"Those postcards Chipp wrote, Nikki."

Three glances crossed stealthily.

"But I fail to see the connection, Mr. Queen," said Dr. Barlowe soothingly. "How are those ordinary postcards a clue?"

"And besides," snorted Bacon, "how could Chipp have been bumped off on June thirtieth and have mailed the cards a full month later, on July thirty-first."

"If you'll examine the date Chipp wrote on the cards," said Ellery evenly, "you'll find that the 3 of *July 31* is crowded between the *y* of *July* and the *1* of *31*. If that isn't a clue, I never saw one."

And Ellery, who was as thin-skinned as the next artist, went on rather tartly to reconstruct the events of the fateful evening of June the thirtieth.

"Chipp wrote those cards in his rooms that night, dating them a day ahead—July first—probably intending to mail them from Slater, Arkansas, the next day on his way to the log cabin——"

"It's true Chipp loathed correspondence," muttered Dr. Barlowe.

"Got his duty cards out of the way before his vacation even began—the old sinner!" mumbled young Bacon.

"Someone then murdered him in his rooms, appropriated the cards, stuffed the body into Chipp's trunk——"

"Which was picked up by the expressman next morning and shipped to the cabin?" cried Nikki.

And again the little chill wind cut through the office.

"But the postmarks, Mr. Queen," said Barlowe stiffly. "The postmarks also say July *thirty*-first."

"The murderer merely waited a month before mailing them at the Slater, Arkansas, Post Office."

"But *why*?" growled Bacon. "You weave beautiful rugs, man—but what do they mean?"

"Obviously it was all done, Professor Bacon," said Ellery, "to leave the impression that on July thirty-first Professor Chipp was *still alive* . . . to keep the world from learning that he was really murdered on the night of June thirtieth. And that, of course, is significant." He sprang to his feet. "We must examine the Professor's cabin—most particularly, his trunk!"

It was a little trunk—but then, as Dr. Barlowe pointed out in a very queer voice, Professor Chipp had been a little man.

Outdoors, the Ozarks were shutting up shop for the

summer, stripping the faint-hearted trees and busily daubing hillsides; but in the cabin there was no beauty—only dust, and an odour of dampness . . . and something else.

The little steamer trunk stood just inside the cabin doorway.

They stared at it.

"Well, well," said Bacon finally. "Miss Porter's outside—what are we waiting for?"

And so they knocked off the rusted lock and raised the lid—and found the trunk empty.

Perhaps not quite empty: the interior held a pale, dead-looking mass of crumbly stuff.

Ellery glanced up at Professor Bacon.

"Quicklime," muttered the chemistry teacher.

"Quicklime!" choked the president. "But the body. Where's the body?"

Nikki's scream, augmented a dozen times by the encircling hills, answered Dr. Barlowe's question most unpleasantly.

She had been wandering about the clearing, dreading to catch the first cry of discovery from the cabin, when she came upon a little cairn of stones. And she had sat down upon it.

But the loose rocks gave way, and Miss Porter found herself sitting on Professor Chipp—or rather, on what was left of Professor Chipp. For Professor Chipp had gone the way of all flesh—which is to say, he was merely bones, and very dry bones, at that.

But that it was the skeleton of Leverett Chisholm Chipp could not be questioned: the medius and index finger of the right skeletal hand were missing to the second joint. And that Leverett Chisholm Chipp had been most foully used was also evident: the top of the skull revealed a deep and rugged chasm, the result of what could only have been a tremendous blow.

Whereupon the old pedagogue and the young took flight joining Miss Porter, who was quietly being ill on the other side of the cabin; and Mr. Queen found himself alone with Professor Chipp.

Later, Ellery went over the log cabin with a disagreeable sense of anticipation. There was no sensible reason for believing that the cabin held further secrets; but sense is not all, and the already-chilling air held a whiff of fatality.

He found it in a cupboard, in a green steel box, beside a rusty can of mouldering tobacco.

It was a stapled pile of neat papers, curled by damp, but otherwise intact.

The top sheet, in a cramped, spidery hand said:

The Mystery of the Three R's
by
L. C. Chipp

The discovery of Professor Chipp's detective story may be said to mark the climax of the case. That the old man had been battered to death in his rooms on the night of June thirtieth; that his corpse had been shipped from Barlowe, Missouri, to the Arkansas cabin in his own trunk, packed in quicklime to avert detection *en route;* that the murderer had then at his leisure made his way to the cabin, removed the body from the trunk, and buried it under a heap of stones—these were mere facts, dry as the Professor's bones. They did not possess the aroma of the grotesque—the *bouffe*—which rose like a delicious mist from the pages of that incredible manuscript.

Not that Professor Chipp's venture into detective fiction revealed a new master, to tower above the busy little figures of his fellow-toilers in this curious vineyard and vie for cloud-space only with Poe and Doyle and Chesterton. To the contrary. *The Mystery of the Three R's,* by L. D. Chipp, was a laboured exercise in familiar elements, distinguished chiefly for its enthusiasm.

No, it was not the murdered professor's manuscript which was remarkable; the remarkable thing was the manner in which life had imitated it.

It was a shaken group that gathered in Chipp's rooms the morning after the return from the Arkansas cabin. Ellery had called the meeting, and he had invited Mr. Weems of The Campus Book Shop to participate—who, upon hearing the ghastly news, stopped beaming, clamped his Missouri jaws shut, and began to gaze furtively at the door.

Ellery's own jaws were unshaven, and his eyes were red.

"I've passed the better part of the night," he began abruptly, "reading through Chipp's manuscript. And I must report an amazing—an almost unbelievable—thing.

"The crime in Chipp's detective story takes place in and

about a small Missouri college called ... Barleigh College."

"Barleigh," muttered the president of Barlowe.

"Moreover, the victim of Chipp's yarn is a methodical old professor of American Literature."

Nikki looked puzzled. "You mean that Professor Chipp ——?"

"Took off on himself, Nikki—exactly."

"What's so incredible about that?" demanded young Bacon. "Art imitating life——"

"Considering the fact that Chipp plotted his story long before the events of this summer, Professor Bacon, it's rather a case of life imitating art. Suppose I tell you that the methodical old professor of American Literature in Chipp's story owns a cabin in the Ozarks where his body is found?"

"Even *that*?" squeaked Mr. Weems.

"And more, Weems. The suspects in the story are the President of Barleigh College, whose name is given as Dr. Isaac St. Anthony E. Barleigh; a local bookshop owner named Claudius Deems; a gay young professor of chemistry known as Macon; and, most extraordinary of all, the three main clues in Chipp's detective story revolve about— are called—'Readin',' ' 'Ritin','' and ' 'Rithmetic'!"

And the icy little wind blew once more.

"You mean," explained Dr. Barlowe, "the crime we're investigating—Chipp's own death—*is an exact counterpart of the fictional crime Chipp invented in his manuscript?*"

"Down to the last character, Doctor."

"But Ellery," said Nikki, "how can that possibly be?"

"Obviously, Chipp's killer managed to get hold of the old fellow's manuscript, read it, and with hellish humour proceeded to copy in real life—actually to duplicate—the crime Chipp had created in fiction!" Ellery began to lunge about the little room, his usually neat hair disordered and a rather wild look on his face. "Everything's the same: the book that wasn't returned to the lending library—the 'readin'' clue; the picture postcards bearing forged dates— the ' 'ritin'' clue——"

"And the ' 'rithmetic clue, Mr. Queen?" asked Barlowe in a quavering voice.

"In the story, Doctor, the victim has found a first edition of Poe's *Tamerlane*, worth $25,000."

Little Weems cried: "That's ' 'rithmetic,' all right!" and then bit his lip.

"And how," asked Professor Bacon thickly, "how is the book integrated into Chipp's yarn, Mr. Queen?"

"It furnishes the motive for the crime. The killer steals the victim's authentic *Tamerlane*—substituting for it a facsimile copy which is virtually worthless."

"But if everything else is duplicated . . ." began Dr. Barlowe in a mutter.

"Then that must be the motive for Professor Chipp's own murder!" cried Nikki.

"It would seem so, wouldn't it?" Ellery glanced sharply at the proprietor of the Campus Book Shop. "Weems, where is the first edition of *Tamerlane* you told me Chipp showed you on the night of June thirtieth?"

"Why—why—why, reckon it's on his shelves here somewheres, Mr. Queen. Under *P*, for Poe . . ."

And there it was. Under *P*, for Poe.

And when Ellery took it down and turned its pages, he smiled. For the first time since they had found the skeleton under the cairn, he smiled.

"Well, Weems," he said affably, "you're a Poe expert. Is this an authentic *Tamerlane* first?"

"Why—why—why, must be. 'Twas when old Chipp showed it to me that night——"

"Really? Suppose you re-examine it—now."

But they all knew the answer before Weems spoke.

"It ain't," he said feebly. "It's a facsim'le copy. Worth about $5."

"The *Tamerlane*—stolen," whispered Dr. Barlowe.

"So once again," murmured Ellery, "we find duplication. I think that's all. Or should I say, it's too much?"

And he lit a cigarette and seated himself in one of Professor Chipp's chairs, puffing contentedly.

"All!" exclaimed Dr. Barlowe. "I confess, Mr. Queen, you've—you've baffled me no end in this investigation. All? It's barely begun! *Who* has done all this?"

"Wait," said Bacon slowly. "It may be, Doctor, we don't need Queen's eminent services at that. If the rest has followed Chipp's plot so faithfully, why not the most important plot element of all?"

"That's true, Ellery," said Nikki with shining eyes. "*Who is the murderer in Professor Chipp's detective story?*"

Ellery glanced at the cowering little figure of Claude Weems.

"The character," he replied cheerfully, "whom Chipp had named Claudius Deems."

The muscular young professor snarled and he sprang.

"In your enthusiasm, Bacon," murmured Ellery, without stirring from his chair, "don't throttle him. After all, he's such a little fellow, and you're so large——and powerful."

"Kill old Chipp, would you!" growled Professor Bacon; but his grip relaxed a little.

"Mr. Weems," said Nikki, looking displeased. "Of course! The murderer forged the dates on the postcards so he wouldn't know the crime had been committed on June thirtieth. And who'd have reason to falsify the true date of the crime? The one man who'd visited Professor Chipp that night!"

"The damned beast could easily have got quicklime," said Bacon, shaking Weems like a rabbit, "by stealing it from the Chemistry Department after everyone'd left the college for the summer."

"Yes!" said Nikki. "Remember Weems himself told us he didn't leave Barlowe until July fifteenth?"

"I do, indeed. And Weems's motive, Nikki?"

"Why, to steal Chipp's *Tamerlane*."

"I'm afraid that's so," groaned Barlowe. "Weems as a bookseller could easily have got hold of a cheap facsimile to substitute for the authentic first edition."

"And he said he'd gone on a walking tour, didn't he?" Nikki added, warming to her own logic. "Well, I'll bet he 'walked' into that Arkansas post office, Ellery, on July thirty-first to mail those postcards!"

Weems found his voice.

"Why, now, listen here, little lady, I didn't kill old Chipp——" he began in the most unconvincing tones imaginable.

They all eyed him with savage scorn—all, that is, but Ellery.

"Very true, Weems," said Ellery, nodding. "You most certainly did not."

"He didn't . . ." began Dr. Barlowe, blinking.

"I . . . didn't?" gasped Weems, which seemed to Nikki a remarkable thing for him to have said.

"No, although I'm afraid I've been led very cleverly to *believe* that you did, Weems."

"See here, Mr. Queen," said Barlowe's president in a terrible voice. "Precisely what do you mean?"

"And how do you know he didn't?" shouted Bacon. "I told you, Doctor—this fellow's grossly overrated. The next thing you'll tell us is that Chipp hasn't been murdered at all!"

"Exactly," said Ellery. "Therefore Weems couldn't have murdered him."

"Ellery——" moaned Nikki.

"Your syllogism seems a bit perverted, Mr. Queen," said Dr. Barlowe severely.

"Yes!" snarled Bacon. "What about the evidence——?"

"Very well," said Ellery briskly, "let's consider the evidence. Let's consider the evidence of the skeleton we found near Chipp's cabin."

"Those dry bones? What about 'em!"

"Just that, Professor—they're so very dry. Bacon, you're a biologist as well as a chemist. Under normal conditions, how long does it take for the soft parts of a body to decompose completely?"

"How long ...?" The young man moistened his lips. "Muscles, stomach, liver—from three to four years. But——"

"And for decomposition of the fibrous tissues, the ligaments?"

"Oh, five years or so more. But——"

"And yet," sighed Ellery, "that dessicated skeleton was supposed to be the remains of a man who'd been alive *a mere eleven weeks before.* And not merely that—I now appeal to your chemical knowledge, Professor. Just what is the effect of quicklime on human flesh and bones?"

"Well ... it's pulverulent. Would dry out a body——"

"Would quicklime destroy the tissues?"

"Er ... no."

"It would tend to preserve them?"

"Er ... yes."

"Therefore the skeleton we found couldn't possibly have been the mortal remains of Professor Chipp."

"But the right hand, Ellery," cried Nikki. "The missing fingers—just like Professor Chipp's——"

"I shouldn't think," said Ellery dryly, "snapping a couple of dry bones off a man dead eight or ten years would present much of a problem."

"Eight or ten years ..."

"Surely, Nikki, it suggests the tenant of some outraged grave ... or, considering the facts at our disposal, the far likelier theory that it came from a laboratory closet in the Biology Department of Barlowe College." And Professor Bacon cringed before Ellery's accusing glance, which softened suddenly in laughter. "Now, really, gentlemen. Hasn't this hoax gone far enough?"

"Hoax, Mr. Queen?" choked the president of Barlowe with feeble indignation.

"Come, come, Doctor," chuckled Ellery, "the game's up. Let me review the fantastic facts. What is this case? A detective story come to life. Bizarre—fascinating—to be sure. But really, Doctor, so utterly unconvincing!

"How conveniently all the clues in Chipp's manuscript found reflections in reality! The lending-library book, so long overdue—in the story, in the crime. The postcards written in advance—in the story, in the crime. The *Tamerlane* facsimile right here on Chipp's shelf—exactly as the manuscript has it. It would seem as if Chipp collaborated in his own murder."

"Collab—I can't make hide nor hair of this, Mr. Queen," began little Mr. Weems in a crafty wail.

"Now, now, Weems, as the bookseller-Poe-crony you were the key figure in the plot! Although I must confess, Dr. Barlowe, *you* played your role magnificently, too—and, Professor Bacon, you missed a career in the theatre; you really did. The only innocent, I daresay, is Ma Blinker—and to you, gentlemen, I gladly leave the trial of facing that doughty lady when she finds out how her honest grief has been exploited in the interest of commerce."

"Commerce?" whimpered Nikki, who by now was holding her pretty head to keep it from flying off.

"Of course, Nikki. I was invited to Barlowe to follow an elaborate trail of carefully-placed 'clues' in order to reach the conclusion that Claude Weems had 'murdered' Professor Chipp. When I announced Weems's 'guilt,' the hoax was supposed to blow up in my face. *Old Prof Chipp would pop out of his hiding place grinning from ear to silly ear.*"

"Pop out . . . You mean," gasped Nikki, "you mean Professor Chipp is alive?"

"Only conclusion that makes sense, Nikki. And then," Ellery went on, glaring at the three cowering men, "imagine the headlines. 'Famous Sleuth Tricked by Hoax—Pins Whodunit On Harmless Prof.' Commerce? I'll say! Chipp's *Mystery of the Three R's*, launched by such splendid publicity, would be swallowed by a publisher as the whale swallowed Jonah—and there we'd have . . . presumably . . . a sensational best-seller.

"The whole thing, Nikki, was a conspiracy hatched by the president of Barlowe, his two favourite professors, and their good friend the campus bookseller—a conspiracy to put old Chipp's first detective story over with a bang!"

And now the little wind blew warm, bringing the first blood of shame to six male cheeks.

"Mr. Queen——" began the president hoarsely.

"Mr. Queen——" began the biochemistry professor hoarsely.

"Mr. Queen——" began the bookseller hoarsely.

"Come, come, gentlemen!" cired Ellery. "All is not lost! We'll go through with the plot! I make only one condition. Where the devil is Chipp? I want to shake the old scoundrel's hand!"

Barlowe is an unusual college.

The Adventure of
the Dead Cat

THE SQUARE-CUT ENVELOPE was a creation of orange ink on black notepaper; by which Ellery instantly divined its horrid authorship. Behind it leered a bouncy hostess, all teeth and enthusiastic ideas, who spent large sums of some embarrassed man's money to build a better mouse-trap.

Having too often been one of the mice, he was grateful that the envelope was addressed to "Miss Nikki Porter."

"But why to me at your apartment?" wondered Nikki, turning the black envelope over and finding nothing.

"Studied insult," Ellery assured her. "One of those acid-sweet women who destroy an honest girl's reputation at a stroke. Don't even open it. Hurl it into the fire, and let's get on with the work."

So Nikki opened it and drew out an enclosure cut in the shape of a cat.

"I am a master of metaphor," muttered Ellery.

"What?" said Nikki, unfolding the feline.

"It doesn't matter. But if you insist on playing the mouse, go ahead and read it." The truth was, he was a little curious himself.

"*Fellow Spook,*" began Nikki, frowning.

"Read no more. The hideous details are already clear——"

"Oh, shut up," said Nikki. "*There is a secret meeting of The Charmed Circle of Black Cats in Suite 1313, Hotel Chancellor, City, Oct. 31.*"

"Of course," said Ellery glumly. "That follows logically."

"*You must come in full costume as a Black Cat, including domino mask. Time your arrival for 9.05 p.m. promptly. Till the Witching Hour.* Signed——*G. Host.* How darling!"

"No clue to the criminal?"

178

"No. I don't recognize the handwriting . . ."

"Of course you're not going."

"Of course I *am*!"

"Having performed my moral duty as friend, protector, and employer, I now suggest you put the foul thing away and get back to our typewriter."

"What's more," said Nikki, "you're going, too."

Ellery smiled his Number Three smile—the toothy one. "Am I?"

"There's a postscript on the cat's—on the reverse side. *Be sure to drag your boss-cat along, also costumed.*"

Ellery could see himself as a sort of overgrown Puss-in-Boots plying the sjambok over a houseful of bounding tabbies all swilling Scotch. The vision was tiring.

"I decline with the usual thanks."

"You're a stuffed shirt."

"I'm an intelligent man."

"You don't know how to have fun."

"These brawls inevitably wind up with someone's husband taking a poke at a tall, dark, handsome stranger."

"Coward."

"Heavens, I wasn't referring to myself——!"

Whence it is obvious he had already lost the engagement.

Ellery stood before a door on the thirteenth floor of the Hotel Chancellor, cursing the Druids.

For it was Saman at whose mossy feet must be laid the origins of our recurrent October silliness. True, the lighting of ceremonial bonfires in a Gaelic glade must have seemed natural and proper at the time, and a Gaelic grove fitting rendezvous for an annual convention of ghosts and witches; but the responsibility of even pagan deities must surely be held to extend beyond temporal bounds, and the Druid lord of death should have foreseen that a bonfire would be out of place in a Manhattan hotel suite, not to mention disembodied souls, however wicked. Then Ellery recalled that Pomona, goddess of fruits had contributed nuts and apples to the burgeoning Hallowe'en legend, and he cursed the Romans, too.

There had been Inspector Queen at home, who had intolerably chosen to ignore the whole thing; the taxi-driver, who had asked amiably: "Fraternity initiation?"; the dread chorus of miaows during the long long, trek across the Chancellor lobby; and, finally, the reeking wag in the elevator who had tried to swing Ellery around by his tail, puss-pussying obscenely as he did so.

Cried Ellery out of the agony of his mortification: "Never, never *never* again will I——"

"Stop grousing and look at this," said Nikki, peering through her domino mask.

"What is it? I can't see through this damned thing."

"A sign on the door. *If You Are a Black Cat, Walk in!!!!!* With five exclamation points."

"All right, all right. Let's go in and get it over with."

And, of course, when they opened the unlocked door of 1313, Darkness.

And Silence.

"Now what do we do?" giggled Nikki, and jumped at the snick of the door behind them.

"I'll tell you now what," said Ellery enthusiastically. "Let's get the hell out of here."

But Nikki was already a yard away, black in blackness.

"Wait! Give me your hand, Nikki."

"*Mister* Queen. That's not my hand."

"Beg your pardon," muttered Ellery. "We seem to be trapped in a hallway. . . ."

"There's a red light down there! Must be at the end of the hall—*eee!*"

"Think of the soup this would make for the starving." Ellery disentangled her from the embrace of some articulated bones.

"Ellery! I don't think that's funny at all."

"I don't think *any* of this is funny."

They groped toward the red light. It was not so much a light as a rosy shade of darkness which faintly blushed above a small plinth of the raven variety. "The woman's cornered the Black Paper Market," Ellery thought disagreeably as he read the runes of yellow fire on the plinth.

LEFT!!!!!!!!!

"And into, I take it," he growled, "the great unknown." And, indeed, having explored to the left, his hand encountered outer space; whereupon, intrepidly, and with a large yearning to master the mystery and come to grips with its diabolical authoress, Ellery plunged through the invisible archway, Nikki bravely clinging to his tail.

"Ouch."

"What's the matter?" gasped Nikki.

"Bumped into a chair. Skinned my shin. What would a chair be doing——?"

"Pooooor Ellery," said Nikki, laughing. "Did the dreat bid mad hurt his—— *Ow!*"

"Blast this—— Ooo!"

"Ellery, where are you? Ooch!"

"Ow, my foot," bellowed Ellery from somewhere. "What is this—a tank-trap? Floor cluttered with pillows, hassocks——"

"Something cold and wet over here. Feels like an ice bucket ... Owwwww!" There was a wild clatter of metal, a soggy crash, and silence again.

"Nikki! What happened?"

"I fell over a rack of fire tongs, I think," Nikki's voice came clearly from floor level. "Yes. Fire tongs."

"Of all the stupid, childish, unfunny——"

"Oop."

"Lost in a madhouse. Why is the furniture scattered every which way?"

"How should I know? Ellery, where *are* you?"

"In Bedlam. Keep your head now, Nikki, and stay where you are. Sooner or later a St. Bernard will find you and bring——"

Nikki screamed.

"Thank God," said Ellery, shutting his eyes.

The room was full of blessed Consolidated Edison light, and various adult figures in black-cat costumes and masks were leaping and laughing and shouting: "Surpriiiiiise!" like idiot phantoms at the crisis of a delirium.

O Hallowe'en.

"Ann! Ann Trent!" Nikki was squealing. "Oh, Ann, you fool, however did you find me?"

"Nikki, you're looking wonderful. Oh, but you're famous, darling. The great E. Q.'s secretary ..."

Nuts to you, sister. Even bouncier than predicted. With that lazy, hippy strut. And chic, glossy chic. Lugs her sex around like a sample case. Kind of female who would be baffled by an egg. Looks five years older than she is, Antoine notwithstanding.

"But it's not Trent any more, Nikki—Mrs. John Crombie. Johnnnny!"

"Ann, you're *married*? And didn't invite me to the wedding!"

"Spliced in dear old Lunnon. John's British—or was. Johnny, stop flirting with Edith Baxter and come here!"

"Ann darlin'—this exquisite girl! Scotch or bourbon,

Nikki? Scotch if you're the careful type—but bourbon works faster."

John Crombie, Gent. Eyes of artificial blue, slimy smile, sunlamp complexion, Olivier chin. British Club and Fox and Hounds—he posts even in a living-room. He will say in a moment that he loathes Americah. Exactly. Ann Trent Crombie must have large amounts of the filthy. He despises her and patronizes her friends. He will fix me with the superior Mayfair smile and flap a limp brown hand . . . *Quod erat demonstrandum.*

"I warn you, Nikki," Ann Crombie was saying, "I'm hitched to a man who tries to jockey every new female he meets." Blush hard, prim Nikki. Friends grow in unforeseen directions. "Oh, Lucy! Nikki, do you remember my kid sister Lu——?"

Squeal, squeal. "Lucy Trent! This isn't *you*?"

"Am I grown up, Nikki?"

"Heavens!"

"Lucy's done *all* the party decorating, darling—spent the whole sordid day up here alone fixing things up. Hasn't she done an *inspired* job? But then I'm so useless."

"Ann means she wouldn't help, Nikki. Just a lout."

Uncertain laugh. Poor Lucy. Embarrassed by her flowering youth, trying hard to be New York . . . There she goes refilling a glass—emptying an ashtray—running out to the kitchen—for a tray of fresh hot pigs-in-blankets?— bong ! . . . the unwanted and gauche hiding confusion by making herself useful. Keep away from your brother-in-law, dear; that's an upstanding little bosom under the Black Cat's hide.

"Oh, Ellery, do come here and meet the Baxters. Mrs. Baxter—Edith—Ellery Queen . . ."

What's this? A worm who's turned, surely! The faded-fair type, hard-used by wedlock. Very small, a bit on the spready side—she'd let herself go—but now she's back in harness again, all curried and combed, with a triumphant lift to her pale head, like an old thoroughbred proudly prancing in a paddock she had never hoped to enter again. And that glitter of secret pleasure in her blinky brown eyes, almost malice, whenever she looked at Ann Crombie . . .

"Jerry Baxter, Edith's husband. Ellery Queen."

"Hiya, son!"

"Hi, yourself, Jerry."

Salesman or advertising-agency man, or Broadway agent. The life of the party. Three drinks and he's off to the races. He will be the first to fall in the apple tub, the first to pin the tail on Lucy or Nikki instead of on the donkey, the first to be sick and the first to pass out. Skitter, stagger, sweat and whoop. Why do you whoop, Jerry Baxter?

Ellery shook hot palms, smiled with what he hoped was charm, said affably: "Yes, isn't it?" "Haven't we met somewhere?" "Here, here, that's fine for now," and things like that, wondering what he was doing in a hotel living-room festooned with apples, marshmallows, nuts, and crisscrossing crêpe-paper twists, hung with grinning pumpkins and fancy black-and-orange cardboard cats, skeletons, and witches, and choked with bourbon fumes, tobacco smoke, and Chanel No. 5. Some Chinese lanterns were reeking, the noise was maddening, and merely to cross the room required the preparations of an expedition, for the overturned furniture and other impedimenta on the floor—cunningly plotted to trap groping Black Cats on their arrival—had been left where they were.

So Ellery, highball in hand, wedged himself in a safe corner and mentally added Nikki to the Druids and the Romans.

Ellery accepted the murder game without a murmur. He knew the futility of protest. Wherever he went, people at once suggested a murder game, apparently on the theory that a busman enjoys nothing so much as a bus. And, of course, he was to be the detective.

"Well, well, let's get started," he said gaily, for all the traditional Hallowe'en games had been played, Nikki had slapped Jerry Baxter laughingly once and British Johnny—not laughingly—twice, the house detective had made a courtesy call, and it was obvious the delightful evening had all but run its course. He hoped Nikki would have sense enough to cut the *pièce de résistance* short, so that a man might go home and give his thanks to God; but no, there she was in a whispery, giggly huddle with Ann Crombie and Lucy Trent, while John Crombie rested his limp hand on her shoulder and Edith Baxter splashed some angry bourbon into her glass.

Jerry was on all fours, being a cat.

"In just a minute," called Nikki, and she tripped through the archway—kitchen-bound, to judge from certain subsequent cutlery sounds—leaving Crombie's hand momentarily suspended.

Edith Baxter said: "Jerry, get up off that floor and stop making a darned fool of yourself!"—furiously.

"Now we're all set," announced Nikki, reappearing. "Everybody around in a circle. First I'll deal out these cards, and whoever gets the ace of spades *don't let on!*—because you're the Murderer."

"Ooh!"

"Ann, you stop peeking."

"Who's peeking?"

"A tenner says I draw the fatal pastboard," laughed Crombie. "I'm the killer type."

"*I'm* the killer type!" shouted Jerry Baxter. "Gack-gack-gack-gack!"

Ellery closed his eyes.

"Ellery! wake up."

"Huh?"

Nikki was shaking him. The rest of the company were lined up on the far side of the room from the archway, facing the wall. For a panicky moment he thought of the St. Valentine's Day Massacre.

"You go on over there with the others, smarty-pants. You mustn't see who the murderer is, either, so you close your eyes, too."

"Fits in perfectly with my plans," said Ellery, and he dutifully joined the five people at the wall.

"Spread out a little there—I don't want anyone touching anyone else. That's it. Eyes all shut? Good. Now I want the person who drew the ace of spades—Murderer—to step quietly away from the wall——"

"Not cricket," came John Crombie's annoying alto. "*You'll* see who it is, dear heart."

"Yes," said Edith Baxter nastily. "The light's on."

"But I'm running this assassination! Now stop talking, eyes closed. Step out, Murderer—that's it . . . quietly! No talking there at the wall! Mr. Queen is *very* bright and he'd get the answer in a shot just by eliminating voices——"

"Oh, come, Nikki," said Mr. Queen modestly.

"Now, murderer, here's what you do. On the kitchen table you'll find a full-face mask, a flashlight, and a bread-knife. Wait! Don't start for the kitchen yet—go when I switch off the light in here; that will be your signal to start. When you get to the kitchen, put on the mask, take the flashlight and knife, steal back into this room, and—pick a victim!"

"Oooh."

"Ahhhh!"

"Ee!"

Mr. Queen banged his forehead lightly against the wall. How long, O Lord?

"Now remember, Murderer," cried Nikki, "you pick anyone you want—except of course, Ellery. He has to live long enough to solve the crime . . ."

If you don't hurry, my love, I'll be dead of natural causes.

"It'll be dark, Murderer, except for your flash, so even I won't know what victim you pick——"

"May the detective inquire the exact purpose of the knife?" asked the detective wearily of the wall. "Its utility in this divertissement escapes me."

"Oh, the knife's just a prop, goopy—atmosphere. Murderer, you tap your victim on the shoulder. Victim, whoever feels the tap, turn around and let Murderer lead you out of the living-room to the kitchen."

"The kitchen, I take it, is the scene of the crime," said Mr. Queen gloomily.

"Uh-huh. And Victim, as soon as Murderer gets you into the kitchen, scream like all fury as if you're being stabbed. Make it realistic! Everybody set? Ready? . . . All right, Murderer, soon's I turn this light off go to the kitchen, get the mask and stuff, come back, and pick your victim. Here goes!"

Click! went the light switch. Being a man who checked his facts, Ellery automatically cheated and opened one eye. Dark, as advertised. He shut the eye, and then jumped.

"Stop!" Nikki had shrieked.

"What, what?" asked Ellery excitedly.

"Oh, I'm not talking to you, Ellery. Murderer, I forgot something! Where are you? Oh, never mind. Remember after you've supposedly stabbed your victim in the kitchen, come back to this room and quickly take your former place against the wall. Don't make a sound; don't touch anyone. I want the room to be as quiet as it is this minute. Use the flash to help you see your way back, but as soon as you reach the wall turn the flash off and throw flash and mask into the middle of the living-room—thus, darling, getting rid of the evidence. Do you see? But, of course, you *can't*." You're in rare form, old girl. "Now even though it's dark, people, *keep your eyes shut*. All right, Murderer—get set—*go!*"

Ellery dozed. . . .

It seemed a mere instant later that he heard Nikki's voice saying with incredible energy: "Murderer's tapping a victim—careful with that flashlight, Murderer!—we mustn't tempt our detective *too* much. All right, Victim? Now let Murderer lead you to your doom ... the rest of you keep your eyes closed ... don't turn ar ..."

Ellery dozed again.

He awoke with a start at a man's scream.

"Here! What——"

"Ellery Queen, you asleep again? That was Victim being carved up in the kitchen. Now ... yes! ... here's Murderer's flash back ... that's it, to the wall quietly ... now flash *off!*—fine—toss it and your mask away ... Boom. Tossed. Are you turned around, face to the wall, Murderer, like everybody else? Everybody ready? Lllllllights!"

"Now——" began Ellery briskly.

"Why, it's John who's missing," laughed Lucy.

"Pooooor John is daid," sang Jerry.

"My poor husband," wailed Ann. "Jo-hon, come back to me!"

"Ho, John!" shouted Nikki.

"Just a moment," said Ellery. "Isn't Edith Baxter missing, too?"

"My wiff?" shouted Jerry. "Hey, wiff! Come outa the woodwork!"

"Oh, darn," said Lucy. "There mustn't be two victims, Nikki. That spoils the game."

"Let us repair to the scene of the crime," proclaimed Miss Porter, "and see what gives."

So, laughing and chattering and having a hell of a time, they all trooped through the archway, turned left, crossed the foyer, and went into the Crombie kitchen and found John Crombie on the floor with his throat cut.

When Ellery returned to the kitchen from his very interesting telephone chat with Inspector Queen, he found Ann Crombie being sick over the kitchen sink, her forehead supported by the greenish hand of a greenish Lucy Trent, and Nikki crouched quietly in a corner, as far away from the covered thing on the floor as the architect's plans allowed, while Jerry Baxter raced up and down weeping: "Where's my wife?" Where's Edith? We've got to get out of here."

Ellery grabbed Baxter's collar and said: "It's going to be a long night, Jerry—relax. Nikki——"

"Yes, Ellery." She was trembling and trying to stop it and not succeeding.

"You know who was supposed to be the murderer in that foul game—the one who drew the ace of spades— you saw him or her step away from the living-room wall while the lights were still on in there. Who was it?"

"Edith Baxter. Edith got the ace. Edith was supposed to be the murderer."

Jerry Baxter jerked out of Ellery's grasp. "You're lying!" he yelled. "You're not mixing my wife up in this stink! You're lying——"

Ann crept away from the sink, avoiding the mound. She crept past them and went into the foyer and collapsed against the door of the closet just outside the kitchen. Lucy crept after Ann and cuddled against her, whimpering. Ann began to whimper, too.

"Edith Baxter was Murderer," said Nikki drearily. "In the game, anyway."

"You lie!—you lying——"

Ellery slapped his mouth without rancor and Baxter started to cry again. "Don't let me come back and find any other throats cut," said Ellery, and he went out of the kitchen.

It was tempting to assume the obvious, which was that Edith Baxter, having drawn the ace of spades, decided to play the role of murderer in earnest, and did so, and fled. Her malice-dipped triumph as she looked at John Crombie's wife, her anger as she watched Crombie pursue Nikki through the evening, told a simple story; and it was really unkind of Fate—if Fate was the culprit—to place Edith Baxter's hand on John Crombie's shoulder in the victim-choosing phase of the game. In the kitchen, with the bread-knife at hand, who could blame a well-bourboned woman if she obeyed that impulse and separated Mr. Crombie's neck from his careless collar?

But investigation muddled the obvious. The front door of the suite was locked—nay, even bolted—on the inside. Nikki proclaimed herself the authoress thereof, having performed the sealed-apartment act before the game began (she said) in a moment of "inspiration."

Secondly, escape by one of the windows was out of the question, unless, like Pegasus, Edith Baxter possessed wings.

Thirdly, Edith Baxter had not attempted to escape at all: Ellery found her in the foyer closet against which the widow and her sister whimpered. Mrs. Baxter had been

187

jammed into the closet by a hasty hand, and she was unconscious.

Inspector Queen, Sergeant Velie & Co. arrived just as Edith Baxter, with the aid of ammonium carbonate, was shuddering back to life.

"Guy named Crombie's throat slit?" bellowed Sergeant Velie, without guile.

Edith Baxter's eyes rolled over and Nikki wielded the smelling salts once more, wearily.

"Murder games," said Inspector Queen gently. "Hallowe'en," said Inspector Queen. Ellery blushed. "Well, son?"

Ellery told his story humbly, in penitential detail.

"Well, we'll soon find out," grumbled his father, and he shook Mrs. Baxter until her chin waggled and her eyes flew open. "Come, come, madam, we can't afford these luxuries. What the hell were you doing in that closet?"

Edith screamed, "How should I know, you old man?" and had a convulsion of tears. "Jerry Baxter, how can you sit there and——?"

But her husband was doubled over, holding his head.

"You received Nikki's instructions, Edith," said Ellery, "and when she turned off the light you left the living-room and went to the kitchen. Or started for it. What did happen?"

"Don't third-degree me, you detective!" screeched Mrs. Baxter. "I'd just passed under the archway, feeling my way, when somebody grabbed my nose and mouth from behind and I must have fainted because that's all I knew till just now, and Jerry Baxter, if you don't get up on your two feet like a man and defend your own wife, I'll—— I'll——"

"Slit his throat?" asked Sergeant Velie crossly, for the Sergeant had been attending his own Hallowe'en Party with the boys of his old precinct and was holding three queens full when the call to duty came.

"The murderer," said Ellery glumly. "The real murderer, Dad. At the time Nikki first put out the lights, while Edith Baxter was still in the room getting Nikki's final instructions, one of us lined up at the wall stole across the room, passed Nikki, passed Edith Baxter in the dark, and ambushed her——"

"Probably intended to slug her," nodded the Inspector, "but Mrs. Baxter obliged by fainting first."

188

"Then into the closet and away to do the foul deed?" asked the Sergeant poetically. He shook his head.

"It would mean," mused Inspector Queen, "that after stowing Mrs. Baxter in the foyer closet, the real killer went into the kitchen, got the mask, flash, and knife, came back to the living-room, tapped John Crombie, led him out to the kitchen, and carved him up. That part of it's okay— Crombie must have thought he was playing the game—but how about the assault on Mrs. Baxter before hand? Having to drag her unconscious body to the closet? Wasn't there any noise, any sound?"

Ellery said apologetically: "I kept dozing off."

But Nikki said: "There was no sound, Inspector. Then or at any other time. The first *sound* after I turned the light off was John screaming in the kitchen. The only other *sound* was the murderer throwing the flash into the middle of the room after he . . . she . . . whoever it was . . . got back to the wall."

Jerry Baxter raised his sweating face and looked at his wife.

"Could be," said the Inspector.

"Oh, my," said Sergeant Velie. He was studying the old gentleman as if he couldn't believe his eyes—or ears.

"It could be," remarked Ellery, "or it couldn't. Edith's a very small woman. Unconscious, she *could* be carried noiselessly the few feet in the foyer to the closet . . . by a reasonably strong person."

Immediately Ann Crombie and Lucy Trent and Jerry Baxter tried to look tiny and helpless, while Edith Baxter tried to look huge and heavy. But the sisters could not look less tall or soundly made than Nature had fashioned them, and Jerry's proportions, even allowing for reflective shrinkage, were elephantine.

"Nikki," said Ellery in a very thoughtful way, "you're sure Edith was the only one to step away from the wall while the light was still on?"

"Dead sure, Ellery."

"And when the one you thought was Edith came back from the kitchen to pick a victim, that person had a full mask on?"

"You mean after I put the light out? Yes. I could see the mask in the glow the flash made."

"Man or woman, Miss P?" interjected the Sergeant eagerly. "This could be a pipe. If it was a man——"

But Nikki shook her head. "The flash was pretty weak, Sergeant. And we were all in those Black Cat outfits."

189

"Me, I'm no Fancy Dan," murmured Inspector Queen unexpectedly. "A man's been knocked off. What I want to know is not who was where when, but—who had it in for this character?"

It was a different sort of shrinkage this time, a shrinkage of four throats. Ellery thought: They *all* know.

"Whoever," he began casually, "whoever knew that John Crombie and Edith Baxter were——"

"It's a lie!" Edith was on her feet, swaying, clawing the air. "There was nothing between John and me. Nothing. Nothing! Jerry, don't believe them!"

Jerry Baxter looked down at the floor again. "Between?" he mumbled. "I guess I got a head. I guess this has got me." And, strangely, he looked not at his wife, but at Ann Crombie. "Ann . . .?"

But Ann was jelly-lipped with fear.

"Nothing!" screamed Jerry's wife.

"That's not true." And now it was Lucy's turn, and they saw she had been shocked into a sort of suicidal courage. "John was a . . . a . . . John made love to every woman he met. John made love to *me*——"

"To you." Ann blinked and blinked at her sister.

"Yes. He was . . . disgusting. I . . ." Lucy's eyes flamed at Edith Baxter with scorn, with loathing, with contempt. "But *you* didn't find him disgusting, Edith."

Edith glared back, giving hate for hate.

"You spent four week-ends with him. And the other night, at that dinner party, when you two stole off—you thought I didn't hear—but you were both tight . . . you begged him to marry you."

"You nasty little blabbermouth," said Edith in a low voice.

"I heard you. You said you'd divorce Jerry if he'd divorce Ann. And John kind of laughed at you, didn't he? —as if you were dirt. And I saw your eyes, Edith, I saw your eyes . . ."

And now they, too, saw Edith Baxter's eyes—as they really were.

"I never told you, Ann. I couldn't. I couldn't . . ." Lucy began to sob into her hands.

Jerry Baxter got up.

"Here, where d'ye think you're going?" asked the Sergeant, not unkindly.

Jerry Baxter sat down again.

"Mrs. Crombie, did you know what was going on?" asked Inspector Queen sympathetically.

190

It was queer how she would not look at Edith Baxter, who was sitting lumpily now, no threat to anyone—a soggy old woman.

And Ann said, stiff and tight: "Yes, I knew." Then her mouth loosened again and she said wildly: "I knew, but I'm a coward. I couldn't face him with it. I thought if I shut my eyes——"

"So do I," said Ellery tiredly.

"What?" said Inspector Queen, turning around. "You what, son? I didn't get you."

"I know who cut Crombie's throat."

They were lined up facing the far wall of the living-room—Ann Crombie, Lucy Trent, Edith Baxter, and Jerry Baxter—with a space the breadth of a man, and a little more, between the Baxters. Nikki stood at the light switch, the Inspector and Sergeant Velie blocked the archway, and Ellery sat on a hassock in the centre of the room, his hands dangling listlessly between his knees.

"This is how we were arranged a couple of hours ago, Dad, except that I was at the wall, too, and so was John Crombie . . . in that vacant space."

Inspector Queen said nothing.

"The light was still on, as it is now. Nikki had just asked Murderer to step away from the wall and cross the room —that is, towards where you are now. Do it, Edith."

"You mean——"

"Please."

Edith Baxter backed from the wall and turned and slowly picked her way around the overturned furniture. Near the archway, she paused, an arm's length from the Inspector and the Sergeant.

"With Edith about where she is now Nikki, in the full light, instructed her about going to the kitchen, getting the mask, flash, and knife there, coming back in the dark with the flash, selecting a victim, and so on. Isn't that right?"

"Yes."

"Then you turned off the light, Nikki—didn't you?"

"Yes . . ."

"Do it."

"D-do it, Ellery?"

"Do it, Nikki."

When the darkness closed down, someone at the wall gasped. And then the silence closed down, too.

And after a moment Ellery's voice came tiredly: "It was at this point, Nikki, that you said 'Stop!' to Edith

Baxter and gave her a few additional instructions. About what to do after the 'crime.' As I pointed out a few minutes ago, Dad—it's during this interval, with Edith standing in the archway getting Nikki's afterthoughts, and the room in darkness, that the real murderer must have stolen across the living-room from the wall, got past Nikki and Edith and into the foyer, and waited there to ambush Edith."

"Sure, son," said the Inspector. "So what?"

"How did the murderer manage to cross this room in pitch darkness without making any noise?"

At the wall, Jerry Baxter said hoarsely: "Look, I don't have to stand here. I don't have to!"

"Because, you know," said Ellery reflectively, "there wasn't any noise. None at all. In fact, Nikki, you actually remarked in that interval: 'I want the room to be as quiet as it is this minute.' And only a few moments ago you corroborated yourself when you told Dad that the first sound after you turned off the light was John screaming in the kitchen. You said the only other sound was the sound of the flashlight landing in the middle of the room after the murderer got back to the wall. So I repeat: How did the murderer cross the room in darkness without making a sound?"

Sergeant Velie's disembodied bass complained from the archway that he didn't get it at all, at all.

"Well, Sergeant, you've seen this room—it's cluttered crazily with overturned furniture, pillows, hassocks, miscellaneous objects. Do you think *you* could cross it in darkness without sounding like the bull in the china shop? Nikki, when you and I first got here and blundered into the living-room——"

"In the dark," cried Nikki. "We bumped. We scraped. I actually fell——"

"Why didn't the murderer?"

"I'll tell you why," said Inspector Queen suddenly. "Because no one did cross this room in the dark. It can't be done without making a racket, or without a light—and there was no light at that time or Nikki'd have seen it."

"Then how's it add up, Inspector?" aksed the Sergeant pathetically.

"There's only one person we know crossed this room, the one Nikki saw cross while the light was on, the one they found in the closet in a 'faint,' Velie. *Edith Baxter!*"

She sounded nauseated. "Oh, no," she said. "No."

"Oh, yes, Mrs. Baxter. It's been you all the time. You

did get to the kitchen. You got the mask, the flash, the knife. You came back and tapped John Crombie. You led him out to the kitchen and there you sliced him up——"

"No!"

"Then you quietly got into that closet and pulled a phony faint, and waited for them to find you so you could tell that cock-and-bull story of being ambushed in the foyer, and——"

"Dad," sighed Ellery.

"Huh?" And because the old gentleman's memory of similar moments—many similar moments—was very green, his tone became truculent. "Now tell me I'm wrong, Ellery!"

"Edith Baxter is the one person present to-night who couldn't have killed John Crombie."

"You see?" moaned Edith. They could hear her panting.

"Nikki actually saw somebody with a flash *return* to the living-room after Crombie's death scream, go to the wall, turn off the flash, and she heard that person hurl it into the middle of the room. Who was it Nikki saw and heard? We've deduced that already—the actual murderer. Immediately after that, Nikki turned up the lights.

"If Edith Baxter were the murderer, wouldn't we have found her *at the wall with the rest of us* when the lights went on? But she wasn't. She wasn't in the living-room at all. We found her in the foyer closet. So she *had* been attacked. She *did* faint. She *didn't* kill Crombie."

They could hear her sobbing in a great release.

"Then who did?" barked the Inspector. His tone said he was tired of this fancy stuff and give him a killer so he could book the rat and go home and get to sleep.

"The one," replied Ellery in those weary tones, "who was able to cross the room in the dark without making any noise. For if Edith is innocent, only one of those at the wall could have been guilty. And that one had to cross the room."

There is a maddening unarguability about Ellery's sermons.

"But how, son, how?" bellowed his father. "It couldn't be done without knocking *something* over—making *some* noise!"

"Only one possible explanation," said Ellery tiredly; and then he said, not tiredly at all, but swiftly and with the slashing finality of a knife, "I thought you'd try that.

193

That's why I sat on the hassock, so very tired. That's why I staged this whole . . . silly . . . scene . . ."

Velie was roaring: "Where the hell are the lights? Miss Porter, turn that switch on, will you?"

"I can't find the—the damned thing!" wept Nikki.

"The rest of you stay where you are!" shouted the Inspector.

"Now drop the knife," said Ellery, in the slightly gritty tones of one who is exerting pressure. "Drop it . . ." There was a little clatter, and then a whimper. "The only one who could have passed through this jumbled maze in the dark without stumbling over anything," Ellery went on, breathing a bit harder than usual, "would be someone who'd *plotted a route through this maze in advance of the party* . . . someone, in fact, who'd plotted the maze. In other words, the clutter in this room is not chance confusion, but deliberate plant. It would require photographing the details of the obstacle-course on the memory, and practice, plenty of practice—but we were told you spent the entire day in this suit *alone*, my dear, fixing it up for the party."

"Here!" sobbed Nikki, and she jabbed the light switch.

"I imagine," said Ellery gently to the girl in his grip, "you felt *someone* had to avenge the honour of the Trents, Lucy."

The Adventure of
the Telltale Bottle

"Now REGARDING THIS folksy fable, this almost-myth, this canard upon history," continued Ellery, "what are the facts? The facts, my dear Nikki, are these:

"It was *not* a good harvest. Oh, they had twenty acres planted to seed corn, but may I remind you that the corn had been pilfered from the Cape Indians? And had it not been for Tisquantum——"

"Tis-who?" asked Inspector Queen feebly.

"—corruptly known as Squanto—there would have been no harvest that year at all. For it took the last of the more-or-less noble Patuxet to teach our bewildered forefathers how to plant it properly."

"Well, you can't deny they decreed *some* sort of holiday," flashed Nikki, "so that they might 'rejoyce' together!"

"I have no desire to distort the facts," replied Ellery with dignity. "To the contrary. They had excellent reason to 'rejoyce'—some of them were still alive. And tell me: Who actually participated in that first American festival?"

"Why, the Pilgrims," said Inspector Queen uneasily.

"And I suppose you'll tell me that as they stuffed themselves with all the traditional goodies other revered forefathers came running out of the woods with arrows through their hats?"

"I remember a picture like that in my grade-school history book—yes," said Nikki defiantly.

"The *fact* is," grinned Ellery, "they were on such good terms with the Indians during that fall of 1621 that the most enthusiastic celebrants at the feast were Massasoit of the Wampanoag and ninety of his braves!—all very hungry, too. And tell me this: What was the menu on that historic occasion?"

"Turkey!"

"Cranberry sauce!"

"Pumpkin pie!"

"And—so forth," concluded the Inspector. He was at home that day receiving Madame La Grippe and he had been—until Ellery unleashed his eloquence—the most ungracious host in New York. But now he was neglecting Madame beautifully.

"I accept merely the and-so-forths," said Ellery indulgently. "If they had 'Turkies' at that feast, there is no mention of them in the record. Yes, there were plenty of cranberries in the bogs—but it is more than doubtful that the Pilgrim ladies knew what to do with them. And we can definitely assert that the pastry possibilities of the Narraganset *askútasquash* were not yet dreamed of by the pale green females who had crept off the *Mayflower*."

"Listen to him," said the Inspector comfortably.

"I suppose," said Nikki, grinding her teeth, "I suppose they just sat there and munched on that old corn."

"By no means. The menu was regal, considering their customary diet of wormy meal. They gorged themselves on eels——"

"Eels!"

"And clams, venison, water-fowl, and so on. For dessert —wild plums and dried berries; and—let's face it—wild grape wine throughout," said Ellery, looking sad. "And— oh, yes. How long did this first thanksgiving celebration last?"

"Thanksgiving day? How long would a day *be*? A day!"

"Three days. And why do we celebrate Thanksgiving in the month of November?"

"Because—because——"

"Because the Pilgrims celebrated it in the month of October," concluded Ellery. "And there you have it, Nikki—the whole sordid record of historical misrepresentation, simply another example of our national vainglory. I say, if we must celebrate Thanksgiving, let us give thanks to the red man, whose land we took away. I say—let us have facts!"

"And *I* say," cried Nikki, "that you're a factual showoff, a—a darned old talking encyclopedia, Ellery Queen, and I don't care what your precious 'facts' are because all I wanted to do was take Thanksgiving baskets of turkeys and cranberries and stuff to those people down on the East side that I take baskets to every year because they're too poor to have decent Thanksgiving dinners tomorrow, and especially this year with prices sky-high and so many refugee children here who ought to learn the American traditions and who's to teach them if . . . And, anyway, one of them *is* an Indian—way back—so there!"

Why, Nikki," mourned Ellery, joining Nikki on the floor, where she was now hugging the carpet, in tears, "why didn't you tell me one of them is an Indian? That makes all the difference—don't you see?" He sprang erect, glowing fiercely with the spirit of Thanksgiving. "Turkeys! Cranberries! Pumpkin pies! To Mr. Sisquencchi's!"

The affair of the Telltale Bottle was a very special sort of nastiness culminating in that nastiest of nastiness, murder; but it is doubtful if, even had Ellery been a lineal descendant of Mother Shipton, who would have called the bountiful excursion off or in any other wise tarnished that silvery day.

For Mr. Sisquencchi of the market around the corner made several glittering suggestions regarding the baskets; there was a lambency about Miss Porter which brightened with the afternoon; and even Manhattan shone, getting into a snowy party dress as Ellery's ancient Duesenberg padded patiently about the East side.

Ellery lugged baskets and assorted packages through medieval hallways and up donjon staircases until his arms protested; but this was a revolt of the flesh only—the spirit grew fresher as they knocked on the doors of O'Keefes, Del Florios, Cohens, Wilsons, Olsens, Williamses, Pomerantzes, and Johnsons and heard the cries of various Pats, Sammies, Antonios, Olgas, Clarences, and Petunias.

"But where's the Indian?" he demanded, as they sat in the car while Nikki checked over her list. The sun was setting, and several thousand ragamuffins were crawling over the Duesenberg, but it was still a remarkable day.

"Check," said Nikki. "Orchard Street. That's the Indian, Ellery. I mean—oh, she's not an *Indian*, just has some Indian blood way back, Iroquois, I think. She's the last."

"Well, I won't quibble," frowned Ellery, easing old Duesey throught the youth of America. "Although I *do* wish——"

"Oh, shut up. Mother Carey's the darlingest old lady— scrubs floors for a living."

"Mother Carey's!"

But at the Orchard Street tenement, under a canopy of ermine-trimmed fire escapes, a janitor was all they found of Ellery's Indian.

"The old hag don't live here no more."

197

"Oh, dear," said Nikki. "Where's she moved to?"

"She lammed outa here with all her junk in a rush the other day—search me." The janitor spat, just missing Nikki's shoe.

"Any idea where the old lady works?" asked Ellery, just missing the janitor's shoe.

The janitor hastily withdrew his foot. "I think she cleans up some Frog chow joint near Canal Street regular."

"I remember!" cried Nikki. "Fouchet's, Ellery. She's worked there for years. Let's go right over there—maybe they know her new address."

"Fouchet's!" said Ellery gaily; and so infected was he by the enchantment of the fairy-tale afternoon that for once his inner voice failed him.

Fouchet's Restaurant was just off Canal Street, a few blocks from Police Headquarters—squeezed between a button factory and ship chandler's. Cars with Brooklyn accents whished by its plate glass front, and it looked rather frightened by it all. Inside they found round tables covered with checkered oilcloths, a wine bar, walls decorated with prewar French travel posters, a sharp and saucy odour, and a cashier named Clothilde.

Clothilde had a large bosom, a large cameo on it, a large black-velvet ribbon in her hair, and when she opened her mouth to say: "The old woman who clean up?" Nikki saw that she also had a large gold tooth. "Ask Monsieur Fouchet. 'E will be right back." She examined Nikki with very sharp black eyes.

"If the Pilgrims could eat eels," Ellery was mumbling, over a menu, "Why not? *Escargots!* Nikki, let's have dinner here!"

"Well," said Nikki doubtfully. "I suppose . . . as long as we have to wait for Mr. Fouchet, anyway. . . ." A waiter with a long, dreary face led them to a table, and Ellery and the waiter conferred warmly over the menu, but Nikki was not paying attention—she was too busy exchanging brief feminine glances with Clothilde. It was agreed: the ladies did not care for each other. Thereafter, Clothilde wore an oddly watchful expression, and Nikki looked uneasy.

"Ellery . . ." said Nikki.

"—only the very best," Ellery was saying baronially. "Now where the devil did that waiter go? I haven't got to the wine. Pierre!"

"*Un moment, Monsieur,*" came the voice of the waiter with the long, dreary face.

"You know, Nikki, less than five per cent. of all the wine produced in the world can be called really fine wine——"

"Ellery, I don't like this place," said Nikki.

"The rest is *pour la soif*——"

"Let's . . . not eat here after all, Ellery. Let's just find out about Mother Carey and——"

Ellery looked astonished. "Why, Nikki, I thought you loved French food. Consequently, we'll order the rarest, most exquisitely balanced, most perfectly fermented wine. Pierre! Where the deuce has he gone? A Sauterne with body, bouquet, breeding . . ."

"Oh!" squeaked Nikki, then she looked guilty. It was only Pierre breathing down her neck.

"After all, it's a special occasion. Ah, there you are. *La carte des vins!* No, never mind, I know what I want. Pierre," said Ellery magnificently, "a bottle of . . . *Chateau d'Yquem!*"

The dreary look on the waiter's face rather remarkably vanished.

"But, monsieur," he murmured, "*Chateau d'Yquem* . . .? That is an expensive wine. We do not carry so fine a wine in our cellar."

And still, as Pierre said this, he contrived to give the impression that something of extraordinary importance had just occurred. Nikki glanced anxiously at Ellery to see if he had caught that strange overtone; but Ellery was merely looking crushed.

"Carried away by the spirit of Thanksgiving Eve. Very stupid of me, Pierre. Of course. Give us the best you have—which," Ellery added as Pierre walked rapidly away, "will probably turn out to be *vin ordinaire.*" And Ellery laughed.

Something is horribly wrong, thought Nikki, and she wondered how long it would take Ellery to become himself again.

It happened immediately after the *pêches flambeaux* and the *demitasse*. Or, rather, two things happened. One involved the waiter. The other involved Clothilde.

The waiter seemed confused: Upon handing Ellery *l'addition*, he simultaneously whisked a fresh napkin into Ellery's lap! This astounding *non sequitor* brought Mr. Queen to his slumbering senses. But he made no remark, merely felt the napkin and, finding something hard and flat concealed in its folds, he extracted it without looking at it and slipped it into his pocket.

As for the cashier, she too seemed confused. In payment of *l'addition,* Ellery tossed a twenty-dollar bill on the desk. Clothilde made change, chattering pleasantly all the while about *Monsieur* and *Mad'moiselle* and 'ow did they like the dinner?—and she made change very badly. She was ten dollars short.

Ellery had just pointed out this deplorable unfamiliarity with the American coinage system when a stout little whirlwind arrived, scattering French before him like leaves.

"Mais Monsieur Fouchet, je fais une méprise . . ."

"Bête à manàger du foin—silence!" And M. Fouchet fell upon Ellery, almost weeping. *"Monsieur,* this 'as never 'appen before. I give you my assurance——"

For a chilled moment Nikki thought Ellery was going to produce what lay in his pocket for M. Fouchet's inspection. But Ellery merely smiled and accepted the missing ten-dollar bill graciously and asked for Mother Carey's address. M. Fouchet threw up his hands and ran to the rear of the restaurant and ran back to press an oil-stained scrawl upon them, chattering in French at Ellery, at Nikki, at his cashier; and then they were on the street and making for the Duesenberg in a great show of postprandial content . . . for through the plate glass M. Fouchet, and Clothilde, and—yes—Pierre of the long face were watching them closely.

"Ellery, what . . .?"

"Not now, Nikki. Get into the car."

Nikki kept glancing nervously at the three Gallic faces as Ellery tried to start the Duesenberg. "Huh?"

"I said it won't start, blast it. Battery." Ellery jumped out into the snow and began tugging at the basket. "Grab those other things and get out, Nikki."

"But——"

"Cab!" A taxicab parked a few yards beyond Fouchet's shot forward. "Driver, get this basket and stuff in there beside you, will you? Nikki, hop to it. Get into the cab!"

"You're leaving the *car?*"

"We can pick it up later. What are you waiting for, driver?"

The driver looked weary. "Ain't you startin' your Thanksgivin' celebratin' a little premature?" he asked. "I ain't no fortune-teller. Where do I go?"

"Oh. That slip Fouchet gave me. Nikki, where . . . ? Here! 214-B Henry Street, cab. The East Side."

The cab slid away. "Wanna draw me diagrams?" muttered the driver.

"Now, Nikki. Let's have a look at Pierre's little gift."

It was a stiff white-paper packet. Ellery unfolded it.

It contained a large quantity of a powdery substance—a white crystalline powder.

"Looks like snow," giggled Nikki. "What is it?"

"That's what it is."

"Snow?"

"Cocaine."

"That's the hell of this town," the cab-driver was remarking. "Anything can happen. I remember once——"

"Apparently, Nikki," said Ellery with a frown, "I gave Pierre some password or other. By accident."

"He thought you're an addict! That means Fouchet is——"

"A depot for the distribution of narcotics. I wonder what I said that made Pierre . . . *The wine!*"

"I don't follow you," complained the driver.

Ellery glared. The driver looked hurt and honked at an elderly Chinese in a black straw hat.

"Chateau d'Yquem, Nikki. That was the password! Pearls in a swinery . . . of course, of course."

"I *knew* something was wrong the minute we walked in there, Ellery."

"Mmm. We'll drop this truck at Mrs. Carey's, then we'll shoot back uptown and get Dad working on this Fouchet nastiness."

"Watch the Inspector snap out of that cold," laughed Nikki; then she stopped laughing. "Ellery . . . do you suppose all this has anything to do with Mother Carey?"

"Oh, nonsense, Nikki."

It was a bad day for the master.

For when they got to 214-B Henry Street and knocked on the door of Apartment 3-A and a voice as shaky as the stairs called out, "who's there?" and Nikki identified herself . . . something happened. There were certain sounds. Strange rumbly, sliding sounds. The door was not opened at once.

Nikki bit her lip, glancing timidly at Ellery. Ellery was frowning.

"She don't act any too anxious to snag this turk-bird,"

said the cab-driver, who had carried up the pumpkin pie and the bottle of California wine which had been one of Mr. Sisquencchis' inspirations, while Nikki took odds and ends and Ellery the noble basket. "My old lady'd be tickled to death——"

"I'd rather it were you," said Ellery violently. "When she opens the door, dump the pie and wine inside, then wait for us in the cab——"

But at that instant the door opened, and a chubby little old woman with knobby forearms and flushed cheeks stood there, looking not even remotely like an Indian.

"Miss Porter!"

"Mother Carey."

It was a poor little room with an odour. Not the odour of poverty; the room was savagely clean. Ellery barely listened to the chirrupings of the two women; he was too busy using his eyes and his nose. He seemed to have forgotten Massasoit and the Wampanoag.

When they were back in the cab, he said abruptly: "Nikki, do you happen to recall Mother Carey's old apartment?"

"The one on Orchard Street? Yes—why?"

"How many rooms did she have there?"

"Two. A bedroom and a kitchen. Why?"

Ellery asked casually: "Did she always live alone?"

"I think so."

"Then why has she suddenly—so very suddenly, according to that Orchard Street janitor—moved to a *three*-room flat?"

"You mean the Henry Street place has——?"

"Three rooms—from the doors. Now why should a poor old scrubwoman living alone suddenly need an *extra* room?"

"Cinch," said the cab-driver. "She's takin' in boarders."

"Yes," murmured Ellery, without umbrage. "Yes, I suppose that might account for the odour of cheap cigar smoke."

"Cigar smoke!"

"Maybe she's runnin' a horse parlour," suggested the driver.

"Look, friend," said Nikki angrily, "how about letting us take the wheel and you coming back here?"

"Keep your bra on, lady."

"The fact is," mused Ellery, "before she opened her door she moved furniture away from it. Those sounds? She'd barricaded that door, Nikki."

202

"Yes," said Nikki in a small voice. "And that doesn't sound like a boarder, does it?"

"It sounds," said Ellery, "like a hideout." He leaned forward just as the driver opened his mouth. "And don't bother," he said. "Nikki, it's somebody who can't go out—or doesn't dare to. . . . I'm beginning to think there's a connection between the cigar smoker your Mrs. Carey's hiding, and the packet of drugs Pierre slipped me at Fouchet's by mistake."

"Oh, no, Ellery," moaned Nikki.

Ellery took her hand. "It's a rotten way to wind up a heavenly day, honey, but we have no choice. I'll have Dad give orders to arrest Pierre to-night the minute we get home, and let's hope . . . Hang the Pilgrims!"

"That's subversive propaganda, brother," said the driver.

Ellery shut the communicating window, violently.

Inspector Queen sniffled: "She's in it, all right."

"Mother Carey?" wailed Nikki.

"Three years ago," nodded the Inspector, drawing his bathrobe closer about him, "Fouchet's was mixed up in a drug-peddling case. And a Mrs. Carey was connected with it."

Nikki began to cry.

"Connected how, Dad?"

"One of Fouchet's waiters was the passer——"

"Pierre?"

"No. Pierre was working there at that time—or at least a waiter of that name was—but the guilty waiter was an old man named Carey . . . whose wife was a scrubwoman."

"Lo the poor Indian," said Ellery, and he sat down with his pipe. After a moment, he said: "Where's Carey now, Dad?"

"In the clink doing a tenner. We found a couple of hundred dollars' worth of snow in the old geezer's bedroom—they lived on Mulberry then. Carey claimed he was framed—but they all do."

"And Fouchet?" murmured Ellery, puffing.

"Came out okay. Apparently he hadn't known. It was Carey all by himself."

"Strange. It's still going on."

The Inspector looked startled, and Ellery shrugged.

Nikki cried: "Mr. Carey was *framed*!"

"Could be," muttered the old gentleman. "Might have

203

been this Pierre all the time—felt the heat on and gave us a quick decoy. Nikki, hand me the phone."

"I knew it, I knew it!"

"And while you're on the phone, Dad," said Ellery mildly, "you might ask why Headquarters hasn't picked up Carey."

"Picked him up? I told you, Ellery, he's in stir. Hello?"

"Oh, no, he's not," said Ellery. "He's hiding out in Apartment 3-A at 214-B Henry Street."

"The cigar smoke," breathed Nikki. "The barricade. The extra room!"

"Velie!" snarled the Inspector. "Has a con named Frank Carey broken out of stir?"

Sergeant Velie, bewildered by this clairvoyance stammered; "Yeah. Inspector, a few days ago, ain't been picked up yet, we're tryin' to locate his wife but she's moved and——But you been home sick!"

"She's moved," sighed the Inspector. "Well, well, she's probably moved to China." Then he roared: "She's hiding him out! But never mind—you take those Number Fourteens of yours right down to Fouchet's Restaurant just off Canal and arrest a waiter named Pierre! And if he isn't there, don't take two weeks finding out where he lives. I want that man to-night!"

"But Carey——"

"I'll take care of Carey myself. Go on—don't waste a second!" The old man hung up, fuming. "Where's my pants, dad blast the——?"

"Dad!" Ellery grabbed him. "You're not going out *now*. You're still sick."

"I'm picking up Carey personally," said his father gently. "Do you think you're man enough to stop me?"

The old scrubwoman sat at her kitchen table stolidly, and this time the Iroquois showed.

There was no one else in the Henry Street flat.

"We know your husband was here, Mrs. Carey," said Inspector Queen. "He got word to you when he broke out of jail, you moved, and you've been hiding him here. Where's he gone to now?"

The old lady said nothing.

"Mother Carey, please," said Nikki. "We want to help you."

"We believe your husband was innocent of that drug-passing charge, Mrs. Carey," said Ellery quietly.

The bluish lips tightened. The basket, the turkey, the

pumpkin pie, the bottle of wine, the packages were still on the table.

"I think, Dad," said Ellery, "Mrs. Carey wants a bit more evidence of official good faith. Mother, suppose I tell you I not only believe your husband was framed three years ago, but that the one who framed him was——"

"That Pierre," said Mother Carey in a hard voice. "He was the one. He was the brains. He used to be 'friendly' with Frank."

"The one—but not the brains."

"What d'ye mean, Ellery?" demanded Inspector Queen.

"Isn't Pierre working alone?" asked Nikki.

"If he is, would he have handed me—a total stranger—a packet of dope worth several hundred dollars ... without a single word about payment?" asked Ellery dryly.

Mother Carey was staring up at him.

"Those were Pierre's instructions," said the Inspector slowly.

"Exactly. So there's someone behind Pierre who's using him as the passer, payment being arranged for by some other means——"

"Probably in advance!" The Inspector leaned forward. "Well, Mrs. Carey, won't you talk now? Where is Frank?"

"Tell the Inspector, Mother," begged Nikki. "The truth!"

Mother Carey looked uncertain. But then she said, "We told the truth three years ago," and folded her lacerated hands.

There is a strength in the oppressed which yields to nothing.

"Let it go," sighed the Inspector. "Come on, son—we'll go over to Fouchet's and have a little chin with Mr. Pierre, find out who his bossman is——"

And it was then that Mother Carey said, in a frightened quick voice: "No!" and put her hand to her mouth, appalled.

"Carey's gone to Fouchet's," said Ellery slowly. "Of course, Mrs. Carey would have a key—she probably opens the restaurant. Carey's gone over with some desperate idea that he can dig up some evidence that will clear him. That's it, Mother, isn't it?"

But Inspector Queen was already out in the unsavoury hall.

Sergeant Velie was standing miserably in the entrance to Fouchet's when the squad car raced up.

"Now Inspector, don't get mad——"

The Inspector said benignly: "You let Pierre get away."

"Oh, no!" said Sergeant Velie. "Pierre's in there, Inspector. Only he's dead."

"*Dead!*"

"Dead of what, Sergeant?" asked Ellery swiftly.

"Of a carvin' knife in the chest, that's of what, Maestro. We came right over here like you said, Inspector, only some knife artist beat us to it." The Sergeant relaxed. It was all right. The Old Man was smiling.

"Frank Carey did it, of course?"

The Sergeant stopped relaxing. "Heck, no, Inspector. Carey didn't do it."

"Velie——!"

"Well, he didn't! When we rolled up we spot Carey right here at the front door. Place is closed for the night—just a night-light. He's got a key. We watch him unlock the door, go in, and wham! he damn' near falls over this Pierre. So the feeble-minded old cluck bends down and takes the knife out of Pierre's chest and stands there in a trance lookin' at it. He's been standin' like that ever since."

"Without the knife, I hope," said the Inspector nastily; and they went in.

And found an old man among the detectives in the posture of a question-mark leaning against an oilcloth-covered table under a poster advertising Provençal, with his toothless mouth ajar and his watery old eyes fixed on the extinct *garçon*. The extinct *garçon* was still in his monkey-suit; his right palm was upturned, as if appealing for mercy, or the usual *pourboire*.

"Carey," said Inspector Queen.

Old man Carey did not seem to hear. He was fascinated by Ellery; Ellery was on one knee, peering at Pierre's eyes.

"Carey, who killed this Frenchman?"

Carey did not reply.

"Plain case of busted gut," remarked Sergeant Velie.

"You can hardly blame him!" cried Nikki. "Framed for dope-peddling three years ago, convicted, jailed for it—and now he thinks he's being framed for murder!"

"I wish we could get something out of him," said the Inspector thoughtfully. "It's a cinch Pierre stayed after closing time because he had a date with somebody."

"His boss!" said Nikki.

"Whoever he's been passing the snow for, Nikki."

"Dad." Ellery was on his feet looking down at the long

dreary face that now seemed longer and drearier. "Do you recall if Pierre was ticketed as a drug addict three years ago?"

"I don't think he was." The Inspector looked surprised.

"Look at his eyes."

"Say!"

"Far gone, too. If Pierre wasn't an addict at the time of Carey's arrest, he'd taken to the habit in the past three years. And that explains why he was murdered to-night."

"He got dangerous," said the Inspector grimly. "With Carey loose and Pierre pulling that boner with you to-night, the boss knew the whole Fouchet investigation would be reopened."

Ellery nodded. "Felt he couldn't trust Pierre any longer. Weakened by drugs, the fellow would talk as soon as the police pulled him in, and this mysterious character knew it."

"Yeah," said the Sergeant sagely. "Put the heat on a smecker and he squirts like whipped cream."

But Ellery wasn't listening. He had sat down at one of the silent tables and was staring over at the wine-bar.

Mr. Fouchet flew in in a strong tweed overcoat, showing a dent in his Homburg where it should not have been.

"Selling of the dope—again! This *Pierre* . . .!" hissed M. Fouchet, and he glared down at his late waiter with quite remarkable venom.

"Know anything about this job, Fouchet?" asked the Inspector courteously.

"Nothing, *Monsieur l'inspecteur*. I give you my word, no thing. Pierre stay late to-night. He says to me he will fix up the tables for to-morrow. He stays and—pfft! *il se fait tuer!*" M. Fouchet's fat lips began to dance. "Now the bank will give me no more credit." He sank into a chair.

"Oh? You're not in good shape financially, Fouchet?"

"I serve *escargots* near Canal Street. It should be pretzels! The bank, I owe 'im five thousand dollars."

"And that's the way it goes," said the Inspector sympathetically. "All right, Mr. Fouchet, go home. Where's that cashier?"

A detective pushed Clothilde forward. Clothilde had been weeping into her make-up. But not now. Now she glared down at Pierre quite as M. Fouchet had glared. Pierre glared back.

207

"Clothilde?" muttered Ellery, suddenly coming out of deep reverie.

"Velie turned up something," whispered the Inspector.

"She's in it. She's got something to do with it," Nikki said excitedly to Ellery. "I knew it!"

"Clothilde," said the inspector, "how much do you make in this restaurant?"

"Forty-five dollar a week."

Sergeant Velie drawled: "How much dough you got in the bank, mademazelle?"

Clothilde glanced at the behemoth very quickly indeed. Then she began to sniffle, shaking in several places. "I have no money in the bank. Oh, may be a few dollars——"

"This is your bank book, isn't it, Clothilde?" asked the Inspector.

Clothilde stopped sniffling just as quickly as she had begun. "Where do you get that? Give it to me!"

"Uh-uh-uh," said the Sergeant, embracing her. "Say . . . !"

She flung his arm off. "That is my bank book!"

"And it shows," murmured the Inspector, "deposits totalling more than seventeen thousand dollars, Clothilde. Rich Uncle?"

"*Voleurs!* That is my money! I save!"

"She's got a new savings system, Inspector," explained the Sergeant. "Out of forty-five bucks per week, she manages to sock away, some weeks, sixty, some weeks eighty-five. . . . It's wonderful. How do you do it, Cloey?"

Nikki glanced at Ellery, startled. He nodded gloomily.

"*Fils de lapin! Jongleur! Chienloup!*" Clothilde was screaming. "All right! Some time I short-change the customer. I am cashier, *non*? But—nothing else!" She jabbed her elbow into Sergeant Velie's stomach. "And take your 'and off me!"

"I got my duty, mademazelle," said the Sergeant, but he looked a little guilty. Inspector Queen said something to him in an undertone, and the Sergeant reddened, and Clothilde came at him claws first, and detectives jumped in, and in the midst of it Ellery got up from the table and drew his father aside and said: "Come on back to Mother Carey's."

"What for, Ellery? I'm not through here——"

"I want to wash this thing up. To-morrow's Thanksgiving, poor Nikki is out on her feet——"

"*Ellery*," said Nikki.

He nodded, still gloomily.

The sight of his wife turned old man Carey into a human being again, and he clung to her and blubbered that he had done nothing and they were trying to frame him for the second time, only this time it was the hot seat they were steering him into. And Mrs. Carey kept nodding and picking lint off his jacket collar. And Nikki tried to look invisible.

"Where's Velie?" grumbled the Inspector. He seemed irritated by Carey's blubbering and the fact that Ellery had insisted on sending all the detectives home, as if this were a piece of business too delicate for the boys' sensibilities.

"I've sent Velie on an errand," Ellery replied, and then he said: "Mr. and Mrs. Carey, would you go into that room there and shut the door?" Mother Carey took her husband by the hand without a word. And when the door had closed behind them, Ellery said abruptly: "Dad, I asked you to arrest Pierre to-night. You phoned Velie to hurry right over to Fouchet's. Velie obeyed—and found the waiter stabbed to death."

"So?"

"Police Headquarters is on Centre Street. Fouchet's is just off Canal. A few blocks apart."

"Hey?"

"Didn't it strike you as extraordinary," murmured Ellery, "that Pierre should have been murdered *so quickly*? Before Velie could negotiate those few blocks?"

"You mean this boss dope peddler struck so fast to keep his man from being arrested? We went through all that before, son."

"Hm," said Ellery. "But what did Pierre's killer have to know in order to strike so quickly to-night? Two things: That Pierre had slipped me a packet of dope by mistake this evening; and that I was intending to have Pierre pulled in *to-night*."

"But Ellery," said Nikki with a frown, "nobody knew about either of those things except you, me, and the Inspector . . ."

"Interesting?"

"I don't get it," growled his father. "The killer knew Pierre was going to be picked up even before Velie reached Fouchet's. He must have, because he beat Velie to it. But if only the three of us knew——"

"Exactly—then how did the killer find out?"

"I give up," said the Inspector promptly. He had discovered many years before that this was, after all, the best way.

But Nikki was young. "Someone overheard you talking it over with me and the Inspector?"

"Well, let's see, Nikki. We discussed it with Dad in our apartment when we got back from Mrs. Carey's. . . ."

"But nobody could have overheard *there*," said the Inspector.

"Then Ellery, you and I must have been overheard before we got to the apartment."

"Good enough, Nikki. And the only place you and I discussed the case—the only place we *could* have discussed it . . ."

"Ellery!"

"We opened the packet in the cab on our way over to Henry Street here," nodded Ellery, "and we discussed its contents quite openly—in the cab. In fact," he added dryly, "if you'll recall, Nikki, our conversational cab-driver joined our discussion with enthusiasm."

"The cab-driver, by Joe," said Inspector Queen softly.

"Whom we had picked up just outside Fouchet's, Dad, where he was parked. It fits."

"The same cab-driver," Ellery went on glumly, "who took us back uptown from here, Nikki—remember? And it was on that uptown trip that I told you I was going to have Dad arrest Pierre to-night. . . . Yes, the cab-driver, and only the cab-driver—the only outsider who could have overheard the two statements which would make the boss dope-peddler kill his pusher quickly to prevent an arrest, a police grilling, and an almost certain revelation of the boss's identity."

"Works a cab," muttered the Inspector. "Cute dodge. Parks outside his headquarters. Probably hacks his customers to Fouchet's and collects beforehand. Let Pierre pass the white stuff afterwards. Probably carted them away." He looked up, beaming. "Great work, son! I'll nail that hack so blasted fast——"

"You'll nail whom, Dad?" asked Ellery, still glum.

"The cab-driver!"

"But who is the cab-driver?"

Ellery is not proud of this incident.

"You're asking *me?*" howled his father.

Nikki was biting her lovely nails. "Ellery, I didn't even *notice*——"

"Ha, ha," said Ellery. "That's what I was afraid of."

"Do you mean to say," said Inspector Queen in a terrible voice, "that *my son* didn't read a hack police-identity card?"

"Er . . ."

"It's the LAW!"

"It's Thanksgiving Eve, Dad," muttered Ellery. "Squanto—the Pilgrims—the Iroquois heritage of Mother Carey——"

"Stop drivelling! Can't you give me a description?"

"Er . . ."

"No description," whispered his father. It was really the end of all things.

"Inspector, *nobody* looks at a cab-driver," said Nikki brightly. "You know. A cab-driver? He—he's just *there*."

"The invisible man," said Ellery hopefully. "Chesterton?"

"Oh, so you do remember his name!"

"No, no, Dad——"

"I'd know his voice," said Nikki. "If I ever heard it again."

"We'd have to catch him first, and if we caught him we'd hardly need his voice!"

"Maybe he'll come cruising back around Fouchet's."

The Inspector ejaculated one laughing bark.

"Fine thing. Know who did it—and might's well not know. Listen to me, you detective. You're going over to the Hack Licence Bureau with me, and you're going to look over the photo of every last cab jockey in——"

"Wait. Wait!"

Ellery flung himself at Mother Carey's vacated chair. He sat on the bias, chin propped on the heel of his hand, knitting his brows, unkitting them, knitting them again until Nikki thought there was something wrong with his eyes. Then he shifted and repeated the process in the opposite direction. His father watched him with great suspicion. This was not Ellery to-night; it was someone else. All these gyrations . . .

Ellery leaped to his feet, kicking the chair over. "I've got it! We've got him!"

"How? What?"

"Nikki." Ellery's tone was mysterious, dramatic—let's face it, thought the old gentleman: corny. "Remember when we lugged the stuff from the cab up to Mother

211

Carey's kitchen here? The cab-driver helped us up—carried this bottle of wine."

"Huh?" gaped the Inspector. Then he cried: "No, no, Nikki, don't touch it!" And he chortled over the bottle of California wine. "*Prints.*" That's it, son—that's my boy! We'll just take this little old bottle of grape back to Headquarters, bring out the fingerprints, compare the prints on it with the file sets at the Hack Bureau——"

"Oh, yeah?" said the cab-driver.

He was standing in the open doorway, there was a dirty handkerchief tied around his face below the eyes and his cap was pulled low, and he was pointing a Police Positive midway between father and son.

"I thought you were up to somethin' when you all came back here from Fouchet's," he sneered. "And then leavin' this door open so I could hear the whole thing. You—the old guy. Hand me that bottle of wine."

"You're not very bright," said Ellery wearily. "All right, Sergeant, shoot it out of his hand."

And Ellery embraced his father and his secretary and fell to Mother Carey's spotless floor with them as Sergeant Velie stepped into the doorway behind the cab-driver and very carefully shot the gun out of the invisible man's hand.

"Happy Thanksgivin', sucker," said the Sergeant.

The Adventure of
the Dauphin's Doll

THERE IS A LAW among story-tellers, originally passed by Editors at the cries (they say) of their constituents, which states that stories about Christmas shall have children in them. This Christmas story is no exception; indeed, misopedists will complain that we have overdone it. And we confess in advance that this is also a story about Dolls, and that Santa Claus comes into it, and even a thief; though as to this last, whoever he was—and that was one of the questions—he was certainly not Barabbas, even parabolically.

Another section of the statute governing Christmas stories provides that they shall incline toward Sweetness and Light. The first arises, of course, from the orphans and the never-souring savour of the annual Miracle; as for Light, it will be provided at the end, as usual, by that luminous prodigy, Ellery Queen. The reader of gloomier temper will also find a large measure of Darkness, in the person and works of one who, at least in Inspector Queen's harassed view, was surely the winged Prince of that region. His name, by the way, was not Satan, it was Comus; and this is paradox enow, since the original Comus, as everyone knows, was the god of festive joy and mirth, emotions not commonly associated with the Underworld. As Ellery struggled to embrace his phantom foe, he puzzled over this *non sequitur* in vain; in vain, that is, until Nikki Porter, no scorner of the obvious, suggested that he *might* seek the answer where any ordinary mortal would go at once. And there, to the great man's mortification it was indeed to be found: On page 262b of Volume 6, *Coleb to Damasci*, of the 175th Anniversary edition of the *Encyclopædia Britannica*. A French conjuror of that name—Comus—performing in London in the year 1789 caused his wife to vanish from the top of a table—the very first time, it appeared, that this feat, uxorial or otherwise, had been accomplished without the aid of mirrors. To track his dark adversary's *nom de nuit* to its historic lair gave Ellery his only glint of satisfaction until that blessed moment when light burst all around him and exorcised the darkness, Prince and all.

But this is chaos.

Our story properly begins not with our invisible character but with our dead one.

Miss Ypson had not always been dead; *au contraire.* She had lived for seventy-eight years, for most of them breathing hard. As her father used to remark, "She was a very active little verb." Miss Ypson's father was a professor of Greek at a small Midwestern university. He had conjugated his daughter with the rather bewildered assistance of one of his brawnier students, an Iowa poultry heiress.

Professor Ypson was a man of distinction. Unlike most professors of Greek, he was a Greek professor of Greek, having been born Gerasymos Aghamos Ypsilonomon in Polykhnitos, on the island of Mytilini, "where," he was fond of recalling on certain occasions, "burning Sappho loved and sung"—a quotation he found unfailingly useful in his extracurricular activities; and, the Hellenic ideal notwithstanding, Professor Ypson believed wholeheartedly in immoderation in all things. This hereditary and cultural background explains the professor's interest in fatherhood to his wife's chagrin, for Mrs. Ypson's own breeding prowess was confined to the barnyards on which her income was based—a fact of which her husband sympathetically reminded her whenever he happened to sire another wayward chick; he held their daughter to be nothing less than a biological miracle.

The professor's mental processes also tended to confuse Mrs. Ypson. She never ceased to wonder why instead of shortening his name to Ypson, her husband had not sensibly changed it to Jones. "My dear," the professor once replied, "you are an Iowa snob." "But nobody," Mrs. Ypson cried, "can spell it or pronounce it!" "This is a cross," murmured Professor Ypson, "which we must bear with Ypsilanti." "Oh," said Mrs. Ypson.

There was invariably something Sibylline about his conversation. His favourite adjective for his wife was "ypsiliform," a term, he explained, which referred to the germinal spot at one of the fecundation stages in a ripening egg and which was, therefore, exquisitely *à propos.* Mrs.

214

Ypson continued to look bewildered; she died at an early age.

And the professor ran off with a Kansas City variety girl of considerable talent, leaving his baptized chick to be reared by an eggish relative of her mother's, a Presbyterian named Jukes.

The only time Miss Ypson heard from her father—except when he wrote charming and erudite little notes requesting, as he termed it, *lucrum*—was in the fourth decade of his odyssey, when he sent her a handsome addition to her collection, a terra-cotta play doll of Greek origin over three thousand years old, which, unhappily, Miss Ypson felt duty bound to return to the Brooklyn museum from which it had unaccountably vanished. The note accompanying her father's gift had said, whimsically: *"Timeo Danaos et dona ferentes."*

There was poetry behind Miss Ypson's dolls. At her birth the professor, ever harmonious, signalized his devotion to fecundity by naming her Cytherea. This proved the Olympian irony. For, it turned out, her father's philoprogenitiveness throbbed frustrate in her mother's stony womb; even though Miss Ypson interred five husbands of quite adequate vigour, she remained infertile to the end of her days. Hence it is classically tragic to find her, when all passion was spent, a sweet little old lady with a vague if eager smile who, under the name of her father, pattered about a vast and echoing New York apartment playing enthusiastically with dolls.

In the beginning they were dolls of a common clay: a Billiken, a kewpie, a Kathe Kruse, a Patsy, a Foxy Grandpa, and so forth. But then, as her need increased, Miss Ypson began her fierce sack of the past.

Down into the land of the Pharaoh she went for two pieces of thin desiccated board, carved and painted and with hair of strung beads, and legless—so that they might not run away—which any connoisseur will tell you are the most superb specimens of ancient Egyptian paddle doll extant, far superior to those in the British Museum, although this fact will be denied in certain quarters.

Miss Ypson unearthed a foremother of "Letitia Penn," until her discovery held to be the oldest doll in America, having been brought to Philadelphia from England in 1699 by William Penn as a gift for a playmate of his small daughter's. Miss Ypson's find was a wooden-hearted "little lady" in brocade and velvet which had been sent by Sir Walter Raleigh to the first English child born in the

215

New World. Since Virginia Dare had been born in 1587, not even the Smithsonian dared impugn Miss Ypson's triumph.

On the old lady's racks, in her plate-glass cases, might be seen the wealth of a thousand childhoods, and some riches—for such is the genetics of dolls—possessed by children grown. Here could be found "fashion babies" from fourteenth-century France, sacred dolls of the Orange Free State Fingo tribe, Satsuma paper dolls and court dolls from old Japan, beady-eyed "Kalifa" dolls of the Egyptian Sudan, Swedish birch-bark dolls, "Katcina" dolls of the Hopis, mammoth-tooth dolls of the Eskimos, feather dolls of the Chippewa, tumble dolls of the ancient Chinese, Coptic bone dolls, Roman dolls dedicated to Diana, *pantin* dolls which had been the street toys of Parisian exquisites before Madame Guillotine swept the boulevards, early Christian dolls in their *crèches* representing the Holy Family—to specify the merest handful of Miss Ypson's Briarean collection. She possessed dolls of pasteboard, dolls of animal skin, spool dolls, crab-claw dolls, eggshell dolls, cornhusk dolls, rag dolls, pine-cone dolls with moss hair, stocking dolls, dolls of *bisque*, dolls of palm leaf, dolls of *papier mâché*, even dolls made of seed pods. There were dolls forty inches tall, and there were dolls so little Miss Ypson could hide them in her gold thimble.

Cytherea Ypson's collection bestrode the centuries and took tribute of history. There was no greater—not the fabled playthings of Montezuma, or Victoria's, or Eugene Fields'; not the collection at the Metropolitan, or the South Kensington, or the royal palace in old Bucharest, or anywhere outside the enchantment of little girls' dreams.

It was made of Iowan eggs and the Attic shore, corn-fed and myrtle-clothed; and it brings us at last to Attorney John Somerset Bondling and his visit to the Queen residence one December twenty-third not so very long ago.

December the twenty-third is ordinarily not a good time to seek the Queens. Inspector Richard Queen likes his Christmas old-fashioned; his turkey stuffing for instance, calls for twenty-two hours of over-all preparation, and some of its ingredients are not readily found at the corner grocer's. And Ellery is a frustrated gift-wrapper. For a month before Christmas he turns his sleuthing genius to tracking down unusual wrapping papers, fine ribbons, and artistic stickers; and he spends the last two days creating beauty.

So it was that when Attorney John S. Bondling called, Inspector Queen was in his kitchen, swathed in a barbecue apron, up to his elbows in *fines herbes*, while Ellery, behind the locked door of his study, composed a secret symphony in glittering fuschia metallic paper, forest-green moiré ribbon, and pine cones.

"It's almost useless," shrugged Nikki, studying Attorney Bondling's card, which was as crackly-looking as Attorney Bondling. "You say you know the Inspector, Mr. Bondling?"

"Just tell him Bondling the estate lawyer," said Bondling neurotically. "Park Row. He'll know."

"Don't blame me," said Nikki, "if you wind up in his stuffing. Goodness knows he's used everything else." And she went for Inspector Queen.

While she was gone, the study door opened noiselessly for one inch. A suspicious eye reconnoitred from the crack.

"Don't be alarmed," said the owner of the eye, slipping through the crack and locking the door hastily behind him. "Can't trust them, you know. Children, just children."

"Children!" Attorney Bondling snarled. "You're Ellery Queen, aren't you?"

"Yes?"

"Interested in youth, are you? Christmas? Orphans, dolls, that sort of thing?" Mr. Bondling went on in a remarkably nasty way.

"I suppose so."

"The more fool you. Ah, here's your father. Inspector Queen——!"

"Oh, that Bondling," said the old gentleman absently, shaking his visitor's hand. "My office called to say someone was coming up. Here, use my handkerchief; that's a bit of turkey liver. Know my son? His secretary, Miss Porter? What's on your mind, Mr. Bondling?"

"Inspector, I'm handling the Cytherea Ypson estate, and——"

"Nice meeting you, Mr. Bondling," said Ellery. "Nikki, that door is locked, so don't pretend you forgot the way to the bathroom. . . ."

"Cytherea Ypson," frowned the Inspector. "Oh, yes. She died only recently."

"Leaving me the headache," said Mr. Bondling bitterly, "of disposing of her Dollection."

"Her what?" asked Ellery, looking up from the key.

217

"Dolls—collection. Dollection. She coined the word."

Ellery put the key back in his pocket and strolled over to his armchair.

"Do I take this down?" sighed Nikki.

"Dollection," said Ellery.

"Spent about thirty years at it. Dolls!"

"Yes, Nikki, take it down."

"Well, well, Mr. Bondling," said Inspector Queen. "What's the problem? Christmas comes but once a year, you know."

"Will provides the Dollection be sold at auction," grated the attorney, "and the proceeds used to set up a fund for orphan children. I'm holding the public sale right after New Year's."

"Dolls and orphans, eh?" said the Inspector, thinking of Javanese black pepper and Country Gentlemen Seasoning Salt.

"That's *nice*," beamed Nikki.

"Oh, is it?" said Mr. Bondling softly. "Apparently, young woman, you've never tried to satisfy a Surrogate. I've administered estates for nine years without a whisper against me, but let an estate involve the interests of just one little ba—little fatherless child, and you'd think from the Surrogate's attitude I was Bill Sykes himself!"

"My stuffing," began the Inspector.

"I've had those dolls catalogued. The result is frightening! Did you know there's no set market for the damnable things? And aside from a few personal possessions, the Dollection constitutes the old lady's entire estate. Sank every nickel she had in it."

"But it should be worth a fortune," protested Ellery.

"To whom, Mr. Queen? Museums always want such things as free and unencumbered gifts. I tell you, except for one item, those hypothetical orphans won't realize enough from that sale to keep them in—in bubble gum for two days!"

"Which item would that be, Mr. Bondling?"

"Number Eight-seventy-four," snapped the lawyer. "This one."

"Number Eight-seventy-four," read Inspector Queen from the fat catalogue Bondling had fished out of a large greatcoat pocket. "The Dauphin's Doll. Unique. Ivory figure of a boy Prince eight inches tall, clad in court dress, genuine ermine, brocade, velvet. Court sword in gold strapped to waist. Gold circlet crown surmounted by a

218

single blue brilliant diamond of finest water, weight approximately 49 carats——"

"How many carats?" exclaimed Nikki.

"Larger than the *Hope* and the *Star of South Africa*," said Ellery, with a certain excitement.

"—appraised," continued his father, "at one hundred and ten thousand dollars."

"Expensive dollie."

"Indecent!" said Nikki.

"This indecent—I mean exquisite royal doll," the Inspector read on, "was a birthday gift from King Louis XVI of France to Louis Charles, his second son, who became Dauphin at the death of his elder brother in 1789. The little Dauphin was proclaimed Louis XVII by the royalists during the French Revolution while in custody of the *sans-culottes*. His fate is shrouded in mystery. Romantic, historic item."

"*Le prince perdu*. I'll say," muttered Ellery. "Mr. Bondling, is this on the level?"

"I'm an attorney, not an antiquarian," snapped their visitor. "There are documents attached, one of them a sworn statement—holograph—by Lady Charlotte Atkyns, the English actress-friend of the Capet family—she was in France during the Revolution—or purporting to be in Lady Charlotte's hand. It doesn't matter, Mr. Queen. Even if the history is bad, the diamond's good!"

"I take it this hundred-and-ten-thousand dollar dollie constitutes the bone, as it were, or that therein lies the rub?"

"You said it!" cried Mr. Bondling, cracking his knuckles in a sort of agony. "For my money the Dauphin's Doll is the only negotiable asset of that collection. And what's the old lady do? She provides by will that on the day preceding Christmas the Cytherea Ypson Dollection is to be publicly displayed . . . on the main floor of Nash's Department Store! *The day before Christmas, gentlemen!* Think of it!"

"But why?" asked Nikki, puzzled.

"Why? Who knows why? For the entertainment of New York's army of little beggars, I suppose! Have you any notion how many peasants pass through Nash's on the day before Christmas? My cook tells me—she's a very religious woman—it's like Armageddon."

"Day before Christmas," frowned Ellery. "That's tomorrow."

"It does sound chancey," said Nikki anxiously. Then she

219

brightened. "Oh, well, maybe Nash's won't co-operate, Mr. Bondling."

"Oh, won't they!" howled Mr. Bondling. "Why, old lady Ypson had this stunt cooked up with that gang of peasant-purveyors for years! They've been snapping at my heels ever since the day she was put away!"

"It'll draw every crook in New York," said the Inspector, his gaze on the kitchen door.

"Orphans," said Nikki. "The orphans' interests *must* be protected." She looked at her employer accusingly.

"Special measures, Dad," said Ellery.

"Sure, sure," said the Inspector, rising. "Don't you worry about this, Mr. Bondling. Now if you'll be kind enough to excu——"

"Inspector Queen," hissed Mr. Bondling, leaning forward tensely, "that is not all."

"Ah." Ellery briskly lit a cigarette. "There's a specific villain in this piece, Mr. Bondling, and you know who he is."

"I do," said the lawyer hollowly, "and then again I don't. I mean, it's Comus."

"*Comus!*" the Inspector screamed.

"Comus?" said Ellery slowly.

"Comus?" said Nikki. "Who dat?"

"Comus," nodded Mr. Bondling. "First thing this morning. Marched right into my office, bold as day—must have followed me; I hadn't got my coat off, my secretary wasn't even in. Marched in and tossed this card on my desk."

Ellery seized it. "The usual, Dad."

"His trade-mark," growled the Inspector, his lips working.

"But the card just says 'Comus'," complained Nikki. "Who——?"

"And he calmly announced to me," said Bondling, blotting his cheeks with an exhausted handkerchief, "that he's going to steal the Dauphin's Doll to-morrow, in Nash's."

"Oh, a maniac," said Nikki.

"Mr. Bondling," said the old gentleman in a terrible voice, "just what did this fellow look like?"

"Foreigner—black beard—spoke with a thick accent of some sort. To tell you the truth, I was so thunderstruck I didn't notice details. Didn't even chase him till it was too late."

The Queens shrugged at each other, Gallically.

"The old story," said the Inspector; the corners of his

nostrils were greenish. "The brass of the colonel's monkey and when he does show himself nobody remembers anything but beards and foreign accents. Well, Mr. Bondling, with Comus in the game it's serious business. Where's the collection right now?"

"In the vaults of the Life Bank and Trust, Forty-third Street branch."

"What time are you to move it over to Nash's?"

"They wanted it this evening. I said nothing doing. I've made special arrangements with the bank, and the collection's to be moved at seven-thirty to-morrow morning."

"Won't be much time to set up," said Ellery thoughtfully, "before the store opens its doors." He glanced at his father.

"You leave Operation Dollie to us, Mr. Bondling," said the Inspector grimly. "Better give me a buzz this afternoon."

"I can't tell you, Inspector, how relieved I am——"

"Are you?" said the old gentleman sourly. "What makes you think he won't get it?"

When Attorney Bondling had left, the Queens put their heads together, Ellery doing most of the talking, as usual. Finally, the Inspector went into the bedroom for a session with his direct line to Headquarters.

"Anybody would think," sniffed Nikki, "you two were planning the defence of the Bastille. Who is this Comus, anyway?"

"We don't know, Nikki," said Ellery slowly. "Might be anybody. Began his criminal career about five years ago. He's in the grand tradition of Lupin—a saucy, highly intelligent rascal who's made stealing an art. He seems to take a special delight in stealing valuable things under virtually impossible conditions. Master of make up—he's appeared in a dozen different disguises. And he's an uncanny mimic. Never been caught, photographed, or fingerprinted. Imaginative, daring—I'd say he's the most dangerous thief operating in the United States."

"If he's never been caught," said Nikki sceptically, "how do you know he commits these crimes?"

"You mean: and not someone else?" Ellery smiled pallidly. "The techniques mark the thefts as his work. And then, like Arsène, he leaves a card—with the name 'Comus' on it—on the scene of each visit."

"Does he usually announce in advance that he's going to swipe the crown jewels?"

"No." Ellery frowned. "To my knowledge, this is the

first such instance. Since he's never done anything without a reason, that visit to Bondling's office this morning must be part of his greater plan. I wonder if——"

The telephone in the living-room rang clear and loud.

Nikki looked at Ellery. Ellery looked at the telephone.

"Do you suppose——?" began Nikki. But then she said, "Oh, it's too absurd."

"Where Comus is involved," said Ellery wildly, "nothing is too absurd!" and he leaped for the phone. "Hello!"

"A call from an old friend," announced a deep and hollowish male voice. "Comus."

"Well," said Ellery. "Hello again."

"Did Mr. Bondling," asked the voice jovially, "persuade you to 'prevent' me from stealing the Dauphin's Doll in Nash's to-morrow?"

"So you know Bondling's been here."

"No miracle involved, Queen. I followed him. Are you taking the case?"

"See here, Comus," said Ellery. "Under ordinary circumstances I'd welcome the sporting chance to put you where you belong. But these circumstances are not ordinary. That doll represents the major asset of a future fund for orphaned children. I'd rather we didn't play catch with it. Comus, what do you say we call this one off?"

"Shall we say," asked the voice gently, "Nash's Department Store—to-morrow?"

Thus the early morning of December twenty-fourth finds Messrs. Queen and Bondling, and Nikki Porter, huddled on the iron sidewalk of Forty-third Street before the holly-decked windows of the Life Bank and Trust Company, just outside a double line of armed guards. The guards form a channel between the bank entrance and an armoured truck, down which Cytherea Ypson's Dollection flows swiftly. And all about gapes New York, stamping callously on the aged, icy face of the street against the uncharitable Christmas wind.

Now is the winter of his discontent, and Mr. Queen curses.

"I don't know what you're beefing about," moans Miss Porter. "You and Mr. Bondling are bundled up like Yukon prospectors. Look at *me*."

"It's that rat-hearted public relations tripe from Nash's," says Mr. Queen murderously. "They all swore themselves to secrecy, Brother Rat included. Honour! Spirit of Christmas!"

"It was all over the radio last night," whimpers Mr. Bondling. "And in this morning's papers."

"I'll cut his creeps heart out. Here! Velie, keep those people away!"

Sergeant Velie says good-naturedly from the doorway of the bank, "You jerks stand back." Little does the Sergeant know the fate in store for him.

"Armoured trucks," says Miss Porter bluishly. "Shotguns."

"Nikki, Comus made a point of informing us in advance that he meant to steal the Dauphin's Doll in Nash's Department Store. It would be just like him to have said that in order to make it easier to steal the doll *en route*."

"Why don't they hurry?" shivers Mr. Bondling. "Ah!"

Inspector Queen appears suddenly in the doorway. His hands clasp treasure.

"Oh!" cries Nikki.

New York whistles.

It is magnificence, an affront to democracy. But street mobs, like children, are royalists at heart.

New York whistles, and Sergeant Thomas Velie steps menacingly before Inspector Queen, Police Positive drawn, and Inspector Queen dashes across the sidewalk between the bristling lines of guards with the Dauphin's Doll in his embrace.

Queen the Younger vanishes, to materialize an instant later at the door of the armoured truck.

"It's just immorally, hideously beautiful, Mr. Bondling," breathes Miss Porter, sparkly-eyed.

Mr. Bondling cranes, thinly.

ENTER *Santa Claus, with Bell.*

Santa. Oyez, oyez. Peace, good will. Is that the dollie the radio's been yappin' about, folks?

Mr. B. Scram.

Miss P. Why, Mr. Bondling.

Mr. B. Well he's got no business here. Stand back, er Santa. Back!

Santa. What eateth you, my lean and angry friend? Have you no compassion at this season of the year?

Mr. B. Oh . . . Here! (*Clink.*) Now will you *kindly* . . . ?

Santa. Mighty pretty dollie. Where they takin' it, girlie?

Miss P. Over to Nash's, Santa.

Mr. B. You asked for it. Officer!!!

Santa (*hurriedly*). Little present for you, girlie. Compliments of Santa. Merry, merry.

223

Miss P. For *me?* (EXIT *Santa, rapidly, with bell.*) Really Mr. Bondling, was it necessary to . . .?

Mr. B. Opium for the masses! What did that flatulent faker hand you, Miss Porter? What's in that unmentionable envelope?

Miss P. I'm sure I don't know, but isn't it the most touching idea? Why, it's addressed to *Ellery.* Oh! Elleryyyyy!

Mr. B. (EXIT *excitedly*). Where is he? You——! Officer! Where did that baby-deceiver disappear to? A Santa Claus . . .!

Mr. Q. (*entering on the run*). Yes! Nikki, what is it? What's happened?

Miss P. A man dressed as Santa Claus has just handed me this envelope. It's addressed to you.

Mr. Q. Note? (*He snatches it, withdraws a miserable slice of paper from it on which is block-lettered in pencil a message which he reads aloud with considerable expression.*) "Dear Ellery, Don't you trust me! I said I'd steal the Dauphin in Nash's emporium to-day and that's exactly where I'm going to do it. Yours——" Signed . . .

Miss P. (*craning*). "Comus." That Santa?

Mr. Q. sets his manly lips. An icy wind blows.

Even the master had to acknowledge that their defences against Comus were ingenious.

From the Display Department of Nash's they had requisitioned four mitre-jointed counters of uniform length. These they had fitted together, and in the centre of the hollow square thus formed they had erected a platform six feet high. On the counters, in plastic tiers, stretched long lines of Miss Ypson's babies. Atop the platform, dominant, stood a great chair of hand-carved oak, filched from the Swedish Modern section of the Fine Furniture Department; and on this Valhalla-like throne, a huge and rosy rotundity, sat Sergeant Thomas Velie of Police Headquarters, morosely grateful for the anonymity endowed by the scarlet suit and the jolly mask and whiskers of his appointed role.

Nor was this all. At a distance of six feet outside the counters shimmered a surrounding rampart of plate glass, borrowed in its various elements from *The Glass Home of the Future* display on the sixth floor rear, and assembled to shape an eight-foot wall quoined with chrome, its glistening surfaces flawless except at one point, where a thick glass door had been installed. But the edges fitted intimately and there was a formidable lock in the door, the key to which lay buried in Mr. Queen's right trouser pocket.

It was 8.45 a.m. The Queens, Nikki Porter, and Attorney Bondling stood among store officials and an army of plain-clothes men on Nash's main floor surveying the product of their labours.

"I think that about does it," muttered Inspector Queen at last. "Men! Positions around the glass partition."

Twenty-four assorted gendarmes in mufti jostled one another. They took marked places about the wall, facing it and grinning up at Sergeant Velie. Sergeant Velie, from his throne, glared back.

"Hagstrom and Piggot—the door."

Two detectives detached themselves from a group of reserves. As they marched to the glass door, Mr. Bondling plucked at the Inspector's overcoat sleeve. "Can all these men be trusted, Inspector Queen?" he whispered. "I mean, this fellow Comus——"

"Mr. Bondling," replied the old gentleman coldly, "you do your job and let me do mine."

"But——"

"Picked men, Mr. Bondling! I picked 'em myself."

"Yes, yes, Inspector. I merely thought I'd——"

"Lieutenant Farber."

A little man with watery eyes stepped forward.

"Mr. Bondling, this is Lieutenant Geronimo Farber, Headquarters jewellery expert. Ellery?"

Ellery took the Dauphin's Doll from his greatcoat pocket, but he said, "If you don't mind, Dad, I'll keep holding on to it."

Somebody said, "Wow," and then there was silence.

"Lieutenant, this doll in my son's hand is the famous Dauhin's Doll with the diamond crown that——"

"Don't touch it, Lieutenant, please," said Ellery. "I'd rather nobody touched it."

"The doll," continued the Inspector, "has just been brought here from a bank vault which it ought never to have left, and Mr. Bondling, who's handling the Ypson estate, claims it's the genuine article. Lieutenant, examine the diamond and give us your opinion."

Lieutenant Farber produced a *loupe*. Ellery held the dauphin securely, and Farber did not touch it.

Finally, the expert said, "I can't pass an opinion about the doll itself, of course, but the diamond's a beauty. Easily worth a hundred thousand dollars at the present state of the market—maybe more. Looks like a very strong setting, by the way."

"Thanks, Lieutenant. Okay, son," said the Inspector. "Go into your waltz."

Clutching the dauphin, Ellery strode over to the glass gate and unlocked it.

"This fellow Farber," whispered Attorney Bondling in the Inspector's hairy ear. "Inspector, are you absolutely sure he's——?"

"He's really Lieutenant Farber?" The Inspector controlled himself. "Mr. Bondling, I've known Gerry Farber for eighteen years. Calm yourself."

Ellery was crawling perilously over the nearest counter. Then, bearing the dauphin aloft, he hurried across the floor of the enclosure to the platform.

Sergeant Velie whined, "Maestro, how in hell am I going to sit here all day without washin' my hands?"

But Mr. Queen merely stooped and lifted from the floor a heavy little structure faced with black velvet consisting of a floor and a backdrop, with a two-armed chromium support. This object he placed on the platform directly between Sergeant Velie's massive legs.

Carefully, he stood the Dauphin's Doll in the velvet niche. Then he clambered back across the counter, went through the glass door, locked it with a key, and turned to examine his handiwork.

Proudly the prince's plaything stood, the jewel in his little golden crown darting "on pale electric streams" under the concentrated tide of a dozen of the most powerful floodlights in the possession of the great store.

"Velie," said Inspector Queen, "you're not to touch that doll. Don't lay a finger on it."

The Sergeant said, "Gaaaaa."

"You mean on duty. Don't worry about the crowds. Your job is to keep watching that doll. You're not to take your eyes off it all day. Mr. Bondling, are you satisfied?" Mr. Bondling seemed about to say something, but then he hastily nodded. "Ellery?"

The great man smiled. "The only way he can get that bawbie," he said, "is by well-directed mortar fire or spells and incantations. Raise the portcullis."

Then began the interminable day, *dies irae*, the last shopping day before Christmas. This is traditionally the day of the inert, the procrastinating, the undecided, and the forgetful, sucked at last into the mercantile machine

226

by the perpetual pump of Time. If there is peace upon earth, it descends only afterward; and at no time, on the part of anyone embroiled, is there good will toward men. As Miss Porter expresses it, a cat fight in a bird cage would be more Christian.

But on this December twenty-fourth, in Nash's, the normal bedlam was augmented by the vast shrilling of thousands of children. It may be, as the Psalmist insists, that happy is the man that hath his quiver full of them; but no bowmen surrounded Miss Ypson's darlings this day, only detectives carrying revolvers, not a few of whom forbore to use same only by the most heroic self-discipline. In the black floods of humanity overflowing the main floor little folks darted about like electrically charged minnows, pursued by exasperated maternal shrieks and the imprecations of those whose shins and rumps and toes were at the mercy of hot, happy little limbs; indeed, nothing was sacred, and Attorney Bondling was seen to quail and wrap his greatcoat defensively about him against the savage innocence of childhood. But the guardians of the law, having been ordered to simulate store employees, possessed no such armour; and many a man earned his citation that day for unique cause. They stood in the millrace of the tide; it churned about them, shouting, "Dollies! *Dollies!*" until the very word lost its familiar meaning and became the insensate scream of a thousand Loreleis beckoning strong men to destruction below the eye-level of their diamond Light.

But they stood fast.

And Comus was thwarted. Oh, he tried. At 11.18 a.m. a tottering old man holding fast to the hand of a small boy tried to wheedle Detective Hagstrom into unlocking the glass door "so my grandson here—he's terrible near-sighted—can get a closer look at the pretty dollies." Detective Hagstrom roared, "Rube!" and the old gentleman dropped the little boy's hand violently and with remarkable agility lost himself in the crowd. A spot investigation revealed that, coming upon the boy, who had been crying for his mommy, the old gentleman had promised to find her. The little boy, whose name—he said—was Lance Morganstern, was removed to the Lost and Found Department; and everyone was satisfied that the great thief had finally launched his attack. Everyone, that is, but Ellery Queen. He seemed puzzled. When Nikki asked him why, he merely said: "Stupidity, Nikki. It's not in character."

227

At 1.46 p.m. Sergeant Velie sent up a distress signal. He had, it seemed, to wash his hands. Inspector Queen signalled back: "O.K. Fifteen minutes," Sergeant Santa C. Velie scrambled off his perch, clawed his way over the counter, and pounded urgently on the inner side of the glass door. Ellery let him out, relocking the door immediately, and the Sergeant's red-clad figure disappeared on the double in the general direction of the main-floor gentlemen's relief station, leaving the dauphin in solitary possession of the dais.

During the Sergeant's recess, Inspector Queen circulated among his men repeating the order of the day.

The episode of Velie's response to the summons of Nature caused a temporary crisis. For at the end of the specified fifteen minutes he had not returned. Nor was there a sign of him at the end of a half-hour. An aide dispatched to the relief station reported back that the Sergeant was not there. Fears of foul play were voiced at an emergency staff conference held then and there and counter-measures were being planned even as, at 2.35 p.m. the familiar Santa-clad bulk of the Sergeant was observed battling through the lines, pawing at his mask.

"Velie," snarled Inspector Queen, "where have you been?"

"Eating my lunch," growled the Sergeant's voice defensively. "I been taking my punishment like a good soldier all this damn day, Inspector, but I drew the line at starvin' to death even in line of duty."

"Velie——!" choked the Inspector; but then he waved his hand feebly and said, "Ellery, let him back in there."

And that was very nearly all. The only other incident of note occurred at 4.22 p.m. A well-upholstered woman with a red face yelled, "Stop! Thief! He grabbed my handbag! Police!" about fifty feet from the Ypson exhibit. Ellery instantly shouted, *It's a trick men, don't take your eyes off that doll!*" "It's Comus disguised as a woman," exclaimed Attorney Bondling, as Inspector Queen and Detective Hesse wrestled the female figure through the mob. She was now a wonderful shade of magenta. "What are you *doing?*" She screamed. "Don't arrest *me!*—catch that crook who stole my handbag!" "No dice, Comus," said the Inspector. "Wipe off that make-up." "McComas?" said the woman loudly.

"My name is Rafferty, and all these folks saw it. He was a fat man with a moustache." "Inspector," said Nikki Porter, making a surreptitious scientific test. "This is a female. Believe me." And so, indeed, it proved. All agreed that the moustached fat man had been Comus, creating a diversion in the desperate hope that the resulting confusion would give him an opportunity to steal the little dauphin.

"Stupid, stupid," muttered Ellery, gnawing his fingernails.

"Sure," grinned the Inspector. "We've got him nibbling his tail, Ellery. This was his do-or-die pitch. He's through."

"Frankly," sniffed Nikki, "I'm a little disappointed."

"Worried," said Ellery, "would be the word for me."

Inspector Queen was too case-hardened a sinner's nemesis to lower his guard at his most vulnerable moment. When the 5.30 bells bonged and the crowds began struggling toward the exits, he barked: "Men, stay at your posts. Keep watching that doll!" So all hands were on the *qui vive* even as the store emptied. The reserves kept hustling people out. Ellery, standing on an Information booth, spotted bottlenecks and waved his arms.

At 5.30 p.m. the main floor was declared out of the battle zone. All stragglers had been herded out. The only persons visible were the refugees trapped by the closing bell on the upper floors, and these were pouring out of elevators and funnelled by a slid line of detectives and accredited store personnel to the doors. By 6.05 they were a trickle; by 6.10 even the trickle had dried up. And the personnel itself began to disperse.

"No, men!" called Ellery sharply from his observation post. "Stay where you are till all the store employees are out!" The counter clerks had long since disappeared.

Sergeant Velie's plaintive voice called from the other side of the glass door. "I got to get home and decorate my tree. Maestro, make with the key."

Ellery jumped down and hurried over to release him. Detective Piggott jeered, "Going to play Santa to your kids to-morrow morning, Velie?" at which the Sergeant managed even through his mask to project a four-letter word distinctly, forgetful of Miss Porter's presence, and stamped off toward the gentlemen's relief station.

"Where you going, Velie?" asked the Inspector, smiling.

"I got to get out of these x-and-dash Santy clothes somewheres, don't I?" came back the Sergeant's mask-muffled tones, and he vanished in a thunderclap of his fellow-officers' laughter.

"Still worried, Mr. Queen?" chuckled the Inspector.

"I don't understand it." Ellery shook his head. "Well, Mr. Bondling, there's your Dauphin, untouched by human hands."

"Yes. Well!" Attorney Bondling wiped his forehead happily. "I don't profess to understand it, either, Mr. Queen. Unless it's simply another case of an inflated reputation . . ." He clutched the Inspector suddenly. "Those men!" he whispered. *Who are they?*

"Relax, Mr. Bondling," said the Inspector good-naturedly. "It's just the men to move the dolls back to the bank. Wait a minute, you men! Perhaps, Mr. Bondling, we'd better see the Dauphin back to the vaults ourselves."

"Keep those fellows back," said Ellery to the Headquarters men quietly, and he followed the Inspector and Mr. Bondling into the enclosure. They pulled two of the counters apart at one corner and strolled over to the platform. The Dauphin was winking at them in a friendly way. They stood looking at him.

"Cute little devil," said the Inspector.

"Seems silly now," beamed Attorney Bondling. "Being so worried all day."

"Comus must have had *some* plan," mumbled Ellery.

"Sure," said the Inspector. "That old man disguise. And that purse-snatching act."

"No, no, Dad. Something clever. He's always pulled something clever."

"Well, there's the diamond," said the lawyer comfortably. "He didn't."

"Disguise . . ." muttered Ellery. "It's always been a disguise. Santa Claus costume—he used that once—this morning in front of the bank . . . Did we see a Santa Claus around here today?"

"Just Velie," said the Inspector, grinning. "And I hardly think——"

"Wait a moment, please," said Attorney Bondling in a very odd voice.

He was staring at the Dauphin's Doll.

"Wait for what, Mr. Bondling?"

"What's the matter?" said Ellery, also in a very odd voice.

"But . . . not possible . . ." stammered Bondling. He snatched the doll from its black velvet repository. "*No!*" he howled. *"This isn't the Dauphin! It's a fake—a copy!"*

Something happened in Mr. Queen's head—a little *click!* like the turn of a switch. And there was light.

"Some of you men!" he roared. *"After Santa Claus!"*

"Who, Mr. Queen?"

"What's he talkin' about?"

"After who, Ellery?" gasped Inspector Queen.

"What's the matter?"

"I dunno!"

"Don't stand here! *Get him!*" screamed Ellery, dancing up and down. "The man I just let out of here! The Santa who made for the men's room!"

Detectives started running, wildly.

"But Ellery," said a small voice, and Nikki found that it was her own, "that was Sergeant Velie."

"It was *not* Velie, Nikki! When Velie ducked out just before two o'clock to relieve himself, *Comus waylaid him!* It was Comus who came back in Velie's Santa Claus rig, wearing Velie's whiskers and mask! *Comus has been on this platform all afternoon!*" He tore the Dauphin from Attorney Bondling's grasp. "Copy . . .! Somehow he did it, he did it."

"But Mr. Queen," whispered Attorney Bondling, "his voice. He spoke to us . . . in Sergeant Velie's voice."

"Yes, Ellery," Nikki heard herself saying.

"I told you yesterday Comus is a great mimic, Nikki. Lieutenant Farber! Is Farber still here?"

The jewellery expert, who had been gaping from a distance, shook his head as if to clear it and shuffled into the enclosure.

"Lieutenant," said Ellery in a strangled voice. "Examine this diamond . . . I mean, *is* it a diamond?"

Inspector Queen removed his hands from his face and said froggily, "Well, Gerry?"

Lieutenant Farber squinted once through his *loupe.* "The hell you say. It's strass——"

"It's what?" said the Inspector piteously.

"Strass, Dick—lead glass—paste. Beautiful job of imitation—as nice as I've ever seen."

"Lead me to that Santa Claus," whispered Inspector Queen.

But Santa Claus was being led to him. Struggling in the grip of a dozen detectives, his red coat ripped off, his red pants around his ankles, but his whiskery mask still on his face, came a large shouting man.

"But I tell you," he was roaring, "I'm Sergeant Tom Velie! Just take the mask off—that's all!"

"It's a pleasure," growled Detective Hagstrom, trying to

231

break their prisoner's arm, "we're reservin' for the Inspector."

"Hold him boys," whispered the Inspector. He struck like a cobra. His hand came away with Santa's face.

And there, indeed, was Sergeant Velie.

"Why, it's Velie," said the Inspector wonderingly.

"I only told you that a thousand times," said the Sergeant, folding his great hairy arms across his great hairy chest. "Now who's the so-and-so who tried to bust my arm?" Then he said, "My pants!" and, as Miss Porter turned delicately away, Detective Hagstrom humbly stooped and raised Sergeant Velie's pants.

"Never mind that," said a cold, remote voice.

It was the master himself.

"Yeah?" said Sergeant Velie, hostilely.

"Velie, weren't you attacked when you went to the men's room just before two?"

"Do I look like the attackable type?"

"You did go to lunch? In person?"

"And a lousy lunch it was."

"It was *you* up here among the dolls all afternoon?"

"Nobody else, Maestro. Now, my friends, I want action. Fast patter. What's this all about? Before," said Sergeant Velie softly, "I lose my temper."

While divers Headquarters orators delivered impromptu periods before the silent Sergeant, Inspector Richard Queen spoke:

"Ellery. Son. How in the name of the second sin did he do it?"

"Pa," replied the master, "you've got me."

Deck the hall with boughs of holly, but not if your name is Queen on the evening of a certain December twenty-fourth. If your name is Queen on that lamentable evening you are seated in the living-room of a New York apartment uttering no falalas, but staring miserably into a sombre fire. And you have company. The guest-list is short, but select. It numbers two, a Miss Porter and a Sergeant Velie, and they are no comfort.

No, no ancient Yuletide carol is being trolled; only the silence sings.

Wail in your crypt, Cytherea Ypson; all was for nought; your little Dauphin's treasure lies not in the empty coffers of the orphans but in the hot clutch of one who took his evil inspiration from a long-crumbled specialist in vanishments.

Speech was spent. Should a wise man utter vain knowl-

232

edge, and fill his belly with the east wind? He who talks too much commits a sin, says the Talmud. He also wastes his breath; and they had now reached the point of conversation, having exhausted the available supply.

Item: Lieutenant Geronimo Farber of Police Headquarters had examined the diamond in the genuine Dauphin's crown a matter of seconds before it was conveyed to its sanctuary in the enclosure. Lieutenant Farber had pronounced the diamond a diamond, and not merely a diamond, but a diamond worth in his opinion over one hundred thousand dollars.

Question: Had Lieutenant Farber lied?

Answer: Lieutenant Farber was (*a*) a man of probity, tested in a thousand fires, and (*b*) he was incorruptible. To (*a*) and (*b*) Inspector Richard Queen attested violently, swearing by the beard of his personal Prophet.

Question: Had Lieutenant Farber been mistaken?

Answer: Lieutenant Farber was a nationally famous police expert in the field of precious stones. It must be presumed that he knew a real diamond from a piece of lapidified glass.

Question: Had it *been* Lieutenant Farber?

Answer: By the same beard of the identical Prophet, it had been Lieutenant Farber and no facsimile.

Conclusion: The diamond Lieutenant Farber had examined immediately preceding the opening of Nash's doors that morning had been the veritable diamond of the Dauphin, the doll had been the veritable Dauphin's Doll, and it was this genuine article which Ellery with his own hands had carried into the glass-enclosed fortress and deposited between the authenticated Sergeant Velie's verified feet.

Item: All day—specifically, between the moment the Dauphin had been deposited in his niche until the moment he was discovered to be a fraud; that is, during the total period in which a theft-and-substitution was even theoretically possible—no person whatsoever, male or female, adult or child, had set foot within the enclosure except Sergeant Thomas Velie, *alias* Santa Claus.

Question: Had Sergeant Velie switched dolls, carrying the genuine Dauphin concealed in his Santa Claus suit, to be cached for future retrieval or turned over to Comus or a confederate of Comus's, during one of his two departures from the enclosure?

Answer (by Sergeant Velie):*

*Deleted—*Editor.*

233

Confirmation: Some dozens of persons with police training and specific instructions, not to mention the Queens themselves, Miss Porter, and Attorney Bondling, testified unqualifiedly that Sergeant Velie had not touched the doll, at any time, all day.

Conclusions: Sergeant Velie could not have stolen, and therefore he did not steal, the Dauphin's Doll.

Item: All those deputized to watch the doll swore that they had done so without lapse or hindrance in the ever-lasting day; moreover, that at no time had anything touched the doll—human or mechanical—either from inside or outside the enclosure.

Question: The human vessel being frail, could those so swearing have been in error? Could their attention have wandered through weariness, boredom, *et cetera?*

Answer: Yes; but not all at the same time, by the laws of probability. And during the only two diversions of the danger period, Ellery himself testified that he had kept his eyes on the Dauphin and that nothing whatsoever had approached or threatened it.

Item: Despite all of the foregoing, at the end of the day they had found the real Dauphin gone and a worthless copy in its place.

"It's brilliantly, unthinkably clever," said Ellery at last. "A master illusion. For, of course, it *was* an illusion . . ."

"Witchcraft," groaned the Inspector.

"Mass mesmerism," suggested Nikki Porter.

"Mass bird-gravel," growled the Sergeant.

Two hours later Ellery spoke again.

"So Comus had a worthless copy of the Dauphin all ready for the switch," he muttered. "It's a world-famous dollie, been illustrated countless times, minutely described, photographed . . . All ready for the switch, but how did he make it? How? How?"

"You said that," said the Sergeant, "once or forty-two times."

"The bells are tolling," sighed Nikki, "but for whom? Not for us." And indeed, while they slumped there, Time, which Seneca named father of truth, had crossed the threshold of Christmas; and Nikki looked alarmed, for as that glorious song of old came upon the midnight clear, a great light spread from Ellery's eyes and beautified the whole contorted countenance, so that peace sat there, the peace that approximateth understanding; and he threw back that noble head and laughed with the merriment of an innocent child.

"Hey," said Sergeant Velie, staring.

"Son," began Inspector Queen, half-rising from his arm-chair; when the telephone rang.

"Beautiful!" roared Ellery. "Oh, exquisite! How did Comus make the switch, eh? Nikki——"

"From somewhere," said Nikki, handing him the telephone receiver, "a voice is calling, and if you ask me it's saying 'Comus.' Why not ask him?"

"Comus," whispered the Inspector, shrinking.

"Comus," echoed the Sergeant, baffled.

"Comus?" said Ellery heartily. "How nice. Hello there! Congratulations."

"Why, thank you," said the familiar deep and hollow voice. "I called to express my appreciation for a wonderful day's sport and to wish you the merriest kind of Yuletide."

"You anticipate a rather merry Christmas yourself, I take it."

"*Laeti triumphantes*," said Comus jovially.

"And the orphans?"

"They have my best wishes. But I won't detain you, Ellery. If you'll look at the doormat outside your apartment door, you'll find on it—in the spirit of the season—a little gift, with the compliments of Comus. Will you remember me to Inspector Queen and Attorney Bondling?"

Ellery hung up, smiling.

On the doormat he found the true Dauphin's Doll, intact except for a contemptible detail. The jewel in the little golden crown was missing.

"It was," said Ellery later over pastrami sandwiches, "a fundamentally simple problem. All great illusions are. A valuable object is placed in full view in the heart of an impenetrable enclosure, it is watched hawkishly by dozens of thoroughly screened and reliable trained persons, it is never out of their view, it is not once touched by human hand or any other agency, and yet, at the expiration of the danger period it is gone—exchanged for a worthless copy. Wonderful. Amazing. It defies the imagination. Actually, it's suspectible—like all magical hocus-pocus—to immediate solution if only one is able—as I was not—to ignore the wonder and stick to that fact. But then, the wonder is there for precisely that purpose: to stand in the way of the fact.

"What is the fact?" continued Ellery, helping himself to

a dill pickle. "The fact is that between the time the doll was placed on the exhibit platform and the time the theft was discovered no one and no thing touched it. Therefore between the time the doll was placed on the platform and the time the theft was discovered *the Dauphin could not have been stolen*. It follows, simply and inevitably, that the Dauphin must have been stolen *outside that period*.

"Before the period began? No. I placed the authentic Dauphin inside the enclosure with my own hands; at or about the beginning of the period, then, no hand but mine had touched the doll—not even, you'll recall, Lieutenant Farber's.

"Then the Dauphin must have been stolen after the period closed."

Ellery brandished half the pickle. "And who," he demanded solemnly, "is the only one besides myself who handled that doll after the period closed and before Lieutenant Farber pronounced the diamond to be paste? The only one?"

The Inspector and the Sergeant exchanged puzzled glances, and Nikki looked blank.

"Why, Mr. Bondling," said Nikki, "and he doesn't count."

"He counts very much, Nikki," said Ellery, reaching for the mustard, "because the facts say Bondling stole the Dauphin at that time."

"Bondling!" The Inspector paled.

"I don't get it," complained Sergeant Velie.

"Ellery, you must be wrong," said Nikki. "At the time Mr. Bondling grabbed the doll off the platform, the theft had already taken place. It was the worthless copy he picked up."

"That," said Ellery, reaching for another sandwich, "was the focal point of his illusion. How do we know it was the worthless copy he picked up? Why, he said so. Simple, eh? He said so, and like the dumb bunnies we were, we took his unsupported word as gospel."

"That's right!" mumbled his father. "We didn't actually examine the doll till quite a few seconds later."

"Exactly," said Ellery in a munchy voice. "There was a short period of beautiful confusion, as Bondling knew there would be. I yelled to the boys to follow and grab Santa Claus—I mean, the Sergeant here. The detectives were momentarily demoralized. You, Dad, were stunned. Nikki looked as if the roof had fallen in. I essayed an excited explanation. Some detectives ran; others milled

236

around. And while all this was happening—during those few moments when nobody was watching the genuine doll in Bondling's hand because everyone thought it was a fake —Bondling calmly slipped it into one of his greatcoat pockets and from the other produced the worthless copy which he'd been carrying there all day. When I did turn back to him, it was the copy I grabbed from his hand. And his illusion was complete.

"I know," said Ellery dryly. "It's rather on the let-down side. That's why illusionists guard their professional secrets so closely; knowledge is disenchantment. No doubt the incredulous amazement aroused in his periwigged London audience by Comus the French conjuror's dematerialization of his wife from the top of a table would have suffered the same fate if he'd revealed the trap door through which she had dropped. A good trick, like a good woman, is best in the dark. Sergeant, have another pastrami."

"Seems like funny chow to be eating early Christmas morning," said the Sergeant, reaching. Then he stopped. Then he said, "Bondling," and shook his head.

"Now that we know it was Bondling," said the Inspector, who had recovered a little, "it's a cinch to get that diamond back. He hasn't had time to dispose of it yet. I'll just give downtown a buzz——"

"Wait, Dad," said Ellery.

"Wait for what?"

"Whom are you going to sic the dogs on?"

"What?"

"You're going to call Headquarters, get a warrant, and so on. Who's your man?"

The Inspector felt his head. "Why . . . Bondling, didn't you say?"

"It might be wise," said Ellery, thoughtfully searching with his tongue for a pickle seed, "to specify his *alias*."

"Alias?" said Nikki. "Does he have one?"

"What *alias*, son?"

"Comus."

"*Comus!*"

"*Comus?*"

"Comus."

"Oh, come off it," said Nikki, pouring herself a shot of coffee, straight, for she was in training for the Inspector's Christmas dinner. "How could Bondling be Comus when Bondling was with us all day?—and Comus kept making disguised appearances all over the place . . . that Santa who gave me the note in front of the bank—the old man who kidnapped Lance Morganstern—the fat man with the moustache who snatched Mrs. Rafferty's purse."

"Yeah," said the Sergeant. "How?"

"These illusions die hard," said Ellery. "Wasn't it Comus who phoned a few minutes ago to rag me about the theft? Wasn't it Comus who said he'd left the stolen Dauphin—minus the diamond—on our doormat? Therefore Comus is Bondling.

"I told you Comus never does anything without a good reason," said Ellery. "Why did 'Comus' announce to 'Bondling' that he was *going* to steal the Dauphin's Doll? Bondling told us that—putting the finger on his *alter ego*—because he wanted us to believe he and Comus were separate individuals. He wanted us to watch for *Comus* and take *Bondling* for granted. In tactical execution of this strategy, Bondling provided us with three 'Comus'-appearances during the day—obviously, confederates.

"Yes," said Ellery, "I think, Dad, you'll find on back-tracking that the great thief you've been trying to catch for five years has been a respectable estate attorney on Park Row all the time, shedding his quiddities and his quillets at night in favour of the soft shoe and the dark lantern. And now he'll have to exchange them all for a number and a grilled door. Well, well, it couldn't have happened at a more appropriate season; there's an old English proverb that says the Devil makes his Christmas pie of lawyer's tongues. Nikki, pass the pastrami."